BELLE SUBMISSION

'What . . . what the hell is a trull?' Trina sobbed.

'What the anglos in New Albion call a trollop. On New Arras, they thrash bad girls for unreasonable behaviour, see? They have all kinds of punishments for unreason, and punishment tools like you'd faint if I described them, for trulls, truants and sluts, until their bare asses are just *squirming* with reason.'

'Elvis, didn't anyone tell you who I am?'

'No,' he said. 'I'm just the mailman, mamselle.'

'I'm going to be in charge of New Arras.'

Elvis shrugged.

'I don't see how that makes any difference,' he said.

BELLE SUBMISSION

Yolanda Celbridge

This book is a work of fiction.
In real life, make sure you practise safe sex.

First published in 2002 by
Nexus
Thames Wharf Studios
Rainville Road
London W6 9HA

Typeset by TW Typesetting, Plymouth, Devon

Printed and bound by
Clays Ltd, St Ives PLC

ISBN 0 352 33728 1

Contents

1

Bag Lady

What to wear? Trina Guelph's bare breasts quivered, without jiggling, as she looked at her nude body in the mirror of her closet and riffled her racks of clothing. Everything was draped neatly, panties, G-strings, skirts, designer jeans, basques and teddies, blousons, garter belts and stockings, all of it, like the generals of a drop-dead clothing army, with the ranks of infantry, footwear from fuck-me stilettos to runners, lined obediently beneath. What to wear? That was always the problem, even in Santa Monica, or especially in Santa Monica. In the power towers of downtown LA, dress was simple, but in sweet old Santa Monica, with how did you act the power, amongst the drifters and movie people and bikinied sand babes, and hot rich women eyeing the beach hunks from their cocktail lounges? Trina paused to look at her sweating nude body, as always, with approval. She'd run five miles on her machine, done a hundred push-ups and a hundred lift-ups, and used her device for ten minutes, for her exercise down there, which always made her antsy for work.

It was 7.30 a.m., already broiling, on this casual Friday. The smooth satin mounds of her jutting thirty-nine-inch breasts trembled only a little when her twenty-two-inch waist moved, with a little roll of her hips, over long, coltish legs that were perfectly smooth, perfectly tanned and shiny as wax. Her long blonde hair swayed over the strawberry peaks of her nipples, its texture a glossy sheen. Her spine tingled, fresh from her session with Gwendoline, her

1

aromatherapist, down in Venice, and who was also an osteopathic chiropractor: a funky, muscular girl, who liked being called a babe and who was the best masseuse in southern California. Her latest therapeutic device was a rack, like a mediaeval instrument of torture, only, of course, it wasn't for torture, really. Having her spine and legs stretched, while her nude body was basted in herbal oils and unguents, was thrilling, especially as Trina's hands and feet were bound by silky cords to the rollers, whose every creak pulled her straining sinews tighter.

Trina got a little frisson when Gwendoline in her fresh tunic, with nothing underneath and two buttons undone to reveal her own titties, almost as full and firm as Trina's own – Trina emphasised the almost – bent close to her nude body, and whispered, joking, that the rack would do proper torture, if required. Whether she meant if Trina required, or if Gwendoline required, was tantalisingly unclear. That added a palpable, weird sexuality to their physical relationship, especially with Gwen so carefree about exposure of her bare skin.

Anything to stay in shape, Trina joked back: in LA, the righteous bod is everything, no matter how much it hurts. She'd seen Gwen changing – clearly, because Gwen wanted to show off her own bod – and her ass had marks, as though she'd been beaten. That had made Trina's pulse race for a moment. She turned, and looked at the full, deep-cleft peach of her butt: ripe, a firm forty inches, the twin, massive silken globes hard as iron. Her bikini lines were vivid: sunbathing, she kept her top on, for she knew bikini marks turned on a certain type of American male, who figured he alone – such power! – was getting to see her juicy tush and boobies. You could be topless at most beaches but, Trina figured, nobody's going to see my merchandise for free.

She stroked the bulging mound of her cropped pubis, and decided the hairs needed just one more trim, so she padded to the bathroom and got her electric trimmer working, until her pubic bush was a neat quarter-inch lawn of designer stubble, a precise triangle framing the heavily

2

extruded crimson lips of her vulva. She pressed her bare pubis to the washbasin, lifted her thigh, and worked on the thick growth of down in her perineum, finally giving her anal pucker one more shave, and rubbing her finger several times through her crack to make sure she was smooth. Running water washed away the few sprouts of trimmed blonde fleece. She resisted the temptation to play with herself – her device brought her to that required heat, where she could be a successful bully broad, her own preferred term. As bully broad executive with sharp claws, at Goody Baggs & Stuff – laid back, west coast, jeans-and-sneakers casual, and one of America's wealthiest companies – she'd long got over grimacing when called a bag lady, for that was how GG Baggs himself called his all-female staff; or, if he felt playful, a goody girl.

Trina's device was a pliable vibrator, revoltingly brand-named 'Smutty Putty' – it was an exercise machine! – which adapted itself to the shape and size of the female vulva. Trina's exercise was to use the muscles of her vaginal walls, and the neck of her womb, to change the shape of her vibrator every morning as she masturbated, skirting her clitoris, hence without fully masturbating. She lubricated the device with extra-virgin olive oil and had to cling tight for it not to escape. To prevent herself cheating, she locked her fingers behind her neck. Then she worked on the huge, cock-shaped thing, squeezing and nipping and pinching, until after ten minutes it plopped out of her in the shape of a corkscrew or hammer or a monkey wrench. Whatever shape it was, it attested cunt power, as she liked to tell Kimmi Lardeau, her office gofer, who lived in a neighbouring apartment block, north of Santa Monica, overlooking the ocean. Kimmi was a kind of wild child, except she was maximum docile. She was big titted, big assed and long legged, and had an all-over tan, but you only noticed those extravagances once her wide feline eyes had alerted you to them, almost apologetically. She seemed to live on olives and cucumber. She was luminous. Trina cabbed to work, but Kimmi swam. Really! She just waded into the ocean in her bra and panties, holding her office wear in her teeth, and swam all the way down the coast, breast stroke, past the snarled traffic. She came into the office in dry clothes and with dry hair, but often her bra and panties were dry too. She admitted she preferred to swim nude and, when far enough into the ocean, stripped off her 'tinies' and held them in her teeth.

'Oh, Trina,' she said, hearing the crude word, with her massive boobies trembling under whatever fabric she'd bothered to cover them with that day – often some man's shirt that she claimed to have just picked up somewhere, and wearing nothing else at all! 'Trina, that's so gross.'

'Yeah, it's gross, Kimmi,' Trina replied. 'I guess you believe men only want us for our bodies.'

'I see nothing wrong in that,' Kimmi said. 'I mean, I like my body, and I'm pleased if someone else does.'

'Kimmi, men don't want us for our bodies. Our bodies are just signposts. Men are livestock. They want us for our cunts.'

'That's kind of nice,' said Kimmi angelically, without a fluttered eyelash, flicker of her long, sunbleached mane or tremor of her breasts.

Kimmi liked to wear corsets, really old-fashioned satin things called 'waspies', which squeezed her waist painfully tight, or so it looked, in a variety of colours. She would have on a corset and bra and a man's shirt and leave the shirt open so you could see the corset, how it pinched her waist. She would wear garters and old-fashioned nylon stockings, too, but never sweated; on casual Fridays, she might wear only a corset, not a waspie, but a huge armoured thing, that covered her titties and her pubis, like a one-piece swimsuit. She wore those, too. In pastel colours, padding barefoot around the office. The corsets constricted her waist to eighteen inches or even seventeen inches, she told Trina. It made her feel like a proper girl.

'We can only beat men with raw sex power,' Trina insisted, 'not trussing our bodies like dolls.'

'Oh, I'd have a problem with that,' said Kimmi. 'I wouldn't like to beat anybody. I might earn a spanking. If a guy likes me for my body, it's a compliment. Maybe that's why you're a director, Trina, and I'm just a file maid.'

They had much the same joshing conversation whenever they visited for jacuzzi sessions at each other's apartment buildings. The jacuzzi meant you could be friendly without totally being friends; on her trips to cold northern states, Trina wondered why people stayed there, instead of coming to warm, fizzy California. At Kimmi's, most people were nude in the jacuzzi after dark, although the foam hid most of you, so it didn't matter; but Trina always wore her bikini, a little eat-your-heart-out affair, scarcely more than wisps of string that hid little, but she wasn't giving anything away. Kimmi refused to be nude at Trina's apartment, in respect, but she wore a demure and clinging one-piece swimsuit that managed to be so demure, she looked nude. Once, at Kimmi's building, Kimmi had doffed her robe and slid into the tub rather faster than usual, but Trina saw her big tan bottom glowing unusually pink. Kimmi blushed when Trina said she'd been overtanning, and said no, a boyfriend had spanked her.

'You're serious?' Trina gasped.

'Just a few taps,' she said. 'And I really deserved it, for being a forward girl. He ordered some more ice for his drink, and I told him it was in the fridge. I wasn't thinking, see. Well, of course, he put me straight over his knee and lifted my skirt up and spanked me on the bare.'

'That's outrageous!' Trina cried. 'Just a few taps?'

'A hundred or so,' Kimmi said. 'His palm got sore, and I suggested my sandal, but he said a hundred was enough. It did me good. I like boyfriends to spank me when I'm forward. We had lovely sex almost straight away. I wonder if that has to do with spanking? A girl's butt being hot, and all . . .'

'Kimmi! We're women, not girls,' Trina blurted.

'I know that, Trina,' Kimmi replied, in her soft southern lilt, 'but I prefer to think of myself as a girl. It makes things simpler, and stops me being forward.'

On another occasion, they were alone in Kimmi's tub, relaxing, with the ocean and stars twinkling, and Kimmi said it was so righteous. Two of her neighbours, guys Trina knew by sight, asked to join them, and Trina was quite happy about that because their eyes weren't fixed on Kimmi's glowing casual nudity but on Trina's bod, tightly packaged as a sex machine in her peekaboo bikini top that pressed her titties together and thrust them up like big quivering jellies. Both guys had bulges in their swimshorts as they slid into the jacuzzi, flanking Kimmi but ogling Trina opposite. Kimmi invited them to get easy, and both pairs of shorts came out of the frothy water. They made small talk and Trina played up those bulging boobies of hers, knowing, just knowing, that the tongue-tied suckers had raging hard-ons only looking at her, and that was all they were going to get, a peek. Kimmi slouched in the water, saying how mellow it was, and her shoulders were writhing, and gradually the conversation stopped, and the guys had their arms beneath the foam. Trina was miffed at being ignored and peered through the steam. Under the water, Kimmi had both her hands around the guys' cocks, and was rhythmically, slowly, jerking them off. Her fingers moved like automata, stroking the coronas of their helmets, and occasionally stooping to stroke their tight ball-sacs, or give sudden firm tugs on the shafts that pulled down their prepuces all the way, before she cupped the whole revealed glans in her palm, grinding the pisshole. The guys were . . . were *groping her*. Their hands squashed her big golden breasts, hard, with the teats squelching and squirming like potter's clay, and stroked her belly, and each had fingers inside the wet crimson purse of her open cunt, for Kimmi had her thighs spread as wide as they would go. The spectacle caused Trina's pussy to juice all over her tight bikini gusset, as sperm spurted from each cock at once, the globules of creamy fluid dissolving in the jacuzzi's froth. The guys were quick to say 'take care now', 'nice talking', and make a speedy exit.

'Kimmi . . .' Trina gasped, 'how could you?'

Kimmi smiled.

'Brad and Greg are going pussy-hunting tonight,' she said, 'and guys so often spoil their act if they come on too horny. So I feel good about mellowing them out. Don't you find diddling really mellows you, Trina? I do myself almost every time I go to the bathroom. Masturbation keeps a girl in touch with her own self.'

Trina admitted she masturbated sometimes, and asked how Kimmi could enjoy the two guys mauling her titties and pussy.

'I guess they enjoy it,' said Kimmi.

'But did you?'

'Obviously, if they did.'

Trina left soon after, vaguely troubled, and, fragrant from the jacuzzi, treated herself to a session with her Smutty Putty – a real session, this time, with the vibrations on max, and the mammoth rubbery cylinder crammed right into her wombneck. She mauled her own bare teats the same as the guys had mauled Kimmi's and found it hurt, but she did not stop, even pinching her stiff nipple plums with her fingernails until she shut her eyes at the pain. She brought herself off, her orgasm making her cry out loud, then towelled the juice from her wet cunt and went straight to sleep.

Kimmi wasn't officially Trina's gofer – she called herself 'maid of the file cabinets' whenever anyone asked, although nobody was ever sure if those big blue eyes and rosebud lips might be joking – but Trina had annexed her without resistance, so that Trina wasn't sure her power had worked exactly right. Trina's bod, and strength down there, gave her power over men and, at twenty-one years old, she was the western personnel director, or 'people relations catalyst', as GG said, of America's largest packaging corporation, in Santa, holy shit, Monica. GG wasn't big on titles; if pressed, he insisted his role as CEO meant 'chief earthling organiser'. GG Baggs smiled whenever a woman suggested moving from the rambling oceanfront property that had run the art deco gamut of hotel, night club, gas station and warehouse into being the unposted HQ of Goody Baggs & Stuff. He would frown and agree a move would be fine. How about El Segundo? El Segundo was where Jive Sacks, the nearest thing GG had to a rival, hung out, and GG called them LYA – light years away. Then he laughed some more, and said he was off to grab some rays on the beach, and why didn't the female come along? He never asked Trina to go to the beach with him, because he said he was scared of her. Trina prided herself on eventually fucking almost every male who spent time at the office, but she didn't hit on GG.

Personnel meant salesmen. Not salespeople, salesmen: big, unreconstructed macho hunks, with a smile and a twinkle and an ecosphere of phoney charm. GG didn't mind being called 'the last hippy', or a relic of the 1960s – it was his granddad who was that, in fact. He said small is beautiful, believed in real, not corporate America and figured that down home real Americans felt comfortable with salesmen who looked like salesmen. GG said 99% of doing a job was looking the part. The salesmen drove outrageous cars gussied up with fins and chrome and, though they ran on solar energy, had a sound system of gurgles and roars, just like a gas guzzler in the old days. Most buyers of anything at all, GG figured, were women, so salesmen had to be men: potential studs descended from dreamland to sell Goody Baggs to the excited women of Pocatello, Idaho, or wherever. Trina's job was to check they had what it took, and that they continued to have it, and use it in the total service of Goody Baggs & Stuff – or, as Trina preferred to think, in service of her own luscious Californian body. The merchandise, once in place, sold itself: getting it in place took an ounce of common sense and a big dick, as Trina encouraged others to say behind her back. Salesmen had to be studs and, to get and keep good studs, you needed a ripe mare. Like Trina.

She travelled a lot, all over the west, to make lightning inspection tours of those remotenesses where Goody Baggs cheered people's lives up, just as GG claimed, and when there she could stun. The full power rig, black suit and stockings, fuck-me shoes, hair sprayed and coiffed, and sometimes wearing a hat and veil, like in those 1940s movies . . . and the local sales guy, if he behaved, got the fuck of the century, until the next time Trina chose to visit.

That was how she recruited salesmen, and how she kept them at peak efficiency: the gift, then the promise, of her body, on her terms. Always her on top, always in control, giving great head but without undressing, as if the male was just another business appointment; or straddling the hunk, making him beg to be brought off, her wet cunt playing with his tool for hours, until she let him spurt – without coming herself. That she attended to with a few deft fingerflicks of her hugely extruded clitoris afterwards. She kept her cell phone turned on, and loved it when some boyfriend called just as she was writhing on another man's cock. 'I'm busy right now,' she'd say. 'I'm bare-ass naked, with a cock in my cunt. It's really so big; it's splitting me . . . listen.' And she'd put the phone right by her pussy, and writhe some more, so the boyfriend could listen to the squelching of the other guy's cock in her wet cunt: 'Uhh . . . talk to you later.' Control. A bully broad. Thinking that made her wet. She called her erotic technique subduction, as when two crustal plates collide, one forcing down the other and producing earthquakes.

Goody Baggs & Stuff did everything the wrong way round. It drove Trina wild, sometimes, but she couldn't argue with her humongous paycheque, which wasn't really a paycheque, but a consultant's fee, because GG Baggs didn't believe in capitalism and had no employees as such. There were computers in the office, but not online. Instead of an IT system, they had real, old-fashioned file cabinets, stuffed with paper! GG explained, smiling, that the best computer was the human brain. Any government agency was welcome to sift through his file cabinets, because a whole generation of screenheads didn't know what a piece of paper was and, anyway, only Kimmi really understood it all.

Instead of 'don't put anything in writing', GG believed in putting everything in writing, as much of it as possible. Paper weighed; gravity, he said, was money. People with bad karma, like tax people, simply didn't have time to go through mountains of paper. GG on purpose overpaid the IRS. If they demanded, say, $1 million, he wrote a cheque for $1.1 million, which they always kept, so that he was then the aggrieved party. That is, he wrote several dozen cheques, on small town banks all over the US, which drove the greysuits nuts. He knew every bank account and company he owned – there was no 'Inc' in Goody Baggs. If there was some financial fact GG felt too bashful to share, he'd advise Trina or Kimmi to 'Bismarck' it. That meant, create an obstacle course of paperwork and excuses, the doomsday weapon being, 'I'm so sorry, GG's gone to Bismarck' – everyone knowing the name, but not exactly where it was.

'Why hide money in Switzerland,' he said, 'when you can hide it in North Dakota?'

GG's name really was Goody Baggs, and that was his legal trademark. He was a genius – his dad had been a genius, even though a screenhead, as GG bemoaned – and his granddad had hung around Haight-Ashbury in the golden age of the 1960s. The name Goody was what screenheads called an easter egg, that is, a joke, but his dad was gracious enough to call him George as well. After becoming even more of a computer whiz than his dad, GG had invented the Baggs nanochip, then stopped. His nanochip, a few molecules wide, created Baggsite, the recycled packaging material that made GG Baggs the world's richest moccasin-wearing man. GG figured that giving was more fun than receiving, and everyone [meaning women] loved bags and boxes and gift wrap, and would buy them without knowing their purpose.

'Packaging makes the world go round,' he said.

A Goody Bagg was a pellet of dark substance which, rubbed a few times to body heat, became a pliable, greaseless dough. There were always new kinds of Goody Baggs. The most basic, placed on top of an object, used nanosensors to expand to a sheet like cardboard, the exact size for the object, form itself into a box meeting US Postal Service specifications, wrap and seal itself, while at the same time extruding a web of gossamer strands, a few molecules wide, to protect the object inside. Touching it made the substance mood-change its colour, like, a happy colour or a wistful one . . . you traced the address with a fingertip, and the box translated your scrawl into neat printing. You could mail a Ming vase from Anchorage to Key West, and it would emerge intact from its Goody Bagg. Other Goody Baggs were tote bags, or purses, or anything, and you could change the colour or design every day; each one was unique – 'a singularity' in GG-speak. From a range called 'Cling Things', a girl could build her own shirt dress, or wet T-shirt – an expanding market, GG gravely observed.

Most important, Goody Baggs were cheap. They came packaged in their own Goody Baggs, imitation felt, silk or leather, which served as earrings or neckwear until a use was found. The display was always the same, in every convenience store throughout America: a totem pole, with twenty-four branches, standing at the angle of an erect cock, and on each branch half a dozen pairs of Goody Baggs, exactly the same as two male balls, chained together. GG, in one of his rare interviews, was asked if that was sexploitation.

'Yes,' he said.

Baggsite, the miracle substance, was produced from organic waste: paper, leaves, potato skins. Filling a Baggs nanochip compressor the size of a trash can, they changed in an hour to the dough, which was manually rolled into pellets, hardening once bagged. The compressors could be anywhere, like a basement, so all merchandise was locally produced.

GG acquired ancient mom-and-pop companies, the Laramie Shoelace Corp or something, and gave them just a tad more work. Everything local, low overheads, cut out big business, employ the good karma folks of real America. When big corporations hurt, GG called them tree-killers and suggested they find another, more American employment, although they were welcome to compete, if they wanted to ruin the righteous folks at the Laramie Shoelace Corp. Why, the Baggs nanochip, GG's idiosyncratic arrangement of molecules, wasn't even patented. GG knew the US was the only country with unapplied patent

11

law, so you could patent something, then bury it, and still keep the patent. So, of course the Baggs nanochip was unpatented, and in the public domain if anyone could find it . . . but every arrangement of molecules that might lead remotely near the Baggs nanochip was patented harder than cast steel.

'American nanochips for Americans,' GG said publicly; or, over a beer, to one of the Santa Monica cops with whom he was friendly, as it was wise to be in Santa Monica, 'Some anti-planet corporation with shitty karma goes up against me, I'll waste the motherfucker – I mean, I'm an *American*,' and the cop would nod sagely.

What to wear? Trina ate breakfast, showered and was back at the closet mirror. A Cling Thing was kind of tacky for a power broad . . . Kimmi instinctively knew what to wear, which was hardly anything, most of the time. But then, Kimmi wasn't after power. At nineteen, she had all the time in the world! She looked after the sales figures, and Trina looked after the salesmen, was their understanding.

Trina stroked her pubic stubble a last time, frowned and slung an array of clothing on her bed. It was so hot, and a chick exec never ever went stockingless, but she could go braless, as it was Friday. She chose a white cotton shirt, sheen flesh stockings in real nylon, and a powder-blue garter belt and straps, with a blue tartan linen skirt fastened by a safety pin at the waist, and showing thigh. Shoes were simple loafers, gold tassel. No panties, for reasons more than aesthetic, although she did like the absence of a panty line on her always clinging skirts or pants, and smooth ass was a potent weapon, facing a male. That, and the swish of her nylon stockings as she crossed her legs, making guys sweat and drool as they pretended they weren't peeking for a glimpse of her haven. She never let her pussy show, but leg-crossing meant that she knew what it was for.

She was doing up her last garter strap when the phone rang. Her answering machine was on and, when she heard a male voice, she grimaced, but lightened up when it was Allan the airline pilot, who rolled into town occasionally and whose light-hearted manner gave her both a smile and a challenge. He'd humour her dominance, even act submissive sometimes, groaning and pleading to come, as she fucked him. Trina Guelph never let a male fuck her – she fucked him. But Allan was always grinning, even when he wasn't grinning. The challenge . . .

'Hey, pick up the phone, Trina,' said Allan. 'No sweat, I'm only in town for the weekend.'

Allan had a good ten inches – Trina sniffed at lesser endowments – and that thought, with moisture already seeping in her quim, made Trina pick up the phone. They kidded awhile, then agreed a date for that evening.

When she got to work, Kimmi had just arrived and was wearing a pink full corset in clinging satin, which squeezed her waist way tight, seventeen inches for sure, clinging to her big firm nipples and showing the crack of her ass, as if she were nude. The corset was wet, so she must have swum to work. She said GG wanted a word with Trina, asap. Kimmi dripped all over the floor, her blonde mane, slightly darker than Trina's, damp at the tips over her bare brown shoulders. Trina reported to GG and came out, thirty minutes later, a cup of latte heavier, and pensive. Kimmi had changed into another pink corset, of filmy, clinging lycra, and her skin was still beaded with moisture – not water but sweat. The corset had a scalloped bra that pushed her almost-bare boobies up to quivering jellies, and the crotch was the wispiest thong imaginable, with the rear cut high to show most of her firm brown ass-melons. The lycra seemed like a mere film of gossamer that clung to her skin, narrowing her waist to pencil thinness, and at the big bulge of her pubis individual clusters of her pubic fleece showed beneath the fabric, as well as the tufts of golden curls that sprouted past the high-cut panty – Kimmi neither shaved nor trimmed her armpits, legs nor vulval area. Trina too was wet, and the thin cotton shirt clung stickily to her own titties, making her feel more of a spectacle than Kimmi.

'I didn't know it was going to be this hot,' she blurted at Kimmi's placid stare. 'Hey, can we talk in my office?'

'Sure, Trina. I'll fetch coffee.'

Kimmi brought coffee and sat on one of Trina's cushioned cane chairs. The desk was there as emblem rather than tool, and Trina sat in a cane chair beside the teenager. The fan brushed the air without cooling it; GG was an enemy of air-conditioning, which he thought the slippery slope to wearing grey suits.

'You're always fetching things,' said Trina as Kimmi, unbidden, extracted bottles of Vittel from the office frigidaire.

'A girl should think of others,' said Kimmi. 'Shouldn't she? You won't mind if I give your ferns a little water?'

She sat, curled in her seat, with her thighs pressed together, as if excited by watering the ferns. Trina told her yes, and watched Kimmi's ass swaying as she swooped to splash French mineral water over the plants. She rejoined Trina, breasts quivering in the strapless one-piece.

'That felt good,' she said breathlessly. 'I'm feeling life-oriented today. I had this wonderful date last night; I think I really made him happy.'

'Anyone special?' said Trina.

'Oh . . . just a guy. All humans are special, like ferns.'

Trina told her what GG had offered, or ordered, and Kimmi's breasts trembled in agitation. GG, who was fond of surprises, had first asked her if she liked crawfish and gumbo and stuff, then said he 'seemed to have bought' the Louisiana Academy of Perruques and Pomades, on a gulf island called New Arras, and he wanted Trina to go down and 'massage it' for Goody Baggs' production. It was a factory and teaching facility at the same time, and had been there 'for thousands of years', and all the staff were girls. GG said it sounded really herbal and righteous, and perfect for Goody Baggs dominance of the deep south. Every exec had to spend time in the field, to get away from the humongous pressures of Santa Monica, so Trina could take the weekend to make her decision.

'I'd be so sad if you were, like, some place that wasn't here,' Kimmi murmured.

Her breasts shook in sympathy, and Trina smiled.

14

'Thanks, Kim. How do you keep that thing on?' she said.

'Oh, it's quite easy,' Kimmi said earnestly, 'with proper breathing control,' and as she spoke, a drop of sweat fell from her chin into the cleft of her breasts, between the two pressed bulbs of gently quivering teat-skin.

Trina wiped her brow and, as she did so, her own breasts rolled in their soaking cotton prison.

'You're very nervous, Trina,' Kimmi said.

'It kind of threw me,' she replied. 'He said I was best for the task – offered more money, profit share and everything, and that I'd be the numera una, you know? But I wonder, in my career curve, if it's a sideways promotion. Sapping my power base by cutting me out of the loop.'

'Oh, Trina, this isn't a big, vicious grey suit corporation,' said Kimmi. 'We don't have loops. GG is sincere.'

She placed her fingers on Trina's nape and squeezed the neck muscles.

'You really are tense. Why don't I give you a herbal massage? I have all the oils back at my place. You – we – could make ourselves comfortable. There's nobody there right now. I mean, we could get naked. It's not the same in a jacuzzi, with other people.'

She blushed.

Trina swallowed, then replied, 'Yes, I'd like that.'

'We can take a cab – shall I go ask GG?'

Trina nodded limply. Suddenly she did want a massage and knew, as she watched Kimmi's buttocks swaying from her office, that she wanted it from Kimmi. Kimmi was a listener; she would understand. The girl was absent for a full half hour before returning to say that GG had okayed it, and they could take the rest of the day off if they wished. She called for a cab, resting her bottom on Trina's desk and keying the numbers with her big toe, whose nail was painted green; all Kimmi's nails were painted different colours.

'You'll love Louisiana,' Kimmi said when the cab was ordered. 'Wish I was going. It's like home to me.'

From the Journal of Mlle Augustine Flageolet, anno 1760 [1]
A sea voyage induces languor of the senses. Sultriness of
the body is tempered by the brisk sea breeze – are these not
the two principles of the human spirit? So soon after
embarkation at Le Havre, we are on the broad Atlantic,
pathway to America, and dreams of liberty enthrall me.
Louisiana! What glorious sunrises await us! The despotism
of France seems far away. We sail to an island of bounty,
where our society of thinking females shall sustain itself by
physiocratic principles, feeding and clothing ourselves
from the fruits of earth and sea, while instructing the mind
and body in the precepts of rational discipline – discipline
which the forces of oppression dare to describe as immodest! Maidens shall grow in this sun-kissed Louisiana, their
bodies in harmony with the discipline of earth and sea and
sky, submissive to nature's reglements and nature's beauty.
The metropolitan fools, ignorant that a girl's duty is to
submit! To nature, to reason, to just chastisement of her
errant flesh.

2

Hardspank

The air was languorous with the scent of tropical flowers and ferns, and Trina breathed deeply of their mingled perfumes.

'First, take all those clothes off,' said Kimmi sternly, as if clothes were some unpleasant modern fad. 'Then, a hot shower before your massage.'

She herself was already stripping off her corset, with a sucking sound as it peeled from her breasts, which sprang aquiver from her ribcage.

'Don't I get time to admire the view?' said Trina.

Kimmi's spacious apartment was on the top floor.

'Later,' Kimmi decreed.

Trina gazed at Kimmi's artless nudity, her corset already folded neatly and stashed, while Trina was still fumbling at her garter straps. Her shirt was off, letting her own breasts sway freely, dripping with sweat over Kimmi's bleached pine floorboards. The garter belt unsnapped; she rolled down her stockings. Kimmi took the underthings, pressed them to her nose and made a face.

'You don't wear panties,' she said, 'so why these? You think it's humid right now, wait till you get to Louisiana.'

'I haven't decided I'm going,' said Trina.

'You're going in the shower,' said Kimmi.

'Are you joining me?' said Trina, shocked at the tremor in her voice and the ripple of electricity in her clitoris at the thought of such closeness to the naked girl.

'Of course,' said Kimmi. 'I'll give you a proper soaping.'

The spray was scalding as Trina felt Kimmi's hands rub scent-free shower gel and soap all over her body. Kimmi's own natural scent pervaded the shower cubicle; the girls were almost, but not quite, pressed together, and as Kimmi's hands touched every inch of her with somehow clinical impersonality Trina's nipples stiffened. Kimmi flicked them playfully, without a word, then washed Trina's cunt-basin and her vulval aperture with shower gel, squirting the liquid into Trina's slit and rubbing the cunt-lips gently as it trickled out. It excited Trina. She was wet, and her come seeped to mingle with the shower gel, yet she felt embarrassed; Kimmi's nipples weren't stiff, and there was no sign of ooze at her gash. Trina's soaping was nurse-like and, when the time came for her to lie face down on Kimmi's futon, so was her very thorough and quite painful massage. After oiling her to gleaming wetness, Kimmi kneaded, thumped, twisted and pounded on Trina's back, thighs and ass, pulling her arms and hands at the sockets, and at times climbing up and walking with precise and dainty toes up and down Trina's spine. Kimmi's big toe pressed the kundalini of her spinal nubbin, dipping into the spread, clean-shaven crack of Trina's ass. Trina's feet were massaged, then her legs bent back until her toes touched her buttocks, and she thought her thighs would burst with Kimmi's full weight on her legs.

'Uh!' she gasped. 'That's very painful.'

'Yes, and that's why you'll feel better. Oriental massage takes you into yourself, absorbs you in your body, your own somatic environment, so that outward things, like where you are on the planet, are an illusion.'

'Is that why you like being spanked?' Trina gasped.

'That's not pain, that's cleansing – like eating a raw tabasco pepper, you know? Folks do that in Louisiana.'

Both Trina's legs were bent fully back, exposing her naked vulva.

'Am I turning you on?' asked Kimmi. 'Your pussy's all shiny. Are you thinking of spanking? Bare ass spanking?'

'Wait a minute!'

'You're all wet, Trina. It's glistening like dewdrops. It's lovely. Hey, I get wet, when I think of being spanked. Most girls do. It's OK.'

'I am kind of excited,' Trina blurted.

'Do you want us to get it on?'

'Wow, Kimmi! Wait a minute . . .'

'We're all flesh, aren't we? I've watched you in the jacuzzi, Trina. I know you.'

'I'm not sure. I've never . . . I'm not lesbian. I've never wanted to, with a girl . . . with any other girl.'

'Sure?'

Trina gulped.

'Except you,' she whispered.

'That's sweet. Being not sure is the best fun. I'll give you the full oriental massage, if you like.'

Without waiting for Trina's assent, Kimmi released her legs and climbed on top, straddling the nude body with her own. She began to slide up and down Trina's quivering back, tickling her with her nipples, which were hard, like tiny pears. She worked her way down to the quivering flans of Trina's buttocks, which involuntarily clenched then relaxed, spreading, to let Kimmi poke each of her breasts fully into the wide ass-cleft, nuzzling her teat between Trina's thighs. Trina's cunt gushed hot oil over the younger girl's stiff nipples. Then Kimmi flipped around and faced Trina's feet. With her own cunt pressed to Trina's nape, she began to trace Trina's spine with her open gash, which was hot and wet and seeping its own copious juice. Trina gasped as she felt Kimmi's erect clitoris, like a hot, fleshy walnut, pressing on the joints of her spine, while Kimmi's breasts caressed her thighs, her calves and, finally, the soles of her feet, with the girl's cunt clutching – actually clutching, with prehensile gash-lips – the last bone in Trina's spine, her nubbin: waves of pleasure and excitement coursed through her throbbing clitoris, her erect nipples, her spine and fluttering belly.

'Feel alive?' said Kimmi.

'Why, that's just how I feel,' cried Trina.

She turned Trina over and straddled her oiled nudity, breast to breast and cunt to cunt. Kimmi plunged her nose into Trina's hair and breathed deeply, while brushing the erect buds of Trina's breasts with her own; their bellies pressed, and Kimmi's pubic bone was hard on the soft wet lips to Trina's womb. Trina's cunt-basin writhed to meet Kimmi's jabbing pressure, her stiff clitoris seeking the caress of the girl's pubic curls.

'Oh . . .' Trina moaned. 'Oh . . .'

Her clitty touched Kimmi's, and Kimmi's body stiffened, trembling. Kimmi's nubbin was heavily extruded from her cunt-lips, and rock-hard. Kimmi made no sound, and her breath was calm, unlike Trina's gasping sighs.

'Oh, do me, Kimmi, do me,' Trina whispered.

'You do want to get it on.'

'I thought this –'

'This is massage. Getting it on is this.'

Kimmi flipped once more, and buried her face between Trina's wet thighs. Trina gasped as Kimmi's tongue entered her anus to an inch and began to poke in and out, while her chin ground Trina's soaking gash. Kimmi's gaping cunt hovered, inches above Trina's own face. Trina grasped the girl's buttocks and pulled her to cover her face; Kimmi allowed the whole weight of her cunt and buttocks to press on Trina's mouth and nose. Kimmi's skin was so silken-smooth, her ass-muscles so ripe and firm and sweetly soft, pulsing beneath the girl's trembling naked moons . . . Trina was smothered in scented wetness, and fastened her lips on the swollen clitty, beginning to chew with rhythmic motions of her nose in the wet pouch. Kimmi prised open the lips of Trina's anus pucker and got her nose inside, while her tongue flicked over Trina's distended nubbin. Trina's belly fluttered, then heaved at Kimmi's expert tonguing; she gulped for air under the writhing of the girl's cunt-basin, grinding her face while slopping it with copious come. Trina's palms pulled Kimmi's buttocks closer to her and she opened her jaws wide to engulf the entire cunt in her mouth. She felt Kimmi's hot come trickle to the back of her throat as she sucked the gash-flaps, with her tongue flicking the nubbin; Kimmi's head bobbed up and down, fucking Trina's gash with her nose, which she intruded fully into the writhing, soaked pouch.

'Mmm . . . Uh . . .' Trina gasped, as she felt her spasm welling up inside her, and then her moans became grunts, then shrieks, long and staccato, as her pussy throbbed and flowed with moisture; moons and stars danced before her eyes as her cunt and belly exploded in orgasm more profound than she could ever remember.

'Wow,' she said weakly, rubbing her eyes, wet with Kimmi's come, as the two bodies disengaged. 'You made me come . . . I've never done it with a girl before. Was it good for you, Kimmi? Coming, I mean?'

'I'm not really into coming,' said Kimmi. 'I pleasured you, that's all that matters.'

'Wait a minute –' Trina's warm afterglow of orgasm was pierced by chilly anger '– I had lesbian sex for the first time ever, I . . . I ate you out, and you didn't come?'

Kimmi grinned impishly.

'Bully broad's sore at me, huh? I enthralled you, but you couldn't enthrall me?'

Trina swallowed, blushing. 'Yeah . . . something like that.'

Kimmi was all serious again. 'Then I didn't give you full pleasure.'

'Oh, Kimmi, you did, but . . .'

Kimmi rose, stretched and yawned. Then she squatted on the bed with her bare ass raised.

'What . . .?'

'Don't you want to spank me? For not coming? That qualifies as disrespect, I'd say.'

'Spank you? I can't do that.'

'You ate me a few moments ago. Don't you want to eat my ass, too? Those big ripe buns, just waiting for your teeth to tear into, and your throat to swallow, washed down by my cunt-juice? That's what guys say, they'd like to eat me up. Well, that's kind of impractical, so the next best thing is spanking me on the bare. It's a very therapeutic power dialogue. Spanking – must be bare-ass spanking – is a tonic to the system. Stimulates the brain and the nerve-ends. You didn't know?'

She stroked Trina's anus pucker.

'A tonic for both of us,' she murmured.

'I came here for a massage and to talk things over, about Louisiana and all,' Trina cried, 'and you're just playing games with me, an excuse to get out of the office. Sure, I'll spank you . . . I'm mad at you. Not just a few taps.'

Trina swung on top of Kimmi and squatted with her still-dripping vulva on Kimmi's nape, forcing the girl's face into the pillow and lowering the cheeks of her ass within easy spanking range. Kimmi did not struggle, not even when the first flurry of spanks from both Trina's palms rapped on her bare ass globes.

Slap! Slap! Slap!

'Mmm . . .' Kimmi moaned; then, her voice muffled by the pillow, 'If I may suggest – start with softer spanks, see, that warms up the nerves in my ass, and then I can take a much longer hardspank.'

'You'll take the spanking I fucking give you,' Trina snarled.

Slap! Slap! Slap!

'Mmph,' Kimmi chirped, her spanked buttocks churning, as they reddened. 'Yeah, that hits the spot.'

Slap! Slap! Slap!

'Ooh . . .'

Kimmi's ass cheeks began to clench before and after each spank, and the squirming buttocks glowed a brighter and brighter red, as Trina's palms slapped both globes of bare, quivering skin. It excited Trina that her fingerprints were discernible on Kimmi's mottled red fesses. She spanked with full force. Slap! Slap! Slap!

'Oh . . . you're really hurting me, Trina.'

The girl's writhing bare buttocks were rapidly brightening to scarlet yet, as Trina continued the bare-ass spanking past fifty slaps, the brightness of the skin ebbed to a dull crimson glow, like a dark star, with the imprints of Trina's fingers raised to puffy swollen ridges of flesh.

Slap! Slap! Slap!

'Ohh! Mmm! My ass is so hot, Trina. Am I red?'

Kimmi's buttocks and back writhed like bloated red eels, as though Trina were squatting on some strange, struggling

22

sea monster. It was no longer a naked girl she was spanking, but two buttocks, blotchy wealed orbs of flesh that danced, squirming in their private agony, detached from the creature trapped between Trina's thighs and crying, 'Ohh . . .' into her pillow. Each spank made Kimmi's buttocks and cunt-basin jerk up, then thud down against the bed, as though to escape the next spank, which made the ass-pears rear up again. The bed under Kimmi's dancing cunt was slimed with her moisture, seeping more and more heavily from her gash. Trina had lost count of the spanks and had forgotten her original miff that had made her wish to spank the girl. Spanking consumed her; only her aching palms and the livid bare drums of skin, dancing to her fleshy batons, existed.

The spanking passed a hundred slaps. Kimmi's arm snaked under her convulsing cunt-basin; its writhing grew faster, the bare ass-cheeks quivering like tomatoes about to burst, as the girl's hand stroked frantically inside her cunt. She made no secret of her masturbation. Trina delivered a furious volley of spanks, unsure if she was pleased or frustrated when Kimmi's voice bleated, 'Oh, oh, oh, yes,' from under her pillow, and her legs and back stiffened, shuddering in orgasm.

'Mmm . . .' Kimmi crooned to herself, and it was only at this dove-coo that Trina realised the spanking had wetted her own cunt, and inflamed her clitoris to a new swelling.

Kimmi was limp, her body serene, while Trina ached to come once more. Still squatting on Kimmi's nape, and with Kimmi's hands now holding and stroking her ankles, Trina masturbated her clitoris with a vigorous stroking until she brought herself off, gasping in surprise at how fast the sweetness drenched her cunt. Her breath rasped and, as she convulsed in new orgasm, Kimmi's eye peeped from under the pillow to watch Trina's fluttering belly and flowing slit.

'That's nice,' she said. 'I guess we'd better get back to the office. Feel better for your massage?'

'Yes,' said Trina uneasily.

She vaguely sensed that Kimmi had used her.

Whatever got into me? I've had my first lesbian sex, and spanked some little flake's bare ass. So what? It's

23

experience, a done deed, and I don't have to go down that road.

'But we haven't talked about Louisiana,' Trina said.

Kimmi rose and stretched. Like a cat. She wiped both hands in her wet cunt, then caressed her puffy spanked buttocks with her juices before putting her fingers in her mouth and sucking her own come. She thrust two fingers right to the knuckle into her pouch and withdrew them, slimed with come. She put them in Trina's mouth and rubbed her tongue and teeth. Trina tasted Kimmi's come, licked the probing fingers and swallowed the fluid.

'Oh, I think we have,' Kimmi said.

Though her cunt still glowed from her orgasms, Trina reflected that her goody-two-shoes little gofer, her sweet sugarfroth, was using her. Pain was repulsive, unless it was mental pain she inflicted on some jealous hunk: getting off on physical pain – inflicting, let alone receiving it! – was unacceptable. How could Kimmi enjoy her bare ass spanked to crimson, then bathe her welts in her own come? Moreover, how could Trina have been enthralled? Her date with Allan that night should put her straight. She'd fuck his brains out, the bully broad way, and make him gasp for more. Spanking? Huh!

She hugged Allan with genuine affection that he didn't know was laced with relief. Allan had just flown in from New Orleans and, when Trina asked him how it was, he said, 'Same old, same old.' Allan was so normal, after the bizarre experience with Kimmi that afternoon. She was so flushed and giggly over dinner that Allan suggested she was taking on too much chardonnay, but she wasn't really – she was just thrilled at the sex they were going to enjoy, part of the thrill being the certainty of it, and knowing that he knew too, so that they didn't need to say a flirtatious word; they were conspirators. They were at a new Italian restaurant in Venice, and got an amaretto on the house for being so obviously a newly in love item, which was nice, although Trina was with Allan once a month, and it had been well over six months now, so they weren't that 'newly'. Afterwards, they wandered around the beach, where a few midnight musclemen were still doing their stuff, with some beach babes oiling them under the moonlight.

'Love southern California,' Allan said. 'So romantic.'

'Depends what you mean by romantic,' said Trina, eyeing the glinting musclemen.

'Let's find out,' whispered Allan.

She drove them back to her apartment in silence; Allan said he was entitled to time out, which he could take that weekend, if Trina liked.

'Let's find out,' she retorted.

She let her hand brush his groin, on its way to giving his thigh a reassuring pat, and breathed deeply, finding the cock straining stiff under his pants, but said nothing. They got into her apartment, with Trina cursing her fumbling key fingers, and she poured them both generous cognacs. Allan lounged on the sofa and she snuggled up to him, blatantly touching his stiff cock. Yeah, ten glorious inches to play with . . .

'Temptress,' he said.

She started to unfasten the big silver buckle of his thick western belt but he moved her hand away.

'Eager beaver,' he said.

'It's not my fault you turn me on, big boy,' she murmured, rubbing her stockinged thighs together and feeling her come ooze into the nylon.

'After all this time?'

'You can't say it isn't mutual.'

'That's right. That's what I've been thinking. You're special to me, Trina. That's what I've decided.'

Trina rubbed the stiff cock hard.

'Special! Lose the big complicated words, lover,' she said. 'Let's get naked.'

Allan lifted her from his lap.

'You first,' he said, with a sly grin.

'Huh?'

'Strip, Trina.'

'Mmm . . .' she said, and licked her teeth with a pouting sulky grin and a flutter of her eyelashes. 'You want some music for me to strip to?'

'No, no,' he said, unsmiling. 'That would spoil it. Just strip.'

'OK,' she said. 'I'll strip, like some trailer park okie, huh? Then you have to catch me.'

'No. Like I said, you're special.'

Trina felt funny, just taking her clothes off, slowly unbuttoning her shirt and unhooking her scalloped peekaboo bra and slipping out of her skirt, until she wore only her satin thong panties and frilly garter belt over black, real nylon stockings – trying to make as much of a show as possible, yet feeling tingly as this erect male just lounged there, ogling her, like some emperor eyeing a slave girl. She couldn't take her eyes off that cock; the memory of her orgasm with Kimmi still warmed her cunt-basin, and she knew he was scrutinising the trickles of come already covering most of her inner thighs and deeply soaking the sliver of fabric that partially hid her swollen dark pussy-lips. She longed for that cock to pierce her right away, longed to straddle him and trap the monster tool with her prehensile vulval walls; yet Allan seemed not in a hurry. Slowly, she slid down her panties and stepped out of them, a soggy scrap on the floor, over which her naked pussy dripped fluid. She stood before him, in only her nylon stockings, garter belt and straps.

'Masturbate,' he said.

'What?'

'Diddle yourself. Rub your clitty.'

Trina swallowed, a fresh seep of come wetting her cunt.

'You want me to bring myself off while you watch?'

'Yeah. Girls like showing off, right?'

Trina smiled.

To obey, or disobey? Obey. He'll pay for it later.

'Mmm,' she said, and put her finger to her extruded, throbbingly erect clitty.

She touched herself gingerly, fearing she would come too fast and give away her power over the male; yet she so wanted her cunt filled, and if degrading herself made him take her, then OK. Her hand brushed and tweaked her stiff nipple-plums, and she moaned.

He's watching me diddle, wet cunt-flesh, a slave in a slave market, strutting my stuff to find a buyer. I want to make him stiff, by masturbating ... I can make any male stiff.

'I don't believe this,' she gasped. 'I like it. What got a hold of you over in New Orleans?' Two fingers were now sliding in and out of her wet cunt, and the juice oozed copiously from her slit to drip on her bare toes.

Showing myself. Being watched. Eyes popping, cocks stiffening ... at my bare flesh.

Allan sighed.

'Like I said, I decided you're special, Trina. I've watched strippers in so many titty bars and done so much sleazy stuff, in places like New Orleans – especially New Orleans – and I wanted to check that I'm not as bored with sex as I think I am. It's fine being rootless, but ... Trina, you're so together! So perfect! Why do you trim your mink so tight and neat? I never thought to ask that before.'

'You never asked me to diddle before.'

'Don't you like it?'

'Sure.'

'Don't you do it when I'm not here?'

'Only when I can't find eleven inches.'

'Touché.'

Still vigorously masturbating – she was really turned on by exhibiting herself, and heard him only dimly – Trina sat on Allan and firmly grasped his belt buckle, undoing it as she rubbed her swollen cunt on his thigh, wetting him with her juices. She unzipped him and prised his stiff brown snake from its lair, then, moaning, bent down and got the glans of the swollen, massive tool between her lips. Her right hand guided the shaft to the back of her throat, while her left had three fingers deep inside her flowing gash and her thumb pounding her clitty. She ran her tongue round the neck of the glans, licked the tender frenulum, then withdrew, and nibbled at his piss-hole with her front teeth, before swooping to engulf the whole cock, tight to the balls. Allan's breath was rapid; he caressed her hair, pushing her face down on his cock as she fellated him.

'It's so cool that you get off on masturbating,' he gasped. 'Kind of an ego trip, imagining you playing with yourself, when I'm not there. I'd like to think I'm as special for you as you are for me. Am I?'

Sucking the monstrous cock, Trina nodded. 'Mmm.'

I'll get off with my fingers, then make him come, and swallow his sperm, then we can mellow out, and when he's stiff again, I can get on top and fuck him all night long. Straddle him, show him my ass, make him want to spank me . . .

'Didn't you hear me?' Allan murmured. 'You aren't jealous?'

Trina laughed, a gurgling laugh, with the back of her throat squeezing on his piss-hole. She had her lips on his tight ball-sac, and began to chew and nibble the orbs as her throat constricted around his throbbing glans. She could feel the cock trembling, about to spurt – the sperm would shoot straight into her gullet. Allan writhed; despite his dippy talk, she had him under control.

'I want more than just sex, Trina,' he gasped. 'I want you, just like I want to be yours. Me alone. Us for us.'

Trina withdrew to the peak of his glans, and spoke with her lips caressing the piss-hole.

'Hey, get real, Allan. You're no saint; me neither.'

'You have other boyfriends.'

It wasn't a question. Trina stopped the fellatio and raised her head, flushed.

'What kind of question is that?'

'I didn't mind, up till now, but . . .'

'You didn't mind? Who the fuck are you to mind?'

Allan pulled her head up by her hair.

'Ow! You're hurting me,' she cried.

'Who are they? How many?'

'Are you crazy?

'How many other guys do you go down on, and say, it's so big, lover? Three? A dozen? That's whore talk.'

'Fuck you, Allan. Sure, I have boyfriends, better fucks than you, and more than you'll ever know.'

Allan wound her hair round his fist and pulled her head down to the sofa, muffling her face in the cushion.

28

'You'll find you're wrong about that,' he said, calm once more. 'And you'll regret talking so forward.'

'Mmm! Mmm!'

Trina was helpless as Allan pulled her on to his lap, and kneed her belly until her bare ass stuck high in the air. Her legs flailed; he pinioned her thighs under his. She felt his stiff cockmeat squashed against her bare belly, which writhed in fear and anger.

'This is just a taste,' he said. 'Don't waste your breath struggling, because it's going to be a long night.'

Slap!

'Mmm!'

Slap! Slap! Slap!

'Oh . . . you're hurting me.'

I can't believe this. He's spanking me, bare-ass.

At first, the shock, the invasion of her private person, overwhelmed the pain of the spanks; when the pain came, it seared her naked ass-skin, and knocked the breath from her. Slap! Slap! Slap!

'Mmm . . . Mmm – wmm.'

She meant to say, let me go, but her face was muffled in the cushion, her whole squirming body trapped helplessly by his grip. The spanks rained on her bare buttocks, a scalding rush of pure pain. Tears sprang to her eyes and she felt her gorge rise, but she was unable to release the scream. Slap! Slap! Slap!

Her buttocks clenched at each spank and her bare ass squirmed and wriggled, her cunt grinding his thigh as though to escape the slaps. Her pubic trim slithered in the pond of her own cunt-juice which, she realised in shock, dripped no less copiously after the onset of her spanking. Slap! Slap! Slap!

'Ahh . . . ooh!' she squealed. 'My ass is burning. Allan, you've made your point.'

'This may teach you a lesson,' he said, 'but you've had it coming. I gave you a chance – I spoke sincerely – but you revealed yourself. You are just a trull. A whore.'

Slap! Slap! Slap!

'Oh . . . mmm . . . you're really, really hurting me.'

Trina's naked buttocks did not stop wriggling as she was spanked, but her squeals ebbed to a long, drooling moan. Fire engulfed her bare ass-flesh; it seemed she had never known such pain, had never known anything on this world but pain. Pain filled her, from her throbbing clitty to her spine, to her tingling breast points, squashed against the sofa. Yet, it was not pain, like a scratch or a headache: it was intimate, buttock pain. Come oozed from her writhing gash even as she was spanked, bare-ass, to deepest humiliation. Her moans became sobs, begging for mercy.

'That's so brutal,' she groaned. 'My ass feels on fire. Oh, it smarts . . . I'm going to look so awful, bruised up.'

'The worst is yet to come,' Allan said mildly.

After an age, in which her spanked bare moons were scalded to agony, the spanking stopped. Trina lay limp on the sofa, crying, with tears running down her face. When she felt Allan rip off her stockings and garter belt, her only reaction was to howl, with helpless floods of tears; neither did she protest when her own wet panties were wadded in her mouth as a gag, secured by one of her torn stockings knotted around her neck. Her hands were secured to a foot of the sofa with the second stocking, and her ankles with her own garter belt.

'Just to make sure,' Allan said easily. 'Some girls don't take well to stropping. Not like Kimmi.'

He lifted his heavy leather belt, and folded it in two. Trina stared and screamed, but it was too late. The leather lashed her helplessly exposed bare buttocks with a dull thud.

Vap!

'Nnggh!'

Her buttocks jerked and bucked, helpless to escape the strop. Vap! Vap! Vap!

'Ah . . . ah . . .' she whimpered.

Vap! Vap! Vap!

'Ohh!'

'I've known Kimmi for a while. Met her in New Orleans, in fact. She's always been a fine friend. We fuck, of course, but what she most likes is a stropping.'

30

Vap! Vap! Vap!

'Nngh . . . !'

'Yeah, Trina, that's fuck, as in get it on. Kimmi's so sweet and submisssive, doesn't play head games. She likes to give service. And stropping as in whip her ass till she's in tears and swears she'll never be disobedient. In return, she tells me stuff. About you and . . . all those guys. She just wants me to know how happy you are when I'm away – bully broad!''

Vap! Vap! Vap!

'Mmm! Mmm . . .' she sobbed.

Trina's flogged bare buttocks danced under the searing lash of the leather, the simple belt transformed in the man's hand into the hardest, most terrifying slaver's whip. She chewed at her panties, tasting her own salty come as her teeth shredded the dainty garment until, at last, her mouth full of threads, she managed to speak.

'Allan . . . please stop . . . I didn't mean to cause you pain . . .'

'But I mean to cause you pain.'

Vap! Vap! Vap!

'Ohh . . . please! I'll do anything.'

'I know you will.'

Trina's naked ass-meat continued its frenzied squirming for an hour before Allan laid down his strop and ran his fingers over the welts and blossoming ridges of her bare croup, still quivering and clenching, in the lash's silence.

'Beautiful welts,' he said. 'They should last, and hurt, for days.'

'What are you doing to me?' she sobbed as she felt his fingers prise her bare moons apart. 'Oh, that hurts.'

'Strange thing to say, after your whipping,' he replied. 'Stay still, Trina.'

'Ahh!'

Trina bucked violently, as her anus bud was penetrated by the man's cock. His glans poked inside her, until her anal elastic enclosed the glans neck; he waited, pushing gently, then thrust again, getting his tool halfway up her passage. Trina screamed and screamed again as his third thrust slipped fully to her rectum, filling her with the monstrous ten-inch cock.

'Oh, stop, please stop,' she gasped.

He pulled his cock from her anus with a plopping sound, and let his pee-hole tickle her pucker for several seconds, while Trina sobbed. Her pucker wriggled, opening and closing, with shiny ass-grease smearing his cock.

'I'm so confused,' Trina whimpered.

Allan sank his tool into her anal elastic, and began to butt-fuck her with hard, pounding strokes, hammering her anal root with his piss-hole while driving the cock right to the balls, with his ball-sac slapping her heaving buttocks at each stroke.

'Oh, it hurts. You're splitting me. Allan, please.'

'I've taken enough shit from bully broads like you, Trina,' he said. 'Down in Louisiana, a girl still knows how to be a girl, a southern belle – sweet and submissive, there to serve men, not to torment them. Kimmi's like that. She fucks to please, not to possess.'

With smooth, ruthless thrusts, his cock penetrated her anus, ramming her root at each stroke and making her body stiffen and shudder; yet come poured from her cunt and Trina's head spun. Her belly fluttered and there was a terrible sweetness in her spinal nubbin.

No . . . no . . . it can't be . . . I'm going to . . .

Allan laughed.

'You like it, don't you? This is what you really want, bitch. A taste of reality.'

'No! No . . . Ahh!'

Trina shrieked as orgasm flooded her, and it was not until the last of her sobbing moans of climax had ebbed to a snuffling whine that Allan slammed her anus with a new urgency and let his sperm jet into her rectum, its hot flood accompanied by a savage, sneering grunt. He pulled his cock from her hole and wiped it on her hair.

'You wanted it, didn't you?' he hissed. 'All of it.'

'Yes,' Trina sobbed. 'All of it.'

'Don't call me, bitch,' he said, to the wealed, naked body on the sofa as he let himself out. 'I'll call you.'

Trina came into the office on Monday morning, dressed in her most awesome power outfit – grey stockings, grey suit, white silk blouse with a black necktie and black designer slingbacks. She wore a smile as bright as the sun, dimmed by the LA smog. Her anus still ached from her buggery, and the welts and ridges on her whipped butt were black and stiff as corrugated cardboard.

'Hey, people,' she said, with a radiant smile at Kimmi, who smiled back, 'let's get to work.'

GG Baggs sauntered out of his office.

'Hi, Trina,' he said. 'You have any thoughts about New Arras, Louisiana?'

'Sure, GG,' said Trina, her smile fixed. 'I've spent the weekend thinking about it – I've done a lot of thinking about my life – and I accept. Any time you want.'

I've been shamed and hurt beyond endurance, and it's made me stronger in every way. A man thinks he can fuck around and it's OK, but a girl has to be submissive and obedient? Piss on that! I'll fuck whom I please. I know I've always been right and, in future, I'll never regret hurting a man. No amount of pleasure from the Kimmis of this world can wash the wounds I'll inflict. What's one dumb butt-fuck, one clumsy whipping, to a bully broad? I know how to kick men where it hurts most, in their filthy macho male chauvinist pride. Now, just let me get to Louisiana and those sweet submissive belles. I'll teach them how to really treat men. I'll clean that submissive pus right out of them and teach them to be strong, like me.

Kimmi brandished a document folder at Trina.

'Your plane to New Orleans leaves in four hours,' she said sweetly. 'Change there for Stennis International Airport, Mississippi.'

'How did you know . . .?' Trina gasped.

'Girl's intuition,' Kimmi said. 'Lots of luck.'

From the Journal of Mlle Augustine Flageolet, anno 1760 2
I had three maids disciplined today, two for surliness and one for unreason. Suzanne Yonne and Alice Foubier

received pertinent chastisements in my stateroom and, afterwards, watched Marthe Gognaud take an exemplary correction in front of ship's complement. Of the three truants, only Alice cried out, at eighteen, the youngest, so I awarded her extra discipline, after which she refrained from noise. Her fesses were quite pink, and she joined the others in thanking me for her humiliance. The good, reasonable girl! A maid's bare bottom is so pretty as it blushes, clenching like flower petals opening to the sun. Admittance to my academy is determined, in part, by academic prowess, although my girls must be able to dress their book-learning with wit but, above all, by excellence of the visible feminine manifestations: that is, the fesses. After examinations in deportment, embroidery, grammar, poetry and other female accomplishments, I make my final selection by inspecting the fesses of the applicant without drawers, shift or petticoats – in a word, completely bare.

It is in the form and carriage of her naked bottom and, eventually, in that bare bottom's comportment under the rod, that a lady reveals her true and most intimate character. Reactionaries, ignorant of nature's laws, dub my academy an institute of lower learning, or, with distressing vulgarity, the academy of the posterior. The fools! France's loss shall be America's gain. There is some debate in our shipboard States General – a decorous and compliant assembly of forty maids – whether I, as intendant, should administer the punishments the court imposes, the court being embodied in my own person. I argued to the contrary, on the grounds that I speak not for myself but for the authority reason vests in me. I admit it is tempting for me to take the wand to those bare croups, since the prescriber of chastisement must naturally think herself best fitted to carry it out.

3

Trull

Trina breathed deeply of the sea air as she watched the Mississippi coastline fade through the heat haze: Biloxi Bay, Gulfport, the white sand beach. She stretched with a contented sigh as the breeze ruffled her hair. *Biloxi seems a dainty place; plenty of time for a vacation later*. The azure of the Gulf of Mexico was calm and flat, with a few oil rigs poking the sky in the distance amongst smudges of islands. She lay back in her lounger, sipping iced tea. Below, Deputy Postal Inspector Elvis Lesieur [which he pronounced 'leisure'] piloted the little jetfoil, the USPS D'Iberville, behind locked doors, which also protected the twice-weekly mail sack for remote New Arras, in the Chandeleur Islands chain. Trina still hadn't discovered why a part of Louisiana was served by a post office in Mississippi – a small concern, compared with her mysterious travel arrangements. The flight to New Orleans was OK, and also the connector to Stennis International Airport, Hancock County, Mississippi, although her buttocks still smarted after Allan's thrashing, and she was happy to climb out of her taxi at the hotel in Biloxi; shower, eat and shower again before sleeping. The heat was stifling, and in the tepid shower she rubbed the hard, crusted welts on her ass, hoping, yet not hoping, they had gone away. *They are part of me*.

She was to go to the Ocean Star Café, at the harbour, at 7 a.m. and ask for 'Mr Elvis', who would convey her to New Arras. The owner, Arlette Sobovica, who spoke with a French accent, explained that the only passage to New Arras for non-residents or the uninvited was the US Postal Service vessel, which was strictly not allowed to carry passengers. *But I am invited!* Arlette had never been to New Arras, but if she could sell the Ocean Star café she might just afford to send her eighteen-year-old daughter Yveline 'for her education', as if Biloxi's high schools provided none.

Trina asked about the Louisiana Academy of Perruques and Pomades, and Arlette said she figured wig-making might well be part of a mamselle's education, though she didn't rightly know. She did know that New Arras mamselles were the finest ladies in the whole south, and she wanted Yveline away from the Biloxi dockside, where too many innocent mamselles ended up common trulls. Arlette's shining eyes announced the breakfast arrival of Elvis; a broad, tanned six-footer, Trina's age, shaggy black hair, wearing blue denims and western boots, with a stetson and red bandanna – and a postal inspector's badge. He grinned lopsidedly and blushed under his tan as he approached Trina and tipped his hat.

'You'd be Mamselle Guelph?' he purred, and Trina nodded. 'Would it trouble you if I joined you, mamselle?'

He grinned that lopsided grin again as he took the envelope of cash, and explained that he was only paid a part-time rate by the USPS, so had to 'eke'. Trina watched as he devoured three servings of sausage, two of bacon, four fried eggs, a hillock of hash browns and a stack of pancakes lathered in maple syrup.

'Real Canadian maple syrup,' he said. 'Arlette gets it from her folks up there.'

Trina began releasing her pent-up frustrations: why hadn't the people in New Arras responded to fax or email or telephone calls, didn't they know she was coming? Kimmi's note said that everything was taken care of, including the rent on her apartment. But she had no copies of any communication, just Kimmi's scribbled assurance, and when she tried to call the New Arras number with the Louisiana area code, she got a busy signal, plus which her cell phone didn't work at all – maybe some horrible southern insect life had got into it.

'I guess they'd know about you,' said Elvis. 'Things get around.'

He stood and placed himself behind her to take her chair.

'After you, please, mamselle,' he said, directing her into the dazzling morning sunshine.

Then, the outrageous, extravagant – yet oddly just – part. To smuggle her aboard the d'Iberville, Elvis explained, she would have to be enclosed in a Goody Bagg, as a properly mailed package, with a stamp, franked and all. Trina had submitted to the indignity – which now, lolling in the sun, she thought wonderfully comic – of lying down, while a blob of industrial-strength Baggsite slowly encased her, its stabilising fronds looping down to hold her tight. Perched on Elvis's shoulder, she had boarded the vessel as a US postal package. When she was unzipped, she asked where the packaging came from, and Elvis said he thought somewhere in 'the Orleans territory'. Well, there was something for her first report back to GG and Kimmi. Inside a Goody Bagg was really quite comfortable. *What if that damned Kimmi already knew?*

They were passing an island to starboard when Elvis did reappear, stripped to the waist, and touched the peak of his sailor's cap. He brought a refill of tea, and said that landfall should be in ninety minutes. Trina was sweating in her far too heavy linen suit, and Elvis cleared his throat.

'I shall not bother you, mamselle,' he said. 'If you want to make yourself at your ease, in this heat.'

Trina looked at the crotch of his jeans over the top of her sunshades. There was a bulge that the tight fabric emphasised. She crossed her legs; was that her imagination, or did the bulge stir? Eleven inches? No – too conservative.

'You couldn't possibly bother me, deputy inspector,' she said, his grin reappearing at the titular usage. 'What island is that one?'

'That's New Albion, mamselle,' he said.

'Do you go there, too?'

'Never!' Elvis cried; then, checking himself, 'They are served out of the Gulfport post office, mamselle.'

'Do people live there?'

'Some, I guess. I only know New Arras, mamselle.'

'Then tell me about New Arras,' she invited, slipping out of her jacket and kicking off her shoes.

'I collect the mail, mamselle,' he said. 'I have quarters there and I empty the mailboxes, then sort, pack and ship out. In Biloxi, I pick up the outgoing. Day and a night in each port. Ladies pretty much run St Arras theirselves, with a US marshal, though it's part of St Bernard parish in the Orleans territory.'

'The what?'

'Uh, the state of Louisiana, mamselle.'

'So, there are only, ah, mamselles living there? That must make you pretty glad.'

'Mamselle!' said Elvis. 'I'm a public servant and, I trust, a Misissippi gentleman.'

'Oh. Of course. I wonder why their mail comes out of Mississippi?'

'I guess, historical reasons, mamselle. Most things round here are historical.'

'Take some iced tea,' Trina said. 'You're sweating.'

Elvis frowned.

'I have to keep the mail within eyeball reach,' he said.

'Why, Mr Lesieur, I am the mail.'

After fetching another pitcher of tea and a glass for himself, he sat on the deck and drank thirstily.

'I have a confession,' she said. 'I'm from California and we have a thing about sun – I mean, when we see some, we just have to tan. Does it bother you if I –?'

'Like I said, mamselle, please make yourself comfortable. Long as I'm satisfied the mail is safe, I'm doing my job.'

'I hope I satisfy a Mississippi gentleman,' murmured Trina, her voice knifing the still air.

She unzipped her skirt and slowly wriggled out of it, then folded it and placed it beside her on the lounger. Her breasts heaving, she unbuttoned her shirt and removed it;

then unfastened her garter things and rolled down her stockings. She sprawled on her lounger, soaking sun, in bra and panties, a flesh-coloured set of sheer translucent voile. Elvis drank tea, staring fixedly towards New Albion. After a long silence, Trina jumped up.

'This tea!' she cried, her teats wobbling in agitation and almost spilling out of the scalloped surround. 'It goes right through me and I need the bathroom.'

'Head's on the lower deck, mamselle,' said Elvis, springing to his feet. 'I'll unlock it for you.'

'Oh! I'm desperate!' she said. 'Mr Lesieur, look away, and I can go over the side.'

'Well, OK,' he replied. 'I guess we're far enough from any New Albion spyglass.'

The deck had two parallel surround rails, about a foot apart, and the top one at waist level. Trina lowered her panties and squeezed her buttocks between the rails, so that her cunt-basin overhung the sea. With Elvis looking away, she sighed as a heavy jet of piss spurted from her vulva, which she held open with two fingers. A sudden gust sprayed the fluid back on deck, soaking her thighs and stretched panties, but she did not interrupt her pee.

'Oh! Mr Lesieur! Help me, I'm stuck!'

Elvis grasped her upper arms and pulled. Trina's ass-melons were so big that she was stuck and had to wriggle to get her hips free of the rails. When she did, she sprang forwards; Elvis slipped in her pee and both bodies slammed to the deck, with Trina straddling Elvis and her crotch against the bulge in his jeans.

'I'm sorry!' she cried, making no effort to move. 'Are you OK?'

'My job is seeing you're OK, mamselle,' he replied. 'I should have swabbed the deck.'

'That was my fault,' she said, giggling and writhing her bare pubis just a little over his. 'I always pee too heavily.'

There was no mistake. The bulge was swelling. Trina unhooked her bra and dangled it away from her body, squashing her massive teat-flans in Elvis's face. The nipples were stiff and she poked the left titty between his teeth, while grabbing his cock and rubbing it through the jeans cloth. It rapidly stiffened to full erection and Trina gasped.

'With a big, bad thing like that, it's time you got more comfortable,' she murmured. 'We have time to kill.'

'Oh, mamselle, I don't know . . .'

His lips fluttered on her erect nipple. Trina smiled, licking her teeth.

'Get those jeans off, sir.'

'Please, mamselle!' he moaned. 'I can't disrespect a lady.'

She grasped his hand and clamped it between her thighs, soaking his fingers in her piss-wet pussy, now oozing oily come.

'See how wet I am,' she said. 'You going to disrespect me by leaving me gasping for that cock of yours? Pants down and cock up, if you please, sir.'

'Please, mamselle, that's trull language,' Elvis protested, but already Trina had unzipped him and had the stiff, monstrous cockmeat glinting bare in the sunlight.

Her fingers scooped at his balls until the whole tool was naked, a monster, at least eleven inches.

'I want respect!' she cried in a strangled gasp, before her head swooped to get her lips around his bulging glans.

He moaned as her tongue lapped his pee-hole.

'No . . . please . . .'

His stiff cock belied him. Politeness abandoned, Trina fellated Elvis, with his cock throbbing inside her throat and her mouth clamped round his corona, licking and teasing, until he sobbed to be brought off.

A southern hunk sobbing! Power . . .

Elvis was putty.

'Promise you won't tell any of the mamselles or the US marshal,' he begged as Trina removed her mouth from his and straddled him, pinching the neck of his glans to get the monster within her gaping wet cunt-lips.

'No promises, sir,' she sneered, then sighed, 'Ahh . . .' as the massive cock penetrated her cunt, right to the wombneck.

She rode him, squeezing his cock with her muscled cunt-walls, until he gasped, writhed and sobbed, gulping air as his loins surged to meet her thrust.

'Uh . . .' he moaned. 'It's so good . . .'

His hands clutched her buttocks, his fingers stroking her welts.

'What are these, honey?' he said, his tone harsher. 'You been stropped? You been a bad little mamselle?'

'Fuck me,' Trina moaned, her cunt spraying oil over his bucking ball-sac. 'Fuck me, sir.'

'That I will,' he said, grabbing Trina by the titties and upending her. 'Those fustigation marks are crude. Maybe that's how they do it in California, but you'll learn proper ladies' ways here.'

'Oh, no,' she moaned, 'you're not a spanker.'

'Why, mamselle,' he said, 'no Mississippi gentleman would spank a lady undeserving, without due process.'

Elvis was on top, forcing his way into her cunt, his cock slamming her slimy wombneck, and his balls clapping on her thighbacks as he fucked her.

'You been stropped; you ain't nothing but a trull,' he panted, fucking her. 'I ain't losing much virtue on you.'

'Oh, yeah, fuck me,' Trina heard herself cry, her head swimming; it wasn't supposed to be like this; she wasn't supposed to lose control.

It was the biggest cock, the most glorious fuck: yet the redneck stud despised her. Her buttocks pumped to slam her belly against him as her ass slithered in her piss.

'Fuck me harder,' she spat, and Elvis slapped her face.

'That's dirty talk.'

'Oh! Fuck me, sir, fuck me.'

Love to talk dirty to men.

Slap! Slap! Slap!

Her face stung.

He's not frightened of hurting me.

'Fuck me, fuck me. I'm wet, sir. Oh, please . . .'

Slap! Slap! Her breast-melons shook under spanks.

'Oh . . .'

My tits are going to bruise . . .

Elvis spanked her bare breasts, which quivered, pinking under his flurry of slaps, delivered with palm and back-handed with the knuckles. Slap! Slap!

41

'Oh! You're hurting me.'

'You don't like it, trull?'

Slap! Slap! Her bruised, wildly flapping teats were reddening with vicious red fingermarks across the erect nipples. Trina groaned, gasping as her belly fluttered and her spine and stiff clitty tingled. Slap! Slap! Her breasts bounced and wobbled under the tit-spanking as she felt the first drop of sperm at her wombneck. His cock bucked, throbbing, and he fucked faster, and he grunted as his spurt of cream came thick and hot inside Trina's gushing cunt, while his hands spanked her naked titties raw. Slap! Slap!

'Oh, yes, oh, I'm coming. Oh . . . oh . . . ohh!'

Elvis withdrew and rose, leaving Trina to slump to the deck, masturbating her flowing cunt in the afterglow of her orgasm. Elvis made her roll over. He inspected the welts on her flogged ass.

'Yeah, a trull,' he said. 'But the mamselles of Arras might turn you into a lady, yet. Slit-poking ain't of much account, down here.'

'What . . . what the hell is a trull?' she sobbed, clutching her groin.

'What the anglos in New Albion call a trollop. On New Arras, they thrash bad girls for unreasonable behaviour, see? They have all kinds of punishments for unreason, and punishment tools like you'd faint if I described them, for trulls, truants and sluts, until their bare asses are just squirming with reason.'

'Elvis, didn't anyone tell you who I am?'

'No,' he said. 'I'm just the mailman, mamselle.'

'I'm going to be in charge of New Arras.'

Elvis shrugged.

'I don't see how that makes any difference,' he said.

Trina was still sobbing, her face red in shame, as she disembarked.

That's never going to happen again! Insulted, disgraced – pleasured! – by a fucking redneck!

Once he had used her, Elvis had taken no notice of her, and her clothing was once more immaculate. She made her own way down the gangplank after he had carted off the mailsack, with a curious glance at her, his lip curled, half inviting, half sneering. Now she stood by the little harbour, surrounded by palms, magnolias, creepers and mosses, with the buzzing of bees and the gaudy scents of flowers, and sweat was pouring from her again under the afternoon sun. She carried a small bag, her instructions having assured her all personal items would be provided on New Arras. There was a long, flat-roofed wooden hut by the start of a track, leading into the jungle, but there was no one around. The sun was high and it was obviously lunchtime. She assumed Elvis had gone inside the hut, over which a flag drooped at full mast – a single star, with a wreath of laurels below – but no Stars and Stripes. Seeing important-looking buildings shimmering in the far distance, past the forest, she made for the track, stooping to pass under a vehicle barrier of a single wooden pole, which refused to swing up at her touch.

'Halt!'

'Oh!'

Trina was stooping under the barrier, with her bottom stuck in the air and her skirt ridden up, so did not see her assailant, but she squealed as she felt something sharp jab her ass-cleft, the prong touching her panties, right at her anus bud. She jerked at the insulting poke, banged her shoulders on the barrier and came out the other side, livid, to face her attacker.

'Who the hell are you?' she blurted to a girl no more than nineteen, wearing a white, short-sleeved military shirt tucked into a white cotton skirtlet that came down only to her mid-thigh.

'Corporal Cindi Kock, of the public watch,' snapped the girl, clicking her heels.

Both her garments were way too tight: the shirt, certainly, for the heavy breasts, with the side-buttoned skirtlet hugging fleshy, muscled thighs, and a waist not more than Trina's own twenty-two inches. At her waist looped a casual belt, which was a whip. Her uniform gleamed, crisply pressed, although dark sweat-stains

43

already marred the girl's armpits and her shirt clung damply to her breasts, revealing her white, apparently scanty, bra, for the tips of wide areolae were wet and visible around her conic nipple buds. From her breast pocket peeped a hairbrush.

Cindi Kock's long black hair was ironed straight, her coltish legs a golden tan, and her shirt, beneath which her heavy breasts bulged, was open to the third button, revealing pressed flans of swelling brown teat-flesh. One shirtsleeve sported two red horizontal stripes. She wore brown leather kneeboots, but no tights, and her bare legs were shaven smooth. The cotton of the skirtlet was more starch than fabric and was already wilted with sweat, so that her panties, like her bra, showed through the cloth: she had a high-cut bikini bottom that barely covered her mound, and her pubic hair stretched on either side of the gusset, like dark sea-fronds. She held up the intrument of Trina's arrest: a cane, three feet long, with a handle of coiled wire.

Cindi joined Trina simply by stepping behind the barrier's hinge and passing unstooped. She grasped Trina's arm.

'You are under arrest,' she said, her teeth sparkling white between full ruby lips.

The accent was fluting, gentle and deep southern, yet not a drawl like Elvis Lesieur's; each word emerged with dainty precision from her lips. Her tongue licked her upper front teeth, after she pronounced 'arrest' as 'array-est'.

'What?'

The girl pointed.

'You crossed the barrier without completing immigration formalities. You are on New Arras territory. If you had waited on the wharf, which is US federal territory –' she shugged '– I have no option but to demand your ID, and detain you for questioning, mamselle.'

'What is this?' Trina blurted, but not resisting as Cindi led her into the hut, where she found herself in a long room with a counter, like a post office.

Behind the counter were several girls, similarly unformed and busy with stacks of papers, upon which they wrote with careful goosequill pens. Behind the counter, and in the room itself, girls bustled, distributing and collecting papers from the various stacks. Those girls were not in military uniform but wore white blouses with flounced collars, black shoes with white stockings, and flowing dark blue skirts, descending to mid-calf. Their skirts were open six inches at the rear, fastened by a bow, tight enough to show only a hint of white panties beneath, while the stockinged thighs and the tips of white garter straps were fully visible.

The wall was bare, but for a portrait of a young lady in eighteenth-century dress and her hair in ringlets. The lady smiled benignly at her portraitist and brandished a cane just like the one prodding Trina, as if to discourage unflattering portrayal. On the desk sat an old-fashioned tear-off calendar, written in ink, with the legend: 'Ishtar-day, 10th Messidor, Year 214'. Above, a ceiling fan whirred lazily, doing nothing to freshen the stifling air. There were tables and chairs around the room, and Trina saw Elvis at the far end, sitting with a blonde girl in a white blouse and long blue skirt, but with the back of her skirt unfastened, so that the garment swirled open, showing her visible panties. Her panties clung to her sweating buttocks, which appeared red under the wet panty fabric. Elvis nodded politely as she spoke.

'Look, I came with El – with Mr Lesieur,' Trina said. 'He'll explain. You see, I'm Trina Guelph, of Goody Baggs, in Santa Monica, California?'

Everyone except Elvis stared at her; Elvis looked away. All were girls, none seeming older than twenty. A second uniformed girl emerged from the shadows and crowded Trina. She was blonde, perky and bright eyed, her coiffe a smooth, lustrous shell that swayed below her ears; she licked her lips as she eyed Trina's sweating body. Her boldly jutting breasts quivered under her moist shirt. Her uniform, too, was too small, trimly hugging the full peach of her ass and the ripely thrusting breasts, while her skirt, sheathing coltish legs, was tighter and shorter than the arresting officer's.

'A spy, for sure,' she said. 'Good work, Cindi.'

'No more than a detainee, until the committee of public safety has established her status,' said the dark girl, 'and it's Corporal Kock, Harriet – I mean, Constable Stooplaugh.'

'Oh, Cindi,' said the blonde girl, making a moue.

'Constable Stooplaugh. *Garde-à-vous*,' Cindi rapped, and the blonde girl sprang to attention, her hand flying to her brow in salute.

'*Demi-tour.*'

The girl's rigid body whirled round, flinging her heavy breasts from side to side.

'Eyes right. Eyes front. *Repos!*'

After each command, Harriet saluted, until she finally stood at ease, her tightly sheathed buttocks quivering and breasts heaving, with the soft outlines of her big plum nipples visibly swollen. Cindi nodded approval, her fingers gliding on her waist-whip, and her tongue flicking gently over her teeth. Throughout the display, her arm remained locked on Trina's.

'Better, constable,' she said. 'My belt can stay tied awhile. Now then, mamselle, please present some ID.'

Trembling, Trina fumbled for her purse, and got her driver's licence and some credit cards. She began to blurt an explanation of the facts and managed to complete it, to polite attention, while the desk officer, whose badge announced her as Sergeant Merlene Makings, held up her pieces of ID and examined them with placid disapproval.

'You have no *laissez-passer*?' she said.

'What's that? No, I don't. I'm an American!'

'Why, I believe we are all Americans,' Merlene replied, to simpers from the girls and a grin from Elvis. 'You say your company has *bought* New Arras?'

Her lilting voice pronounced it 'New Airs'.

'Yes! If you'll just take me to whoever's in charge – I mean, whoever *was* in charge?'

'With the treasure of New Arras, it is us that buy other people,' said Merlene. '*Purchasing* New Arras –' she chuckled '– such a revendication would be a matter for the

46

directorate of the council of reason, who would instruct the committee of public safety to issue the correct orders, but I have had no instructions on such a matter.'

'Is it possible the affair could have been regulated by the committee of public safety itself, without reference to the directorate?' said Cindi.

'They often do that,' Harriet added, 'on sub-regulatory business that the directorate hasn't time for.'

'A revendication is scarcely sub-regulatory business,' said Merlene, 'and anyway, we've had no orders from the committee, one way or the other.'

'Maybe they are in the stacks,' said Cindi, pointing to the several piles of paper on the counter and the desks behind.

'Maybe they are indeed,' said Merlene, 'in which case, every officer of the public watch shall have copies in triplicate, and we will do our job within reasonable time. Meanwhile, we must consider the new arrival an illegal alien, examine her case, according to the immigration laws, prepare a report for the committee, with copies to the directorate, and await authorisation of further action.'

'Sergeant Makings, may I suggest it would be appropriate to report to the directorate directly, with copies to the committee?' Cindi said.

'Go over the heads of the committee?' said the sergeant.

'On such a matter as this,' said Cindi. 'It could indeed be a case of espionage.'

'Which would place it under the *ultimate* jurisdiction of the directorate, but the *immediate* jurisdiction of the committee,' said Harriet. 'Uh, sergeant.'

Cindi glowered at her. Merlene tossed her flowing auburn mane and smiled, with a little shiver of her tan melons that seemed to jut in competition with Cindi's, and which peeked under a full four undone buttons, allowing a glimpse of the sergeant's lacy scalloped white brassiere.

'If we do have a situation here, time is of the essence and the directorate would expect the committee to make an appropriate unilateral response, so the committee must reasonably expect us to make a similar response,' she said.

'Search her, and write me a priority report, corporal. You may take Constable Stooplaugh to assist. Confiscate and itemise the mamselle's clothing and belongings, and convey her to the detention centre, in the customary manner, taking reasonable care of her unclad person.'

'Must we give her pertinent chastisement, sergeant?' asked Harriet, her eyes gleaming.

'Not at this stage,' replied Merlene, 'until the full facts are in our possession, at which point, I suspect, the committee may consult with the directorate to obtain a decree of formal judicial chastisement, most likely exemplary correction, the act of illegal immigration being automatic malfeasance, under article eighteen of the reglements. She's certainly no scholar, as we'd have a memorandum from the academy, and anyway, scholars arrive by appointed transport. Any judicial chastisement might be severe, so I think it wise to refrain from pertinent chastisement, which the detainee might represent in tribunal as prejudicial, therefore voiding a certainly harsher judicial penalty – unless, of course, she is troublesome, in which case you may apply reasonable provisional correction. I don't think she looks troublesome. You are a reasonable person, aren't you, mamselle?'

'No, I am not a reasonable person!' Trina shrieked. 'Stop this fucking charade. If this is one of GG's jokes, it's gone on long enough. I'm tired and filthy and I want a shower, and – ugh!'

Her mouth was clasped by Harriet's palm, and the two girls frog-marched the struggling Trina past Elvis, lolling with the full-breasted blonde girl in the blue skirt. She was kneeling on a chair opposite the male, gazing up at him, with her skirts parted, seeking fan breeze on her bottom. The ripe pears of her ass rippled as she spoke, and stuck to the wet panties, glistening with sweat. She plucked at her waistband to peel the panty fabric away from the dark ridges on her bottom, where it clung. She grimaced.

'You're sure you weren't mad at me, that last time?' the girl murmured shyly, gazing at Elvis. 'I mean, it sure felt like you were mad at me. I've only four more days of half shame, then I can bowtie my skirt again. It's full shame that's the worst of it all, sir, having to go unfastened and unpantied, and showing bare. All those maids, ogling my naked melons! Ooh!'

'I just do my duty, Mamselle Persimmon,' Elvis replied.

They watched Trina being led into an adjacent cell, whose door the smirking Harriet propped open; girls clustered to spectate as Trina was shown an oblong wooden table with rubber straps dangling from each corner.

'What the hell do you expect me to do?' she blurted.

'Why, undress, of course,' said Corporal Cindi Kock.

'We can't strip-search you unless you're bare-ass naked,' Harriet explained.

'You're out of your fucking minds,' Trina retorted.

Corporal Cindi turned to the onlookers and shrugged.

'An insult to officers of the people?' she sighed. 'You leave me no choice but to have you forcibly stripped, and I warn you that further unreason may justify provisional exemplary punishment.'

'Get your hands off me,' Trina cried, but to no avail; Harriet had her in a half-nelson and forced her face down on to the table.

Trina shrieked in protest as Cindi carefully pulled her clothing from her body, placing each item in a neat stack. She wailed as her panties came off, exposing the writhing bare moons of her ass. Only her bra was left, squashed under her wriggling titties, and Trina cried out as Harriet ripped it from her breasts.

'Cindi – Corporal Kock – please let me administer punishment,' Harriet gasped. 'This is one subversive trull – look, she's been stropped before, and crudely, too. Those fesses beg for proper lashes.'

'No,' Trina whimpered. 'This is grotesque.'

'You heard the constable,' Cindi said. 'One last chance. You have been stropped recently and that changes things, not in your favour – such crude stropping looks like New Albion work so, chances are, you're an ecaped felon. Are you going to behave and submit to reasonable search, or

49

do we have to restrain you in straps, like some malfeasant who can't take a whip on the bare without wetting herself? It's your choice – we shall search you either way.'

Harriet twisted Trina's arm higher and Trina gave a gasp of pain.

'OK,' she sobbed, 'you win. I'll be quiet. Just don't tie me up – anything but that.'

Nude, Trina clutched the table with white fingers as the two watch officers donned rubber gloves, oiled them with water-based jelly and proceeded to inspect her anus and vagina. Trina gasped and swallowed as Harriet got two rubbered fingers, then three, into her anus, tickling the root of her ass for over two minutes. She squirmed and winced as her bare titties and belly slapped the table. Her legs were splayed rigid.

'Isn't that enough?' she moaned. 'It's agony. I'm not hiding anything.'

Harriet withdrew from her anus, leaving her cunt-basin free for Cindi to probe her vulva. Trina sobbed, unresisting and helpless; Cindi penetrated her gash with four fingers, then fanned them to stretch the helpless cunt wide open, and used index and forefinger to stab and pinch the walls of Trina's cavern, right to the wombneck, where Cindi's fingers remained for over a minute.

'Mmm,' Trina moaned. 'Please . . . it tickles.'

'Your kind gets more than tickling on New Arras, mamselle,' said Cindi, her voice icy. 'Our lubricant jelly was superfluous – it seems your cunt interprets our search as lesbian behaviour and is accordingly excited.'

'No! That's gross.'

Cindi removed a wet rubber finger from Trina's cunt.

'Mmm!' Trina gurgled, as Cindi rammed the finger into her throat.

'Do you deny it?' she rasped.

Trina tasted her own come on the invading finger. Gagged by Cindi's knuckles, she sobbed, and shook, no.

'That shall be entered in our report,' said Cindi grimly.

Elvis Lesieur allowed his lips to crease in a sneer.

'Oh, please, sir, tell me about that mamselle,' said Jewel Persimmon, fanning her wet bare buttocks with her sticky panties, so that Elvis glimpsed flesh.

'Nothing much to tell.'

'Alone on a boat for so long! You are a tease, sir.'

'Not me, mamselle. Coming here with all those crazy ideas in her head, that trull got to be dumber 'n' a barrel of hair. Of course, I'm only the mailman,' Elvis said.

From the Journal of Mlle Augustine Flageolet, anno 1760 3
The female bottom is sculptured for the rod, and application of the cane to bare buttocks is therefore a natural and rational duty. Does it not follow that the crimes meriting corporal chastisement are also part of the natural order? A girl unspanked is untrue to her nature. The physiocrat Dr Quesnay, consultant to Mme de Pompadour, advised me the lady was accustomed to a weekly emetic, after which a scourging of birch rods was applied to her naked buttocks, the effect of which was to produce copious dunging and, she averred, a sensation of physical pleasure. His Majesty Louis XV was kind enough to appreciate her subsequent ardour in the royal bedroom. Up to thirty strokes of a birch sheaf produced a notable discoloration and hardening of her posterior flesh, which she said was pleasant to the touch, after the discipline. Dr Quesnay opined that the female body is like a field. For true fecundity of mind and body, its hindquarters must be ploughed with rods. Not entirely inexperienced, I readily consented to the experiment of birching, and found it rigorous but healthful, although – or perhaps because – my naked buttocks smarted for days after each application. Like Mme de Pompadour, I found the tingling and crusting of the weals agreeable to the fingertips. That encouraged me to found my rationalist school for young ladies at Arras, where industry was not unrewarded by punishment.

4

The Public Weal

Sweat rolled down Trina's nude body, tickling her between her breasts and dripping through her pubic forest into her bare quim. She clung to the sides of the perching-rail that bit between the flaps of her vulva as the clanking, mule-drawn wagon jolted over the track. Constable Harriet Stooplaugh and Corporal Cindi Cock sat at either end of the rail, squashing Trina between them.

'Please tell me where we're going?' moaned Trina, her voice muffled by the holeless paper bag on her head.

'You have no need for fear, detainee,' barked Cindi, 'but you are beholden to silence. Consider our favour, transporting you in a closed tumbril, your arms unroped and your legs free of gyves.'

The cart, a furnace, had canvas walls, hiding Trina's nudity from the excited onlookers, who announced their presence by a babble of girls' voices, randomly but briefly silenced by the crack of a whip and a girl's cry of, 'Labour, sluts!'

'She is lucky, being bare-ass,' grumbled Harriet. 'I wish —'

'Harriet,' Cindi interrupted, 'I hope you didn't plan to speak unreasonably. If the committee wishes us to go bare, then it shall promote us to the security corps. For a watchmaid to think of shaming herself by nudity is — well, I am proud to wear watchmaid's uniform. Perhaps vicious trulls deserve caning by corpsmaids in the nude, for their shame, but I don't like girls to cry, even the worst trulls.'

'I do,' said Harriet.

The cart lurched with particular violence on the rutted track and the three girls were thrown together. Trina squealed and struggled from their forced embrace.

'No,' she cried. 'Enough. Let me go, now.'

'I warned you, mamselle,' hissed Cindi.

'Shall we do her, corporal?' said Harriet.

'I must say yes. Rioting merits exemplary punishment.'

'No!' screamed Trina, wriggling as the two officers pinioned her on the floor of the cart, with Harriet squatting on her thighs and Cindi astride her neck, holding her wrists high behind her back.

'We have time to strop her a hundred before we reach the palace of justice. Fifty each, Constable Stooplaugh.'

'Would not the cane be more reasonable, corporal?' murmured Harriet.

'It would, but these quarters are cramped and the detainee is sturdy. Remember the sergeant's warning about prejudicial punishment.'

'Yeah,' said Harriet. 'Worth waiting to see that juicy lesbian ass officially caned raw. Vertical or horizontal, corporal?'

'Mmm!' Trina squealed, writhing under the girls' heavy buttocks, and with her bare titties and cunt squashed to the splintered wooden floor.

'Vertical.'

'Mmm!'

Trina squirmed, the paper bag rustling noisily on her bagged head.

'Paired or in turn?'

'In turn. I'll lead. You take the left, constable.'

Whap!

'Ah!'

Trina yelped, as the back of Cindi's dainty enamel hairbrush cracked on the bare meat of her right buttock.

Whap!

'Ah! Oh!'

She yelped louder as Harriet's strop took her right on the same spot. Her ass-cheeks clenched as she wriggled helplessly under the watchmaids' bodies. Whap! Whap! Whap! Whap! Four more taps with the two hairbrushes landed in the same place, on bare mid-fesse, the impact centre seared hot and stinging on the naked skin.

'Constable!' snapped Cindi. 'I said, you take the left buttock.'

'That is the one to my left.'

'But it's not to my left.'

'Geometrically, corporal –'

'Follow my example. We must start over.'

'No,' wailed Trina. 'It hurts like hell. You've no idea how much my ass smarts, after . . . after . . . I'll behave, I promise.'

'I imagine you will see reason,' Cindi remarked, as she lifted her hairbrush over Trina's quivering bare flans.

Whap!

'Uh . . .'

Whap! The stinger from Harriet's hairbrush bruised her unmarked left globe.

'Uh . . .'

Whap!

'Oh! Please stop, please, please. I can't take it.'

'Your welts speak otherwise,' said Cindi, 'and I see that your breasts were spanked recently. Perhaps we are dealing with a pervert, Harriet.'

Whap! Whap!

'Oh!'

Trina's scarlet buttocks writhed and jerked in a frenzy, but she could not wriggle free from her chastisers' crushing buttocks. The paper bag heaved in and out as she gasped under each blow from the brushes. Her scarlet bare turned darker, with black, puffy patches ripening around the tender left haunch and top left buttock, where Harriet concentrated her impacts; Cindi was content to beat the fleshy centre of her squirming right flan, also darkening to crimson.

Whap! Whap!

'Uh! Oh, no . . .'

A hissing sound filled the confined space as Trina lost control of herself, and a spray of steaming hot piss puddled the floor, the golden liquid squirting between her quivering thighs and filling the crack of her ass. Cindi Kock wrinkled her nose and asked Harriet how many slaps Trina's croup had taken, adding that she was a dirty trull, and her pissing would be included in the report.

'I thought you were counting, Cindi.'

'Harriet, you're the duty constable.'

Cindi sighed.

'We must start over,' she said, 'and count properly, Harriet. I'm so mad at you! You wait till we're off duty.'

'You going to punish me with the cane, Cindi?' murmured Harriet. 'I hate that so much.'

'That's the idea.'

'I mean, it hurts me to whip your bare ass crimson, the way you like it,' Harriet hissed, 'and you weep and squall and everything. It really does. My back aches and my arm gets so tired. You submissive bitches are so demanding.'

The girls shifted on top of Trina and made the sound of sloppy kisses, with moans from Cindi.

'Mmm . . .' Harriet murmured.

'Oh! Don't stop,' whispered Cindi.

'You've the loveliest tits in New Arras, corporal,' said Harriet, 'and the best ass. You know I love to see those melons glow.'

'For sure?'

'Honest.'

On her bare thighs and neck, imprisoned under the crushing weight of the watchmaids' cunt-basins, Trina's skin moistened with hot trickles, as come oozed from the officers' cunts. *And they called me a fucking lesbian . . .*

'Mmm.'

'Yes. Frot me. Oh, yes . . .'

Trina listened, helpless, as the maids masturbated each other to orgasms, whose noise rose above the clattering of the cart. *No!* Her nipples and spine tingled and her clit swelled, with her own cunt helplessly gushing come over the rough wood. She began to writhe, rubbing her stiff clitty against the knotted floor; her belly fluttered, and come gushed from the two tribadists' cunts over her thighs and shoulders, conjoined by streams of hot come from her own gash. *I'm going to get off . . . yes . . .*

Whap! Whap!

'Oh!' Trina screamed as the two watchmaids began to beat her squirming bare buttocks afresh. 'Oh, yes. Oh . . .'

She was sobbing convulsively, her cunt-basin writhing in her spasm of orgasm, as the cart drew to a halt. Her bare buttocks glowed fiery and dark with weals and had taken over a hundred and fifty blows of the hairbrush. Her belly still glowed and fluttered as the watchmaids led her meekly from the tumbril into the palace of justice, past a crowd of jeering girls. Cindi had to unleash her whip and crack it several times on air or on girlflesh, crying, 'Desist, citizens!' and then, 'Get back, you trulls, or I'll whip you to the bone.' Laughter followed that, and Trina wailed as a tomato, then an egg, splashed on her glowing red ass.

'Yee-haw!'

At Harriet's rebel yell, there were cries of alarm, as the blonde watchmaid charged into the crowd. There were screams, thumps and kicks, then a flurry of cane-strokes on bared flesh and a girl's screams. Cindi cried to Harriet to desist, but Harriet obeyed only when she had completed her task, leaving one individual sobbing and howling. The crowd was docile.

'That bitch Devora Dykes is the ringleader,' Harriet said, smacking her hands. 'I hear the committee is to sentence her to public torture next week on another matter. I'd love to see those big titties stretched.'

Swiftly, the girls hustled Trina inside the palace of justice, where Cindi explained the case to a female addressed as Prefect Funger. Asked why the prisoner was naked in shame, yet ungyved, Cindi said Sergeant Makings had not thought her a risk to public safety, despite her abnormal revendication of New Arras.

'Yet I see from her croup,' said the prefect drily, 'that you effected provisional exemplary punishment.'

'The detainee was being unreasonable,' Cindi said.

'Enough to warrant charges of riot? You'd have to wait until a corpsgirl can administer pertinent flogging.'

'Mamselle prefect, with respect, a brief passion must have overcome her. Being unfamiliar with passion, Anglos are untrained to resist it.'

'Very well. She is an abnormal detainee, not a charged prisoner, and I need not waste a prisoner's uniform on her. She can remain naked in shame. Public servants Felt and Acajou! Transport the abnormal detainee to cell 501.'

There was a rustle of papers and the scratch of a pen, with two copies of signed orders handed to the unseen watchmaids, who now escorted Trina, half carrying her, through the fetid heat of the palace of justice and into a cooler corridor winding steeply below ground. The palace sounded and smelled like a bus station, but now in the cell block there was only an occasional girl's moan or sob. Far away, she heard a rhythmic tap-tap and a series of yelps, followed by a long, sobbing groan, and she shuddered in the public servants' clutch.

'Please,' she groaned, 'tell me what's happening? How long am I going to be here?'

'The committee of public safety will study your dossier and make a recommendation to the council of reason, who will debate your case and instruct the committee what to do with you.'

'But –'

'Silence!'

Whap! Whap!

'Oh . . .'

Public servants Felt and Acajou slapped her breasts and buttocks several times.

'I'll make you a deal,' Trina blurted, cringing. 'You heard about my – my revendication. Well, it's true.'

No spanks were administered.

'Yeah! In a few hours, the misunderstanding will be cleared up and I'll be in charge of this place and, you know, I could do you some favours.'

The girls halted.

'Public servant Felt, do you bear witness to an attempt at corruption?'

'Public servant Acajou, I do. Attempting to suborn two public servants in the excecution of their duties. I suggest an oral as well as written report to the prefect, and copies for each member of the committee of public safety.'

Trina heard the clanking of keys and the creak of a door opening. From inside came a warm, sensual perfume.

'Didn't public servant Pageant deliver a condemned prisoner to cell 501 yesterday?' said Felt.

'501 is what we have in writing,' replied Acajou. 'You going to argue with writing?'

'No,' said Felt. 'Is she to remain bagged?'

'The headbag is the property of the public watch and must be returned to them.'

The paper bag slid from Trina's head, and she gulped air, looking at two svelte maids, aged maybe nineteen or twenty, their big titties and croups swathed in clinging uniforms like Cindi's and Harriet's, only in grey denim. Like them, they wore whips and hairbrushes, and their shirts were unbuttoned, showing tanned jellies squeezed by flimsy white cotton brassieres, drenched in sweat.

'Sign this, bitch,' snarled Acajou, the taller of the two, and gave Trina a scroll of paper with a quill pen tipped in a blob of ink. 'It's a deed of abnegation, stating that you no longer claim responsibility for your state-issued head-gear and acknowledge safe delivery to your place of lawful confinement.'

'Fuck that,' said Trina, her face flushing. 'I'm out of here!'

Her spurt of escape was useless. The two jailers grabbed her, and Acajou kneed her in the vulva, doubling her up; as she gasped and wheezed, Felt slapped her bare nates six times, quickfire.

'We already have you on corruption,' Acajou said. 'You want to add riot? We can play games until the corpsgirl gets here to give you pertinent chastisement.'

She kneed Trina again between her thighs. Trina shrieked and, eyes blurred by tears, reached for the crazy goose quill and scrawled a signature on the crazy piece of paper. As she straightened up, Felt delivered a rapid breast-spanking of a dozen slaps, while Acajou stuck a sharp index fingernail into Trina's ass-cleft and wedged it two inches inside her anus. Throughout the breast-spanking, she stabbed Trina's rectum, then jerked her finger out of the anus and wiped it clean on Trina's hair.

'Fuck you!' Trina howled.

'You'll hang for that, bitch,' said Felt and Acajou together, pushing her into the shadows of her cell.

The door clanged shut and was locked from the outside. Trina sank to the stone floor, curling herself up into a ball and rubbing the flood of tears from her eyes. Sobbing, she uncurled and stood shakily to see a shadowy chamber, fifteen yards by ten, illumined by a shaft of light from a barred window. She grabbed the bars and stuck her nose through the window, looking up towards the hulking tower of the palace of justice, three hundred feet above; below, there was a pit of craggy ochre rock. Opposite were the windows of other cells; she was in a hollow prison skyscraper. Faces peered from barred windows; one girl stuck her bare breasts through the bars and rubbed herself obscenely, while another mooned Trina with her bare croup.

Grimacing, she looked away and searched the shadows for the source of the perfume. A bowl of tropical flowers stood on a writing table at the cell's far end, which contained a bed, toilet things, water and a scented candle burning beside the flower bowl. Beside the candle, a teenage girl sat meticulously scripting a document with her quill pen. Her body flickered in the shadows of the candle light. She had long, combed, sandy hair, falling over heavy breasts and trim shoulders, encased in a sleeveless canvas tunic, its front loosely laced over her naked torso. Her long skirt was of the same grey material, which fell away from her wide bare buttocks so that they pressed the cane chair. The prison dress was like the bowtied blue skirts of the girls at the watch post but its back was open, without ties; her buttocks were permanently visible in shame and accessible for punishment. Pot-pourris hung round the walls, adding to the pungency of candle and flowers.

'Hi,' said the girl, smiling and looking up. 'Blush Coynte's my name. Who are you?'

The girl spoke with the familiar southern lilt.

'Didn't expect your company, but glad of it,' Blush said. 'You'll have the cell to yourself soon. I shan't be here long. I'm to be hanged this afternoon, and I'm just busy with my last will and testament. You can be a witness, if you like.'

'Sure,' said Trina weakly.

Hanged? This is complete insanity. Oh, no. Maybe they mean it. Maybe insanity must be complete to be real.

'What are you to be hanged for, Blush?' Trina asked.

'Oh, same old,' said Blush, with a shrug. 'I'll get over it – I always do. It's the shame that really hurts, afterwards. If you're really a spy, they'll hang you too, but if you're lucky they'll deport you straight away and you won't have to endure naked shame. Unless you have a thing about tar and feathers.'

'Wait a minute,' said Trina faintly. 'This doesn't chime – you're talking about hanging, then shame?'

'Blush Coynte wrinkled her nose.

'Poo, you stink of tinkle,' she said, moving closer, and Trina retorted that she didn't smell so good herself.

Blush laughed and said she hadn't washed or wiped her ass for five days, ever since sentence was passed, because if a condemned girl's stink was strong enough the hangman wouldn't come too near her to apply secondary torture on the scaffold.

'Like to wash? I'll help soap you. There's drinking water, and if you're hungry there are some egg salad sandwiches in the fridge.'

Trina wolfed two sandwiches, washing them down from the jug of cold water; all the while, Blush touched the furrows of her bare wealed ass.

'Who did that?' she said. 'It's awesome. They must be really cruel over on New Albion. Let me show you my welts.'

'I'm not from New Albion,' Trina snapped. 'I'm from California.'

Blush shrugged, pouting.

'A king of Spain's maid? Oh, sure. Have it your own way. You'll sing under torture. You must be a spy, for you're nude. My, you have gorgeous titties, and such an ass, I just have to wash you. A condemned girl so misses washing.'

Blush poured a bucket of cold water over Trina and began to work on her breasts with a bar of soap. Trina let the younger girl massage her, sighing and relaxing as the soapy fingers tickled her armpits, rubbed her belly and mons, then strayed between her thighs, touching the fleshy cunt-lips. Blush seemed amazed that Trina trimmed her pubis. As Blush's skirt flapped around her bare buttocks, Trina gasped at the heavy tracery of weals and dark ridges carved on the girl's nates, the hard skin stripes meshing with the exploring tendrils of her pubic jungle; she quivered, realising that Blush's soaping was more caress than massage.

My cunt can't be so pissy she needs to soap it over and over, but it feels nice.

Trina remarked carefully that Blush seemed very relaxed for someone about to be hanged, and asked what exactly did being hanged entail? Blush passed her fingers casually up and down the crack of Trina's ass, then took a gobbet of soap in her fingernail and rammed it up Trina's asshole, making her squeal. The girl began to ream her anus until it was slimy with soap and Trina's cunt began to ooze gently. Blush's soapy fingers traced the puffed ridges clustered across Trina's bare fesse-flesh, and she whistled every time Blush's fingernail gouged a particularly deep welt. Blush shuddered and said she didn't like to think about hanging, as she would have to endure it soon enough, but if Trina was so curious, why, being hanged meant just what it said – being strung up by the hair, or the ankles, wrists, or nipples and quim, and flogged on the bare by the hangman.

Trina laughed nervously.

'There's nothing funny about being hanged, mamselle,' said Blush frostily, 'as I'm sure you'll find out.'

Just a crazy bunch of cracker lesbians, playing weird fantasy games, that's all. Even lesbians can make Goody Baggs. A game, except my welts from the hairbrush still hurt.

'Humour me, Blush,' said Trina. 'Pretend I am a spy from New Albion and tell me everything I should know.'

'I'm due punishment, so what have I to lose?' said Blush. 'I can say anything I like, about the committee and all, and nobody'll believe a thing you tell them, even when you're screaming under torture.'

'Exactly,' said Trina.

The star and laurel was the flag of the Republic of West Florida, of which New Arras and, Blush said in a whisper, New Albion were the remnants. In the eighteenth century, there was confusion about who owned the territory – whether the king of Spain or Napoleon of France – and then the USA made the Louisiana Purchase, only nobody knew for sure what Louisiana was, or whose it was to sell, so folks on the mainland got tired and proclaimed the independent republic of West Florida, in the month of Vendémiaire, Year 19, by the French republican calendar of 1793, 'or September 1810, mainland reckoning'. New Arras threw in with West Florida, because the Feminine Republic of Reason had been established on the island fifty years before, by Mamselle Flageolet, exiled from France because of her love of female education. A love not shared by the Anglo bitches from Maine over on New Albion – Blush didn't like to speak of New Albion, as they were scumbags.

'You might be one of them,' she said, 'but your bod's so virtuous. Such righteous fesses.'

After the speedy collapse of the RWF, New Arras made a deal to be a commonwealth, or *état libre et associé*, of the USA. New Arras still considered itself the Feminine Republic of Reason, but was officially an academy, as those men in DC couldn't abide a feminine republic and laughed at the notion of feminine reason – Blush said men could be twittle-pated sometimes. New Arras lived off its own produce, augmenting its income by the manufacture of wigs, pomades and hand-crafted furniture; providing assistance to mariners; and schooling young ladies in submission to the laws of reason and the manners of southern belles. With a US marshal as federal ambassador, the council of reason and its directorate ran New Arras, with law and order assured by the committee of public safety, the public watch and the security corps. Beauty of buttocks was the sole test of entry to the academy.

'We teach old-fashioned feminine virtues,' Blush said as she soaped Trina's naked breasts, 'and, truth be told, I don't know what the USA would do without us.'

'Which virtues?' Trina gasped, for Blush's nimble fingers made her belly tingle, as come oozed from her soaped cunt.

'Modesty, decorum and submission to reason, which make a perfectly submissive southern belle. As we are at war with New Albion, reason must be harsh for the benefit of the public weal. The flapjacks of New Albion want to get their hands on Mamselle Flageolet's treasure in the Bank of New Arras. There are spies everywhere, but I'm a gallows-bird, so I don't care. I solemnly give Mamselle Pure the finger. Yee-haw! Let New Albion enslave us! Hey, listen, the jailers will be here soon and I must get my will finished.'

Blush disengaged and recommenced her writing, leaving Trina to rinse, shivering, with the cold water. The girl sucked the end of her quill, before dipping it in the ink.

'Hmm . . . let me see.'

She began to scratch, muttering.

'To my best friend Emily Cawdor, I leave thirty lashes with the bullwhip. To my other best friend, Jewel Persimmon, I leave fifty strokes on the bare fesses with the hickory switch, split end. To my other best friend, Devora Dykes, I leave a titty-thrashing of forty with the cane, and twenty strokes of the double ashplant on the bare fesses.'

She looked up, saw Trina shivering and, as Trina opened her mouth to assure the maid she wasn't shivering from cold, Blush stripped naked and wrapped Trina in her bulky canvas uniform.

'Take it till you warm up,' she said. 'Why, I'm as hot as a June bride in a feather bed.'

Trina eased her arms through the sleeves, and knotted the skirt around her waist, leaving her ass bare. The garment stank of Blush, the odour of her piss and

unwashed asshole being powerful, yet stimulating Tina to
bend over Blush's head and tickle her hair with her breasts.
She asked what bequest Blush was making.

'A hanged girl is made bankrupt after her correction and
forfeits all her currency in the bank of New Arras,' she
explained, 'unless she gives it away to her best friends.
Currency can't buy you off a hanging.'

'You're giving away whipstrokes?' Trina said, aghast.

'A pile,' said Blush, pulling a face. 'I hope I do so well
when they string Devora up, or Jewel. Poor Emily's an
unlucky creature and rarely gets fustigation, so her bottom's not very rich. You can get rich fast, if you're
prepared to serve in the Stella Maris mariners' hostel by
the harbour, or if you have juice with a committeemaid,
who'll stroke you privately, with attestation. But Emily is
too shy to have juice, and she wimped out on a term in the
Stella Maris – which was a pity, for that kind of frightened
submissive is popular with males. The Stella Maris is way
better than a tour as guardsmaid in the prisoner of war
camp. Yuk!'

Blush shuddered.

'OK, that about winds things up. The jailers will be here
soon. I . . . I hope you don't think me bold, or forward, but
I noticed my touch was making you wet in your chatte, so
do you want to diddle before they hang me? I know I do.
We just have time. I'd so love to touch your quim. It's so
beautiful, under that funny trim, all red and glowy. Would
you like to touch mine? It's OK for condemned prisoners to
be forward. Do you like my gash? Look.'

She stood, and raised her right leg straight up, so that
her calf touched her cheek. She hugged her leg to her face,
her big eyes beseeching Trina, and the cunt-basin stretched
open for her inspection. Trina gasped as she saw the
furrow of the ass-cleft, the brown pucker of the anus, puffy
and crinkled like a prune, and almost as large; the curved
slit between the full red gash-flaps, dribbling clear, shiny
come that slimed Blush's perineum. The cunt-lips twitched,
creased, formed a smile, then creased the other way, to
make a frown: smile, frown, smile. Blush giggled.

'Oh . . . I'd like to, very much,' Trina moaned.

Blush plunged her hand beneath Trina's prison skirt, rapidly finding her gash, which was indeed slimy with ooze, and clucked with pleasure. She drew Trina's trembling fingers to her enormous pubic mane, and Trina delved into the pungent mass of hair, to find a clitty as throbbing, and a cunt as swollen and wet, as her own.

This is crazy. Do these girls do anything but masturbate?

The two girls frotted, fingers probing wet pouches and thumbs pressing clits, until each gasped and writhed her cunt-basin against the other's touch.

'Oh, yes,' said Blush. 'Do me, diddle my cunt, oh yes . . .'

Trina got her whole fist into Blush's cunt and was reaming the walls of the pouch with alternate fast and slow jabs until the nude maid's toes were off the floor, and she danced with her cunt on Trina's forearm. Her breasts flopped up and down, as she smacked her swollen erect nipples, blushing like dark plums on her creamy teat-flesh. Trina felt her ooze turn to a stream as the girl's agile fingers twitched and nipped her throbbing clitoris, and her belly heaved under the stiff canvas, drenched in her sweat.

She writhed under her canvas top to rub her nipples against the stiff fabric and, with a whirl of her torso, had the buds as hard and swollen as the nude maid's. Blush's hands darted from Trina's gushing quim to cup her buttocks, oiling them with Trina's cunt-slime. Her fingers slid up and down the marks of Trina's naked spanking, and Trina's own fingers explored the full, ripe ass-peach, ridged and furrowed with hard weals.

'Such beautiful petals,' Blush gasped. 'So firm and hot, and sliced deep, oh, oh yes, I'm going to come. Oh!'

Trina swallowed and said nothing; as Blush Coynte's body shuddered in orgasm, her come poured over Trina's frotting fist, and Trina's own cunt sluiced with a torrent of slimy cunt juice as she moaned in the stabbing, swooning joy of her own climax. Keys rattled at the door and it was flung open. Surveying the two *frotteuses* were public servants Acajou and Felt, along with Prefect Funger and a tall, blonde girl, ripely fessed, massively teated and with smouldering grey eyes, no older than Trina, and whose regal carriage proclaimed her authority. Her waist narrowed to a taper over big, jutting buttock pears; she wore a white blouse and dark blue skirt, like the girls at the watch post, but her stockings were of pure nylon fishnet and in black. Her skirt did not billow but clung to her broad buttocks, revealing that she had no panties, and the skirt was smooth at the back with no bowstring. Her gleaming black pointed boots shone so brightly that they mirrored the pink and blonde of her naked pubis.

'All rise for Mamselle Zealla Pure, chief officer of the committee of public safety,' announced Prefect Funger. 'Citizen Blush Coynte, the committee has decreed that you be transported to a place of execution and there hanged, until correction has been applied to your naked person. I order you to accompany public servants Acajou and Felt at this time.'

The blonde female spoke in a soft purr as Trina gaped in astonishment.

'I believe the prisoner has been masturbating with the detainee. That is a serious offence.'

'Oh!' Trina gasped. 'It was my fault, honestly. Don't blame the kid, I mean –'

'How reasonable of you to confess, mamselle,' said the blonde. 'Your chastisement shall be augmented after you are hanged.'

Acajou and Felt approached Trina and seized her arms.

'Let's go, Citizen Coynte,' said Acajou.

'Wait,' Trina shrieked as they dragged her, wriggling, to the door. 'I'm not Coynte, I'm Trina Guelph. I'm . . . I'm an illegal immigrant, that's all. Blush, tell them who I am.'

'Whoever the detainee is, she is naked and in shame,' said Zealla Pure, 'so her statements mean nothing until confirmed by torture. Citizen Blush Coynte was confined here wearing prisoner's raiment, and the mamselle in prisoner's raiment is therefore Citizen Blush Coynte.'

'Yes, Mamselle Coynte,' said Blush, 'best take your punishment like a lady. Think of me, an unwilling spy for New Albion, tortured and screaming under the whip.'

Trina turned to Acajou and Felt, begging them to admit that they had delivered her here only an hour before.

'Is that true?' hissed Zealla Pure.

'Our report, stamped by Prefect Funger, says we delivered a naked detainee,' replied Felt, 'so although the derrière welts of the nude female resemble those of Citizen Blush Coynte, scholar of New Arras, the prisoner for execution must be this one.'

Elvis Lesieur appeared at the door.

'Thank goodness you're here,' cried Trina. 'Tell these maniacs I'm Trina Guelph! Tell them I came in your boat this morning, please!'

Elvis tipped his peaked cap to the ladies.

'All I had on the boat was a mail sack, Citizen Pure,' he said. 'Didn't look to see if there was a mamselle inside.'

Everybody laughed, except Trina.

'No . . .' she sobbed as Acajou and Felt pinioned her hands behind the back of her neck.

'Thanks for the diddle, New Albion spy,' said Blush as Trina was dragged away. 'How sweet, you already know Elvis.'

'She'll get to know him a lot better, Blush, in the next couple of hours,' said Zealla Pure.

She turned to Trina, whose eyes were still staring at Zealla, a perfect lookalike for Kimmi Lardeau.

'Elvis is our public hangman, you see,' Zealla added.

From the Journal of Mlle Augustine Flageolet, anno 1760 4
To banish vice from polite society, we must remove the notion of cause and effect. Virtue does not produce happiness, nor crime punishment. Strokes descend on bare buttocks, as rain descends from the sky. Virtue is to accept and relish the inevitability of strokes, for why did nature create the sublime sculptures of a girl's bare croup, if not to display it red and aquiver under flogging? If only Mme de Pompadour had prevailed, to preserve my academy from the viperish tongues of Flanders and Artois!

Today, I had Annique Ducrueil lashed at the mainmast, fifty strokes on the bare back, with a stockwhip. Her offence was laziness in the furniture workshop. Whipping on the back is arguably less ladylike, hence more shameful, than strokes on bare nates, as it affords less occasion for delicious blushes and squirms. The delicacy of our pieces requires teamwork and, when we have access to the treasure of American hardwoods, our exportation of stocks, stools, racks, gibbets and other flagellant utensils must reap vast profits from the academic institutions of Europe, as well as discerning friends of the rod in the New World. I had her stripped to her petticoat, with her torso bare, and was interested that her nipples stiffened during her whipping, also that there was a damp stain at her crotch afterwards. Can corporal punishment have to do with voluptuous pleasure? In which case, where is the line drawn between punishment and delight? Annique's skin was discoloured, but she did not shriek. Afterwards, I laced her in a green satin corset, fastening her waist to sixteen pouces, but the brave girl did not cry out. Suffering adds a poignancy to female beauty.

5

Melons Up

The sultry air matted Trina's mane, damp with sweat, against her brow. Pinioned, she was unable to brush the locks away.

'I believe your offence was wetting your palliasse, Mamselle Coynte,' said Zealla Pure, striding in front of Trina and her guards. 'Again . . . the rule book specifies a chastisement of pertinent flogging, but makes it a hanging offence for unreasonable repetition.'

'I'm not Blush Coynte. You *know* I'm not, mamselle,' Trina blurted, as she hobbled along. 'Please tell me, do you have relatives named Lardeau?'

Zealla Pure stopped the cortege and smiled without replying.

They stood in the middle of Central Place, a large square, framed by the palace of justice, the courthouse, the academy of sciences and the Bank of New Arras, its hanging sign showing a girl in eighteenth-century costume, skirts and petticoats lifted, and a cane swishing her bare bottom, with an older inscription beneath: Banque du Nouvel Arras. The buildings drooped with kudzu vine and yellow Carolina jasmine, whose fragrance shimmered in the sweat-moist air, the creepers intermeshing and the plants rooting in the stonework. The group of girls attracted only mild or frightened curiosity from the numerous girls hurrying towards the square's end, and dressed either in official uniform or else the flowing scholar's robe that bared or modestly hid the unpantied croup.

In the centre of the square stood a plain rectangular frame of southern white oak, fifteen feet long and six high; from the crossbar dangled half a dozen sets of rubber wrist-cuffs, with one occupied. The exposed girl was nude and hung limply from her bonds, with both back and buttocks bearing stripes of recent flogging. Her body twirled and as her front swayed into view Trina saw big, jutting dugs covered in thick whipmarks; the belly too, with the same pink slashes covering the tops of the thighs, and the pubis itself, swollen and red under a thick, straggling blonde fleece, wet with the girl's exudations. A low, mewling sob came from the paper bag that shrouded her head, with hanks of blonde mane clinging wetly, beneath the bag, to her wealed back and shoulders.

The robed girls lowered their heads as they passed the nude figure, but with quick looks at her weals and making wide eyes of fear. The officers, in white or grey uniform, ignored the flogged girl. From Central Place, a cobbled street led to a larger square, in whose centre stood a scaffold, dimly visible in the heat haze, and surrounded by a mass of girls – scholars, in white blouse and blue skirt. The shamed, with bottoms exposed, mingled with the modest, whose skirts were drawn tightly over their fesses, and around the crowd stood white-uniformed officers of the public watch, their whips uncoiled. Zealla poised her cane over Trina's buttocks, bared by the canvas shame dress. She nodded towards the hanging girl of Central Place.

'Julie Pageant received a pertinent flogging this morning,' she hissed, 'for telling such lies. She was leader of a circle of lesbian *frotteuses*, disgraceful in a public servant, and foolishly tried to deny it. A normal sentence for unreasonable masturbation is fifty canestrokes on the fesses, but for conspiracy to masturbate she got one hundred lashes with a cattle whip, fifty on the back and fifty on the croup, and she only had enough strokes in the bank to buy thirty-two of them away. Blush Coynte is rich, but the foolish trull must forfeit her bank balance yet again. No currency can buy a girl off a public hanging. And you claim you're not Blush Coynte? Your prison garb says you are, mamselle – reason says you must be. The maids expect to see a uniformed prisoner stripped and shamed, and they shall.'

Vip! Vip! Vip!

'Uh!' Trina grunted, as three cuts from the ashplant sliced fresh pink weals on her bare. 'Piss on you, I'm Trina Guelph, you dumb fuck.'

The naked buttocks clenched in a frenzied squirm and her legs danced, alternately stiffening and buckling, as her bare croup tried to dissipate its pain.

Vip! Vip! Vip!

'Ah! No, please!'

The ashplant raised crisp, vivid weals on her naked ass-flesh. Vip! Vip! Vip!

'Uhh . . .'

'Who are you, malfeasant?' Zealla said.

Trina shuddered in a choking sob; her loins and bare buttocks danced, her legs and feet jerking, with her toes tapping the ground as her jailers held her up by her pinioned arms. Vip! Vip! Vip!

'Oh . . . oh . . . I'm – I'm Blush Coynte, OK? Anything, just please stop.'

Vip! Vip! Vip!

'Oh!' Trina wailed as her flogged bare fesses trembled and a hissing golden stream of piss spurted from her cunt, spraying the earth and soaking her canvas dress.

Zealla Pure wrinkled her nose and put away her cane.

'Truants should not make unreasonable requests,' she said daintily. 'That malodorous display would earn you stripes, save that you are already beyond quota.'

Trina sobbed, trying to rub her buttocks, but was restrained by the jailers, who dragged her along the cobbles. They entered the second square, flanked by edifices of five or six floors in the Grecian style, which Zealla called Republic Place. She poked Trina's anus with the tip of her cane, advising her to walk erect to her place of execution, on pain of further pertinent chastisement before her torture and hanging. Trina wailed and sobbed, but managed to steady herself and hobble upright.

71

Be cool. When this fucking misunderstanding is cleared up, I'll be boss of these crazy bitches.

Elvis climbed on to the scaffold, where a watchmaid handed him a black canvas hood and a whip, consisting of a handle with a flail of knotted rubber thongs two feet in length. Elvis stripped off his shirt and gave it to the maid, who curtsied. Her motion caused her top shirt-button to pop and her bare breast spilled out. Elvis cupped the teat with a swift slap of his palm. He inclined, secured the shirt and packed the errant breast back in its covering, making sure to tuck it in firmly and rolling the maid's flesh against the heel of his hand, which rubbed back and forth on her nipple. The maid blushed and Zealla Pure's lip trembled; her nostrils flared as she turned her head away. The maid curtsied again.

'I'm an American citizen,' Trina wailed. 'You can't treat me this way. I demand to see the US marshal.'

Zealla smiled as Trina mounted the scaffold, stumbling up the steps and steadied by her guards beside the polished wooden rack. Elvis stood in front of her, tucked the handle of his whip down the front of his pants and released her wrists from their neck cuff. She wept copiously, screwing her fists into blurred eyes. Slowly, Elvis unfastened her prison tunic, finally ripping the cloth from her breasts and drawing a low wail from Trina as he bared her upper body. He took a teat in each hand and began to squeeze her breasts, kneading them painfully and drawing the nipple-flesh between his fingernails to pinch the nips to white buds. Trina trembled, but remained rooted to the spot.

'No, don't,' she gasped, as Elvis pinched her teats harder. 'Oh! You motherfucker, stop. You fucking bastard.'

Elvis grinned his lopsided grin, and reached behind her. With one pull, her skirt was undone, and fell to her ankles, revealing her nude buttocks, glowing with the weals from Zealla's cane. Elvis stroked the jagged gashes of the canemarks, applying his fingernails to rake her sores and making her groan. He swayed his hips, so that the tips of his scourge dangled, brushing against Trina's fleece and belly.

'You motherfucker,' she sobbed, 'you motherfucker. Ahh!'

At her obscenity, Elvis dug his claws sharply into her cooze, and began to rake the inside of her slit.

'Oh . . . oh . . . don't . . .'

He plunged his fist inside her, penetrating her to his wrist. Trina widened her thighs to permit his penetration, and sobbed louder as his wrist quickly slimed with her cunt-oil. After two minutes of fisting her cunt, Elvis withdrew and held up dripping fingers. The crowd murmured excitedly, all the maids standing quivering to attention, arms rigid at their sides.

'You bastard,' Trina wailed.

She did not resist as the hangman's maids bound her wrists and ankles to the rollers at each end of the rack. Trina's screams and frantic wriggling as a new, terrified jet of piss burst from her cunt made the crowd buzz. Elvis donned the black leather hood, and stood over Trina with only his eyes and mouth visible. The two sweating, braless girls in public servants' uniforms stood beneath Zealla at either end of the rack, grasping the driver wheels. The rack was stained with fluids of previous victims.

'I am the US marshal,' said Zealla. 'Carry out sentence, Citizen Lesieur.'

Trina screamed and pissed herself once more, very heavily, as she was strapped down. Elvis gave the order to crank up the rack. Ratchets squeaked; Trina stretched herself fully, as if to charm away the pain for as long as possible. Elvis's eyes were lazy slits, staring at the driblets of golden fluid from Trina's gash.

'Ahh!'

Her spine and legs stretched, bones cracking, and the pain seeped into her body.

'Ahh! No . . .'

Her teats stretched to tight melons, billowing in the languid breeze above her chin. Her breath came in furious, frightened gasps.

'Oh, please, enough,' she groaned. 'Whip me then. Please whip me and have done with it.'

Zealla stared down at her.

'Not until you confess,' she murmured.

'OK, I confess,' sobbed Trina, rattling at the ropes which bound her. 'Anything. I'm guilty. Just please, oh please, get this nightmare over with.'

'A detailed confession,' said Zealla, 'or you'll find your nightmare is only beginning.'

'Ahh!' Trina screamed as the rack creaked tighter; her spine arched and her gaping cunt, between thighs bound apart, dribbled hot come into the crack of her ass.

Zealla put a finger to her anus and scratched her, which made Trina moan, then lifted the finger, glistening with Trina's dripped cunt-slime. She put the finger into the back of Trina's throat, ordering her to suck her own juice.

'The only way you may persuade us you are not Blush Coynte,' she said, 'is to describe your true self. From your reactions to chastisement, it seems you are that most despicable of creatures, a submissive pervert. Confess fully to your nature and we may believe you are not Citizen Blush Coynte, not even a New Albion spy, merely a deluded enthusiast of pain, who imagined she would enjoy our reasonable punishments. Such a confession means baring youself, intruder. Every detail of your perverted history – otherwise, Blush Coynte you shall remain.'

A hangman's maid, on signal from Zealla, upended a squirming cloth bag into Trina's cunt. From the bag spilled clams, flicking from open shells, and scuttling spider crabs. Trina screamed, as her cunt was invaded by the crustaceans, and the maid clamped her gash-lips tight shut with a two-inch-long iron cunt-clamp.

'Every detail. Now,' Zealla snapped.

Trina began to sob her story, including her mission to New Albion, and insisting her predicament was a terrible misunderstanding, but fervently agreeing her perverted nature might be responsible. She blurted her games with Kimmi and Allan and everything before that, her cruel and dominant sex practices with males. She insisted that the truth would prove her no submissive but a tyrant, a dominatrix. Her cunt-basin wriggled from the cargo in her pouch, with her wet ass thumping the base of the rack, as the crustaceans fought inside her cunt. Trina shrieked as shell splinters ripped her gash-meat, and mingled fluids dripped from her squirming slit. Scholars and watchmaids craned to hear Trina's words. Their arms twitched at their sides, clutching skirts and knotting the fabric into balls, wet with perspiration. The maids scratched themselves at their half-bared breasts or in the cracks of their asses, shifting on trembling legs.

'For one so bold, you seem to fear pain,' said Zealla.

'I hate pain. I do hate to be hurt, so very much.'

'Do the crusties hurt?'

'You know they do.'

'A rhetorical question. And another: what if your story is a lie, presenting yourself as cruel and unreasonable simply to get the flogging you crave?'

'You're crazy! Who would want this – and whipping? I can't believe it. Oh, please, mamselle, enough.'

'Why, no maid wants whipping,' said Zealla, 'which is why they like to watch. It could be them . . .'

The girls turned the rack; Trina's back soared in an arch and she screamed. Droplets of her torturers' sweat landed on her face and belly. Zealla sniffed and turned her head in disdain. Upon her orders, Trina's jaws were forced open and a shaven tennis ball wedged between them, the gag fastened around her nape by a tight rubber cord.

'Mmm, mmm,' she gurgled, as the rack notched tighter, splaying her ribs hard against her skin and stretching her teats to envelopes.

The cunt-vice was wrenched from her bruised gash-flaps, and the first rack maid kneeled between Trina's thighs. She looked up at the tortured girl and licked her lips. Then she buried her mouth in Tina's cunt and fastened the lips between her teeth. Her jaws engorged the whole of Trina's vulva, and her teeth scraped on Trina's throbbing naked clitoris.

'Ngnh . . .' she moaned.

The girl began to suck, only pausing to prise Trina's cunt open with her fingers and extract the scuttling crustaceans from her pouch. There was a cracking as the girl crunched the creatures whole, slurping their juices mixed with Trina's steadily gushing cunt-oil.

'My turn,' barked her colleague, and the girl gave way.

The second maid guzzled the shellfish until Trina's bruised cunt was empty, save for the river of cunt-slime she exuded, with little cries, as the hot droplets smeared her quivering bare thighs. When the maid rose, her mouth was bulging with molluscs; she sprang to Elvis's face and planted a kiss on his lips. Elvis did not start but opened his mouth to meet hers and calmly took her whole cargo of creatures, which he crunched thoughtfully, looking down at Trina's trembling body. He patted the donor's ass and let his fingers stray inside her cleft as he swallowed. Then he took his scourge from his belt and sliced the air with the cluster of heavy rubber thongs.

Trina screamed as the rack winched her tighter, and Elvis advised the rack maidens to leave some screaming for his whip. Zealla stood inches from him, her hand amid the thongs of his dangling quirt, stroking and rubbing the gleaming rubber. The rack creaked and Trina squealed. Zealla laughed.

'The rack has scarcely tightened,' she said. 'A mere one twentieth of one degree. The idea of pain enthralls you. You demand whipping, like a submissive.'

The crowd began to murmur.

'Whip her! Whip the trull!'

Girlish voices rose in a crescendo of lust and fury.

'They want your ass to bear their scars,' said Zealla. 'To crave punishment of another's flesh is desire to punish one's own. They crave even your scheduled chastisement, hanged from ropes clamped to nipples, mane and *chatte*, slanted at forty-five degrees, with legs fully splayed, to take whipping on the bare fesses, back, ass-cleft and thighs.'

The rack maidens began to unfasten Trina's bonds; Elvis raised his scourge high, and brought it cracking on the deck, inches from Trina's face, with a smack that made her shudder, shrieking.

'Mmm,' she gasped, as control vanished, and her stream of piss was punctuated by a plop of dungs. 'Mmm! Mmm!'

She lay, wriggling in her own exudations, her naked body lathered in sweat, tears and drool that trickled from her gagged mouth. Piss dribbled from her gaping cunt, mingled with a copious stream of come, which slopped her upper thighs and dripped into her ass-crack. She sobbed; Zealla smiled again and reached beneath her skirt. She drew out a sheaf of documents, with photographs, which she took some time to inspect. The maids raised the freed body of Trina and held her pinioned and upright in front of her tormentors. Come and piss dribbled unchecked down the sobbing girl's bare thighs and puddled between her toes. Zealla turned her round and traced the pattern of fresh weals on her buttocks, the most recent being the plump trenches raised by her own cane. After a while, she nodded and pursed her lips. Then she reached forwards and ripped the gag from Trina's lips. Trina squealed and jerked, but the arms of the rack maidens held her fast.

'Let me go,' she whined. 'Please, mamselle.'

'Of course, Mamselle Guelph,' said Zealla. 'As soon as you are calm enough for your own safety.'

'Uh?'

'Why, there has indeed been a misunderstanding,' Zealla purred, 'though not an unreasonable one. Yes, I have been expecting Mamselle Trina Guelph, but the watchmaids were not informed, as we figured you would arrive in pomp and style, not sneak ashore like some illegal migrant, wanting to sell her body at the Stella Maris! You will agee that your ripeness of figure, mamselle, invites suspicions of sex migrancy at the very least – possibly a spy, into the bargain. Now that I have seen you bared, shrieking and fouling yourself, and inspected your buttocks, I recognise you as the Mamselle Trina Guelph described. I am honoured to invite you to occupy the intendant's palace, as lawful intendant of New Arras.'

Her hand cupped Trina's left buttock, and kneaded her weals, the palm stroking and squeezing Trina's fesse-meat.

'You have a flagellant's ass,' she purred, 'the skin satin-smooth, the welts a neat mosaic and the buttock beautifully tense, firm and ripe, without spare fat – unlike so many mainland females. You are a submissive and crave the lash, mamselle. Clenching under cane is the perfect isometric exercise.'

'Let me see that,' Trina whimpered.

Zealla swept the documents away but a few papers fluttered to the ground. As the rack maids picked them up, Trina saw a naked girl, spanked and flogged on the bare, her ass livid with welts and her limbs contorted in agony. *Who did this? Allan? Kimmi?*

'That's not me,' she shrilled.

'I think it is,' Zealla retorted.

'I wasn't informed,' Elvis murmured sullenly.

Zealla turned to him with a radiant smile.

'Why should a mere public official be informed, sir?' she said. 'You might have guessed, if you learned to focus more, instead of pawing any girlmeat that takes your eye. Mamselle Guelph, we shall proceed to the palace at once. How fortunate that your behaviour under torture revealed who you really are, at the last moment, before the whip kissed your bare. It is with satisfaction and some relief that I shall hand to you the scroll of supreme authority. I realise my behaviour may have seemed uneasonable to you as a mainlander, so I'd understand and expect it if you wanted me whipped. I'm bound to say my chances of getting a majority of the committee to oppose my summary chastisement on bare are slim.'

She licked her teeth as Trina, her gasps diminishing and her trembling eased, was freed from the rack.

'Whip you, mamselle?' she said. 'Why, no.'

Zealla smiled.

'You aren't tempted by my buttocks?' she murmured. 'Think of them, naked and red, squirming under your cane, mamselle intendant.'

Zealla curtsied to Trina, bowing low and showing the firm jellies of her teats, quivering brown against white straining bra-fabric. There were murmurs from the maids standing to attention under the baking sun. Their ranks began to sway as they relaxed in defiance of the watchmaids' canes. Random canestrokes seemed to further inflame the watching girls.

78

'There is to be a fustigation,' remarked Elvis, 'and if they don't get one you'll have trouble, mamselle. I'm easy – you can pay me for strokes whipped or strokes unwhipped, don't make no difference.'

'So, Mamselle Guelph,' Zealla said, 'your first duty as intendant shall be to select a malfeasant for hanging. Mr Lesieur gets cranky any day he hasn't whipped a girl's bare melons. There are enough who deserve it.'

'How can I? I don't know them or who has committed crimes.'

'They all have. Are you sure you don't want me flogged, citizen?'

Smiling, the blonde rubbed her breasts, licked a finger and dabbed the air. The crowd growled louder and louder.

'No. I'm going to reform this wacky system,' Trina declared. 'Stop all this flogging and brutality and barbaric shit, like eating crusties from a girl's pussy.'

'Best think on it, mamselle,' Zealla said. 'Right now, I'd be reasonable and name a victim for Mr Lesieur.'

The girls in the crowd began to chant, their voices drowning the tap of canes on fesses and the little shrieks of the victims. Trina looked desperately for a solution to the problem; saw faces avid to witness flogging. One girl, a heavy-breasted blonde, turned suddenly and mooned the group on the scaffold, drawing jeers and cheers from the girls around her. Trina saw a perfect ass-peach, its golden skin neatly pinked in lattices of canestripes.

'The scholars expect you to ... establish credibility,' Zealla said. 'I can suggest a few names, if you wish.'

'Unnecessary,' Trina hissed. 'I am in charge – right?'

'Right,' Zealla said.

'Bring Devora Dykes up here, and hang her,' Trina said.

The girls cheered and there was a struggle, the air peppered with screams and curses. At last the girl Devora Dykes was carried by watchmaids up on to the scaffold. Her clothing was in disarray so that she was half nude, big teats flopping, even before she was stripped and strapped, groaning, into the rack, still warm and piss-soaked from

Trina's own body. She was the girl who had mooned them minutes before.

'Wise choice,' Zealla said. 'May I ask how you knew –?'

'No, you may not,' Trina rapped. 'I am the intendant.'

'Of course. Maid, fetch a robe for the new intendant.'

Trina raised her arm.

'It's too hot for clothes,' she said sweetly. 'Isn't nudity shameful, here in New Arras?'

'The most shameful of things,' Zealla replied.

'Then I shall travel nude to my palace,' said Trina, licking her teeth. 'I am a mainlander, right?'

Elvis leered but Zealla's face crisped, pale in anger.

'Your privilege, mamselle intendant,' she said, curtseying, 'but remember that all officials are subject to the constitution, and one who sports shame may retroactively accrue the punishment leading thereto.'

Trina said she would take her chances. Nude and cheerful, she folded her arms and spread her legs to watch the chastisement of the squealing, cursing Devora Dykes. An hour later, she stumbled away from Devora's inert and silent body, lathered in sweat and glowing with welts. Still nude and pale of face, she was escorted by Zealla and a dozen watchmaids to the intendant's palace perched on a wooded hillock overlooking the harbour.

Zealla Pure invited the committee of public safety to hear and heed their new intendant.

'I don't ever want to witness such a hideous thing again,' Trina blurted. 'I thought I'd been brutalised, but what Devora endured . . .'

Droplets of golden tea spilled from the cup to her saucer.

Zealla Pure shrugged.

'That was nothing, mamselle intendant,' she said, and the committee murmured agreement. 'Devora is no stranger to the lash, or to nipple- and quim-clamps.'

'She screamed so,' Trina said faintly.

'Not as much as you would have, mamselle intendant,' said Zealla sweetly and the other maids laughed, while Trina blushed furiously, knowing it was true.

'Nor was her juice so copious,' said Sirena Toitte, a silky brunette with ruby lips and large conic teats quivering in braless merriment.

The committee consisted of four other directresses, costumed like Zealla: Sirena Toitte, Alice Frequemme, Heidi Absorb and Dorita Carawn, all scarcely – perhaps not yet – out of their teens. All were ripe maids with the same swelling titties and ass sported by Zealla, the confidence of youth and beauty and the gravity of those accustomed to power over other bodies. With full breasts ballooning inside tight blouses, buttoned to the neck, they sat at a rectangular rosewood table, each girl with a stack of papers before her, a quill pen and inkpot, and a slave – politely, a thrall – in attendance. Thralls kept their heads down, wore shame dress of only skimpy bra and panties and were barefoot on rough floorboards. Their croups, almost fully exposed by their loinstrings, bore marks of recent caning, and the directresses sat with their canes of office hung on the chairbacks behind them. Trina sat alone at the table's head.

'You'll want a senior thrall as your secretary and some drudges under her,' Zealla said. 'You subdue thralls by playing them off against each other, with promise of reward or punishment. Thralls are indolent scum, but the threat of a return to the prisoner of war camp or, at the least, unpaid duty in the Stella Maris, is enough to quell the boldest. The more harshly you treat them, the more they worship you, especially New Albion prisoners. I think most Anglo trulls from New Albion are lesbians.'

'That sounds like slavery,' Trina said.

'You have a problem with that?'

'Why, yes.'

'Slavery of humans is forbidden on New Arras and always has been. Anglo trulls do not qualify as human. They are lustful, dirty animals, prey to the most obscene vices, of which lesbian perversion is the mildest.'

Trina was robed in a power business suit, not unlike her normal workwear: linen, with a white cotton blouse and white scalloped bra and string panties, and nylon stockings, which Zealla assured her were essential for an intendant – although, like the rapidly soaked panties and bra, they clung to her skin and dripped sweat in the high humidity. Her thin blouse was translucent and Trina shifted in her chair, unable to hide her bosom, plastered to the scanty bra, with her nipples bulging against bra and shirt fabric.

'I feel so guilty. I had to watch poor Devora take a hundred strokes with the rubber quirt . . .' she gasped. 'And hung so cruelly, by her flaps and nipples, but with clamps beneath her, and her ass-melons strung up.'

'Then you approve, mamselle intendant,' said Zealla briskly, 'and we may proceed to business – your rapid induction into the laws and traditions of New Arras.'

'But I don't approve.'

'Mamselle intendant chose to watch the chastisement in the nude,' said Heidi Absorb drily: a hard-muscled blonde, with her mane in bangs. 'Was mamselle intendant excited by the spectacle? Enough to moisten?'

There was more giggling until Zealla suggested mamselle intendant called the meeting to order. Her lip trembling, Trina did so and allowed each directress to lecture her on the nuances and structure of New Arras life. Her attempts to remind them they were now thralls of GG Baggs – she couldn't help using their terminology – were greeted with tolerant smiles. Her questions as to who had made this takeover deal – and how, in the absence of phones, computers or faxes – were brushed aside. She slumped in her chair while china tea and petits fours refreshed her and the sleek quintet lectured her on her duties. Beyond the mullioned windows in the intendant's palace, her new home, tendrils of white clematis, trumpet creeper and Carolina jasmine jostled to penetrate the conference chamber. Sun darted through the thick glass, its hard light turning the sweating girls' breasts into shimmering prisms. Dust was heavy in the scented air. The directresses swayed like flowers as they spoke, shifting buttocks on wood chairs, crossing bare legs with a swish of skin that echoed the rustle of Trina's soaked nylons.

Sirena Toitte directed the department of justice and prisoners of war; Alice Frequemme, the public watch, which was also the army and navy; Heidi Absorb ran the academy and the Stella Maris therapeutic institute; Dorita Carawn, the Bank of New Arras and the bare-breasted canewielders of the security corps, separate and in rivalry to the watchmaids. The former intendant Zealla Pure was now overall directress of discipline and commander-in-chief of the armed forces general staff, staying in residence at the intendant's palace – 'for the safety of the head of state', she reassured Trina. Sirena Toitte observed that the state was at war, and it behoved all citizens to pull together for the common weal. Trina must provide herself with a personal maidservant or secretary as her thrall. Sirena offered to send the least despicable prisoners of war for the citizen intendant to select her staff.

'Remember to cane them naked and melons up before you make your choice,' she said. 'A girl can never lie under caning.'

'Must they all be prisoners?' Trina asked.

'It is customary,' said Zealla.

'Reason suggests it,' said Dorita Carawn, a haughty, sloe-eyed brunette who flicked an imaginary speck of dust from her right nipple-plum as she spoke.

'In fact,' Zealla continued, 'I have already selected a suitable –'

'Hold up,' Trina said. 'I can pick my own staff, thanks, mamselle. I want a maid of my own choice to voluntarily accept the position of secretary and personal assistant.'

'Some might think you forward, mamselle intendant, after such short residence,' said Zealla acidly.

'Directress Pure,' Trina declared, 'please summon Constable Harriet Stooplaugh, whom, I trust, Directress Frequemme will release from her duties as watchmaid.'

The directresses looked at each other sullenly. Only Zealla smiled.

'Of course, mamselle intendant,' she said.

Trina sat back, smirking.

'However,' Zealla continued, 'may I remind you that you still have a debt to pay – one which I do not think the committee will derogate in your case.'

Sirena, Alice, Heidi and Dorita shook heads.

'By debt, I mean chastisement. Public servants Acajou and Felt have you on a charge of bribery and corruption, and not even the intendant is above the law.'

'That's crazy! Sure, I offered them a favour, whenever I got things straight, but –'

'Corruption is unconditional, even suborning maids on your own staff. Plus which, I surprised you *in flagrante delicto*, masturbating with a prisoner of the republic. So if you decide to thrash me in compense for your ordeals this day, it may be that as directress of discipline I shall first have the pleasure of flogging you, mamselle intendant. Melons up.'

From the Journal of Mlle Augustine Flageolet, anno 1760 5
I have taken to inflicting punishments simultaneously for the good of my maids. Where triple or quadruple canings are required, it seems merciful to inflict the strokes all at once, with the girls bent over a lowered ship's mast, or tied by hands and ankles to the rigging, in order to instil *esprit de corps*. Dorette Lapune, a cheeky minx whose bare bottom is well marked by cane welts, argued for solitary punishment, since part of the punishment is waiting and witnessing of other maids' bottoms as they redden under strokes. I accused her of egoism, and she admitted it excited her to be the centre of attention as she took a naked flogging. She said all females like to exhibit their bare bodies; in hypocritical bourgeois society, modesty forbids them, which is why they commit crimes, inviting lashes on the bare, in order to enjoy such exhibitions beyond control of their modesty. In particular, girls like the cane on naked buttocks, whose reddening shows their beauty of form. Helpless, she may indulge – indeed, the pain of lashes obliges her to indulge – in wriggles and pouts of her naked buttocks, tantalising any observer sensitive to beauty, and otherwise forbidden by bourgeois modesty. The bare nates of a flogged girl are the hillocks and waves, trembling in a breeze of strokes, of nature herself; or the smooth orbs of moons and planets, virtuously pocked by

celestial hail. Lashes on the back are arguably less painful but more humiliating, as they make the naked breasts shudder to an immodest degree. I awarded Dorette a caning of sixty strokes on the bare buttocks, in public, to satisfy her ego.

6

Skin Abacus

It was cool in Trina's chamber. A soft, velvet dusk shrouded her open balcony windows, and below her the chirps of insects and birds mingled with girls' voices, shrilling the languid tropical night. The room was airy, its stone floor devoid of furniture, save for a rosewood four-poster bed with plump pillows and sheets; wash things in a cubicle, with a Turkish-style toilet; high chairs and a writing table; and a curious X-shaped frame, like an ironing board, the size of a human body, carved from a single piece of mahogany and standing on four metal legs. Otherwise, the room was as spartan as Blush Coynte's jail cell. Trina stripped, preparing to bathe before dinner. Scented, tepid water was brought in buckets up the stone staircase by a serving maid, clad in a frilly short skirtlet that came only inches below her pubis; black shirt and crossover suspenders for the skirt, with a white ruff at her bosom.

Harriet Stooplaugh was on secret duty, an *affaire d'état*, Alice Frequemme had explained in some embarrassment and, begging the intendant's pardon, but a temporary thrall would be sent. Muted but hissing argument among the committee of public safety, accompanied by viperish exchange of documents, with much signing and counter-signing, found a thrall to attend Trina that evening. The intendant's palace brimmed with staff, but Zealla informed Trina they could not leave their specific tasks without reports being filed, requisition forms completed and the duty roster amended in the public censor's office, presently closed. Zealla hinted that the intendant herself was merely one piece of the palace's complex puzzle.

The maid was barefoot and her long tan legs were nude of tights. Her lush sandy mane straggled unkempt on her shoulders, its ends flicking the hillocks of ripe breasts straining under their cloth enclosure, and her fesse-melons bulged, bouncing against the frilly slip of her skirt which revealed that she wore no panties or else a string too small for comfort. Her eyes were downcast, acknowledging her mistress by fear, and Trina cast aside her own clothing with no attempt to conceal herself from the maid's eyes. The fabric clung to her sweating skin and peeled off with a sticky plopping sound. The maid watched Trina dung, squatting naked over Turkish porcelain, and when her stools had plopped from her smeared buttocks wiped and perfumed her anus. Trina stepped outside on to the balcony, standing back to hide her nudity in shadow, and touched the tops of her breasts, stiffening in the breeze from the Gulf of Mexico. She stroked the weals, still smarting, that were her legacy of her first day on New Arras. A smile creased her lips: the selection of Harriet Stooplaugh as her secretary, and her insistence thereon, had surely established her dominion over the committee of public safety. Harriet would be hers the next day.

There was neither electricity nor internal combustion engine on New Arras, although the palace had butane gas lighting, and otherwise there were candles and oil lamps, made in the republic's own factory. That was the factory making wigs and pomades, technically part of the academy and under the sway of Heidi Absorb, who also controlled the Stella Maris therapeutic facility. Heidi seemed the only committee member without a say in law and order, until Trina learned the Stella Maris had its own elite corps of vigilantes, with special uniforms: the guardians of virtue. Trina's hand strayed to the goose-bumps on her bottom and stroked the weals dealt her during the day. They had hardened to crisp ridges of puffy skin and tingled at her touch, not unpleasantly, as her fingers awoke the bruised skin and the welts throbbed, warm and insistent. She cupped her left fesse with one palm, squeezing her meat and clenching the buttocks to trap her fingers in her ass-cleft, itself severely welted. The serving maid paid her no attention, keeping her head and gaze downwards, even when Trina quietly mooned her, with her massage of the crimson flesh quite blatant.

'Tell me about yourself, maid,' she said, selecting a walnut from a silver bowl and cracking it with her teeth, then washing the nut down with a sip of iced water.

She ran the shell fragment along one peaked nipple, drawing a thin white line of scratched skin on the red nip-flesh; then the other nipple, pressing the jagged point of the fragment into herself until her teat-buds swelled to full erection. Rapidly blinking, Trina sucked breath. The maid stared at her briefly with her eyes wide and white.

'At your orders, mamselle,' she said and then was silent, until Trina realised it had been a question.

'Of course, on my orders,' she snapped. 'I am the intendant of New Arras, and everything I say is an order.'

'Then mamselle knows that slave maids may not speak without orders, on pain of caning,' the girl mumbled.

Her name was Beulah Beaucoup, from Pritchard, Alabama; she was a scholar, and a worthy member of the New Arras part-time militia, or tried to be, but had spent the last three months a slave maid, deemed recusant after whipping failed to reform her of her wicked practices. She hesitated to name her offence, until Trina ordered her.

'Playing games with other maids, mamselle. Shameful games.'

'Masturbating?'

'Yes. I couldn't stop. So many girls join the militia just for that. But I wouldn't snitch on my partners – I just got caught, that's all, with Devora Dykes. We were diddling each other in the woods under a sweet gum tree, and we'd taken off all our clothes, and – we couldn't deny it. We were daubing each other all over, like, on the titties, and in our pussies, with the liquid amber, you know, that comes out of the bark, like – I guess like girl's come, only real sweet and aromatic and sticky – you know? – and that's off limits to maids, on account of it's used for the pomade and perruque manufacture. Constable Stooplaugh caught us, thrashed us on the bare, twenty-four strokes each, in six squares of four, then said she must report us. Mamselle Stooplaugh is truly the harshest law enforcement officer I've ever known, mamselle intendant.

'Those strokes really hurt, because we took them with gum all over our bare asses, and it smarts so much more on the wet, doesn't it, mamselle? She poked tubes of gum right up our buttholes, and that felt all sticky and irritating, but kind of ticklish, too. And we'd no choice but to link hands round the tree-trunk, buck naked in shame, and get stickier while she lashed us on the bare. She said if we wanted to complain, like some sassy mainland lawyer, she'd loose a colony of ants on to us, and then we could giggle at the gum up our holes. So we took it in silence – or not exactly in silence, because those slices with a hickory switch smarted so. I moaned out loud as each cut striped my skin, I confess. I'd never been thrashed so savagely and Stooplaugh took such delight in lashing bare skin, mamselle! Devora just grunted; she was used to lashes more than I was. Swish! Swish! Swish! Devora and me, clutching hands as we slammed against the gummy tree bark, and our pussy-hair getting tangled in it, and all. Devora – well, she got away with it, somehow. She makes friends easily. And enemies. But my grievous offence was racketeering – trading in black market canestrokes. I was hanged publicly for that, whipped one hundred with the quirt and broken to a slave, with my skirts ripped to shreds. I have to stitch every piece of my uniform back together before the committee will even consider me for parole. But it wasn't true, mamselle intendant, I swear! All my strokes were noted and accounted for! Some filthy trull sneaked my stroke book, that's all. A New Albion spy, I'd bet.'

'You weren't charged with lesbianism?' Trina said drily.

'Why, no, mamselle, how filthy. Diddling is a crime, but it's not lesbianism. More like a misdemeanour. Your bath's ready, now, mamselle. Have you further use for me, or do you elect to thrash me?'

'Why would I elect to thrash you?'

'It's normal, mamselle. Slaves are flogged in submission, regularly and at whim. But it's not as it seems,' Beulah blurted. 'Slave maids get no benefit of strokes, as we cannot have bank accounts.'

'Stay awhile,' said Trina, sliding into the warm, scented water. 'Racketeering? Explain. And sponge my back.'

Beulah flicked back a lock from her forehead and began to rub Trina's skin. Racketeering was a heinous crime, akin to high treason against the republic, she explained, for it was tantamount to forging the currency and inflating the money supply regulated by Mamselle Carawn and the governesses of the bank. Girls offered their buttocks for unofficial caning or flogging on the bare and received black market fessignats, or strokes, as the New Arras currency was familiarly known. The value of those strokes fluctuated and, as a result, so did the value of official strokes. A girl claiming wealth by showing the bruises on her bare bottom could not be asked to prove if her weals were official currency. Stripes were fessignats; mottled or blushing bruises were small change. The deemsters of the bank valued each very harsh welt at several fessignats.

'If I may speak, mamselle, and without rebellious intent, your own fesses suggest you enjoy great wealth.'

Trina laughed.

'You mean because I've been whipped, Beaulah? I've had too hot a welcome here in New Arras and, as intendant, I intend to put a stop to all this ... this fustigation. This place is quaint, granted, but we're still Americans, and these barbarous beatings must stop. I took the most savage treatment today – think of my surprise at Mamselle Pure's misunderstanding – but I'm a little older than you girls.'

'I don't rightly know what you mean, mamselle,' stammered the girl, blushing deeply. 'How else can we learn to be ladies? You could take your chastisement because you already are a lady.'

'I forbid you to say that. You wouldn't wish to be charged with lesbianism.'

'Oh, mamselle.'

Trina stared at the girl's heaving breasts and crimson bunched face, shutting back her tears. She reached out and pushed up Beulah's skirtlet. The maid's bare buns were sheathed in the tiniest of loinstrings, a rubber cord that bit harshly into her perineum and gash, while her full bare buttocks bore numerous livid cane scars, many of them fresh. Trina began to stroke the girl's bare and Beaulah trembled.

'Do you have marks on your titties, Beulah?' Trina said.

'Everywhere, mamselle. My pussy, especially. They are cruel, because I like to masturbate so much.'

'Hey, Beulah, every girl masturbates. I masturbate.'

'You are the intendant.'

'I wasn't yesterday,' Trina said.

Her hands brushed Beulah's titties, swelling under the tight cloth and soaked in sweat. Trina twanged a suspender strap against her breast, and the girl shuddered.

'Stop shaking, maid,' Trina said. 'You stink.'

'Slaves may not bathe, mamselle, so that males will shun us. A hungry man indeed for a cheesy quim, that's what Mamselle Pure says.'

'Yuk. Get in the bath.'

Beulah nodded and placed her foot in the water.

'You have to strip naked,' Trina said.

'Oh. Yes, mamselle.'

Beulah undressed with her back to Trina and, as she dropped her skirtlet and rolled down the tight, chafing string, Trina stared at the massive and cleverly striped buttocks, each cane welt laid in deft sequence to form a series of squares, so that the girl's flogged moons could very well have represented an accounting device or skin abacus. Smiling shyly, but making no move to cover her quim or huge, jutting breasts, Beulah stepped daintily into the bath beside her mistress.

'Haven't you ever thought of escape, Beulah?' Trina said.

'That would be unreasonable, mamselle.'

'You could go back to Alabama.'

'Whatever would I do there?'

The two nude girls caressed: daintily at first, and then their caresses grew feverish. The bathwater slopped around Beulah's floating breasts, which Trina slapped together with a wet crack. They explored each other, Beulah with her eyes closed, moaning as she felt Trina's weals, and Trina's tongue licking the tracery of welts that crisscrossed the bare Alabaman breasts, thighs, cunt and ass. The big pink nipples, domed like soft plums, were impacted with a fine spray of curving, deep weals, as though from a tiny cane or wire. The gash-lips themselves, strongly extruded from a tangled pubic forest, bore whip slices; the belly, the substance of the teats and the back were all ripe with marks, carefully laid in a mosaic. Beulah shifted her ass so that Trina could cup the melons in her hands and Trina gasped, saying she scarcely needed to look, as it was like feeling corrugated leather.

Beulah had her eyes shut and moaned as Trina probed her body, the fingers sliding nearer her cunt, with the cunt-basin shifting and the swollen red gash-flaps opening moistly at Trina's approach. She brushed the lips tenderly at first, then more aggressively, until the come seeped into the bath suds, pooling with the oily unguents. Trina let her fingers enter the girl's pouch and jerked as she felt hesitant fingers clasping her own swelling cunt-flaps; she snatched breath as Beulah's thumb touched her swelling, erect clitoris. In a moment, she had her thumb pressing Beulah's own; her hand, freed from the buttocks, was squeezing and kneading Beulah's creamy tanned teat-flesh, pinching the nips and eliciting faint little cries from the slave girl.

'Maybe I should spank you,' she whispered as her belly writhed and her own come flowed from her throbbing cunt. 'I should be tired in this heat, and after such a whirlwind of a day, but I'm not. This climate is enervating; this warmth tempts me. And . . . your bottom.'

'It is the humidity, mamselle,' Beulah gasped as Trina tongued her nipples, 'freshened by sea air. Do you really want to spank me? I must obey you totally. You are intendant of New Arras and, with sublime reason, can do anything you like.'

Trina's fingers brushed, then rubbed and clawed at the heavy welts on Beulah's bare buns, eliciting moans from the squirming girl. Come poured from Beulah's cunt over Trina's wrists and oiled the bath suds.

'Yes, you must obey me. Anything I like. Mmm . . . do you desire spanking?' she whispered.

'Slaves may not desire, mamselle.'

'But if you were free?'

'I should like it, mamselle. Begging pardon, mamselle, my fesses thirst for your spanks.'

Beulah's lips parted, gasping as she poked two fingers into Trina's copiously juicing slit.

'Mamselle's pussy is wet at the thought of spanking me bare? They say that girls who like to spank are really spanking *themselves*.'

'How dare you? Fucking trull,' Trina hissed.

'I didn't mean – oh!'

Trina grabbed Beulah's waist, pulling up her buttocks, and forced her head beneath the water. She raised her arm to the full and brought her palm down across the quivering bare moons. Slap! Slap! Slap! The water bubbled and frothed as Beulah's pinioned head shook and her buttocks clenched, their spank-weals glowing pink. Slap! Slap! Slap! Trina spanked the bare, holding the girl's nape and cracking her wet flesh until, after thirty slaps, she had raised a mottle of crimson on the skin. Beulah's fesses were parted wide as they wriggled, revealing her jungle of pubic hair straggling through her perineum and its fronds caressing her writhing anal pucker, with the whole ass-cleft slathered in the copious come gushing from her cunt. Slap! Slap! Slap!

'Ohh,' Beulah gurgled, her cunt-basin threshing as Trina dragged her up from the water.

The maddened girl punched Trina on the breasts, repeating her blows until Trina grabbed her by the wrists and forced her under water again, with her crimson fesses sticking into Trina's face, and smothering her mouth and nose in wet cunt-hairs. Trina extended her tongue and got it an inch into the girl's anus, then two inches, and began to ream the narrow, acrid channel. Beulah writhed; Trina took her tongue from the tight asshole and licked the perineum and the gash-hairs all the way to Beulah's heavily juicing cunt. She plunged her tongue inside the slimy pouch and began to gamahuche Beulah, allowing the maid's face to bob up from the water, with her fingers probing her own oily gash and her thumb vigorously rubbing her extruded clitty. As Trina masturbated, so too did the upended girl, her fingers rapid on her clit and brushing Trina's lips, pressed to the swollen flaps at the mouth of her gushing cunt-pouch. Her legs came up and pinioned Trina's neck in a hammerlock; then Beulah dived once more under the water, this time for her face to make contact with Trina's cunt. Trina moved her masturbating fingers a little to allow the girl's eager tongue to penetrate her cunt to its full length and begin gamahuching Trina. The wet tribadists clung to each other's slippery nude trunks, as their tongues worked on come-slopped cunts.

'Oh . . . oh . . .' Trina moaned, her cunt-basin writhing in the water, and spilling suds on to the stone floor.

Beulah's gash spurted slime as Trina chewed the clitty and gash-flaps, and the girl stiffened, heaving and threshing the water with a stream of orgasmic bubbles bursting over Trina's breasts. Trina shut her eyes, stifling a squeal and opening her thighs to the full as the girl's teeth fastened on her cunt-lips. Her belly heaved and she began to mewl, then groan, as honey engulfed her. Beulah splashed noisily into the air, gasping and writhing, with her hand blatantly masturbating between her legs. She put her other hand on Trina's gash, slid three fingers into her slit and poked, while thumbing the swollen clitty. She bent, fastened her teeth on Trina's left nipple, then bit hard.

'Oh!' Trina groaned. 'Oh, yes, I'm coming, oh, yes . . . Ah! Ahh! Let's be friends, Beulah . . .'

'No, mamselle!' cried the slave. 'Don't speak unreason!'

The door opened quietly and it was a few moments before Trina opened her eyes and, gasping, looked round to inspect the intruder. She cried out when she observed Zealla Pure, dressed in a full corset of shiny black latex that left her teats almost bare and powerfully upthrust, with the nipple-plums starkly outlined beneath the thin latex; the sides of the garment were cut high and thin over the swollen pubic hillock, so that tendrils of pubic forest sprouted, curling around the rubber thong, and so lush as to nearly engulf it. The waist pinched Zealla to eighteen inches at most. She wore black thigh-boots and cradled a cane in her fingers.

'Do you require assistance, mamselle intendant?' she said, curtseying. 'I came to remind you that dinner awaits your presence.'

Moaning, Beulah leaped from the bath in a spray of suds and prostrated herself in a cross shape, arms and legs wide, on the floor at Zealla's feet. Zealla kicked the fesses, glowing from Trina's spanks, and Beulah groaned.

'The thrall was oppressing and importuning you, mamselle intendant,' she stated coldly.

Trina gasped that everything was under control but Zealla raised her cane, kicking the prone girl's bare ass twice more with sharp silver toe-points viciously, so that she squealed. Zealla swished her weapon in the air.

'Do you like my new whipple?' she said. 'Very light, but pliant and stingy, of the best Missouri ash. Emily Cawdor made it for me today, the sweet thing. She begged me to test it on her bare. Poor Emily. Always poor . . .'

She swished the air again, sending a rush of air to ruffle Beulah's mane.

'It's especially good for delicate *pointillage*,' she said. 'I think I shall try her on the juicy buns of this filthy little lesbian slave.'

'Wait, mamselle!' Trina said. 'I'm in authority here.'

'Not in matters of pertinent discipline, mamselle indendant,' Zealla drawled. 'Do you know, I relish my new authority – though lesser than intendant, I am broader in pertinent power. You, mamselle, must rule by the book.'

'If the girl is guilty of lesbian perversion,' Trina said icily, 'then so am I. More so. I seduced the trull.'

'Impossible, mamselle, because against reason. The intendant, embodying reason, cannot betray it. Beulah, rise and spread thighs in position, touching toes.'

'No,' Trina cried, rising from the bathtub. 'I forbid it.'

'Mamselle, you may only forbid things after a plenary committee meeting and a debate of the council of reason,' Zealla said.

Beulah stumbled to her feet and rubbed her bottom, red with spanks and bruised by the blonde girl's kicks. She bent over and grasped her toes, spreading her thighs wide to show her ass-cleft still dripping come.

'Beulah knows,' Zealla said, raising her left arm to full height, with the whipple quivering almost to the ceiling.

Vip!

'Mmm . . .' the girl moaned, a long, despairing wail, as her bare ass clenched, taking the slice of the whipple.

Vip! Vip!

'Oh, mamselle.'

Vip! Vip! Vip!

'Ahh!

Beulah's rump squirmed frantically, the strokes laid on bare forming a neat grid.

Vip! Vip!

'Ooh! Mamselle, that's tight.'

The tracery of lines on Beulah's frantically clenching bottom was deep and red, with the strokes laying a pattern of interlocking squares. Her ass-flesh quivered before and after the slices, and after each impact clenched several times, awaiting the next. As Zealla flogged, her breasts danced in their slender prison, threatening to burst from the confining latex. Her nipples were swollen.

'Vip! Vip!

'Oh, please, no . . .'

'Mamselle, that's enough,' Trina gasped.

Vip! Vip!

'Aah!' Beulah screamed, and burst into a frenzied sobbing; yet she did not budge from submissive position, clutching her toes with her mouth a rictus of pain.

Her brow wrinkled and her eyes tightly shut dripped with tears. The tears were mirrored by a steady seep of come exuding from Beulah's shivering ass-cleft and oiling the tops of her thighs. Zealla breathed deeply and smiled.

Vip! Vip! Vip!

'Ooh!' Beulah gurgled, her scarlet bare melons clenching and wriggling; the fabric of the slender cane suddenly shredded at the tip, and beneath glinted metal. Trina sprang forwards and grabbed the cane.

'That's not right,' she exclaimed.

'The directress of discipline decides what's right, mamselle intendant,' Zealla snarled. 'Do you want me to bind you? That is within my powers.'

She waved at the ceiling, walls and four-poster bed.

'These quarters were mine until a week ago. I moved out without a murmur when I heard of a new intendant's arrival and got this post in return. Intendant! A zero, compared to directress of discipline, one too powerful to be removed, mamselle.'

'Put down that cane,' cried Trina. 'It's weighted – that's not just.'

Her nostrils flaring, Zealla thrust her face an inch from Trina's. Her eyes sparkled.

'But it is reasonable,' she spat. 'Slave! Rise and assist me in binding the intendant for her own safety. Her reason has temporarily deserted her.'

The bruises on Beulah's caned bare bottom now glowed a livid crimson, darkening to purple, the puffy, ridged flesh forming a quilt of squares. The flogged slave jumped to her feet and, before Trina could protest, clapped her hand over her mouth, pinioning her in a choke hold. The struggling Trina was dragged to the X-table and made to lie face down with Beulah's naked bottom crushing the small of her back, while her ankles and wrists were lashed to the extremities of the cross by coarse hempen ropes.

'Stop!' Trina yelled. 'I'll call the guard.'

'I *am* the guard,' Zealla hissed. 'Gag her, slave.'

'No, please no!'

Trina wriggled and howled as Beulah wadded her mouth with her stinking panty-thong and tied the gag in place with cord.

'Mmm,' Trina moaned as she felt the tip of Zealla's metal-weighted cane trace a delicate path down her bare spine, linger at her spinal nubbin, then descend into the cleft of her ass to prise open Trina's squirming melons and poke, teasing, at her anal hole and cunt-lips.

Zealla ordered the slave girl to resume position, with her buttocks proximate to Trina's face. Her back to the door, she resumed the caning on Beulah's bare, the whipple whistling inches from Trina's eyes. Vip! Vip! Zealla looked at Trina as she flogged the slavegirl.

Vip!

'This –'

Vip!

'– is how we treat –'

Vip!

'– unreasonable –'

Vip!

'– trulls!'

Trina smelled the girl's sweat and the unmistakable odour of come, gushing copiously from her swollen gash-flaps. The girl's melons wriggled as the strokes lashed her bare nates, their subtle pattern defined by hard, crisp ridges of bruised skin, puffing to purple. At each third stroke she allowed the cane to rest, hot from Beulah's ass, on the quivering melons of Trina's own buttocks. Zealla said nothing; she smiled. Trina was mute, trembling and no longer struggling against her bonds. She gazed at the shuddering bare melons of the flogged girl, as her tariff of canestrokes rose: thirty, forty, fifty . . .

A trickle of come seeped from Trina's quim and crawled to the edge of her platform, then dripped to the stone floor with a plop as it began to puddle. Zealla laughed. Slowly, she unfastened the buttons at her vulva and opened the flap of rubber to let it dangle loose, exposing her entire cunt and pubic jungle glistening with her sweat and oozing come. She ripped down the flimsy restraint of her breasts, allowing the teat-jellies to spring bare and jut, quivering, as she flogged. Zealla's free hand alternately caressed her quim and nips, sliding up her rubbered belly between canestrokes. She fingered her clitty, drawing it from its pouch to display the erect, swollen nubbin amid fleshy red folds of cunt-meat, and slapped her breasts together, clawing at her nipples with sharp nails. Her face flushed and her smile widened as Trina's eyes darted from Beulah's flogged bottom to the blatant masturbation of the discipline directress.

'Yes, I diddle,' Zealla drawled. 'Going to snitch? Who'd believe you, without witnesses? A slave cannot witness anything.'

Vip! Vip! Vip! The caning neared seventy strokes and Beulah's legs jerked rigid at each slice, her naked bottom now ploughed with crusted purple welts. Zealla's masturbation grew rapid, her breath heavier and her taut, muscled belly heaving as she approached climax. She placed one foot on the side of the bed, spreading her cunt-lips wide to show Trina the glistening pink meat within her pouch. Her quim made gurgling sounds as she swayed her cunt-basin, and squeezed her flaps together to squirt funnels of come over Beulah's bare back. Trina writhed, rubbing her cunt against the polished wood of her X-frame and pressing her clitty against the wood, slopped in her come. Zealla signalled her climax by deep grunts of satisfaction, and after a valedictory six canestrokes, delivered in a flurry on Beulah's squirming bare nates, declared the caning terminated. She clawed the welts on the girl's buttocks, making her squeal and sob, and called them a warning to other lesbian sluts.

Trina sighed and ceased frotting, allowing her cunt to rest in a puddle of come, soaking her thighs and pubis. Beulah rose, grimacing through her tears; curtseying, she thanked Zealla for her chastisement. She kneeled before the directress and fastened her corset over the titties and dripping cunt, while Zealla played her cane up and down Trina's back, buttocks and thighs. Trina trembled, staring wide at the dominatrix, and beneath her cunt a fresh seep of come shone.

'You want the same, mamselle intendant?' Zealla asked.

Trina shook her head violently.

'I see your come, mamselle. I think you do, and must oblige you.'

'Mmm! Mmm!' Trina squealed, as Zealla lifted her cane.

Swish! The cane slashed air; Trina clenched her fesses and shrieked into her gag. The cane did not connect with her skin but passed an inch from her left haunch. Swish! The next stroke skimmed her right haunch without touching: and so on, for twenty-five strokes, each a hair's breadth from Trina's bare, but leaving her unwhipped. Her eyes knotted tightly closed and her teeth fastened on her panties gag until it sprang loose, as she had chewed right through it.

'Please,' she wailed. 'Stop this.'

'Does your croup smart, mamselle intendant?' Zealla said.

I want it to smart.

Behind her, the slave girl, drooling, gazed at Trina's quivering bare. Unseen by the directress, she masturbated, with her hand penetrating her wet cunt in deep thrusting punches and her thumb rubbing her swollen clitty. She smiled lustfully at Trina, who wailed.

'Let me go, I order you, mamselle. I am in charge here. The committee of public safety shall know this disgrace.'

'Why, of course, mamselle intendant. Your wish, my command.'

I want it so. Thrash me, thrash my bare ...

Zealla snapped her fingers and the door opened to admit Sirena, Alice, Heidi and Dorita. They stood laughing at the squirming bare girl, naked and come-slathered on her X-frame, as Zealla flogged her in mime.

'Enough of this terrible show,' Trina gasped.

'At your command, mamselle intendant,' said Zealla.

Vip!

'Ahh!'

Her stroke lashed Trina in the spread ass-cleft, slicing fesse-meat, and slamming both her exposed anal bud and the juicing folds of her gash. Trina shuddered, her buttocks clenched, and she moaned as a golden stream of piss spurted from her pussy.

'No ... no ...' she wailed.

Thrash me, thrash me ...

'A mistake, mamselle intendant,' Zealla cried, 'and one which demands pertinent chastisement, at once.'

The other committee members clapped. Zealla threw her cane to Beulah and bent over, showing her melons bare, but for the thin rubber thong embedded in her cleft. Beulah lifted the cane and dealt her a single slashing stroke across mid-fesse and cleft, so hard that Zealla's ass-thong snapped in two. The stroke painted a wide pink stripe on Zealla's bare. She took it without a sound, without clenching her buttocks or trembling. She rose and smiled, saying she felt much better. Lifting her broken thong, she wondered out loud who was guilty of such wilful destruction of the republic's property. Taking Beulah by the hair, she forced her to her knees and ground her anus with her toe until she confessed, with a plea for mercy.

'Excellent,' Zealla said. 'A hanging offence, I think.'

'No, mamselle,' Beulah wailed.

'Beulah,' Trina cried. 'I promise I'll help you get out of this, back home to Alabama. Just be brave.'

Beulah stared at her in puzzled distaste.

'New Arras is my home, mamselle,' she said.

Zealla raised her cane and lashed Trina on the bare.

Vip!

'Oh . . .'

I'm juicing . . .

'The heat forces our –' vip! '– intendant –' vip! '– to talk –' vip! '– unreason,' Zealla said. 'Are you joining us for dinner, mamselle intendant? We should be honoured.'

Zealla used her cane tip to slice open Trina's cords and Trina got to her feet. She sobbed, rubbing the fresh weals on her caned ass and turning away from the committee to conceal the smears of come oozing from her gash.

'Enough misunderstandings. Do you wish to dine nude and in shame, mamselle intendant?' said Zealla. 'A curious whim, but one which we all must follow. Or you may choose to be robed. The committee likes and approves you, and feels we shall have a happy friendship. All of us have endured taming to become citizens of the republic.'

'Yes. I mean, yes, I'll be robed.'

'Yes, and?'

Zealla's cane whistled in the air.

'Thank you. Thank you,' Trina said.

From the Journal of Mlle Augustine Flageolet, anno 1760 6

Today, I had Sophie Despreux flogged to one hundred on the bare back, suspended from a newly finished gibbet, a chastisement I felt obliged to administer myself. She wriggled superbly as her back wealed but did not cry out, other than gasps and moans. Her head sank halfway through her stripes, but she did not lose consciousness, thanks to frequent dousings in sea-water, whipping on wet flesh being doubly painful. Her extravagantly large breasts did wobble as she was flogged, the immodesty adding to her shame, as she freely admitted. After my exertions, I felt an agitation of brain and body; a flush and trembling which I assuaged by caressing my *bassin intime*, in particular my 'clitoris', and experienced that sublime sensation, the enjoyment of which is every female's right and duty, within moderation. I encourage my maids to 'masturbate', as the ancients call it, in order to expel irrational humours from the brain, a healthy exercise, but one which must be carried out thoughtfully and even frugally, for its healthful benefits and raptures to be savoured; preferably by groups of girls together, in orderly and rational social fashion. Certain physiocrats argue that judicious female masturbation can cure the female lust for male caresses, whose ruinous social consequences are so often seen amongst our European nobility. Surely, a generous bourgeois husband, who encourages his wife to masturbate and whips her regularly on the bare to subdue her female unreason, is preferable to a debile and nervous aristocrat, addicted to 'romantic love' and other perversities?

7

Hot, Clean and Raw

It's not so bad, really. The committee are nice American girls at heart. Nothing like a good dinner to relax. Hey, they're genuinely sorry for all the misunderstandings. Alice even said it was best to get them over with the first day. And they seem to know I'm boss. Watch Zealla, though – friend or foe? The others aren't like her; they know she has attitude. Some funny ideas, like that zany French republican calendar, retro but cute. Too free with the cane or whip, but there's time to change things and teach them to be good bag ladies. Hasten slowly. I have time, and power . . .

The slut parade – Zealla's term – which the discipline directress ushered into Trina's chamber next morning, confirmed her power: six maids in frilly French maids' uniforms, hosed in nylon, with tightly scalloped brassieres thrusting their generous titties high and close, and their long legs teetering on high stilettos, served her breakfast and kneeled to watch her eat. Their teat-flesh thrust upwards to form shiny domes of skin, scarred with tiny geometric patterns of thin pink weals. One maid, Prudence Vile, a coltish blonde from Laurel, Mississippi, with wide lips, big hair and big jutting teats, waggled her bosom and asked half sassily and half incredulously if they were to go uncaned for faults. Trina said she had no intention of caning anyone, upon which she had to sign six releases attesting that their pure bottoms were 'within reason'. The sluts left with lips sullen.

They want me to cane them! Am I right in refusing? They are victims of the system. Or, of their own perverted lusts?

There was a rap on the door.

'Come in,' Trina said, closing her diary, laying down her quill pen and pushing away her breakfast things.

Harriet Stooplaugh entered, wearing her watchmaid's uniform, freshly laundered and as casually buttoned as on the day before. She carried a folder of documents but wore no hairbrush, cane or whip. She curtsied gravely. Trina was still in her frilly dark blue nightshirt, one of several such garments in her armoire which she had chosen, eschewing those fashioned of string or rubber. She put her elbows on the table and pressed her fingertips together. Harriet placed her documents on the table, stepped back and curtsied again.

'For you to sign, mamselle,' she said, with lowered gaze. 'Copies of my contract of employment to the committee of public safety, the prefect of the watch, Sergeant Makings and Prefect Funger.'

Trina took up her pen, and perused the papers.

'Lots of "wheretofores" and "hereinafters",' she said.

'It's a standard personnel transfer contract, mamselle,' Harriet said. 'I've signed it already. If you'll just – here, here and here . . .'

Trina stopped at a paragraph headed 'remuneration'. Constable Harriet Stooplaugh was to be paid two hundred and ten fessignats per week, with a further two hundred and ten fessignats to be paid by bank transfer from the intendant's account to the account of the public watch, in recompense for Constable Stooplaugh's services. Harriet's two hundred and ten fessignats were to be delivered from the intendant's private purse, and Trina asked what that meant exactly. Harriet smiled and tossed back her blonde mane. She fingered the undone top buttons of her uniform shirt, beneath which her taut breasts quivered, braless. She wore a gaudy red carnation of tissue paper in her mane.

'You have to give me the strokes personally, mamselle,' she said. 'At the watch, we used a rough exchange rate for one fessignat – it equals one deep whiplash or canestroke, or two slaps with slipper or paddle, or four hardspanks with bare hand, or any combination thereof.'

'I have to cane your bare ass thirty strokes every day?' Trina said, swallowing as Harriet's firm rump shifted, under the thin cotton.

'Of course, mamselle,' said Harriet, 'but it's only twenty-one strokes a day. The week has ten days and is called a decade, and there are three decades every month. Mamselle Flageolet adopted the rational calendar, in solidarity with her revolutionary sisters in France. Her friend Mr Franklin wanted to have it adopted on the mainland, but the Pennsylania Germans were against it.'

'So, I have to whip you on the bare twenty-one strokes a day.'

'Or all in one session, or in a combination of spanks and strokes, mamselle, as it pleases you, and you may choose to reward me with a tip of extra strokes.'

'It seems girls here are obsessed by caning,' she said.

'Beg pardon, mamselle, but people in the Orleans territory are obsessed by money. Lashes are our money.'

Trina swallowed again and mopped her brow.

'I intend to change New Arras – this brutal code of corporal chastisement in particular. My own bare is still smarting from – well, frankly, the idea of girls beating each other on the bare buttocks is . . . is . . .'

'Unacceptable, mamselle?'

'No, that means something you are powerless to change. I'm not powerless. I shall face down the committee, the directorate and the council of reason.'

'They are the same people, mamselle, Zealla and her gang, sitting in different chairs. The citizens may not support you. We like our spanks. You think us quaint?'

Harriet licked her teeth, smiling.

'Maybe I needn't proceed too fast. Your stroke stipend is no problem, I guess, if you're comfortable.'

'If I wanted comfort, I'd have stayed home in Savannah,' Harriet said.

Trina eyed the twin melons of Harriet's ass, wobbling pantiless under her sheer skirtlet.

'Is that why you are wearing no underthings?'

'It is for your convenience, mamselle, as and when I merit correction.'

She leaned across the table and her eyes met Trina's; Harriet shook herself so that her blouse fell away from her naked breasts, beaded with sweat, which slapped wetly together. She shook the red paper carnation from her hair so that it fell between her breasts; flexing her pectorals and triceps, she squashed the flower between her bare teats. Trina swallowed, breathing heavily, and said they must go to the intendant's office, on the first floor, directly beneath them. All round were the sounds of serving maids scurrying in the palace, with an occasional bark from Zealla, giving orders; or the tap of a cane on bare skin and a girl's moan. Harriet said that if the new intendant desired a tour of the island, she would liaise with the secretariat of ceremonies to arrange it.

'As and when,' said Trina as Harriet's ass-peach swayed before her.

'The citizens will be eager to see your face, mamselle.'

Harriet's lips creased in a smirk and she licked them, then ran her tongue between her pearly white teeth. Trina drew a deep breath, jogging her robe so that it slipped down her breast, uncovering half her bare jellies.

'You probably wonder why I picked you as my secretary, Harriet,' she said. 'It's because you're sassy.'

Harriet leered at Trina's bared breast, with the nipple edging towards the air and stiffening visibly, clinging to the damp fabric of the robe. Trina shifted in her seat, crossing her legs with a wet slithering sound.

'But I won't have too sassy,' she said.

'Anything you say, mamselle intendant,' Harriet replied, curtseying again.

'People have seen I can endure what they endure. So my reforms aren't some cissy thing. I won't be a . . . a flogger and whipper and torturer. The girls in this place shall have proper instruction and proper employment.'

'Mamselle,' said Harriet, putting her hands to her lips, 'please don't think me forward, but could I have a portion in advance? I owe that trull Cindi Kock some spanks.'

'What, now?'

'Mamselle, I was insolent just now. I should be punished anyway, in a pertinent chastisement creating no currency, and thus outside my appointed stipend. Please give me strokes on account? You don't want citizens to accuse you of weakness after the other things they say. Look.'

Harriet stood and unbuttoned the middle buttons of her blouse, allowing her bare breasts to spring up and reveal the paper flower, a mush of sodden sweat.

'Watch property, and I've sabotaged it! You'll have to punish me and write a report.'

'What do they say about me?'

'Why, that you're a lesbian and a submissive, that you like men to thrash you before they give you a cornholing.'

Harriet's face was stony and bland as she delivered the barbed tidings, but her eyes twinkled. Trina sprang to her feet, her face white. She did not bother to replace her robe, which fell to her waist, baring her own quivering breasts. The two girls faced each other down, Harriet pouting and smirking, and Trina with flared nostrils and a frown. Their titties, each with nipples pointed and swollen stiff, came within an inch of touching.

'You fucking trull,' she spat. 'Yeah, I'll thrash you, so that you'll never ask for your fucking stipend again. Get up on that X-frame. Now, bitch.'

Silkily, Harriet loosened her skirt and let it drop to the floor. Nude, she padded to the closet, opened it with familiarity and withdrew a whippy little ashplant, like Zealla's whipple, from the rack of canes that shone within. She swivelled, smiling.

'It's a nice, all-purpose cane, and good for close work,' she said. 'Or would you prefer an imported Scotch tawse, mamselle? There's a Georgia oak, Tennessee ash, Virginia hazel, Kentucky willow or a two-holed paddle of Carolina hickory. That really hurts.'

'The cane is fine,' Trina blurted.

She crossed her thighs as a thin trickle of come stained her robe, just above the dangling tendrils of her cunt-fleece. Harriet handed her the cane and swung on top of the flogging frame, fitting her hands into the straps. She wriggled her bare melons to get them raised for her beating and turned her head, tossing her mane.

'Not too hard, mamselle? Please?'

'You dare ask, after yesterday.'

'I was doing my duty, mamselle.'

'You seemed to relish your duty – and, I gather, whipping poor Cindi's ass in your spare time.'

Harriet closed her eyes and breathed a deep lungful through flared nostrils.

'That submissive bitch Cindi deserves it and wants it,' she said. 'As for me, *peu importe* where the cane lands, as long as it whistles and slices skin and leaves its imprint hot, clean and raw. It's the beauty of the thing that counts. When I lash a girl's ass raw, I feel part of beauty, like an artist. If it's my own bare – well, the same, I guess. There's no beauty like a girl's bare ass, mamselle, all red and trembling and about to burst with weals. None at all. Not even . . . cock in asshole.'

'Mr Elvis Lesieur's cock,' Trina spat.

Harriet shrugged, pouting and with her tongue caressing her lips. Trina raised the cane and swished the air, causing the girl to shudder, close her eyes and clench her ripe, firm buttocks. Harriet's body perfectly fitted the X-frame and she stiffened rigid as the whipple lashed the air. Trina reached down and let her palm brush the satin surface of the naked buttocks, her fingers stroking an inch inside the ass-cleft. Harriet's croup wore a pattern of mature bruises in overlapping squares. Trina rubbed the scarred skin, poking into the perineum and the folds of the gash-flaps, allowing her fingers to moisten with the oily come seeping through the hairy forest adorning Harriet's crimson cunt.

Her palms cupped the naked ass-globes and squashed them together, while her fingers delved deeper into Harriet's pliant holes, brushing the wrinkled anus pucker and massaging the outer flaps of the vulva.

Harriet shifted her cunt-basin, whimpering as Trina's caress became more insistent. A finger entered the anus and met no resistance: Harriet squirmed to open the channel and permit Trina's deeper penetration. Breathing heavily and wiping the sweat from her brow to plaster it on her naked breasts in lieu of kerchief, Trina sank her index finger into the elastic passage of the girl's anus, which suddenly slackened, then gave way, sucking the finger right inside to the anal root. Her mouth slack and drool oiling the left corner of her lips, Trina reamed the ass-channel, her finger caressed by silky smoothness and bathed in viscous ass-grease. A second finger joined the first, easily penetrating the butthole, and then a third: Trina had the three fingers clenched in a spear, massaging, reaming and stabbing at Harriet's anal root and making the girl wriggle in response to each thrusting caress.

'I'm not the only visitor you've had in that asshole,' she blurted hoarsely.

'No, mamselle.'

'Buttfucked?'

'It's normal, here in the south, mamselle.'

'Enjoy it?'

'That would be forward, mamselle. I strive to be a belle – we all do.'

'Submissive belle?'

'If you wish, mamselle. Oh! that's so good. Yeah, fingerfuck me . . . oh!'

Come dripped from Harriet's cunt on to the X-frame and soaked her squirming pubic fleece. Trina put the cane's handle against her own cunt and shuddered, closing her eyes and sighing. With an abrupt plop, she removed her fingers from Harriet's anus. Harriet's cunt-basin and buttocks continued to writhe, blatantly rubbing her clitoris on the flogging frame.

'To business,' Trina blurted. 'Bare caning.'

'How many, mamselle?' Harriet gasped.

'I . . . how many do you need?'

'Forty-two, mamselle? Only two days' stipend?'

'No. One day. Twenty-one is enough,' Trina gasped, her fingers tucking the wet hem of her dress between her gash-flaps.

'Yes, mamselle. May I suggest, if you please, that you stripe me in triangles? It makes such a cute pattern on my skin. Mamselle Pure always whipped me in triangles.'

Trina raised the cane to full arm's length and Harriet's body tensed rigid. The whipple whistled as it slashed the air. Vip! A thin pink worm appeared on Harriet's mid-fesses.

'Uh,' she gasped, as her fesses clenched tight, so that the weal appeared jagged on either side of her cleft. 'You're mad at me, mamselle.'

'Yeah, I am, some.'

Vip!

'Ooh! That's tight,' Harriet gasped.

Vip!

'Uh! That's good, mamselle.'

Vip!

'Ah! Ooh!'

'You mean my caning, or that I'm mad at you?'

Vip!

'Uh! Both, mamselle.'

The come from Harriet's quivering bare cunt was now a stream; Trina asked her if beating always made her wet.

'Why, yes, mamselle. Doesn't it you?'

'You fucking slut,' Trina hissed.

Vip! Vip!

'Oh, mamselle, my ass is so hot . . .'

'Cunt.'

Vip! Vip!

'Oh . . . please, mamselle . . .'

Vip! Vip!

'Ah! That's savage.'

Harriet's bare ass-cheeks squirmed in an uninterrupted clenching. Trina angled the cane so that her weals

110

appeared in two closely interlocking triangles, slightly to the north on the naked buttock skin, and after several strokes had scarred the bottom applied the cane solely to existing weals, which deepened rapidly to puffy crimson trenches. The bare fesses squirmed, wriggling, although Harriet's wrists and ankles jerked only slightly in her straps, as though the fesses had a life of their own. Harriet's spine and legs remained rigid, the stiff spine crisscrossed neatly by old whipmarks, purplish in colour, that travelled up to her shoulders and nape. Vip! Vip! Vip!

'Oh! I'm really smarting.'

Three sharp slices made one triangle luridly brighter than the other.

'Oh, mamselle . . .'

Vip! Vip! Vip!

'Ohh!'

Now both triangles glowed, their sides puffy ridges, with the crisp lines already mottling to a crimson blotch. Harriet was panting deeply, her mane limp and soaked in sweat. At each cut to her bare, she jerked her head up, in time with the clenching of her sweat-slimed buttocks.

Vip!

'Uh . . .! You trying to make me piss, mamselle?'

Vip!

'Uhh.'

'Insolent bitch.'

'That's twenty-four, mamselle. You giving me two days' stipend?'

Vip! Vip! Vip!

'Ooh . . .'

Harriet's puffed red buttocks now squirmed, two carved melons shivering and dancing under Trina's whipple. Her breasts, bunched under her ribs, were squelched in and out by the maid's rasping breaths.

'No, bitch! This is pertinent chastisement. You don't get paid.'

Vip! Vip! Vip!'

'Oh! For what, mamselle?'

'For juicing, you fucking little lesbian.'

Vip! Vip! Vip!

'Ahh!'

The pattern of red all over Harriet's churning nates overflowed the delicate geometric tracery: her whole buttock-pan was a single mottled mass of red with blackening welts where the cane had touched bare on the tender haunches and far north buttock. To the south of her melons, the underfesses wore vivid stripes which cascaded over on to her rigid, trembling bare thigh-backs, the weals extending four inches down the squirming flesh, shining with the lubrication of Harriet's gushing cunt-come.

Trina flogged the bare croup to fifty strokes, with Harriet's shrieks growing louder and her raucous gasps turning to gurgles in her throat. Her hips slammed the X-frame at each canestroke; jerking in her bonds, she bruised her arms and ankles against her chafing ropes of restraint, and at each impact and each new stripe raised her hips high, with her clenching bare buttocks thrust towards Trina's face. Panting, Trina laid down her cane at the fifty-first stroke to a whining shriek of protest from Harriet.

'Just . . . just one more, mamselle,' she pleaded through clenched teeth. 'I'm nearly there. Oh . . . Yes . . .'

'You fucking slut.'

Vip! Vip! Vip! Vip!

'Ah! Oh, yes, more, more . . .' Harriet gurgled, as come spurted from her writhing cunt lips, and her spine and belly convulsed.

Trina snarled and bent down, grasping Harriet's hips. She threw aside her cane and plunged her face into the maid's ass-cleft, getting her nose into the writhing anal pucker then into the flowing oil of Harriet's cunt. She hoisted herself on to the X-frame, which creaked under her weight. Her cunt straddling Harriet's shoulders, she fucked Harriet's slit with her nose, while her tongue probed and penetrated the anus hole. Harriet groaned, whimpering, and closed her anus on Trina's tongue, trapping it and sucking it fully up her shaft to brush the writhing plug of her ass-root. Trina's nose pushed against the girl's

112

throbbing, stiff clitty and her head slammed up and down the wet slit, sliding in the gash-channel between Harriet's trembling swollen cunt-petals. Her naked breasts danced on the hot, raw weals her cane had drawn on Harriet's bare nates.

'Uhh . . . uhh . . . Yes, yes! Yes!' Harriet shrilled, as her cunt-basin jammed against Trina's face, soaking her in come, and the girl wailed long and high in her orgasm.

Trina's fingers darted between her own thighs. Eyes closed, she groaned as she found her swollen clitty. With her wrist bathed in her own flowing come, she began to masturbate, thumbing and reaming her erect nubbin until she had to stifle her cries of shivering climax. She leaned, panting, with her hands on Harriet's ass-melons.

'I never came so hard before, mamselle,' Harriet whispered. 'Thank you for picking me to be your slave.'

'I didn't –' Trina began, then sighed and inserted her fingers between Harriet's crushed bare breasts.

She withdrew the red paper flower, now a sodden mass. Unseen by Harriet, Trina rammed the ball into her cunt and pressed her lips shut, holding them tight; she reattired herself in her robe before releasing Harriet from her bonds. The beaten girl at once kneeled at Trina's bare feet and began to lick them with a fervent wet tongue. She looked up, with wide puppy's eyes.

'I'll be so obedient, mamselle,' Harriet murmured. 'I know about obedience. That's our second currency, after canestrokes. There is so much politics here – the war party, and the peace party, each of them will try to snare you. Beware the security corps – they can punish anyone, including you, as a threat to state security. They go bare-breasted, for their flogging ease, and to show they are not belles and have no shame. I took a scourging last month – they came into the watch barracks and selected a maid at random, and it was me. They ripped off my uniform and flogged me on the bare with my own whip, to fifty strokes, in front of Cindi and Sergeant Makings and all the other maids. They said it was to discourage traitors. The security corps want the glory of going to war with

New Albion, see? There was never a peace treaty signed between the two republics in two hundred and fifty years.'

'But why this hostility?' Trina asked.

'Maybe it's because they are flapjacks, no-brain yankees, and we are southern belles.'

'There is usually money involved in any conflict.'

'New Albion doubloons are hard currency, just like our own, mamselle,' Harriet said. 'Two strokes for one of ours. Then, there's trade. They have the wood and we have the manufactures. You'll have to lead the trade mission and get drunk with Lady Juliet Gorges while you watch maids flogged in demonstration – demo girls are very proud, with big rewards in fessignats.'

Harriet assisted Trina in dressing. It was optional for the intendant to wear bra and panties and Trina chose to do without, shivering at the silky cling of her tight blue skirt and thin blouse as Harriet slid them over her naked body. The garter straps and silk stockings were not optional, and the too-tight garter belt and straps pulling the stocking fabric taut made her unpantied cunt moisten. Harriet invited her to choose her cane of office, and Trina agreed to carry the whipple, still warm from flogging Harriet's bare. She agreed too that Harriet might carry a whip, knotted at her waist, in testimony to her reputation as the hardest flogger among the watchmaids.

'I shall be very cruel in your service, mamselle,' she murmured, 'and I beg you to discipline me accordingly.'

'Why?' Trina asked. 'You, a dominant female – like me – why do you crave the lash on your own fesses?'

'So I can think like a filthy submissive,' Harriet drawled.

Harriet leaped on Trina, pinioning her arm behind her back, and in a swift movement forced her to bend, while Harriet's hand plucked Trina's skirt.

'Stop! What the –?'

Trina wriggled but could not resist Harriet's placing her over her knee, croup raised in spanking position. The maid raised her hand; Trina craned to look as the girl brought her palm down in slow motion and cupped her mistress's left bare buttock. She left her palm on the naked flesh, sweeping the skin in tender brushing movement before raising her arm over her head. She repeated her slow caress, this time on the right melon. Her fingers penetrated the ass-cleft and stroked Trina's anus and the lower cunt-flaps, getting further and further inside the wet vault until Harriet had four fingers inside Trina's cunt. Holding Trina by the cunt, she lifted her arm for spanking and brought it down in a caress, repeating the movement six times. Trina moaned and stopped wriggling.

'You are a bitch. Let me go,' she gasped.

Harriet released her and crouched at Trina's feet.

'Are you mad at me, mamselle?'

'I was helpless. You could have spanked me and you didn't. Yes, I am mad at you.'

'Then you won't deny me lashes? Hot, clean and raw?'

Panting, and smoothing down her skirt, over her cunt fleece moist with new seepage of come, Trina blushed.

'Damn you, I guess not.'

'Such an honour, mamselle intendant,' purred prefect Sophie Petrarque, beneath the festoons of ivy wreathing the door of the the academy of pomades and perruques.

The lofty Grecian palace lay off the main thoroughfares and Trina had reached it through a maze of passageways broadening into an elm-lined avenue, with the gates to the Parc Flageolet at the end, beyond which seagulls swooped. The academy, giving right on to the cobbled street, abutted the high, crumbling limestone walls of the park, and the dense foliage of kudzu vine, clematis and bougainvillea enveloped the walls of both. Prudence Vile and three other thralls chosen by Harriet accompanied the intendant and her secretary on a twenty-minute walk whose informality Trina approved. She said to Harriet that her first impression of New Arras was of some antique yet strict backwater, like a sleepy Mississippi town, all classical courthouses and prisons, and yet away from the grand, crumbling palaces of Republic Place the town was livelier, its haphazard alleys and nooks almost mediaeval. The girls, though uniformed, seemed frisky away from the guardians of order.

'That's more like it,' Trina said.

After her second week as intendant, she had expressed herself weary of official receptions and banquets, always distracting her from GG's agenda. In private, she dutifully fulfilled her obligations to her secretary, keeping her bare nates in a state of constant redness. Most of her public duties seemed to be signing warrants for thrashings or torture, and she wanted to go out and see New Arras for herself. Trina's buttocks had been uncaned for those two weeks.

'I'd expected some fanfare,' said Trina.

'People are busy, mamselle. There's only fanfare when lashes are given,' was Harriet's reply.

'They don't look busy,' Trina said, acknowledging curtsies from girls in military uniform – blue or grey denim – who lounged in the doorways of wine shops or coffee houses; some had their shirts undone, and even their bras, showing bare breasts dripping with sweat.

'Sailors and soldiers on leave,' Harriet said. 'Scum, all of them, and disrespectful of the watch. Only the security corps has authority to discipline them with unlimited pertinent chastisement. Our strokes are limited by the rule book and we must make a report of any chastisement – as you know, mamselle. The darn security corps need not report. I blame the politicians.'

'I'd like to stop and talk.'

'With respect, mamselle, it is beneath your dignity, and would be the subject of a report – official or otherwise.'

A clattering approached rapidly from Republic Place, and the girls loitering over pots of wine shrank into their doorways. A squad of bare-breasted girls, carrying canes and whips and wearing only clinging white athletic shorts and white calfskin jackboots, ran down the street in military formation. Their shorts bore gold braid, depicting a whip and cane crossed over two moons of female buttocks. The leader nodded and they dived into a doorway to extract the wriggling form of a wine-bibbing girl, who had no time to cover her undraped breasts before her entire uniform was ripped from her. Squalling and kicking, she was strapped to the clattering engine: a simple,

116

wheeled flogging frame of wood, consisting of a top bar and a lower bar, four feet in length. The girl was bent over the frame, with her ankles and wrists knotted by ropes to the lower bar and her bare fesses exposed. Her body was longer than the frame and her heavy bare breasts drooped quivering over its end, while she had to hold her head up unsupported. Her melons and cunt-basin writhed as her pubic folds were ground into the bar.

Without a word, the leader of the security corps detail lifted her cane and began to thrash the girl's bare buttocks. Her strokes were a rapid volley, tap-tap-tap-tap-tap, and when she lowered her cane her place was taken by her second. Again, the girl's squirming bare endured five slashes of a willow wand, her naked fesse-skin darkening rapidly from pink weals to crimson. The whippers' breasts jerked and bounced in the rhythm of their canestrokes. The third corpsmaid concentrated on the north buttocks and haunches, striping them purple, and the girl's moans became shrieks, then screams. The fourth caner took her on the lower buttocks and the backs of her thighs, reducing her whole naked body to shuddering, with her legs jerking rigid beneath tightly clenched melons at each stroke. A fifth security maid took her, finishing the beating with repeat strokes in the existing livid gashes and darkening the whole bare buttock-flesh to a uniform blotchy purple. The girl's ropes were undone and she was pitched, wailing and sobbing, face down on the cobblestones. Only when the corps girls had departed at a trot, and without looking at Trina or anyone else, did the wine shop girls venture out to collect the bruised body of their friend.

'Fucking trulls,' Harriet hissed. 'Fucking martial law. Fucking war.'

'Doesn't anyone want peace?' Trina asked.

'What would be the point of that?' exclaimed Harriet.

The rest of their promenade was placid, though Harriet had to press Trina away from little shops selling trinkets, caps, knitwear, baubles, tacky plaster figurines of bare girls flogged, illustrated books and pottery, saying they were just souvenirs for tourists, from the mainland.

'I hope you enjoyed your promenade through our little *cité*, mamselle intendant,' said Sophie Petrarque, loosening her blouse, open two buttons at the top, to show her full tit-jellies glistening with beads of sweat.

Tall, tanned and blonde, a couple of years younger than Trina herself, she resembled the maid Prudence Vile, only with her breasts and rump fuller and less bony under her tight white blouse and blue scholar's skirt, bow-tied at the back to show the minute thong of her string panties clenched by a muscular ass-cleft. Sophie's skirt was open only two inches by her bow, yet those inches revealed delicate pink weals on her nut-brown naked buttocks. Without ceremony, Sophie ushered Trina into her office, obliging her to accept a cup of tea served by a maid in a short, frilly French uniform, with her breasts bare, the nipples studded with sequins, and her skirt drawn up at the front, showing her pantiless pubis and a pubic fleece so big Trina gasped that it could not be real: a jungle of sleek cunt-hair that stretched from her navel and dangled well below her cunt-lips over the nylon fishnet stockings sheathing her thighs. Sophie said it was a *vison*, or pubic wig. Trina duly admired 'Sophie's trophies' as the directress called them: hung on the walls, beneath the portrait of Mamselle Flageolet, were models of flogging stools, racks, caning chairs, whipping frames and other apparatus of discipline, together with rows of shaggy hairpieces like the serving maid's.

'Some committee members would rather we built military equipment,' Sophie said, 'but how would mere girls learn to build siege engines and the like? Happily, my superior Mamselle Absorb, the supreme directress of the academy, is of my opinion. Our furniture is the best weapon New Arras can have.'

Trina asked how Sophie would feel about switching production to bags.

'Body bags?'

'No! All sorts. Like packaging.'

'Hmm,' said Sophie, tapping the bare tops of her breasts and crossing her legs with a slither of nylon stocking, 'like the Trojan horse – body bags in pretty colours, for raiding parties to infiltrate our enemies. I like it.'

She escorted Trina and her party down a corridor bustling with girls in pleated white tennis skirts and matching bras with laced Moroccan sandals.

'We'll see the furniture room first, mamselle,' Sophie said, 'and of course witness a testing. Then, the *vison* room, that is, our wigs. Devora Dykes was thrice-shaved yesterday, and I think she's just your colour. You'll forgive me, mamselle, for knowing that your mound is a little ticklish – those cropped hairs, how very mainland! – and will hopefully accept a fleece of new hairs from Devora, who will be very proud her hairs adorn the intendant's hillock. She's a lustful animal, I admit, but a useful auxiliary in the marines, and must shave for combat, lest she fall in battle and New Albion scum scalp her pubis. The savages!'

'I'd like to see the pomades,' said Trina.

Sophie blushed.

'Is mamselle sure?' she said.

When Trina insisted, Sophie explained that corners of New Arras still hid irrational superstitions, one being that the pomade could only be produced – or its production witnessed – by nude girls blindfold. Only pomade monitors, subject to the Bank of Arras, could witness the proceedings they supervised under oath of perpetual silence. Trina might observe the pomade-makers if she donned monitor's uniform, that act equal to swearing an oath. Trina said she would be glad to enter into the spirit of things, and that she wasn't scared of pomade, and what was it used for, anyway?

'Why, the ingredients are oils from garden and forest, unique to our island, mamselle,' Sophie said, 'and another, which we believe also unique, to southern belles. Southern gentlemen use it to sleek their hair, as a refreshing body rub or anywhere that fragrant and effective lubrication is required,' Sophie said.

'Like a pick-up truck?' Trina murmured, at which Harriet made a face, and Trina apologised for her mainland coarseness.

119

'Mamselle the intendant cannot be coarse!' Sophie retorted. 'Making New Arras pomade is in no way scary, in fact quite pleasurable – just a little tiring, perhaps.'

From the Journal of Mlle Augustine Flageolet, anno 1760 7
By a unanimous vote of our States General, the crew is permitted to watch public chastisements on deck, and maids are permitted equally to watch the floggings of the matelots, taken on the back with the cat-o'-nine-tails. It is natural for healthy young girls to stir at the striping of a muscular male back and allow their hands to wander under their shifts or petticoats, for only those garments are worn in this sweltering heat, their filmy substance leaving the body almost bare. Any masturbation, to which the sight of flogging stimulates them, must however be effected in a controlled, decorous and ladylike manner, preferably under the eye of a senior demoiselle, who may choose to take part. I tell my scholars that unfettered masturbation leads to fettered chastisement, and they applaud my wit. I confess that a flogging causes my own hands to wander inside my shift or petticoats, to find a pouch moist at the spectacle.

8

Butt Stud

The vast woodworks buzzed with drills, adzes, saws and hammers as over fifty girls, all in white bra and panties, and with wooden clogs painted blue, fashioned disciplinary furniture: stools, frames, stocks, pillories, racks and gibbets. Monitors in blue uniforms with high blue jackboots, and wielding two-foot whipples, supervised the workers; their one-piece cotton tunics consisted of shorts and a halter top, carrying a name badge, and baring shoulders, arms and upper breasts. All the girls, monitors and workers alike, curtsied at the entrance of Trina, Harriet and Mamselle Petrarque. Trina wrinkled her nose at the clouds of sawdust and the acrid stench of varnish.

'Mamselle Henek,' said the prefect.

'Mamselle.'

A tall monitor with cropped auburn hair sprang to attention. As her palms slapped her bare thighs, the flesh quivered, with her heavy breasts responding, the jellies quivering in their narrow halter cups.

'The new intendant wishes to see a demo. How many pieces are in condition?'

'Seven varnished and ready, mamselle.'

'Are miscreants expected?'

'There has been no word from class, mamselle prefect.'

'It's not really necessary –' Trina began.

'Oh, but it is,' said Sophie Petrarque, her face flushing. 'Mid-morning already, and no mistakes in grammar or cosmography? You'd think me deceitful, and then it should be *my* fesses bared for the demo.'

Her laughter was throaty and made her breasts dance under her tight white blouse, translucent with sweat and showing bare nipple.

'Mamselle Henek, inform mamselle the professeuse that the new intendant wishes to honour her with a greeting.'

A girl in her underthings was jerked from her task of sanding a flogging-horse, which another girl was drilling to fix bolts for straps and handcuffs at its end. She received instructions, covered her exposed body in a canvas sheet, and departed. Sophie showed Trina the workshop, inviting her to feel woodwork, suppleness of hinge and joint, polished cavities for cupping buttocks, chin or breast. They came to a half-finished rack.

'I wonder if such an extent of correction is necessary,' Trina said, shivering.

'The rack is mainly for export, for those brutes in New Albion,' Sophie replied. 'The only language they understand. Trash, all of them – if you visit the POW stockade, you'll find they don't even curtsey. We have a few flapjacks here, on loan from the stockade. We can't use them in the candle shop, because the beasts use the candles as dildos.'

She pointed to the corner of the hall where the fumes of varnish were strongest. Trina saw a group of fully nude maids, their bodies dripping with lacquer, busy varnishing the frames and furniture frames under the raised canes of the monitors. Every nude girl had a croup well laced with fresh weals, and most had stripes across their upper backs.

One, a coltish blonde, with a full mane and huge pubic fleece streaked and stuck with brown varnish, raised her head and gazed sullenly at Trina; three monitors brought down their canes all at once on her bare fesses. Vip! Vip! Vip! echoed in the hangar, yet no girls looked towards the POWs. Her face twisted in a grimace as she doubled up, but she did not cry out or drop her paintpot. Instead, her jellies and melons trembling, and raw pink stripes streaking her bare buttocks, she curtsied to Trina, biting her lip and her grimace twisting to a smile. Sophie glared, hissing that the girl was the sassiest of POWs, but a good worker, being so strong. Odette van Kram, undoubtedly a *nom de guerre*, had been captured on a solo night raid from a fishing boat. Bent on theft and sabotage, nude and her skin blacked, she had refused to confess, even under repeated caning, back-whippings and the rack. Yet, without giving reasons, she refused to be traded for a New Arras POW, as if preferring the regime of corporal punishment on New Arras. She worked in the academy as a security measure, for Mamselle Toitte feared her wanton beauty exerted a lesbian influence over the camp guards.

'I can bear witness that the rack is not just for export,' Trina said.

'Well, I guess the occasional hanging for the really incorrigible,' said Sophie, before her hand flew to her mouth. 'Oh, mamselle intendant, I'm so sorry! You yourself – what a welcome to New Arras! But you understand, in wartime, with so many spies around . . .'

Trina laughed and said she fully understood, and was no worse for racking.

'The rack was uncomfortable? Painful?' Sophie asked.

'Decidedly so. Real agony . . .'

'Thank goodness,' Sophie said.

The messenger returned, stripped off her canvas robe and returned to work. A scholar maid entered, head hung low and her hands folded at her crotch, but unescorted. She was scarcely nineteen, and her long dark mane sheathed a swelling breastwork, while the loose bowtie at her croup and the skimpy film of her high-cut white panties did little to shield two ripe melons, the unpantied portion of the moons liberally scarred with old welts.

'Clara Latasse, again,' Sophie exclaimed. 'What now?'

'Please, mamselle prefect, I said there were ten planets, and the professeuse said there were only nine. She said nine is a significant number, but I think ten is reasonable.'

'A repeat offence, then,' Sophie hissed. 'You are here to learn what is reasonable, not to think it. Last week, you took twenty on bare, with a maple rod, for just the same thing. Do you enjoy being caned?'

'No, mamselle,' Clara mumbled, a tear forming in her eye, and her breast-jellies trembling.

'Yet your behaviour invites the cane. Very well. Thirty strokes on the bare croup for the offence and a further fifteen on teats for insolence in repeating it.'

'Yes, mamselle,' Clara said.

'You may apologise to the intendant.'

'With respect, mamselle, it would be unreasonable of me to naysay my belief, until it is beaten from me.'

Sophie looked at her in disgust.

'You'll take your thirty *à la baignade*, in sets of ten, with thirty seconds' pause between sets. Wet buttocks,' she rapped. 'Unless you prefer to go before a tribunal and risk double sentence?'

'The sentence is reasonable, mamselle,' gasped Clara.

'The flogging to be with a hickory wand.'

'Yes, mamselle,' Clara murmured, and curtsied.

Sophie rubbed her brow and loosened the top buttons of her clammy shirt, fanning the air around her breasts, which bobbled loosely, slapping against the moist fabric.

'So hot today,' she gasped. 'Not your dry mainland heat, mamselle. It is moist and invades the loins, warming girls to frenzy, unless they are disciplined . . .'

'Please, not for my benefit,' Trina said.

'It is for the benefit of New Arras, mamselle,' Sophie rapped. 'Dissent must be punished, for it leads to treason. If we were enslaved by the goddammees of New Albion, mere caning would be light relief from punishment.'

'Can't she buy her way off strokes with fessignats?'

'Academy corrections are not on treasury account. They are internally earned and administered in house.'

Monitor Dolores Henek led Clara to a short table three feet high, with indentations for belly, breasts and thighs. Clara took off her shoes then unfastened her croup bowtie, allowing her skirt to billow and expose her panties. She took the hem of the skirt and tied it together in front of her in a larger bow, so that her buttocks were exposed. She rolled down her panties, stepping out of them to reveal her massive tangle of wet pubic curls spilling over dark red, swollen cunt-flaps that glistened wet. After folding her panties and handing them to Henek, she stood croup bared for punishment. Henek grasped her neck and forced her face down on to the shiny new flogging bench. A second monitor, Jennifer Tans, strapped her stockinged ankles to the corners of the bench, with her wrists behind her and her arms folded over the small of her back. The wrist rope extended to a rubber cord fastened around her waist.

The workmaids lined up before a wooden pail; each squatted over it, lowered her panties to span her knees and pissed into the pail. After ten girls had spurted their piss, Henek placed the brimming receptacle below the top of the table at Clara's head. Henek raised her cane above Clara's naked buttocks; Tans upended a pitcher of drinking water over Clara's bare, making sure every crevice was soaked. Clara was sobbing, with little gasps and a choked, mewling sound, and her bare fesses trembled violently, clenching even before a single stroke lashed her. Lattices of old welts crisscrossed her wet nates, and Trina asked why a hardened offender should so dread further punishment. She had heard of women who even relished the lash on bare.

'She is undoubtedly one,' Sophie said, as Jennifer Tans grasped Clara's mane and wound it around her fist. 'They relish the idea of the lash on bare, but not the process. Nudity of the caned buttocks makes for shame. It is the subject's naked bottom, her female essence, which is touched; while the caner must face the squirming, the bruises, the reddening of flesh ... and must be doubly virtuous to resist pride and desire. Bare fesses are such defiance, such intimacy.'

As her head was jerked towards the piss pail, Clara looked up and cried to Trina:

'Don't *you* tremble before bare-ass beating, mamselle intendant?'

Trina paled. She looked at Sophie, then at Henek and Jennifer. Every girl in the workroom stared at her, including Odette Van Kram, the caned POW who had impishly curtsied.

'Lay it on hard, mamselle,' Trina snapped to Henek, who saluted; Harriet, quivering, clutched Trina's arm.

Jennifer dragged Clara's head by the hair, plunging it under the surface of the liquid in a flurry of bubbles until the piss lapped her nape.

'One,' Sophie cried.

Vip! The cane landed athwart Clara's wide, full melons, and the naked buttock-meat clenched, jerking, as the rod gouged a livid pink weal on the satin skin. The girl's skirts billowed; her head banged the side of the pail and bubbles surged from the piss. Sophie's voice rang out once more. Vip! The cane landed right in the same weal and Clara's body jerked rigid, her roped arms struggling against her rubber waist cincher. The pail of piss frothed as her head shook beneath the liquid. The buttocks clenched rapidly after the cane was lifted, having remained caressing the weal for over a second. Vip! Vip! Vip! The beating continued, every stroke delivered to the same welt, now a jagged gash darkening to purple, and the whole roomful of girls was silent, clutching their faces as the flogged maid squirmed helplessly on her table.

'Look at her quim, mamselle,' Harriet whispered. 'She was wet before the first stroke, and now . . .'

Clara's billowing skirts revealed her bare pubis, slimed in a lake of oily come. Trina clutched Harriet's hand, shifting her thighs to conceal the moisture seeping from her own quim as she gazed at the writhing bare buttocks framed by the flounced skirt. At the tenth stroke, Jennifer wrenched Clara's head from the pail by her hair.

'Ugh! Ugh!'

The girl spluttered, her face bright scarlet. Her buttocks continued to clench for the full half minute, until she had caught her breath and was plunged once more into the foaming liquid, her wail drowned in the bubbles of girl piss. Vip Vip! Vip! Trina panted, gasping, as Sophie's voice called out the strokes and Henek lashed the squirming bare nates, now in a second weal crossed over the first. Without relinquishing the flogged girl's hair, Jennifer refreshed her wet bottom from the water pitcher, and Sophie murmured to Trina that a wet caning was superbly painful. The caner's muscles and breasts heaved as she brought the rod down with a squelching slap on the bare wet nates, spraying water, mingled with Clara's sweat. The second set ended with a deep purpling gash stretching across the first weal, which was now puffing to a high ridge of blackened skin. Trina swallowed and wiped her brow.

The third set began. Henek laid five strokes to vertical, then five horizontal, forming a star shape on Clara's bare. Trina clutched Harriet's hand, jumping at each stroke, and started as, at the twenty-eighth, Henek's breasts burst from her bodice. She continued the caning bare-breasted, her firm, jutting jellies jumping at each stroke of the cane on Clara's writhing bare ass. Trina sighed, moaning, as the girl's head was dragged from her pail of seething piss, and as Henek unfastened her ankle ropes, without attending to her own bare teats, Jennifer ripped open Clara's blouse, scattering buttons. Clara was bound anew by the feet, face up and with Jennifer holding her head down by her hair. Her arm pinion remained in place. Jennifer ripped open her bra, tearing it – 'She'll have to pay for that on account,' Sophie whispered – and Henek raised the cane over the trembling bare jellies, whose big cherry nips stood pointed and erect.

'Free delivery to fifteen, mamselle,' Sophie called.

Vip! Vip! Vip! Vip! Four rapid strokes slashed Clara's bare breasts, right across the points of her nipples.

'Ah!' the girl screamed, wriggling so that her bunched dress fell away from her pubis, revealing her massive cunt-bush, soaked in the come that dripped from her swollen gash-flaps; her clitoris poked above the vulva, the crimson bud throbbing, hard and extruded.

Breathing heavily, Henek shouldered her cane and pinched the girl's scarlet nipples, then ground the heel of her fist against the girl's cunt, crushing the swollen clitoris.

'Oh . . . oh . . .' she moaned.

'That must hurt dreadfully,' Trina gasped.

'I imagine so,' Sophie replied.

Vip! Vip! The teat jellies writhed as weals coloured them above and below each nipple.

'Ah . . .'

Vip! Vip!

'Ohh!'

There was a hiss as a flood of golden piss spurted from Clara's cunt, spouting all over her thighs and belly and dripping in a lake. Her ankles strained against their bonds as the piss soaked her and she wailed, sobbing.

'Dirty bitch,' said Sophie.

Vip! Vip! Vip!

Clara's flogged breasts were a patchwork of crimson weals, their jellies shaking uncontrollably as her belly writhed, her legs sticking rigid from her hips, and the telltale flow of piss continuing to dribble from her cunt, its lips gasping. Trina blurted that she needed the bathroom, and Sophie asked Harriet to escort her.

'Harriet was an honours student here,' she said, 'until she opted for life in the watch.'

The bathroom was large, shaded and airy, with the scent of soaps and unguents. There was a tin bathtub and a porcelain toilet pot. Trina scrabbled to unfasten her skirt and had rolled her panties down, slopped with come from her gaping cunt, when she saw Harriet still present.

'I didn't think you'd want me to leave, mamselle,' Harriet said impishly. 'We're both the same. You first, mamselle, or both of us together?'

'What . . .?'

'You need to masturbate, don't you, mamselle?'

Trina closed her eyes, swallowing, as her fingers plunged towards her oozing cunt-flaps and erect, swollen clitty. She thumbed the throbbing organ, jerked as a flood of electric pleasure jolted her and began to frot herself. She looked at Harriet, who had her panties already down and her cunt-lips between her fingers. With wide, sweeping strokes Harriet began to masturbate, staring at Trina's wet cunt. Trina nodded.

'Both together,' she whispered.

The snip-snip of shears was the only sound in the bathroom, above the gurgling of pipes, save for the sobbing of naked girls. They sat, roped by wrists and ankles in dentists' chairs, with their thighs wide, showing naked cunt-basins. Workmaids of the academy, clad in bra and panties and barefoot, carefully sheared the pubic fleeces, the clusters of curls falling to the floor where they were swept up and each girl's hairs placed in separate buckets. When a girl's pubis was completely bare, including the downy hairs of her perineum and anus, she was released from her bonds and permitted to dress. She had to don her scholar's skirt backwards, so that the parting showed not her buttocks but her shaven hillock, and the flaps of her dress were pinned back to fully expose a pair of gauze panties that revealed her pubic nudity. They sat huddled on a bench beside a row of sewing machines, tended by seated sewing maids who stitched the shorn hairs into pubic wigs. Sophie picked up a glossy *vison* from a pile, by one of the sewing maids, and sniffed it.

'A hybrid,' she said. 'Made from the hairs of two or more maids – I would say Florence Glow and Virginia Marble, two of our most succulently hairy maids.'

The hairs of the enormous *vison* were both blonde, but not the same shade: one a corn yellow, the other an ash hue, the colours mingling in tufted ribbons. The wig was designed to cover not only the pubic mound but to stretch its fur as far up as the navel and dangle luxuriantly beneath the cunt-flaps, while crawling generously to the rear over anus and perineum, with little curling fronds to peek at the bottom of the ass-cleft. Some of the cunt-hairs were mere kiss curls, while others were sprawling lianas six inches in length.

'We call that a pompadour,' said Sophie. 'Yours, mamselle, fashioned from the hairs of Devora Dykes, will be a *maintenon*, with hairs from only one maid. Dykes is quite our most prolific sprouter.'

The monitor in charge beckoned to one of the shorn girls, who rose, trembling and sobbing. Her naked cunt-mound was red from the shears and razors and she scratched it incessantly, until the monitor brought her cane cracking across her fingers and laid a thin stripe on the plump bare mons, at which the girl's sobs were broken by a whimper. The girl put her hands behind her back to be swiftly fastened by twine, and she lowered her head as ropes uncurled from the ceiling. Sophie handed the pompadour to the monitor, who ordered the girl to squat, parting her legs. A scholar in her underwear crouched and fitted the wig against the girl's cunt, poking its every tendril into the folds and niches of her buttock-cleft and cunt-flaps, until the cunt was visible only by the thick red lips that swelled above the blonde billows of the vison. She removed the wig, and a second scholar slopped pungent magnolia sweet gum on to its skin backside; after twenty seconds, the crouching maid slapped the *vison* in place, pressing it firmly around the girl's cunt and buttocks, then slapping it hard as the girl wailed. The dangling rope held a metal bolt in which a dozen or more knotholes were punched. Both maids kneeled to loop strands of the newly fitted *vison* through the holes, knotting them tightly until the bewigged maid was hoisted to her tiptoes by her tethered hairs. A rubber cord from the ceiling was looped around the girl's waist. At a signal from the monitor, the rope jerked, abruptly hoisting the maid into the air where she dangled, shrieking and sobbing, and the skin of her mons pulled into a tight envelope inches above her pubic bone. She dangled, squirming, before the rubber rope sprang up to slacken the pull on her cunt-hillock. Thereafter, her wig hairs stretched taut but did not snap as they took her full weight when the protective rubber strap sprang away, yielding her to the rope's suspension. For moments, she hung by her cunt-mound alone.

'Give her twelve minutes,' Sophie said to the monitor, who curtsied. 'The glue comes from New Albion; I dread to think what they put in it.'

She ushered Trina out of the bathroom; behind them, the suspended girl screamed and sobbed and a stream of piss spurted between her thighs. Sophie laughed.

'Yes, it withstands any kind of ordure. She'll foul herself, probably, but you don't want to see that, mamselle intendant.'

130

'No,' Trina blurted. 'Let's see the pomade room.'

Harriet and Sophie exchanged glances.

'As you wish, mamselle intendant,' they said together.

The pomade room announced itself first by its smell, like Tennessee chestnuts in blossom, then by the sighing and whimpering of girls behind its metal doors. And the faint but unmistakable sound – tap, tap, tap. Trina shivered and she tensed her thighs against the seep of come that oozed from her cunt at the noise of bare chastisement. Trina, Harriet and Sophie reached it by winding corridors, where oaken doors with barred windows led to classrooms, Sophie explained. Whenever there was the unmistakable tap-tap of cane on bare flesh, followed by a maid's groan, Sophie smiled coyly and said she hoped Trina agreed bare-buttock caning was the only tongue submissive belles properly understood.

Trina begged to know if Sophie was herself experienced in bare-bottom discipline, and received the answer that no mistress should be ignorant of what she administered.

'Yet you accept me as intendant,' Trina replied, 'without knowing me.'

She felt Harriet's fingers squeeze her butt, right at the lower cleft, and gasped. Harriet and Sophie exchanged glances.

'Virtue is its own swift rumour, mamselle,' Sophie said. 'We are cognisant of you. The Bank of New Arras, under instruction of Mamselle Carawn, maintains an intelligence service in the Orleans territory and elsewhere.'

'Like Los Angeles?' Trina mumured. 'I guess you can't tell me about secret agent Kimmi Lardeau.'

'Correct, mamselle – *supposing* I knew of such a maid,' Sophie replied, putting her finger to her teeth.

Two monitors stood on guard, at the bolted metal doors to the pomade chamber. Both girls were nude, save for an armour of metal and rubber straps, with spikes seven inches long extending from steel toecaps, knees, ankles, wrists, shoulders; from their naked cunts, with the *visons* trimmed to an inch of pubic crewcut, and from the points of their conical and fur-trimmed steel brassieres. They had canes in scabbards at their waists, and rawhide cattle whips coiled to four lengths at the hip, whose steel crotch-thong was also trimmed with fur. Their manes were cropped like their pubic thatches, and they wore spiked helmets with half-face visors slitted for eyes and nose. They turned to unlock the doors and revealed their bare buttocks criss-crossed by a harness of straps, bristling with spikes across fesse and haunch, and with the stoutest, sharpest spike poking right out of the anus, or seeming so. Sophie said they wore battle dress to guard one of the most precious secrets of New Arras. The fur trimming was for good luck, taken from the pubic shavings of those maids who had shown themselves bravest and most silent under bare-bottom correction. Trina said it must be difficult for them to sit down.

'Warriors do not sit down,' Sophie answered.

They entered the pomade chamber, and the doors clanged shut behind them. They stood in a vestibule, where a doorway draped in fur hid the main chamber. Harriet opened a closet and withdrew a complete monitor's uniform. Sophie invited Trina to strip and put it on. Trina stripped naked, sweating profusely in the cramped vestibule and brushing often against the limbs of the other girls. She asked why they were not undressing and Harriet said that, with respect, the intendant must enter the chamber alone: only one *fausse* monitor might enter at a time to preserve the natural harmony of the work. Trina shivered as the girls strapped her in the several harnesses, the spikes fitting snugly at her limbs, and winced as the steel bra cut the sides of her teats. Harriet strapped it so tightly that Trina murmured in a protest, which the girl ignored. Her buttocks were sheathed in spiked straps, and then Sophie brandished two larger spikes, each with a handle like a scythe's. She told Trina to open her buttocks and bend over. Trina obeyed. Harriet grasped Trina's head and held her down with one hand, while the other prised open the buttock-melons. The girl wiped a long, slow finger across Trina's cunt and perineum and anus, then held the finger to Trina's lips. It was slimy with her own come. Harriet smiled.

'Now, wait,' Trina began, 'this is getting – oh!'

Her body jerked as the spike, lubricated with her own come, penetrated her anus to a few inches then jammed.

'Relax, mamselle,' said Sophie.

Harriet rammed the spike again.

'Oh! Oh!'

The heavy steel shaft penetrated Trina's insides and her bare moons quivered violently; Harriet said she was properly stuck and permitted her to rise. Trina winced as the burning pressure of the shaft filled her anus, yet behind her she saw her defensive spike pointing proudly from her ass-cleft.

'The quim should be no problem,' Harriet said briskly, 'as you're already so wet, mamselle intendant.'

'Uhh . . . yeah . . .'

I am wet.

Trina's clit was throbbing as she parted her thighs and leaned backwards for the second prong to penetrate her. The steel tube slid easily up her moist cunt, slamming the neck of her womb. Between her legs, Trina sported a spiked sword. Sophie buckled a scabbard with a whipple cane at her waist, and Harriet said she regretted not having a cattle whip available, but the armament was only for show, anyhow. Finally, she wedged the steel pod of the helmet over Trina's mane, which bristled out on either side. Without ceremony, she hustled Trina through the fur drapes into the perfumed chamber. The drapes closed with a zip behind her. She heard a whisper, Harriet's voice – watch out for the butt stud, mamselle – and giggles.

The room was in shadowy green candlelight; bodies moved and Trina stood still, adjusting her eyes. Her feet crunched a covering of sawdust on the dirt floor. A machine, like an outsize food blender, whirred at the far end of a trough five feet long. Three nude maids, heads sheathed in tight green rubber hoods, leaned over the trough at an angle of sixty degrees, with their feet in shackles bolted to the floor. Their heads were held up by ropes extending from the low ceiling, to which their manes were knotted, with their torso weight taken by their hair pulled to its roots. Each maid had one arm pinioned behind her back, the wrist pulled upwards and fastened by a chain to a spiked neck collar. Behind each maid stood a uniformed and helmeted monitor, her spikes and harness flashing as she caned the bare bottom of the bound girl. The girls writhed to the rhythm of their flogging by the snappy little whipples, drawing traceries of red welts on their bares.

As they were flogged, each girl masturbated, fingers delving into swollen cunt-lips and tangled with wet pubic hairs as a steady stream of come dripped from her cunt into the trough. On a bench by the wall, three more nude maids sat, hooded, with their knees held up by a two-by-four roped around the backs of their necks. Their wrists were tied to their raised ankles, and they shivered at each canestroke to the bares they could not see, but whose owners yelped loud. Telltale trickles of come seeped beneath the naked girls' buttocks, streaking the bench with cunt-oil.

One of the three monitors put down her cane and approached Trina. Her eyes were stone as she turned her bottom towards her and clashed ass-spikes; then repeated the greeting by flapping her cunt-spike against Trina's. The two other monitors did likewise, and the second gestured to Trina that she should take her place at the come trough. Trina hesitated; the girl drew Trina's whipple from her scabbard and impatiently thrust it between her fingers, pointing at the scarred, squirming nates she had been flogging. Trembling, Trina took up position behind the naked girl and perceived further movement in the far depths of the smoky chamber. She raised her cane; the bare buttocks clenched and quivered, and a sob escaped the lips of the girl, who mewled under her hood.

There was an exclamation of disgust from the monitor, who grabbed Trina's forearm and brought the cane smartly across the girl's bare, adding a further stripe to the numerous bruises already mottling the flesh. The girl groaned. Trina shook off the monitor's hand, which delved at Trina's groin, coming up shiny and oily with her own come. The monitor grinned. Trina swallowed and forced herself to grin back. The plugs were tight, *so very tight*, filling her cunt and butthole . . . The monitor gestured once more to the girl's squirming bare. The other monitors watched Trina. The prisoner snuffled and yelped, wriggling her bottom as if pleading for welts. *This weird shit . . .!* Trina snorted, raised her cane and lashed the naked moons. Vip!

'Oh . . . Oh . . .' the girl crooned, sobbing.

Vip!

'Oh . . .'

Vip! Vip!

'Ah!'

Trina began to cane the naked girl without pity, watching the flow of come spurt after each canestroke and feeling her own cunt slippery with her slime. Sweat poured from her, dripping on to the spikes from her cunt and ass, which flashed in the candle's glow, and which in turn sprayed droplets of her sweat. Vip! Vip!

'Uh . . .' came the writhing girl's whimper, muffled by her hood as she masturbated faster.

Vip! Vip!

'Oh . . .'

The full bare moons danced in the smoky light, the ridges etched by Trina's cane puffing to purple, and the buttocks squirming like twin kaleidoscopes. Vip! Vip! Vip!

'Ahh!'

Trina's cane rose but did not yet lash.

'Ooh!'

A second scream tore from the darkness in the far depths and Trina craned to look. She saw two naked bodies, one hooded: an elfin, hard-muscled slip of a girl, prostrate, with her hooded face in the dirt, and manacled, her teeth clawing at sawdust and raw earth, which she chewed and swallowed as the masked figure behind her slapped his loins against her wriggling buttocks. The male withdrew after every cockstroke, his tool dripping with ass-grease, while the girl masturbated her cunt, sending torrents of come dribbling into a gutter, which led to the churning blender. Trina stared at the sweating male body, the enormous, hideous cock cleaving the tiny girl's anus before a wooden throne. He fucked tirelessly, slamming the girl's helpless body with each penetration; her legs jerked rigid at the cockthrusts; her moans turned to shrieks, then gasps of orgasm, and come poured from her frotted cunt as she masturbated harder and harder. He did not come himself, nor cease to crack his hips on her quivering ass as she slid from the spasms of one orgasm towards another. The ruthless buttfucking continued, and her cries shrilled again, as the enculing cock brought her off once more.

'Elvis . . .?' she murmured.

The male looked up without ceasing to buttfuck the prostrate, wriggling girl. Trina saw his mask and screamed.

'You dare to address the butt stud, bitch?' hissed the first monitor.

The monitors rushed her, jabbing at her ass and teats with their cunt- and buttock-spikes, while immobilising her. Flailing and helpless, Trina screamed again. The enculing male was wearing a rubber mask with the face of Trina Guelph.

From the Journal of Mlle Augustine Flageolet, anno 1760 8
Forcibly, our crew is male, and my design to keep them in docility has worked perfectly. There is the promise of five gold pieces held for them in the Bank of Geneva on their return to Europe, with my written accreditation. My academy of reason can well afford the sum, possessed as it is of my treasure. I let no one see the treasure, not even the bankers who finance my endeavours, for I know that what those greedy periwigs imagine is more potent than reality. Most important is the crew's daily servicing by my virgins of Ishtar, the lustful goddess, queen of the universe, protectress of prostitutes and patroness of wine shops. I have long been an admirer of Ishtar. Her cult worship included temple prostitution, the sublime art of feminine power, by total submission. which tames men, by draining their juices. I teach my girls to submit totally to the male principle of power, for it is only by female submission that

hear she is quite the martinet, her cane ever lashing, and that in two weeks she has left a trail of scarred melons. Possibly including her own. It seems she arrived smooth-cunt, but has grown a fleece to rival Zealla Pure's.'

'You hear much, your ladyship,' Sirena said.

Juliet laughed and shifted on her divan, its only ornament, apart from her nude body, being a red telephone.

'And know but little. There are rumours she is enthralled by the vicious trull Harriet Stooplaugh, some say her appointed tribadist. I do know a martinet is a dominatrix, but also a girl whose bare ass craves the cane. Our English language has such subtleties. Mmm! Good, Duane.'

Sirena nodded, grimacing. Sweat dripped from their brows and dampened their nylon blouses, clinging to their low-cut scalloped brassieres; their nylon stockings slithered wetly as the two women crossed and uncrossed their legs. Behind them, under the eyes of two cane-wielding guards, shyly stood three girls of eighteen years, all clad in a new military uniform of black tunic and mini-skirt, with bare legs and black rubber ankle-boots. None carried a whip or other weapon and the tightness of their garments indicated none had underwear. The guards had corporal's and sergeant's stripes tattooed on bare upper arms, and were uniformed in black rubber bikinis and jackboots, the bra cups steel cones, with spikes at buttocks, breasts and toecaps.

Beneath the open balcony windows of the first lady's chamber, squadrons of uniformed girls drilled and practised combat on the parade ground beyond Lady Juliet Gorges's patio where, among arbours and flowers, stood tiny gibbets, flogging stools, stocks and a pillory. Those held strapped nude girls, their faces sullen with shame, with bodies striped by the whip and stained with pelted ordures.

Beyond them, at the crest of a hillock, stood an eight-foot brass cannon looking out to sea. A naked maid was strapped to the cannon, her wrists and ankles roped beneath the barrel, and her buttocks gleamed with a panoply of fresh red welts. Her head slumped on the gunmetal, wet with her tears, and the juices oozed from her quim. The sun was rising in the morning sky, a fierce azure, across which white clouds scudded in the brisk sea breeze. The soldier girls wore combat dress of black spikes jutting from oiled nude bodies. The spikes were fixed by rubber cords clustering around teat and vulva, and were most concentrated at the bare fesses. Those drilling marched at a goosestep, carrying whips held taut against their breasts. Those at combat dodged and dived, cracking their whips, in efforts to lash each other's bodies, the spikes both for armour and attack, for when a girl had lashed out with her whip and lost momentum she was laid open to a spinning croup assault and a clash of spikes aimed at fesses, gash or titties.

Sirena and Alice watched the display with stony faces. The black-spiked girls moved in perfect harmony and utter viciousness; a beaten girl, pinioned on the ground, refused to beg for mercy as her victrix whipped her spikes from her body. Once denuded, she lay flat in the dirt for her bottom to be striped by the quirt, and the bare fesses not clenching – save when it was over, and her wealed ass-flesh leaped into frenzied, pent-up shuddering, like flapjacks on a griddle, origin of the New Arrasiennes' derogatory nickname for girls of New Albion. When the flogged ass made flapjacks, the victrix thrust with her bottom and hoisted the flogged girl by her spikes, driving her off the parade ground by a flurry of spiked thrusts to her anus, with the nude, shamed victim passing a gauntlet of buttocks, each spiked and thrusting at her anus or vulva. She bowed to the flag of New Albion, swaying on top of a pole thirty feet high: it was a nude girl, bound at the breasts and loins by hempen ropes, with her eyes covered, her mouth gagged by a rubber strap and ball, and wrists and ankles roped behind her. Sirena and Alice made a moue.

'How barbaric,' murmured Sirena.

'Pig-sticking is a noble battleground tradition,' said Lady Juliet. '*Vae victis!* Woe to the conquered. Nevertheless, see how lightly armoured our troops are. So easy for an enemy – naming no one – to flog them to submission.'

'Our troops abjure pig-sticking, Lady Juliet,' said Alice, 'and yours have metal in their whipthongs.'

'Why, that would be forbidden by the Biloxi convention! Mmm . . . yes, Duane, continue. Higher. Mmm . . .'

'Shall we to business, your ladyship?' Sirena said, sipping her glass of ale and poking at her plate of greasy fodder. 'We have some formal diplomatic notes to deliver.'

'My secretary, Abby Musquonset, shall receive them, as usual,' said Lady Juliet, nodding to the blonde in black military uniform.

The coltish blonde girl, eighteen years old, wore a tight short skirt clinging to her bare thighs. Above the waist she was naked, save for a brassiere whose black rubber straps encased her bulbous teats in two sharply pointed conical cups of gunmetal, each breast ringed by spikes in the same metal, six inches long, while from the tip of each bra-cup jutted a thicker spike. Untrimmed fleeces poked from her armpits. She wore a cane at her waist and a whip curled around her torso, passing through the crease of her big, sweat-damp breasts. Her feet wore calf-length black boots in shiny latex, with a steel spike at the toe. Sirena handed her a paper scroll bound in a string. She leered and stuck the scroll behind the left cup of her bra.

'The republic of New Arras protests the repeated incursions into our territory and waters by the New Albion armed forces,' Sirena said. 'We desire only peace, but the behaviour of New Albion obliges us to remain on a war footing. We further protest the haven given by New Albion to fugitives from New Arras justice.'

'An outrageous provocation,' said Lady Juliet, 'which we reject utterly. Abby has *our* diplomatic note. In it, we protest your detention and imprisonment of innocent New Albion mariners lost in the fog. Also the incursions of spies into our territory, masquerading as political refugees, who our Anglo-Saxon humanity obliges us to welcome.'

Abby Musquonset parted her thighs and raised her right leg until her knee was at her chin. Her minge was fully spread and exposed, showing the fleshy red cunt-lips nestling amid a jungle of blonde pubic thatch that trailed up her belly and down between the cheeks of her bottom, almost covering her anus. She poked a finger inside her anus and withdrew a rolled paper gleaming with her ass-grease. Sirena accepted it frostily. Juliet and Abby smiled.

'We commend your subtlety,' said Sirena, grimacing. 'New Arras has no choice but to detain as POWS those armed insurgents, bent on violent overthrow of our state, under orders of New Albion high command. Therefore we reject your outrageous suggestion and demand the return of so-called refugees – in reality felons, or civilians, kidnapped as slaves.'

'Outrageous! That is a lie, peddled by the warmonger Zealla Pure and her faction. Is Zealla still diddling Devora Dykes, by the way? I hear that the new intendant has grown a cunt-fleece that puts Devora's to shame, and that the imperialist dictator Pure is avid for hot new bushes, as well as new croups to lash, and juicy new quims to suck. Anyway, there are no slaves on New Albion.'

'Preposterous! There is nothing but,' said Sirena. 'As for your despicable slur on citizen Pure's morality, she is without equal in her devotion to reason and the common weal. I suggest we get down to the real business. You have advertised certain disciplinary instruments to be supplied for humanitarian purposes.'

Lady Juliet Gorges clapped her hands, and the guards pushed the three soldier girls forwards, towards a flogging chaise longue six feet in length, with straps for ankles and wrists at the extremities. Its rosewood sides and table curved to meet the undulations of a female body and the centre was a hillock to thrust the buttocks up, with slopes to force the thighs wide open. Each of them stood trembling with her head hanging low and her hands crossed at her pubis. The sergeant flicked each of them under the chin with her cane, and they raised their heads. All had moist eyes and slack lips.

'You maids know why you are here,' Lady Juliet said, sucking a greasy fragment of chitlin and sipping ale.

The girls nodded.

'It is a singular honour for new recruits,' said Juliet, 'and each of you will explain that to our diplomatic guests.'

'I'm recruit Mandy Huxtable, from Biddeford, Maine,' said the first, a muscular blonde, 'and I've never had my bottom caned or spanked, and I'm honoured to serve New Albion in this way. My bare croup is ready to be flogged. Hail Gorges!'

'I'm recruit Claudine Butreaux, from Lowell, Massachusetts,' said the raven-haired, big-titted girl beside her, 'and I've never been punished on the bare, and I'm happy to undergo my induction rite into the defence forces of New Albion. My bare can take the most! Please whop me hardest, ladies. Hail Gorges!'

'I'm recruit Donnette Spinks, from Ithaca, New York,' said the third, a petite, wiry girl, smaller than Claudine, but with jutting dugs, long, coltish legs and two ripe melons that strained her clinging black skirt. 'I've never been chastised on the bare, or caned or even spanked, as a soldier, I mean, and –' she licked her teeth '– I'm looking forward to serving my country. Hail Gorges!'

'Each contestant shall have the honour of demonstrating one new product,' said Juliet. 'Please choose, ladies.'

Each girl unbuttoned her shirt and removed it, allowing her bare breasts to spring free. She slid off her footwear and unfastened her skirt, letting it drop to the floor. Nude, she exhibited her bare bottom, spreading the cheeks blatantly to show pink as she bent to pick up her skirtlet. The maids stood naked in a row, winking and pouting and wriggling to show off titties and ass. Each swivelled, hands on bare fesses, stroking the bare, goose-bumped skin, then clawing aside the buttock-meat to show the anus bud and the straggly, quim-damp pubic hairs that infested the slit of her perineum. Each sported a cunt-jungle as luxuriant as Abby Musquonset's.

Alice and Sirena rose and touched the girls' naked bodies, pinching the nipples to stiffness, brushing the clits, which all stood erect, and wiping the cunt-slits, to test the come oozed by all three gashes. They paid most attention to the ass-melons, stroking and caressing the satin-smooth rumps, until the three candidates blushed and crossed their legs to hide their seeping cunts.

Lady Juliet announced the demonstration of three implements: a cane, a switch and an Aroostook birch. Mandy was to take the cane and Claudine the switch. They chose Donnette Spinks for the birch, as her melons were largest and possibly not virgin to corporal punishment. Mandy and Claudine glowered, exchanging glances, and each licked her lips as she curtsied to the diplomats. Donnette paled, then shuddered, hearing that the implements were to be tested on the bare by each contestant in turn on the croup of the next.

'Aren't they something, ladies?' purred Juliet, stroking the shiny skin of the three woods and coming last to the birch. 'Cane of real Vermont ash, the hardest and springiest model we have yet designed – the switch, or yankee quirt, four tongues of the supplest New Hampshire willow, perfect for close work – and this Aroostook birch, culled from the finest Maine saplings, and bushier than any before, with at least twenty twigs bonded at the hilt by maple gum. Look at these naked girls. Look how their fesses swell and their haunches sway with that lovely satin gleam in the morning sun, just begging for welts to furrow the flesh. What finer meat could test such fine implements?'

'You have chosen well,' said Alice. 'I wonder how?'

'That's simple,' Juliet said, wiping the chitlin grease drooling from her lips. 'Tell the ladies, Donna.'

Donna blushed.

'I don't rightly know –' she began, then squealed as Abby's cane flicked her gash. 'We were caught diddling – not each other, but Mr Carvalho, there.'

She caught the eye of the masseur, who did not blink.

'We were told new recruits had to do it . . . as a dare, you know?'

'Do what, Donna?' Juliet murmured.

'We snuck up to Mr Carvalho when he was asleep, and did him – brought him off, you know? He was asleep, and bare-ass naked, and Mandy tickled his balls while Claudine squatted with her bare cunt over his nose, diddling herself to make her juicy and smelly, while I took his cock-tip in my mouth and licked it. Idea is, he thinks he's dreaming

144

and isn't supposed to wake up when he comes. Mandy was stroking his balls and he got a massive boner – he's very big, begging your pardon, milady – and I started rubbing his shaft with my fingertips while I got his whole helmet in my mouth, and was sucking him, with my tongue licking at his peehole, and my lips squeezing the neck of his helmet, and ... I guess I got too excited. Mandy was diddling herself, so that her come trickled into his nose, and Claudine was licking his balls, so we all got carried away. I felt a drop of sperm from his peehole, and the next thing I had his cock right to the back of my throat and I was milking his sperm, while he woke up ejaculating. Mandy lowered her cunt right on to his face and squatted on him, and my lips met Claudine's at his balls; she had taken them fully into her mouth and was sucking on them. He came and came, like a horse! I swallowed every drop, too.'

'Really,' said Sirena, wrinkling her nose. 'It pains me to consider such Anglo-Saxon grossness. These trulls deserve lashes for their criminous lusts.'

'Of course,' said Juliet. 'For the crime of getting caught.'

Donnette was to cane Mandy, then Mandy was to lash Claudine with the yankee quirt, after which Claudine would birch Donnette. Mandy lowered herself on to the flogging chaise and Abby Musquonset helped the sergeant bind her hands and feet in overlapping rubber thongs. The girl looked round, her face pale, as her pink gash-meat shone wetly between her stretched thighs and her ripe bare melons strained, thrust upwards by the curve of the flogging chaise.

'Splendid furniture,' said Juliet. 'One of yours, of course. Captured on a reprisal raid, after your pirates had a New Albion skipper strapped to her mainmast and whipped to the bone, by a male, who afterwards buggered her.'

Juliet shuddered.

'I object,' said Sirena. 'Our committee of enquiry showed –'

'Bah!' Juliet snorted. 'She did not submit. Our sailors are taught to endure buggery and the lash.'

145

'I was that sea captain,' hissed Abby Musquonset, showing her naked croup, deeply scarred with whip welts, and the distorted pucker of her asshole. 'I hate the candy-butts. There will never be peace until they submit to our whips forever.'

Donnette lifted the cane, stroked it and lashed the air; the cane whistled and Mandy's buttocks clenched, shuddering.

'Please don't be too cruel, Donnette,' Mandy whispered.

'Strokes without limit,' said Juliet, her mouth full of chitlin, 'until our guests decree them sufficient. Our policy of silent and unsquirming punishment is suspended for this demonstration, and the submissives are encouraged to clench, squirm, wriggle and squeal, as they wish. That is the way New Arras maids take their canings.'

'Really,' snorted Alice.

'The full portion of the buttocks must be marked by the implement and remember, Donnette, that includes the birch,' Juliet concluded.

Donnette winced, looking at the bushy birch, and lashed Mandy's bare with the cane.

Vip! Donnette's bare titties wobbled as she flogged.

'Ooh!'

A thin pink weal appeared in the perfect centre of Mandy's fesses. Vip! Vip! Two more sliced her top buttocks. Vip! Vip! Vip! Vip! Two each to the haunches, and a pattern of welts began to mottle Mandy's satin skin.

'Oh! Oh!' she gasped, her bottom squirming fast and the cheeks continuing to clench between strokes.

Donnette flogged hard and efficiently and after the thirtieth canestroke Mandy was sobbing and gasping, with her spine and legs jerking rigid at each cane welt, while her darkening fesses continued their frantic clench. Alice and Sirena watched from close quarters, their faces flushed, and poking with their noses almost in Mandy's ass-cleft as they examined her marbling of welts.

'Most interesting fesses,' Alice said thoughtfully, prising the clenched buttocks apart with her fingernail to reveal the come-slopped cunt-bush and the juicy red meat of

Mandy's gushing slit. 'It appears that chastisement has unusual side effects on your troops, Lady Juliet.'

'Fascinating, that a rod, a mere wisp of a thing, can cause such agitation,' Lady Juliet mused. 'We Anglos pride ourselves on our corporal punishment, the vigour given by robust flogging on the bare, a tonic to mind and body – not the lustful and prurient fascination of you Frenchies.'

'Let the treatment continue,' Sirena said.

'Oh, no, please,' wailed Mandy.

Vip! Vip!

'Ah! I can't take any more, honest. It smarts terribly.'

Vip! Vip!'

'Ooh!'

Her bare flogged nates jerked up and down, in metronomic rhythm.

'Yes,' sighed Juliet, 'a delightful blush. A tad more oil, Duane. You ladies may cast your French primness aside, if you like. This is no-nonsense Anglo territory, so please feel free to diddle if Mandy's juicy buttocks, ah, turn you on.'

'What?'

'The very idea . . .'

Lady Juliet laughed and slapped her rump. Mandy's caning proceeded to eighty strokes, by which time the flogged melons were dark crimson, mottled with black streaks. The girl was shaking her head from side to side with her wealed nates squirming and slamming her soaked pubic bush against the chaise. She screamed, 'No! No!' as each of Donnette's canestrokes bit the deep furrows of her weals; hands beneath their skirts and faces red, Alice and Sirena were vigorously masturbating their quims. Abby sprawled in her seat, legs wide open, and made no secret of her own masturbation, diddling her massively extruded clitty with long, lazy strokes of her thumbnail, and sliding fingers in and out of her wet gash.

Claudine looked on, trembling, and with legs pressed together but with come streaking both inside thighs. At the eighty-fifth stroke to Mandy's flaming bare ass, she bit her lip and plunged her hand between her swollen cunt-lips to vigorously diddle her clitty. Sirena and Alice agreed that one hundred was enough; the sergeant knocked Claudine's masturbating fingers from her cunt while Abby rose and released the wailing Mandy from her wrist and ankle straps, four of them burst open. Claudine sighed, shivering, as she was strapped to the chaise, still wet from Mandy's cunt-juices, which pooled with new come from Claudine. Rubbing her wealed bottom, and still shivering violently, but with nostrils flared and a gleam in her eyes, Mandy took the four-thonged yankee quirt. She pushed the ridges of her welted bottom into Claudine's face.

'Mandy, it wasn't me who striped you,' whimpered Claudine.

'But you diddled watching me . . . slut.'

Vap! The quirt slapped hard on Claudine's bare.

'Ooh! That hurts so . . .'

Her bare bottom clenched, writhing and slapping her cunt against the hard wooden chaise as she sobbed. The four slender rods of the quirt left four pink weals, slanting on her naked buttocks in a cross.

Vap! Vap!

'Ah!'

Eight new stripes joined them and already the bare bottom was a mass of mottled bruises blurring into each other. Sirena and Alice continued to masturbate and Abby's cunt was gushing come as she sat with her thighs thrown open. She slipped off her left boot and bent her leg to toe her clitty. Donnette, breathing heavily, diddled her streaming slit, while the sergeant stood stiffly with a dark stain of come seeping at her groin. Vap! Vap!

'Oh! I can't take it! I never knew –'

Vap! Vap!

'Ohh . . .'

A loud hiss accompanied a heavy spurt of piss from Claudine's writhing cunt-lips soaking the chaise and sprinkling the feet of her caner.

'Why, you bitch,' Mandy snarled.

Vap! The quirt slapped the girl's naked ass-flesh with a dry, explosive crack.

148

'Ahh!' Claudine screamed, the heaving globes of her flogged bare bottom shining darkly, with fifty-two separate welts.

As her flogging continued, her screams ebbed to a constant, choking sob; her hips thumped against the chaise at each impact and her gash oozed copious come, sliming the rosewood. At the thirtieth stroke, equalling one hundred and twenty separate cuts, the visitors deemed her chastisement sufficient; both Arrasiennes were wet with come as they masturbated and eyed the lush bundle of birch branches. Abby rose and, still diddling, used her prehensile toes to release Claudine from her rubber straps; the sergeant bound Donnette in her place. Donnette masturbated until the last moment of her strapping, then continued, rubbing her juicing cunt in the pool of come on the flogging chaise. Her nostrils flared as, rubbing her wealed nates, Claudine lifted the birch sheaf. Donnette licked her teeth.

'Never been spanked, Donnette?' Lady Juliet drawled.

'Not as a soldier, milady,' Donnette said.

'Never been birched?'

'Not at all, milady.'

'Looking forward? Your wet gash says so, miss.'

Swish! The birch lashed hard, crackling across Donnette's bare buttocks.

'Ah!' Donnette squealed.

'Tight?' said Sirena, openly masturbating and her face a foot from Donnette's blushed, clenching bare.

'Yes, miss. It smarts like crazy.'

Swish!

'Ooh! I'll say it's tight. Please, milady, I don't know if I can take a bare birching . . .'

'How tight?' Alice asked, her own fingers twitching at her throbbing clitty, visible under her rolled-up skirt and lowered, come-soaked panties.

'It's worse than anything,' Donnette gasped. 'It's not clean and sharp, like a cane, or heavy, like a paddle. It doesn't feel like much, just a tickle, and then it kind of creeps up and your ass is all flames, like a whole bunch of little fiery tongues were licking your bare . . .'

Swish! Swish!

'Ah! Ah! Ooh!'

Her naked bottom writhed, mottled with the cluster of red birch cuts, deepening to a dark, veinous mosaic.

Swish! Swish!

'Ahh! It's agony . . .'

Donnette's buttocks squirmed as her cunt dripped more and more copious come; Claudine birched with one hand, her titties bouncing as she whipped, while her fingers rubbed her gushing cunt.

'Be thankful it's not a titty-birching,' said Lady Juliet. 'A beastly, perverted, French sort of thing.'

Swish! Swish!

'Uh . . .! Thank you, milady,' Donnette sobbed.

As the women masturbated, Donnette's birched bare bottom darkened from red to puce, to purple, and then to a crusted black filigree of deepening welts. At the fiftieth stroke, Sirena and Alice stopped the birching.

'I would like to test the efficacy of this instrument . . . on the subject's naked breasts,' Sirena panted, her hand inside her come-slimed quim. 'If I may . . .?'

Lady Juliet nodded, and Sirena took the birch from Claudine.

'Noo . . .' wailed Donnette, as the sergeant unstrapped her from the chaise, then suspended her wrists from a hook drawn down from the ceiling on a thick chain.

Her naked body hung wriggling with her toes inches from the floor. Swish!

'Ahh!'

A pattern of pink welts sprang up on Donnette's bare, massively wobbling breasts. The chain jangled as her naked body writhed and swayed helplessly. Swish! Swish!

'Ah! No! Please! Not my titties . . .'

Her bare titties darkened with livid welts, with the erect nipples bruised black. Sirena masturbated so hard, her bare breasts snapped a button and burst from her shirt. Swish! Swish!

'Uh! Please, no more . . .'

Sirena birched Donnette on the breasts to twenty-five strokes, then handed the birch to her masturbating colleague. Still pounding her stiff clitty, Alice lashed the darkening teats a further twenty, until Donnette screamed and pissed herself, her steaming yellow fluid spattering her wriggling toes.

'Mmm . . .' said Juliet. 'Just a little higher, Duane. Ah . . .'

At the fiftieth cut of the birch to Donnette's jiggling bare teats, Alice put down the birch. She conferred with Sirena, who said they wished to order a gross of canes, a gross of quirts and three gross of birches.

'Why, thank you, ladies,' said Juliet. 'You mustn't leave without a little sweetener.'

Abby and the sergeant leaped forward and pinioned the two protesting Arrasiennes, then forced them to bend over Lady Juliet's oak dining table. Abby pulled their skirts up, shrouding their heads, and pulled their panties off. The two women were pinioned at half-nelson.

'I believe I am ready to come, Duane,' Juliet said to her masseur, 'but I forbid you to sperm.'

Behind the prone, nude woman, her masseur grunted as his cock rammed harder into her anus. A few thrusts and Juliet clawed her divan, mewling and with drool appearing at the corner of her mouth.

'Yes . . . yes . . . harder . . . fill my rectum; fuck me hard; fuck my ass . . . yes! yes! yes!'

Lady Juliet shuddered in orgasm and no sooner had her spasm stopped than the naked Duane withdrew his massive stiff cock, gleaming with ass-grease, from her anus. He approached the bared buttocks of Sirena, fingered her cunt to get lubricating come for his cock and, with his tool shining, plunged the member to the balls, right into her anus. Sirena screamed as he began to fuck her with short, vigorous stabs and her ass swayed, thrusting against his balls, to meet his rhythm. Duane reached under her cunt-basin and began to frot her clitty; her thighs streamed with come. After a minute's enculing, he brought her to orgasm, then withdrew and plunged his cock between Alice's fesses. Once more, he penetrated the anus with a single thrust and reduced the squealing female to a helpless spasm of climax in less than a minute.

'I'm no cunt-hound,' Duane grunted. 'Some guys get off on split beaver, but give me melons and a juicy cornhole.'

He left Alice's squirming anus with a plop, his still-erect cock copiously slimed with come and ass-grease. Picking up the birch, he applied it quickfire to Alice's rump. The swishes blurred into each other as Alice screamed, and a dozen lashes were given; then Sirena's bare received the same. Twigs crackled and flew off the birch as the wriggling bare asses jerked and reddened.

'This is monstrous,' wailed Sirena as she was released.

'How could you?' sobbed Alice, rubbing her flogged bottom and sweeping aside her skirt after one touch to the glowing, wealed fesses.

'Thank you for your business, mesdemoiselles,' said Lady Juliet. 'Shall I expect you next month, at the usual time?'

'Yes, milady,' gasped Alice.

'Uh, make that four gross of birches,' Sirena added.

When the ladies had departed, Duane requested permission to sperm.

'Why, yes, Duane. You are a dutiful butt stud. Take that suspended trull,' said Juliet.

Duane seized Donnette's hips and slammed his cock between her splayed buttocks. His helmet penetrated the anus in one stroke; meeting resistance, he growled, withdrew and rammed the cock inside until Donnette screamed, parted her buttocks to the full and allowed him ingress to her anus in a single stroke. He began to pump, shaking her hung body and making her teats wobble violently. Donnette's cunt sprayed the floor with come. As she watched Duane encule the moaning Donnette, Lady Juliet, playing with herself, said she was glad Duane's duties as ambassador to New Arras left him with ample sperm.

'Thank you, milady,' Duane gasped as a flood of sperm frothed at Donnette's anus, and for several seconds he pumped her anus full of his cream.

'I must liaise with my director of counter-intelligence,' said Lady Juliet, swallowing another chitlin. 'Harriet! You may show yourself.'

Harriet Stooplaugh emerged from behind the drapes, bare-breasted and with a wet smear of come staining her pleated white tennis skirt.

'Were you masturbating, Colonel?' said Juliet.

'In the line of duty, milady,' Harriet said.

'I shall birch you for it,' Juliet said. 'Tonight – one on one – in the line of duty. It is criminous to excite me so. Naked, of course, perhaps gagged and strapped. I'll see . . .'

She took a chitlin from her slimed cunt and handed it to Harriet, who curtsied and put it in her mouth.

'Thank you, milady,' she replied.

The sergeant released the groaning Donnette, who was helped from the room by the two other victims; after Duane's enculing, she could not stand. The red telephone rang. Abby Musquonset picked it up, listened and handed the receiver to Juliet.

'The hot line, milady,' she said.

'Zealla!' cried Juliet. 'How nice to hear you! I've just concluded business with your two mamselles . . . yes, most satisfactory, I'll send you the flogged girls as slaves. Yes, they took it well, but they whimpered. Useless to us . . .'

She listened for a few minutes.

'I see . . . I see . . . so this new intendant is a bit of a troublemaker. Certainly, my guarantee of no intervention when you mount your coup. Bye, Zealla.'

'That Zealla is becoming a diplomatic embarrassment,' she said to Harriet. 'Might be worth considering her seduction and submission. How many strokes do you think it would take?'

Harriet frowned.

'Many floggings,' she said. 'Zealla's ass is tough.'

'Perhaps a campaign of disinformation,' said Juliet. 'A highly placed traitor plotting to oust Zealla and the committee of public safety. New Arras in chaos, we step in to save the regional balance of power, as permitted by the treaty of Gulfport. Activate the usual double agents.'

'Certainly, milady,' said Harriet, bowing, 'but that will be unnecessary. I have just the mamselle for the job. She won't know a thing about it – a useful idiot, as Lenin said.'

'Her name?'

'Trade secret, milady.'

'You bitch. How do I know you're not a double agent?'

'You don't, milady. I'll expect my birching tonight?'

She cupped her palm on Juliet's bare ass; Juliet trembled.

'And I'll expect mine,' she murmured.

From the Journal of Mlle Augustine Flageolet, anno 1760 9
For a long time, ever since our expulsion from Arras by the *procureur du roi*, it has been my custom to take a daily roll call of my students – and not by their faces, for in early morning a lady never looks her best – but by the enduring and ever beautiful portion of a female, in which her true nature and spirit resides, viz. her buttocks. Woman is a fickle and fleeting creature! Our faces assume a thousand masks at whim, yet our croups never lie. I can tell all forty maids from their bare fesses, trembling and adorably pimpled as the morning dew clears. I have maintained this practice aboard ship, much to the curiosity of the mariners, and they attend respectfully as forty bottoms are bared at my command. We must look to nature, I tell Capt Stouplois, from Roscoff – not to the fleeting appearance, the paint and frippery of woman in society, but to the naked and eternal truth of her bare rump. He has begun taking roll calls of his matelots, whereby they drop their breeches, and their 'cannons' are inspected. There is much jesting about 'small bore', or 'heavy gauge', yet it cannot be denied that the nature of a male lies in his genital organ, to which a female must pay homage. Capt Joliot has a Breton sense of humour.

10

Come Detail

'Is this some kind of joke?' Trina whimpered.

The three monitors glowered at her, squirming hopelessly in their grip.

'Who the fuck are you, bitch?' snarled the tallest and most ripely figured, her teats heaving under their tight rubber straps and making her steel bra-cups quiver as she shook her mane free.

'Don't you know? I'm the intendant, and –'

Her words were drowned by raucous laughter, echoed by the hooded girls awaiting punishment on the bench, the nude victims, bound over the come trough, and the elfin girl writhing on the end of her buttfucker's cock. A gauntleted hand ground the steel left cup of her bra against her ribs, and Trina shrieked.

'Oh! You're hurting me.'

To more laughter, a hand grasped her right bra-cup, screwing its sharp edge into her flesh.

'Better take that fucking bra off you, so,' said the tall girl.

'Who are you?' Trina squealed.

Vap! Vap! The girl's hand slapped her, backhand and forehand, across the mouth.

'Who are you, mamselle,' she said.

'I'm sorry – please, mamselle –'

Vap! Vap!

'Don't you know me, bitch? They call me Devora,' spat the girl. 'And that's Cindi Kock and Prudence Vile. We're punishment monitors, the come detail we call it, supervising these submissives. Masturbating bitches! We got to whip them to jerk off, the dirty trulls, because if they don't foam up good and make their quota, we have to fill the fucking bucket with our own juice and diddle each other till we drop. That's why it's a punishment detail. As if having my cunt-hairs shaved wasn't punishment enough! We were expecting Jewel Persimmon until you opened your ugly fucking mouth.'

'We were sent here for diddling, Devora,' said Cindi Kock. 'I was caught diddling Jewel, behind the Stella Maris, by Sergeant Makings.'

Clang! Devora's cane lashed harmlessly the steel spikes adorning Cindi's naked butt.

'Mind your fucking mouth, you fucking sub. Whore like you belongs in the fucking Stella Maris, taking it up the ass from every redneck and his beer bottle, why, you and that bitch Stooplaugh – the whole republic knows about you, taking dildos up the ass and drinking her come as she whops your bare. Mamselle goody fucking two shoes of the public fucking watch, huh?'

'Why the . . . the buttfucking?' gasped Trina, ceasing to writhe and turning to the masked figure, now slamming his cock into the slender girl's anus once more to her redoubled screams.

'Whipping makes them come; ass-ramming makes them flood,' growled Devora Dykes. 'All got to take turns.'

'Uh, including us, Devora,' whimpered Cindi Kock.

Vap! Devora's cane lashed her bare thigh.

'Oh! Devora, no . . .'

'Won't you shut the fuck up, bitch?' Devora snarled. 'We get that stud to spurt enough, he won't have jism enough to get it up for your butt, swamp blossom.'

The masked man gave no sign of spurting, with his elfin victim impaled on his tool, which he used as a broom handle, mopping the floor with her bare teats and face.

'What is the Stella Maris?' Trina blurted.

'What ain't it?' snorted Devora.

She thrust her hand down Trina's cunt-spike, and pinched the folds of her gash, which exuded a bubble of come.

'Seems like you belong there, too, slut,' she said. 'Well, juice is down, so we'll tan your hide to fill that bucket.'

'No,' Trina wailed. 'I'm the intendant. Prudence, you remember serving me.'

'I serve and don't look. Best strip the noisome bitch,' drawled Prudence Vile.

'Cindi, you arrested me.'

'I arrest so many sluts,' said Cindi. 'You are a forward maid, no mistake.'

The three girls reached gingerly for Trina's rubber thongs, careful to avoid her spikes, but Devora cursed when a wriggle of Trina's cunt-basin snagged her finger.

'Listen, trull, you can get slaps or kisses,' she said, 'doesn't matter much to us. Strict or soft, up to you.'

'Sophie! Harriet! Help!' Trina screamed.

Devora snarled and wadded an oily hot rag between Trina's teeth, filling her mouth and nose with the scent of cunt-meat; her gag was a slimed pair of girl's panties. Trina moaned and began to sob. The girls stripped her of her body armour, piece by piece, but left her helmet and boots. She renewed her struggle, moaning beneath her gag, but could not prevent the three monitors from strapping her over the come trough beside the three other nude maids. Her legs were forced wide into cuffs bolted to the floor, and Devora knotted her mane around a meathook dangling from the ceiling. Sweat poured from every girl's body as Trina's writhing grew still; her body drooped, and she whimpered as her left arm was pinioned and knotted to her spiked collar. Her spread cunt-lips, gripping the handle of her spike, gaped directly over the oily runnel, while behind her the ass-prong shivered like a pennant. Devora lifted a hacksaw and began to saw through her ass-prong, the blade cutting swiftly through the metal until a fraction of jagged steel peeped from Trina's anus. She removed the frontal spike in the same way, the hacksaw blade brushing hot against Trina's bush and belly as sparks flew, until her cunt-prong dropped into the sawdust. Trina's nostrils puckered at the reek of wig glue spurting into her cunt and anus – the resinous substance quickly hardening to block the anus fully and the cunt halfway.

'Diddle, bitch,' said Devora.

She lifted her whipple.

Vip!

'Uh . . .'

The cane slashed Trina's bare fesses.

'I said, diddle, bitch. Strop that clitty, or . . .'

Vip! Vip!

'Urrgh!'

Trina's bare rump jerked as two livid pink weals scarred the skin. Her head tugged at her mane, pulling the hair to her roots. Vip! Vip!

'Uh . . .!'

Trina sobbed, her body shuddering as her naked ass-melons squirmed with vivid welts crisscrossing the skin. Vip! Vip!

'Mmm! Oh, please don't flog me, please?'

She lowered her free right hand to her cunt and a finger entered her slimy, half-blocked pouch, already filled with come that squirted gleaming on her perineum and stubbled cunt-hairs.

'More, bitch. Did no one ever tell you to diddle before?'

Vip! Vip! Her bare ass jerked; frantically, she got two fingers inside her gash and a thumb on her clitoris, already throbbing and swollen. With a long, deep sigh, Trina began to masturbate as Prudence and Cindi awaited their turn at caning her. Vip! Vip! Trina's bare buttocks began a sinuous, swaying dance, clenching and jerking as the cane bit their bare meat. Her cunt juiced copiously as her fingers worked faster and more firmly within the narrowed slit and on the raw erect clitoris, which she rubbed and mashed with heavy thumbing. Vip! Vip!

'Uh! It really smarts. That's enough! I'm hurting so. I'll masturbate without beating, OK?'

A torrent of come gushed over her wrist, soaking her.

'Your cunt's juicing pretty good, slut. Thrash the bitch harder,' said Devora.

Vip! Vip! Vip! Vip! Four stingers, two each from Prudence and Cindi, took Trina in an existing welt just north of mid-fesse, which at once furrowed to a livid purple gash, jagged at the edges.

'Mmm!' she shrieked.

At each impact slapping her bare, her spine arched, her legs splayed rigid as the ass-cheeks frantically clenched, and her whole body shook in a spasm, spraying the gushing cunt-juice from her slit and wetting her boots. Tears streamed on her face, wetting her cunt-slimed gag, and her slit spewed a shiny torrent of come. Trina's fingers pumped within her gushing pouch; her clitty was huge and extruded as her thumb pounded the erect, swollen nubbin. Come trickled on the first inch of her inner thighs, then, pushed forwards by its mass, dripped below her cunt-basin to fill the runnel. Its puddle of come turned to a stream flowing towards the churning blender. As her fingers worked, and the vicious hiss of strokes to her wriggling bare nates echoed in the fetid chamber, Trina's belly heaved her breath came in gasps and her hand slopped in a faster and wider flow of juice from her cunt.

Vip! Vip! Vip! The beating neared thirty strokes . . . Vip! Vip! Vip! . . . Forty . . . and beyond, and as Trina's bare bottom was caned to dark crimson, edged with a delicate crisscross of black ridges, her panting grew hoarser, until she shrieked and her cunt flowed come in a rapid plop! plop! into the runnel; the caning did not stop, even when Trina buckled at the knees, her face a rictus of pain, and shuddered in orgasm. Her cries were drowned by a bellowing from the corner; the enculing male impaling the wriggling elfin body upside down on his cock rammed harder and faster. As her come gushed, Trina saw sperm bubble from the girl's buggered anus and drip into the fresh scarlet cane weals on her flogged melons. The buggered girl's gash writhed on sawdust and mud, caking the dirt to a pudding of come and piss spurting golden from her flapping cunt-lips.

'You dirty fucking slut,' Devora hissed. 'You're a real dirty diddler, coming like fucking Niagara.'

Trina sobbed helplessly, not resisting as her torturers released her from her bonds and dragged her by the hair before the throne of the enculing male.

'Eat dirt, diddler,' Devora cried, putting her boot on Trina's nape and forcing her head into the mud and sawdust, puddled by the elfin girl's piss and come.

That girl lay on the floor, rolling in the paste of her own fluids and masturbating as she crooned to herself. Vip! Vip! Trina lurched forwards, banging her teats and brow on the floor as a new flurry of canestrokes striped her bare buttocks with white hot weals. Devora ripped the gag from her teeth. Vip! Vip!

'Uhh . . .!'

'Eat dirt.'

Trina ground her teeth into the floor and began to chew the come-soaked mud.

Vip! Vip!

'Ah . . . have pity.'

'Swallow, bitch.'

Gagging, Trina forced the muck down her throat. Her caning continued for three minutes as her bare flogged buttocks writhed helplessly on the dirt floor and her mouth frothed with the come-soaked muddy slop. Vip! Vip! Vip! Each stroke to her flailing buttocks slammed her cunt against the dirt and made her writhe, jarring her clitty so that a new seep of come dripped from her cunt. Devora wrenched her up by the hair and flung her at the male's feet.

'Suck him hard, slut.'

The buttfucker's cock still glistened with his victim's ass-grease. Trembling, Trina cupped the balls and manoeuvred her lips on to the half-flaccid, massive glans; a few licks from her tongue and the organ swelled, rising to new massiveness and almost choking her as it filled her throat. She sucked the cock, acrid with the girl's grease, to shivering stiffness, pausing to gasp for air before taking the giant flesh once more to the back of her throat, sucking powerfully with her tongue playing at the corona and neck of the glans. She felt Devora's boot tip slapping her erect clitty and the hot seep of her come oiling her thighs.

If only I can suck him off . . . it's Elvis, I'm sure! There can't be another cock like this . . .

Laughing, the butt stud pulled her mouth off his cock and doubled her over with her head pressed to the seat of his throne and her thighs straddling the low wooden arms, thus parting her quim-lips to the maximum extent. Devora took the spike she had sawn from Trina's gash and plunged it into her anus, making her scream and frantically widen the elastic walls; there was a rip as her plug of glue was shredded and Devora withdrew the spike. She had no time to contract her anal elastic before the male plunged his cock fully into her hole, slamming her anal root and making her jerk as he pulled her hair back, with his body weight pressing on her buttocks and the chair arms biting her splayed thighs. He began a vigorous buttfucking, his hips slapping her flogged raw buttocks, stinging her weals as his tool penetrated her clinging anus now slimy with her own ass-grease. Devora stood at the side of the throne, staring at Trina's grimace and her finger diddling her erect clitty, extruded over the prong of her cunt-spike. A steady trickle of come dripped from Devora's shaven gash into her boots as she masturbated.

'Oh! Oh! He's splitting me in two,' Trina squealed. 'Devora, how could you?'

'Masturbate? If you could look round, you'd see every trull diddling herself at the sight of your flogged ass and that tool stoking you. Even the POWs awaiting treatment are diddling. And your own cunt? I can see your come. You're something else, slut.'

'Ohh . . .' Trina wailed.

Her buttocks pumped and squeezed, in time with her bugger's ferocious rhythm, her anal elastic embracing the hard cockmeat and teasing him to spurt into her rectum; at each stroke, he wrenched the tool from her hole with a loud sucking plop before slamming it in to the balls. He began to spank her bare at each filling of her anus. Tears sprang from her eyes as her cunt spurted new floods of come and her fesses jerked under the slaps.

'Oh . . .' Trina moaned, 'don't stop . . . fuck me . . . harder, harder . . . I need it so much . . .'

Her belly heaved and her moans grew to shrieks.

'Oh! Oh! Ohh! Fuck me . . . split my ass!'

'Mmm,' Devora said, masturbating hard. 'Do as she says, sir, I'm almost there.'

The male grunted and Trina felt a hot trickle of sperm at the root of her anus. Her sphincter sucked harder on the giant cock until her own belly fluttered and, as she felt a massive, hot jet of sperm splash her anal walls, her come splashed the seat of the stud's throne and she howled in long, sharp yelps as orgasm flooded her. Devora had one foot perched on the throne's arm and her cunt was stinking in Trina's face, with her come-soaked cunt-spike bobbing as she thumbed her erect clitty; she growled in orgasm as her cunt squirted come. Behind her, Cindi Kock had her tongue at Prudence Vile's clitty, while Prudence flicked Cindi's with her forefinger; both maids were slathered in sweat and shivered as their cunts melted together in climax. The male pulled his still-hard cock from Trina's anus and wiped it on her hair before disappearing into the shadows.

'I'm so ashamed . . .' Trina wailed. 'Why won't you believe me? I'm Trina Guelph, the new intendant! Elvis could have vouched for me . . . he didn't have to torment me with that dumb hallowe'en mask.'

'I know you're Trina Guelph,' said Devora. 'The way your ass wriggled under cane, and that buttfuck action! But that joker wasn't Elvis. He wears a mask because he thinks we don't know . . . he's the ambassador of New Albion.'

'They send an ambassador, while we're at war?'

They sat in Sirena Toitte's court chambers, adjoining the palace of justice. All committee members had their own palaces and meetings took place in each, by turn. Trina, like the other committee members, wore scholar's blue, with an unopened rear vent, black nylon stockings, white blouse – Trina wore a white scalloped bra, as thin as possble, to satisfy both comfort and modesty, while the others were braless – and a ceremonial whipple in a cane scabbard at her waist.

'Civilised dialogue is always appropriate, even in war-time, mamselle intendant. More tea? Sugar?'

'Yes . . . too bad you don't have artificial sweetener.'

The committee of public safety collectively giggled.

'No lady deprives herself of sugar, mamselle,' said Zealla, serving Trina's tea. 'We are so sorry for yesterday's misunderstanding at the academy. There was a mix-up in the inter-service paperwork. Of course, if you venture outside the normal channels –' she shrugged '– anyway, I have ordered Sophie Petrarque whipped fifty lashes on the back, with a six-thonged scourge of Florida ivy.'

'Oh! there's no need. I intend to cut down bureaucracy. The GG Baggs business plan comes first.'

Zealla waggled her foot and shook off her boot, revealing her nylon stocking with her big toe poking through a hole. Her skirt slipped up almost to her pubis, with a sliver of white panty visible and lush hanks of pubic hairs sprouting from the frilled hem of the garment. She tutted, pinched the stocking fabric to cover her toe and slipped her boot on. She smiled at Trina.

'Sentence was carried out at dawn today by Sergeant Merlene Makings of the watch,' she said. 'I trust you are pleased with your *vison*?'

'Most honoured. I haven't got around to . . .'

'At your own convenience, mamselle. The miscreant Dykes will sprout another fleece in no time. She has been caged in the Stella Maris for indefinite service without pay, subject to your executive clemency. No doubt you have dealt with any malfeasance by your secretary.'

Trina blurted that she had caned Harriet on the bare that morning during breakfast.

'In addition to any merited canestrokes?' Zealla asked. 'My apartments in the palace are within earshot of your own, mamselle. By the way, there is no need to specify that correction was on the bare. It would be a breach of our constitution, otherwise.'

'Then you must know I caned her a hard forty,' Trina said, 'with twenty unpaid, and I beat her bare ass – sorry, her ass – as hard as I could, with an English muffin in my mouth. I'm aware that my treatment was a misunderstanding – I don't want to cause a reign of terror.'

'Ah,' said Sirena Toitte, '*la terreur*. That was long ago.'

'Though several bottoms still bear the scars,' murmured Alice Frequemme, wiping her brow and loosening the third button of her blouse, beneath which her soaked bare jellies quivered; she shifted in her seat with a squeak as sweat slopped her nylon-stockinged thighs.

'This heat. Why must we wear real antique nylon, mesdemoiselles? Mamselle Flageolet surely made do with cotton hose? It's no secret that I train my soldiers and sailors in the nude for greater efficiency.'

'For shame,' said Dorita Carawn. 'You are too soft with your troops, mamselle, due to misplaced sympathy. Do you suggest we should go about like Albion beasts?'

'Your security corps are almost nude, mamselle,' gasped Alice.

'Almost is the thing, mamselle,' retorted Dorita. 'The sex is sheathed for modesty, the breasts bared for ease of whipstrokes. I seem to recall that during the terror you were a humble scholar, a ringleader in the revolt of the *sans-culottes* – and were well flogged for your insolence, with your big bare moons truly *sans* their *culotte*.'

Alice rubbed her buttocks and grimaced.

'Some might have thought you over-zealous, mamselle, as a mere grunt in the security corps,' she said.

'A security corpsmaid's flogging arm cannot be too zealous, mamselle,' replied Dorita.

Alice flushed. Zealla interrupted the delighted laughter by rapping the rosewood table with her knuckles.

'Mesdemoiselles, as directress of discipline, I must ask you if you are in dispute, and if so whether you wish to settle the matter summarily or before the states-general.'

Alice glared at Dorita.

'I say summarily,' she said. 'The bitch has a thrashing due.'

'No white trash calls me bitch,' snarled Dorita.

Zealla licked her teeth and sighed loudly, though her eyes sparkled.

'I take it we have a contest?' she said. 'You know the rules, mesdemoiselles, according to the law of the republic of West Florida. Nude but for stockings. No weapon save the cane, no shoes and no armour. Strip off and go to it when I whistle. First submission decides.'

Alice was the first to slither out of her clammy garments, which she ripped from her sweat-slimed body and stood, jellies trembling, to spit at her opponent. Dorita took her time, smiling in contempt at her rival, similar in age and strength, but a few inches shorter – though Alice's breasts, thighs and buttocks were fuller and heavier with muscle than Dorita's sinewy whipcord. Both girls had stiffly erect nipples and the sunshafts darting into the dusty chamber illumined smears of come at their cunt-lips. Alice turned around and bent over, pushing her bare moons almost in Dorita's face. Her fesses were striped with a geometric pattern of old, deep welts, still ridged and puffed to dark grey. She brandished her cane and slapped air.

'I still bear your cane scars, you vile torturer. You'll have them back with interest –'

Vip!

'Ah!'

Alice spun, clutching her bare breasts, which bore a vivid pink stripe of Dorita's suddenly flashed cane. The taller girl finished folding her skirt and whirled to face the sobbing Alice, still rubbing her teats and staring in disbelief.

'That's not right! She didn't wait!' Alice cried to Zealla, who shrugged.

Dorita sprang, and her cane slashed. Vip! Vip!

'Ah! You fucking bitch.'

Alice danced in agony with two cane welts sliced to her cunt-flaps. She flailed with her own cane and caught Dorita on the left haunch, tracing a thin pink weal. Dorita grimaced. Their forearms shielding their faces, the two girls danced around each other, thrusting and parrying, the sunlight glinting on their nylon stockings which clung to their rippling thighs, damp with sweat. Suddenly, Alice lowered her head and charged under Dorita's flailing canestrokes to butt her in the cunt-basin. Dorita shrieked and could not prevent Alice from seizing her hips, clawing at the exposed folds of her bare gash and grappling her to the floor, where Alice sat on Dorita's neck and applied canestrokes to her wriggling bare bottom, which striped at once with sinuous crimson welts. Vip! Vip!

'Ah! You fucking trull!'

Vip! Vip!

'Ah! Stop, please!'

'Chickenshit!' Alice hissed.

As she caned, Alice twisted Dorita's hair round her balled fist and pulled it to its roots. Vip! Vip!

'Ahh!'

Dorita's legs began to bang the floor, drumming separately and exposing the jagged red scar of her cunt-lips, juicing heavily and with a thick smear of cunt-slime trickling between her legs. Alice's quim, too, was juicing, and as her flow shone more copiously, her strokes increased in vigour as the squirming bare buttocks threshed beneath her wand. Vip! Vip! Vip!

'Ahh! For pity's sake . . . !'

Dorita's legs thumped the floor and Alice raised her arm at an angle.

Vip!

'Ah! Oh!'

The stroke of the springy little whipple took Dorita squarely in the centre of her gash, the red wet lips writhing like anemones as the wood slashed the wet folds of the cunt-slit within. Vip! Vip! Two more strokes to the cunt had Dorita sobbing in frenzy, and as Alice slapped the cane down on her writhing anus pucker Dorita's ass leaped, glowing with weals, and a long, steaming jet of piss erupted from her caned vulva. Vip! Vip! Alice's cane made a wet, sploshing sound, as she caned the pissing cunt-flaps while wrenching Dorita's hair. Zealla and Heidi craned to watch, each with pressed thighs and fingers at their quims. Their arms rippled as their fingers jerked between their legs. Trina stared, her own stockings moistening with come as she watched the naked combat. *They're diddling!* Panting, Trina allowed her fingers to brush her throbbing clitoris, then got her fingers wedged in the folds of her pantied cunt and began to masturbate through the cloth.

'Oh! Ah! Oh!' shrieked the tortured girl, her whole naked body dripping with sweat and spraying the beads from her as she shuddered in the pool of her piss.

'Submit, bitch.'

Sobbing and gasping, Dorita shook her head.

'Drink slime, you cunt.'

Alice's breasts heaved as she forced Dorita's head into the piss-lake, now gleaming with droplets of Alice's own come. Her clitoris shone raw in arousal at the other's humiliance; yet Dorita's nubbin too was erect and her cunt juiced as heavily as her tormentress's. Alice slipped and Dorita scrambled from beneath her slithering body to kick the cane from her grasp and mount her. Alice was face up, struggling, as Dorita's cunt pressed hers and the taller girl's fists smashed her breasts, punching the nipples with hard, vicious jabs, then unfolding the fingers, to rake scratches across the existing raw cane weals on Alice's naked, bouncing titties. Dorita bucked as she rode the helpless victim, her clitty mashing Alice's as her pubic bone smashed the girl's massively hairy cunt-hillock. Both pubic fleeces were soaked in piss and come; Dorita swivelled and flopped over the screaming girl until her face was in the pool of pee. She grabbed Alice's own whipple and began to thrash the bare, squirming buttocks, with her foot on Alice's back and her cunt-basin squatting inches above her face. A second stream of piss spurted from Dorita's cunt, drenching Alice's hair and face. Heidi and Zealla masturbated openly, and Trina parted her thighs to poke her quim and clit through her panties.

Vip!

'Ah!'

Vip!

'Ah!'

The beating slowed as Dorita carefully flogged the buttocks in their existing welts, of which she was the distant authoress. She lowered her piss-soaked cunt and squirmed on Alice's writhing back, her face reddening as she squashed her stiffened clitty in the jerking runnel of Alice's spine.

'Yeah, I remember that one,' she panted. 'That was so cool, flogging your ass while your spine and titties were all stretched out and you groaned on the rack, you bitch!'

Vip! Vip!

'Ahh! You mean, fucking whore, my ass has never taken such welts. They smart like fury . . .'

Alice's naked croup writhed, slamming the soaked floor, and her whole body twisted; Dorita, intent on her diddling, fell once more, and this time Alice did not leap for dominance but darted her head between Dorita's flailing thighs. Zealla bared her teeth, masturbating with firm, voluptuous strokes between her parted thighs, while Heidi, flushed, dribbled drool and come, and moaned. Trina had her thumb and forefinger fastened on her own clitty and tugged hard, her belly beginning to flutter.

'Ahh!' Dorita screamed as Alice's teeth fastened on her erect nubbin and bit. 'Ah! No! Ahh . . .'

'Submit, pig?'

'No . . . no . . .'

'Submit!'

'No . . . Oh! Stop.'

Alice tightened her grip on Dorita's clitoris and her hands grabbed the swollen nipples of her foe; she nipped and pinched the plums and Dorita's mouth went slack, with drool spurting from the corner of her lips. Alice's tongue massaged her enemy's nubbin, licking and stroking and chewing the erect clit. One hand left the shivering titties and dove into the ass-crack, finding the anus bud with a sharp fingernail.

'Ahh!' Dorita roared, as Alice's index penetrated her anal hole and thrust in right to the knuckle. 'No! Ahh!'

A second finger joined the first; with forefinger and index, Alice reamed Dorita's butthole, while clawing at her erect, bruised nipple, and chewing on the come-slimed clitty. Dorita's belly started to heave and her squeals grew to high moans; drool cascaded from her lips. Alice withdrew from the twitching teat and raised her palm above Dorita's buttocks. Slap! Slap! She began to spank the quivering bare fesses in a strong, regular rhythm.

'No . . . please don't, pretty please . . .'

The spanking continued as come gushed from Dorita's cunt, lathering her torturer's chin, until Dorita erupted in a savage wail, followed by a dozen anguished yelps, and her belly heaved in spasm. Zealla and Heidi quivered in the climax of their masturbation; Trina thumbed her throbbing clitty and gasped, biting her lip, as orgasm drenched her.

'By the laws of the republic of West Florida,' Zealla said drily, 'Mamselle Dorita has submitted.'

Alice raised her face, dripping Dorita's come; then, lowering her hand to her own gash, gave herself a few deft flicks to the clitty and grunted as she brought herself off.

'To business, mesdemoiselles,' said Zealla, when both combatants had dressed, sponged their bodies of fluid and rejoined the table. 'If mamselle the intendant would care to call the meeting to order?'

Trina did so, riffling the four-inch stack of copperplate papers before her. All the others had similar stacks.

'I'd like to say something first, about the future of New Arras, as I see it,' she began, when Zealla held up her hand.

'Begging your pardon, mamselle, but on a wartime footing we may only discuss urgent business. Our first item, before the petty assizes, is a review of our tourist programme.'

'Tourist programme? Hold up –' Trina began.

'Mamselle, the survival of New Arras is at stake,' panted Dorita. 'The exchequer is low. Hence, as mistress of the bank, I propose extending our range of tourist spectacles, since we are so in need of US dollars. A new boatload of tourists arrived this morning, so time is of the essence. If you will look at page three of your documents?'

While the committee perused their papers, nodding, Zealla explained that tourists were permitted to visit the wine shops and buy souvenirs – soft toys of girls under correction, or after correction, or on the gallows, and other harmless gewgaws. They might visit the Stella Maris, whose revenues accrued directly to the state, and which were estimated at two-thirds of the total spend. Mamselle Carawn proposed admitting tourists to the courts of assizes and to witness both exemplary punishments and any pertinent chastisements carried out immediately after sentence. In addition, they should be able to witness public hangings and even – after proper security clearance – the cells in the palace of justice, public corrections in Republic Place, the POW camp, with access to all discipline, and all facets of Mamselle Absorb's academy.

'Really!' exclaimed Heidi. 'I let them into the Stella Maris – well and good, the comfort of travellers is its traditional function. Even when the lickspittles want to pay in fessignats for my maids to cane *their* bare asses. Males, too, for shame. I demand Yankee dollars for all treatments, of course. But the secrets of my academy . . .'

'It goes way beyond the academy, mamselle,' said Zealla. 'The Stella Maris is our main concern. We propose that the treatments should extend further than carnal comfort and the witnessing of punishment. Mamselle Flageolet decreed that the witnessing of chastisement might teach the uninstructed from the Orleans territory in the ways of reason, but, such are the times, I fear we must accept a certain lubricity in mainlanders' enjoyment of corporal punishment. Lesbianism we may disapprove, but lesbianism accompanied by Yankee greenbacks has the allure of reason. Those females who wish to commit lesbian indecencies, and bare their *own* asses to virtuous cane, must be able to – paying in fessignats, rated at an exchange of one fessignat for five dollars. A correction of one hundred strokes on the bare would therefore earn some perverted Yankee mamselle one hundred fessignats, purchased for five hundred dollars cash.'

'I shall open my POW camp to male and female tourists alike – "guard for a a day" – including discipline and free carnal usage of the prisoners' bodies,' Sirena said.

'Or, "prisoner for a day", added Alice, 'also including discipline. There must be extra whippings, in either case.'

'What about prisoners' rights?' blurted Trina.

'Prisoners? Rights?' Zealla gasped. 'They are bottoms to be flogged, mamselle. No girl demands rights when she can enjoy showing off her bottom.'

From the Journal of Mlle Augustine Flageolet, anno 1760 10
At twenty-four, I am senior to my oldest maid by only
three years, and I become aware that seniority must be
earned, when bodies and minds are so nearly alike. Of
course, I have had the benefit of wealth and education, the
better parts of which I try and instil in my charges, but
does that excuse me from sharing the tribulations – and the
delights? – of their training? My two years at the Gentle-
women's College of Gant's Hill in England taught me the
effectiveness of the rod in the moulding of young ladies.
How well I remember the gentle eyes of Miss Blacker as
she prepared to flog me! She apologised for the pain her
birch was about to inflict on my bared fesses, and the
shame of having my agony witnessed by my peers, yet I
must comfort myself that a single birching did more for a
girl's character than all the Latin and Greek in creation,
and that as the rods striped my bare I should rejoice in the
knowledge that I should watch another girl's bottom
redden on the morrow. Few days went by without one or
more birchings, always on the bare, and for the most
trifling of offences – skipping, whistling, eating too fast, or
the like. It was not the gravity of the offence which
counted, but the necessity of punishment meted to a girl's
naked bottom. Guardians of my friends would visit and
enquire not about prowess in learning, but about the
chastisements their girls had taken. If one confessed to
dreadful crimes, and had been birched to twenty-five
strokes on three or four occasions, that delighted her
guardian, and obtained extra spending money for her;
especially if she lifted her skirts and petticoats and showed
her scarred bare bottom.

Birchings were taken at the block, a dreadful slab
of wood, before which a girl must kneel with her hips
supported by the head of the block, her ankles clasped
in leather straps, and her arms in front of her, supporting
her upper body. The girl kneeled and awaited the ripping
away of her garments of modesty, the cool wind on
her bare fesses, and the awful whistle of the birch.
The pain was indescribable. Each stroke seemed to sear

the bare buttocks with molten lead, and each stroke thereafter was worse and worse. It was not uncommon, and not despised for a girl to lose control of her bladder, or even her bowels. Curiously – as it seemed then – birched friends whispered to me that to calm the inflammation of the birched buttocks they had to repair to a water closet, and while dunging masturbate their intimate parts to relief. The English, however uncultured, have a certain earthy sense, particularly in disciplinary matters. I was birched frequently for trifles, but only once before the whole school. In truth, I had grown accustomed to birching, and felt irritated if my bottom went a full week without stripes. I now know that my bottom *craved* naked birching, a craving as healthy as that for spring water. My offence was dalliance with one of the ostlers – a crude, smelly fellow, but irresistible, because of his massive virility. Girls, of course, sense these things. We formed our alliance in the stables, amid the dungs, and he swived me with the utmost vigour, yet allowed me to retain my virgin hymen, for his taste was the nether hole. He was whipped, and I was birched – thirty-five strokes, an agony. I released my waters at the twentieth stroke. Afterwards, I locked myself away, and masturbated thrice, to exhaustion, then fell into a pure, dreamless sleep.

11

Full Bare Skin

Trina shifted, drawing her own nylons closer, and aware that the trickle of moisture between her thighs was now oily and more than her dripping sweat. Dorita, Alice and Sirena nodded in agreement, followed by a sheepish Heidi, who said she needed to devise a tariff for 'the pomade chamber experience'.

'Admirable,' cried Zealla, clapping her hands. 'I am sure mamselle intendant will accede.'

Trina looked at the shining, eager faces of the sweating committee members. Downstairs, there was the tap-tap of canes; excited voices and footsteps approaching.

'I guess so,' she said, 'but I want to ask about the war? As intendant, I want to know what peace measures have been taken and what vested interests oppose them. I want to speak freely with POWs, and –' she gulped, blushing '– the ambassador of New Albion, and convene a special meeting of all armed forces commanders, and –'

A knock on the door interrupted her. Public servants Felt and Acajou entered holding a girl pinoned between them, with head paper-bagged and her nut-brown body clad only in a powder-blue bra and panties, the panty scarcely more than a thong, pushed out by her jungle of pubic tendrils, and the massive teat-jellies overspilling the skimpy, scalloped bra, so that one broad strawberry nipple was half exposed from the bra-cup. Her arms were hooked up, strapped to an ox yoke over her shoulders. Each custodian held her cane drawn, with a hairbrush dangling at her waist thong, and bore a sheaf of papers hanging around her neck from a rubber cord. The maid's bare, quivering haunches were pink with cane weals, and her bare moons, flanking her rucked-panty bottom, bore the wide pink imprint of twin hairbushes.

'Prefect Funger is downstairs, with a party of ticketed paying tourists as spectators, mesdemoiselles,' said Acajou, managing to curtsey. 'We have five prisoners for judgement and this one is the first, mamselle Emily Cawdor, the wicked slut, and she deserves a purple bottom and *pendaison sévère*, if you'll pardon my French, mamselle.'

Whap! Whap! Whap! Whap!

Drawing her hairbrush, she slapped Emily on her big, dangling breasts, which soon glowed crimson with fresh bruises, while the nipples, beaten by the brush, sprang into trembling stiffness. The maid howled and burst into tears.

'Your French is fine, Citizen Acajou,' said Zealla. 'Bring the criminal in and the tourists. They should soon have confession, sentence and punishment of this guilty bitch.'

'Has the accused no rights?' asked Trina.

'You may not be aware, mamselle,' said Sirena Toitte, 'that Louisiana is the only one of your fifty states with Roman law, not English common law – yuk. Many flags have flown here – we've had French law, Spanish law, most lately, republic of West Florida law . . .'

'Isn't an accused still innocent until proven guilty?'

'No,' Zealla said. 'The republic of West Florida didn't have any laws.'

'This way, ladies and gentlemen,' said Prefect Alana Funger, ushering the bevy of chattering tourists into the courtroom.

The visitors were young, tanned and casually dressed, in T-shirts, jeans and loafers. Females slightly outnumbered males, most females being with partners, but some clustered in self-conscious girl groups. At Alana's order, they filed into the tiers of benches and placed their cameras on the desks in front of them, assured they would be permitted photo opportunities. Trina sat in the deemster's box, like a pulpit, and the rosewood surround engraved with

174

carvings of chastisement: the gallows, the rack, the flogging horse, the ducking stool. Behind her, the same, very real devices of correction stood in polished splendour. Beulah Beaucoup squatted, wearing only panties and buffing the implements with the swaying jellies of her bare breasts, until Zealla ordered her to quit; the slave maid retreated on her knees. Below and beside Trina sat the prisoner, Emily Cawdor.

The girl squatted on a plain stool with her back exposed and her teats squashed between two holes in the high front piece. Her back and neck were rigid as she perched bolt upright, in her bra and panties, bearing her yoke on her shoulders. A hangman's noose enclosed her neck, draped loosely on her collarbone, and stretched upwards to a meathook dangling from the beams of the ceiling. At Trina's either side, Heidi and Alice fussed with sheaves of papers, Heidi as prosecutor and Alice acting for Emily's defence.

Trina, as intendant, was the deemster. Like counsel, she wore a long judicial robe, but unlike the two committee members she remained clothed beneath. Before the arrival of the public, Heidi and Alice had unconcernedly stripped bare, save for their boots, black nylon stockings, garter belts and straps, but no panties; they donned the billowing black robes over their naked bodies. Zealla, the clerk of the court, stripped after counsel and donned a short black gown, buttock-length, over a white rubber corset, tightened to eighteen inches, which left her buttocks and jellies naked and allowed her ass-melons to peep through the latticework of her high-backed chair. She explained that counsel must be in shame, for humility before the court; the deemster remained clad until the moment of passing sentence, which she must pass in the same humility. Trina might extemporise or read from the traditional script before her, used by Mamselle Flageolet herself, and which included all variables of disapproval, condemnation and sentencing.

'What if the prisoner is found not guilty?' Trina said.

'The court does not decide guilt or innocence,' Zealla explained. 'The court decides *how* guilty.'

Dorita, dressed like Zealla, with her skimpy gown flapping over the spanked melons of her glowing bare ass, was the sergeant-at-arms; Felt and Acajou, constables of the court, and Prefect Funger the usher. The door opened again and two custodians entered, leading a gang of prisoners in their snowy underthings and on a neck-chain; the custodians wore uniform of tight shorts with security corps flashes – only the shorts were black – with black laced knee-boots. Their bare breasts shook as they flicked their canes over the prisoners' pantied buttocks and the nipple points, thinly protected by shallow brassieres. The custodians, flicking canes over the bras and panties of their charges, were Julie Pageant and Blush Coynte, both leering at Trina as they seated the girls on a bench next to the prisoner and sat one at each end of the bench.

'What is the meaning of this?' Trina hissed to Zealla. 'They are miscreants!'

'Sometimes miscreants make the best muscle maids, mamselle. They serve in the security corps punishment battalion and are not graded – they carry no hairbrush.'

Zealla stood, allowing the flaps of her gown to sweep back from her bare breasts.

'The citizens will rise!'

The spectators lurched to their feet, gazing at Zealla's titties bouncing with her intonation, and she proclaimed:

'Oyez, oyez, Federal court of the republic of New Arras, 3rd district, in the county of Rousseau, 2nd circuit, in the parish of Marat. This court is now in session, citizen intendant Mamselle Guelph is deemster presiding. You may sit. The first case concerns citizen Emily Cawdor. Citizen, how do you plead?'

'Guilty, mamselle,' whispered Emily, ashen-faced.

'What is the charge?' Trina hissed.

'You have the dossier before you, mamselle citizen,' Zealla said rather coldly. 'It is up to the miscreant to confess, and see if her confession matches her dossier.'

She smiled at the spectators and slowly ran her palms over her naked breasts, squeezing the jellies so that they sprang back to firmness, quivering as they jutted from her drawn-in ribcage. Her big plum nipples were tall and swollen. The salon thrilled with excited murmurs.

'Order in the court,' Trina said, banging her gavel.

'You must invite citizen Absorb to open the case for the prosecution,' Zealla whispered.

Trina obeyed, and Heidi swirled into centre stage, clutching her papers. She raised her arms, allowing her robe to fall back, with her naked breasts and cunt pointing straight at the public gallery. Staring fiercely at the public, then at Trina, she pointed at the quivering Emily Cawdor.

'It is our intention,' she declared, 'to prove the defendant guilty of malfeasance with criminous intent, concerning disloyal and scandalous apportionment of uniform clothing; for which we shall demand *peine forte et dure*, with fustigation and circumligation to the maximum severity the law permits. The sentences to be carried out publicly and forthwith, and on full bare skin.'

The crowd clapped; the men and women alike, bright eyed, the males with bulges at the groin, and the females with darkening patches of damp at the crotch of their jeans or the laps of their frilly short skirts as they crossed and uncrossed their thighs. Trina looked at their faces.

That's what they've come to see, a girl whipped and tortured. Rednecks, yet Americans, like me.

She asked Zealla, in a whisper, what *peine forte et dure* meant, and learned that it was crushing with a heavy weight – 'say, a dozen girls sitting on her,' Zealla said, 'and her body slopped in sweet gum, so they don't slide off.'

'Also, there is the graver charge of treason,' Heidi thundered, 'for which we shall demand the supreme penalty of public hanging.'

There was a buzz from the public benches, with females clasping their aroused males and pressing their thighs together. Heidi stepped back to the front row of spectators and suddenly swirled to face them, her face red and her heavy bare breasts bobbing. She parted her legs, then slipped her gown off her shoulder and balanced it on the end of her finger, twirling it for several moments before once more draping it on her back.

177

'In a court of law,' she declaimed, 'to get at the truth, we may sometimes use language that shocks. I make no apology. This heinous maid – this slut, this trull – is guilty of the foulest abominations, which I must name. *Diddling*, ladies and gentleman, or to call it scientifically, masturbation – a practice much observed in the basest form of female, a crime against reason, and one which a young scholar of the republic must learn to eschew, to master, to suppress, in her goal of becoming a submissive southern belle – a lady! Sluttish dress is no lesser crime – to parade in unseemly raiment, the hose torn, the brassiere or panties with rips and holes, betokening vice of the most abominable kind, which I must refer to by its true name – one that base females adore, and addict themselves to, making thralls of helpless males, slaves of their own animal vigour – buggery, ladies and gentlemen. That is, anal sexing, where the depraved female opens her anal orifice to the sex organ – naked and erect! – of the hapless victim of her seduction, and brings him to sperm in her nethermost cubicle! Fighting between lustful females adds to her woeful litany of offences: sluts, inflamed by those sorry pleasures, prepared to abandon their dignity as submissive belles, strip naked in shame, then kick, gouge and claw each other's pure bodies, in dispute over – I must say it – *cock!*'

The audience gasped. Heidi's naked teats rose and fell like bellows.

'Such crimes merit reasonable torture to extract the truth. Yet the prosecution can show exhibits and present witnesses to confirm what the prisoner – this miserable, mewling slattern – shall confess to the court of her own free will and without any torture yet applied.'

The crowd sighed. Emily Cawdor's face was a grimace and tears rolled from her eyes. She shivered, with goosebumps covering her bare, trembling breasts, and her shaking swayed the rope round her neck.

'I present exhibits A, B and C,' Heidi called and public servant Felt scurried to fetch and deposit the items on the table: a torn white cotton stocking, a pair of ripped and heavily stained white panties and a monstrously gnarled rubber cylinder in the shape of a magnolia trunk but resembling a man's cock, and unmistakably a dildo, fifteen inches in length, and a girl's fist wide.

Heidi held up the stocking, showing the tear, and accusing Emily of vile sluttishness and disregard for the unifom of a scholar and the treasury of the republic, which had borne the cost of that uniform. The same applied to the shredded panties, save that their *déchirement* indicated the porcine delights of buggery, confirmed by the hideous stains, where no submissive belle should even *think* of having stains. Heidi poked her finger through the holed panties and waggled it, ripping the garment some more.

'She was so hot, ladies and gentlemen, she couldn't wait to strip her panties off,' Heidi said. 'She had her ass on some boy's cock faster than a fat lady on a milkshake.'

She picked up the dildo and held it at arm's length, squinting in distaste.

'Doesn't this confirm the slut's depravity? She'll tell you about it much better than I can, but can you imagine, ladies and gentleman, what it feels like – what maid would degrade herself so – to have this stuck up your most shameful private area?'

Heidi turned and crouched with her gown over her shoulders and her buttocks spread, showing her anal pucker gaping open. She brought the tip of the dildo within an inch of her anus and mimed reaming and thrusting motions, before allowing the dildo to touch her pucker and slip half an inch inside – at which she recoiled from the tube with a gasp.

'Oh! What a dreadful mistake!' she panted. 'I let that monster creep inside my crack by accident! So cold and filthy and painful, ladies and gentlemen! Imagine a girl who would let her tiny passage be filled, filled to bursting, and mutilated, by such a thing, for twisted, perverted pleasure! But I must not allow my testimony to colour the judgement of the court. The accused bitch shall damn herself by confessing, and torture may be applied afterwards at the discretion of our learned deemster.'

The audience buzzed.

'With her permission,' Heidi concluded, 'I give the floor to my learned friend for the defence, such as she is able to muster, in such an open and shut case.'

Trina crossed her thighs and nodded. Alice Frequemme sauntered to the front of the court, her mouth moving in a sardonic leer as if chewing gum. Casually, she let her robe fall from her shoulders and selected her left breast for examination. She took her nipple between finger and thumb and rolled it, pinching, until both nipples stood erect from her swelling bare titties. Only then did she look at the audience with a sly smile. She let her entire nudity show, with her gown swept back, and put one boot on the guardrail, opening her gleaming wet cunt-flaps only inches from the front row of spectators. She scratched her left nylon stocking with a rasping sound, and then her right, the operation extending right to the stocking-tops and then extending up her taut garter straps, with her fingernails brushing the gash-lips.

'Well,' she drawled, in her lilting Southern accent, 'I guess there's not much I can say to dent my learned friend's reasoning. Might as well just hang my client out to dry and have done with it. Pity. Those dreadful vices she spoke of, and to which my client is surely going to confess, are abominations all right.'

She scratched her stockings again and then her fingernails brushed on the swollen folds of her wet cunt itself, where her clitty was visible, erect, moist and stiff.

'My, it's hot in here, isn't it?' she said. 'You folks from the Orleans territory don't know really hot. Makes a girl itchy. Makes her do all kinds of things she doesn't mean. Why, darn it, look what I've gone and done!'

Her finger poked through a hole in her stocking at the thigh.

'And that was just from innocent scratching in this infernal heat. Of course, in court, everything is *sub specie modestiae*, which means I can do anything I want, with courtroom privilege, and my stockings are my own furbishment, bought from Beauregard's haberdashers in Biloxi, but had I innocently scratched myself, in this heat, a foot beyond that door there, ladies and gentlemen –' she pointed dramatically '– should I hang for it? Hmm. You might think panties are a different matter, but don't you all sometimes get an itch down there – I mean way inside? And you just have to scratch way inside? Now a submissive belle, a good Southern lady, like my client, must never ever scratch her butt, because that is what uncouth, tobacco-chewing men do – but she still got to scratch that itch, way inside – and what better, what more ladylike way of solving the problem, than to use a thing like this?'

She picked up the dildo, squatted, as Heidi had done, and placed its gnarled tip firmly on her anus bud. She began to tickle her pucker, which dilated and opened. Parting her buttocks with splayed fingers, she drove the dildo an inch into her butthole and began to waggle it.

'Ahh . . . that's better. But don't forget, I still have my panties on, for a Southern belle never removes her panties, and that pesky itch is still there, way inside, and making me madder than a possum in a beehive. So . . .'

There was a gasp as Alice pushed the shaft right to the hilt, a good eight inches of it penetrating her anus, and began to thrust vigorously in and out.

'See?' she gasped. 'That's a real good way to get rid of that itch. But itches are pesky critters, and they can spread just any old place. So, while I'm having an innocent and decorous scratch, with my panties on, I get an itch here in front, and have to put on a pair of my best cotton gloves to get rid of it with another innocent scratch.'

Alice spun, showing the audience her spread cunt, with her fingers rubbing her clitoris, and copious come seeping down the insides of her thighs into her stocking-tops. She continued to frot herself for a minute, until she snapped her thighs shut with a squelch of cunt-juice and stood.

'No masturbation and none of this here buggery – which plain folks like you and me know as cornholing, and there are those that say no Southern lady should be ignorant of what's done in every cotton field twixt here and Natchez! I just know my client's confession will reveal the truth of

181

what I've said,' she added, with an encouraging smile at Emily, while Heidi glowered, her arms folded. 'But I don't rest my case, for there's the accusation of treason. My learned friend didn't make much of that, did she? Wants to hang an innocent girl on trumped-up charges of this here masturbation, while the more serious charge slips by.'

She opened her thighs an inch and let a forefinger play on her cunt, the fingernail slipping inside the moist fat slit, then slicing her erect clitoris.

'Now, it's no secret that my client recently served time in the Stella Maris therapeutic institute. Dare say some of you visitors are familiar with it. Get all kinds in there, aside you good tourist folk . . . unlawful migrants from New Albion, female or male, even spies. Place is a hotbed of intrigue. My learned friend is going to accuse my client of passing secrets to the enemy, I don't doubt. But how does a hard-working scholar get to know state secrets, unless she has them from a higher authority?'

Two fingers penetrated her oily quim, with a thumb jabbing the swollen nubbin. Come dripped copiously down her quivering thighs and into her stocking-tops.

'And why should she give them away, unless she was ordered to for reasons of state? My learned friend knows full well, for citizen Heidi Absorb is directress of the Stella Maris. She corrupted my client, a simple everyday miscreant serving hard time and taking her reasonable whippings like a good citizen, promising her a lighter sentence if . . . uh . . .'

Alice pumped her pulsing gash with three rigid fingers, penetrating the hole right to the knuckle, while her thumb pounded and squashed the erect, come-shiny clitoris. Her thighs parted wide and she hooked a foot over the guardrail, with her exposed spread quim inches from the gawping faces of the front row of spectators. Come flowed, gleaming wetly on her bare thighs; her soaked stocking-tops slithered as her hand slapped and stove her cunt, awash with come, and her thumbnail flicked the clitty in a staccato blur.

'If . . . yeah . . . if she'd pass secrets to the enemy! Yeah!'

Come spurted from her cunt down her thighs.

'Yee-haw!' said several spectators.

'Objection!' cried Heidi, springing to her feet.

Trina looked at Zealla, who mouthed 'overruled'.

'Overruled,' said Trina, thumping her gavel on the wood. 'I think it is time to hear the maid's confession.'

Alice's mouth hung slack and drooling as she slowly plopped her fingers from her clinging wet slit and waved them at the glowering Heidi.

'Go on, maid, say your piece,' said Trina.

She watched Alice enfold herself in her gown, with just her stiff nipples peeping, and her breasts rising and falling with her hot breath. Trina shifted her buttocks, with moisture slimy between her stocking-tops.

'It was like counsel said, mamselle,' Emily quavered. 'I'm guilty of all charges, even treason, but it was involuntary treason.'

'The ripped stockings and panties, and the . . . the dildo, are related, so deal with them first,' Trina snapped.

'Pardon me, mamselle, but they are all related. I am the victim of a misunderstanding, I swear. It's very hot at night in the Stella Maris, and I was scratching myself, for there is no fan in the prisoners' dormitory. But I was careful not to rip my garments! They are the property of the public watch, you see, and I am still technically a watchmaid, though I was sentenced to a month in Stella Maris for another misunderstanding! Sergeant Makings assigned me to the vice squad, and I was undercover. I heard of a diddling ring – masturbatresses, mamselle – and I infiltrated it successfully. Of course, I had to go along with their diddling games until I caught the ringleaders, who were Devora Dykes and Julie Pageant, and I was just about to bust them – we were playing three-handed clitty rubbing, mamselle, when a troop of security corpsmaids arrived and arrested us all. Only Devora was let go, because she had snitched on us to the security corps! It was a bureaucratic foul-up and I sent a petition to the committee of public safety, copying Sergeant Makings and the then intendant, Mamselle Pure, but I don't think they had time to read it. Because it was a corps arrest, I forfeited the right to trial on grounds of national security and got a month, arbitrary, in the brig – that's the Stella Maris. With my career as a watchmaid in ruins!'

Emily sobbed, and made as if to wipe her streaming eyes, but her bound wrists jerked against her yoke.

'Who gave you the dildo?' Trina said.

'It was another slave, mamselle,' Emily wailed. 'I don't know who, honest, because it was dark – I couldn't help it. It wasn't me who ripped my panties and stockings; it was her. She wanted to help me find my itch and before I could say no she was . . . she was diddling me, mamselle.' She ripped off my panties and tore off my stockings and started to masturbate my clitoris. Then, when my pussy was all wet, she stuck the dildo inside me. First in my quim, then in my butthole. It was horrible – I was so raw, after my shift – four cocks in each hole, mamselle, and thirty canestrokes, separate delivery, in sets of ten, on each bare fesse – oh! She cornholed me with that dreadful thing for at least forty minutes, until I pissed myself twice, in agony.'

'You didn't resist?' Trina barked, her thighs slithering together, as she crossed and uncrossed her legs.

'I couldn't, mamselle judge, the maid was sitting on my face.'

'Bare-ass?' Trina murmured.

'Yes, mamselle.'

'And how did you respond, prisoner?'

'I was licking her pussy, mamselle. She made me suck her clitty, and swallow her come.'

'*Made* you? You swallowed her come.'

'Yes, mamselle.'

'And did you come?'

'Yes, mamselle,' Emily sobbed. 'I was scared. She threatened to get me assigned to the punishment battalion, leading the upcoming assault on New Albion. She said the first wave would surely be captured and tortured by the Anglos. She said any maid with sense would surrender to the Anglos, for the war fever was just a ruse to cover up the coming devaluation of the fessignat – too many maids were baring up for black market strokes, which devalued the currency. Lady Juliet Gorges had spies everywhere on New Arras, ordered to lash as many bares as possible, without payment at the official rate, and if we couldn't beat her we should join her. She said the ringleader of the black market and Anglo spy, was . . .'

Emily stopped her babble and paled as Zealla stared at her and emitted an audible hiss.

'Was who?' Trina said.

'Oh! I don't remember, mamselle.'

'Citizen judge,' cried Zealla, 'as commander in chief of the general staff, I deem it a matter of national security that your interrogation be continued in private. May I respectfully suggest that the charges of lewdness and destruction of government property provide sufficient basis for sentence to be carried out. The slut is one of the vilest I have heard in any public court, and no crimson can be deep nor weals hard enough for her bare fesses.'

Alice rose.

'Hearsay, innuendo and oppression,' she cried. 'I move that all charges be thrown out.'

Heidi leaped to her feet, smirking.

'My learned friend forgets the state has a witness,' she said. 'I seek permission to call citizen, and security corps captain, Harriet Stooplaugh.'

'That is in order,' whispered Zealla.

'Very well,' Trina said.

Harriet Stooplaugh entered the court, bare-breasted and wearing the white skirt and jackboots of a security corpsmaid. She took the witness stand, swore her oath on the copy of Mamselle Flageolet's reglements and returned Trina's gape of astonishment with a bland smile, wriggling slightly so that her naked titties swayed and the pert, erect nips winked at Trina, who swallowed as moisture trickled from her quim into her stockings. Questioned by Heidi, Harriet said she was an undercover security corpsmaid, under discreet attachment to the public watch, and sometimes posing as a slave in the Stella Maris to elicit information from tourists who had recently visited New Albion, and to sniff out revolt amongst the slave maids. Trina demanded if discreet attachment meant spying, and Harriet agreed that it did; pressed, admitted that her role as Trina's secretary was also discreet attachment. Trina wished to know if Alice, as head of the public watch, and Dorita of the security corps, had knowledge of such things. Both girls shrugged.

'It may go on, mamselle,' said Dorita, 'but only as a result of mistakes in paperwork, by inept clerical staff.'

Alice agreed.

'I am more interested in the damaged panties,' she said.

'Cawdor should not have been wearing those panties,' Harriet said, 'but should have turned them in to the ordnance store. However, since they had entered slave premises, they were technically slave panties, whatever their provenance, and their destruction is sabotage.'

'Did you cause that destruction, Harriet?' Trina stammered. 'Did you masturbate her?'

'Yes, citizen judge, but only when she begged me to. The dildo was hers; the first rips in the garments were hers. She complained the customers weren't rough enough for her taste. She wanted me to spank her, slap her around.'

'Did you?'

'Yes, mamselle, I did, for *raison d'état* I spanked her bare for about thirty minutes, and her titties about the same, while I had my quim on her mouth, and she was sucking my clitty. She twisted round so that I could slap her ass. While I spanked her, she orgasmed twice, and she told me the stud Duane Carvalho on New Albion was twice as virile as Elvis Lesieur, and that's why she was scheming with tourists, to get her out, so she could defect and satisfy her perverted craving for anal sex. She was planning to bring Lady Juliet the secret of sweet gum in return for Duane's services, as he is known to be the depraved Lady Juliet's favourite stud.'

'Did you enjoy her sucking your clitoris?' Trina said.

'Why, no, mamselle,' replied Harriet. 'It was all in the line of duty.'

Emily wailed and burst into fresh tears.

'Yours is the only clitoris I've ever enoyed sucking, mamselle,' Harriet murmured.

'Yee-haw!'

The audience clapped and cheered.

'It's all lies!' shrieked Emily. 'She made me spank her and thrash her on bare, first with a whipple, then a studded belt that she said was Duane Carvalho's, and she had it from the Albion spy, Duane's buttfuck partner, Mamselle Zealla Pure.'

There was uproar; Zealla alone remained calm.

'Of course, if the slut's outburst has any truth, it merely shows what an excellent *agente provocateuse* the corps Captain Stooplaugh is,' she said smoothly. 'Intelligence work is subtle – it surely helps national security for the Anglos to believe I am Duane Carvalho's mistress, while that gentleman thinks I am Mr Lesieur's.'

She turned to smile winningly at Trina.

'I must confess, I have never enjoyed the pleasure of that gentleman's cock,' she said, 'although our agents on New Albion have let the lustful pervert understand that my anus is longing for it. Now, mamselle intendant, there are other cases to consider – if you care to pass sentence on the felon who has pleaded guilty?'

Trina called counsel to the bench and expressed her dissatisfaction with the proceedings, and that rumours of war peddled by some kind of dirty tricks department were kept from the public and, not least, herself. Harriet sat in the witness box, smiling at the audience and juggling each bare breast up and down while pinching her nipples.

Trina called her to order.

'Pertinent chastisement is the least you can expect when I get you alone. You'll be screaming, mamselle, as I whip your bare ass raw,' she hissed, and Harriet bowed her head.

'We'll shine the treason thing, if you'll go for the lewdness and disorderly ya-de-da,' Heidi said to Alice. 'That's enough to give these rednecks their show.'

'Works for me,' Alice replied. 'If you'd care to pronounce sentence, mamselle judge?'

'Just a minute –'

'I suggest page seventeen of the reglements, mamselle,' Zealla said.

'Please, mamselle judge,' cried Emily Cawdor, straining at her noose, and her breasts bobbing, their nipples erect and goose-bumped. 'To delay my chastisement would be cruel and inhuman.'

The audience buzzed agreement.

'The slut is juicing for it right now,' said Harriet. 'I can see a trickle of come on her thigh.'

Numbly, Trina turned her book to page seventeen. Zealla leaned across her, brushing her breasts over Trina's eyes, and fingered the passage. Trina read.

'Emily Cawdor, you have been found guilty as charged, and must suffer exemplary correction of one hundred strokes of the cane on the naked buttocks, while strapped in restraint on a public flogging bench; followed by *peine forte et dure*, on full bare skin, at court's discretion.'

She looked up to see Blush Coynte's bare teats bobbing as she stripped off her custodian's uniform.

'Yee-haw!' shouted the rednecks.

'Blush is going to cane her here and now?' Trina gasped.

Nude, Blush handed the uniform to Trina, and curtsied.

'No, mamselle judge, you are,' Zealla answered.

From the Journal of Mlle Augustine Flageolet, anno 1760 11
Arlette Dupuis pleasantly surprised me today. She fashioned a delightful rack of burnished teak, all by herself, being jealous of her creation. Of course, such egoism merited chastisement, so she was the first to offer her person on the device. She took her stretching very well – entirely naked – suffering both face down and face up. In the former position, I personally birched her twenty-five on the buttocks, and in the latter caned her twenty-five on the bare breasts, a refinement of discipline Capt Stouplois much admired. He complimented me on my flagellant prowess. It is so difficult to draw the fine line between ego and reason! In these tropics, I masturbate two or three times a day, and of course I encourage my girls to

masturbate frequently, singly or in groups, but always rationally and in a social manner. Baring the buttocks for anal penetration is similarly governed by reason, and the rules of the virgins of Ishtar – modesty, obedience to the male, and without vainglory. Yet reason is abandoned when these healthy pursuits become lustful and driven by sensation. Arlette taunted me that I dared not bare myself in worship of Ishtar or, more properly, in obedience to the male force I admired so much. I caned her a further fifty strokes on the bare nates, bent over a ship's mast, for that insolence. Nevertheless, it stung.

12

Peine Forte et Dure

It was the reglement that pertinent chastisement was carried out on the spot by the sentencing judge. *The fucking reglements*, Trina cursed, as she stripped – that too, was in the reglements – under the eyes of the court – *drooling rednecks!* – and donned Blush's shorts, which were too tight at the crotch, hugging her ass-pears and vulva, and presenting her cunt-basin neatly wrapped.

I must stop this whipping fever, this war mania. It's not healthy for girls to crave flogging so, nor the other thing . . . cock in butthole, indeed! How do I explain all this to GG?

The courtroom air was fetid on her big, swaying breasts, whose downy hairs quivered in the eddies of hot breath. Sweat beaded the teats and she raised her hand to rub the flesh, brushing droplets from the big – stiffening! – plums of her nipples and drawing appreciative murmurs from the audience. Zealla noticed her arousal and said it was reasonable and healthy for a whipper to be aroused by a beating, as it made her strokes sting more and the miscreant's bare buttocks smart more handsomely. She handed her a four-foot hickory switch, gnarled and unpolished. Trina wriggled, trying to get the shorts comfortable; there were no panties and the gusset was soggy with Blush's cunt-oils. She looked angrily at the nude Blush, who smiled, flaring her nostrils, and crooked her finger just over her luxuriant growth of cunt-fleece, where her swollen clitoris stood red and glistening raw.

*The bitch was masturbating! Why her shorts? Yeah –
Zealla knew they would fit. What doesn't she know?*

Alana Funger supervised Julie Pageant hauling an
oblong teak bench, colonial in style, and with legs eighteen
inches high, into the centre of the courtroom. There were
rubber straps dangling on each side and at each end, with
extra straps at the foot of each leg. The body of the bench
was of solid wood, a foot deep, but rose, curving, to an
altitude of two feet underneath the hips, so that the
buttocks were presented raised for flogging, for greater
ease of the whipper. Trina's lips wrinkled as the heavy
thing was dragged to mid-stage: it was not some lounger
or long chair, pressed opportunistically into the service of
chastisement, but lovingly handcrafted furniture, whose
only purpose was to lodge a victim for flogging on the
buttocks. The prisoner Emily Cawdor was unyoked and
led by her noose to the flogging bench where, snuffling and
sobbing, she lay face down. Prefect Alana Funger unfastened her bra and pulled it free from the big squashed
teats, then ripped her panties down to her knees; Emily
raised her hips and legs, permitting Alana to complete the
garment's removal. At a signal from Dorita, the clerk of
the court, the rednecks lifted their cameras and flashes
began to pop.

The condemned girl's bare buttocks trembled, covered in
goosebumps, and with the downy hairs clustered in her
cleft standing straight. Her body draped the flogging
hillock like a crescent moon, with the buttocks in promi-
nence over her head and feet; she raised her head aw-
kwardly. Julie, in black shorts clinging damply to her ripely
swelling mons, and Blush, nude but with moisture plainly
visible at the dark red slash of her quim, strapped the girl
to the body of the bench. Long straps of rubber crossed
over her skin, holding her by the backs of her knees and
by her waist, just above the buttocks. They fastened her
wrists and ankles to the bottom of the legs, which stretched
her arms fully and held her buttocks parted. The fat red
slice of her naked vulva and her anus bud were fully
exposed to her chastiser, and telephoto lenses hummed to

focus on her wet gash-meat. Swish! Trina lashed the air, the cane passing inches from Emily's top buttock.

'Ohh . . .' Emily moaned. 'Oh, I'm sorry, I didn't meant to . . .' and a jet of steaming yellow pee bubbled from her cunt-flaps, sluicing up over her ass-peach and puddling the floor and Trina's boots.

There was a flurry of camera shutters.

The fucking bitch, putting me through this . . .

Vip!

She lashed Emily hard across the middle of her bare melons and Emily screamed, her buttocks clenching shut, then open, half a dozen times; a thick red welt flamed across both ass-cheeks. Her mons banged against the teak bench, slopping her cunt in her pee. Vip! Vip! One to each haunch, delivered forehand and backhand.

'Oh . . . oh . . .' Emily sobbed, her face a rictus, and her eyes shut tight, squeezing copious teardrops.

Vip! Vip! Vip! One to the fleshy underfesse, and two stingers to the taut thin skin at top buttock. The bare fesses jerked harder at each stroke, anus and quim-lips disappearing in a deep, clenched furrow that sprang open and closed. Cameras clicked incessantly.

'Ah! Ah! Ohh . . .' Emily squealed. 'Oh, please, no . . .'

Trina's bare breasts bounced and jiggled at each stroke to delighted gasps from the rednecks; she looked round to see the men and women staring half at Emily's wealed bottom and half at her own naked teats. Vip! Vip! Vip! She caned two more at top fesse and another across the backs of the upper thighs.

'Ah! Oh! It's so tight, mamselle. Oh, I don't think I can take a full hundred, mamselle. Please have mercy.'

'Shut the fuck up, bitch,' Trina hissed. 'You think I like beating you?'

Yeah. I do. I want that bitch's melons to swell up crimson. I want to hurt her as I've been hurt. Make her feel my pain.

Vip! Vip! Vip!

'Ahh! It hurts. It hurts me so.'

One to each haunch, and another stinger deepening the weal at top fesse. Emily's buttocks jerked in a frenzy, clenching madly at each stroke, and the ripe envelopes of buttock-meat slammed into each other as though to devour her ass-cleft, even though the strokes avoided the fleshy mid-fesse. Her arms and pinioned legs leaped, straining the rubber cords that bound her. Vip! Vip!

'Oh! Oh!'

At the fourteenth stroke, Trina halted for breath. The girl's bare croup continued to clench, churning her cunt-basin against the piss-soaked wood, and with an oily trickle of come seeping into the pee. The buttocks were marked by a grid of pink and crimson weals, rapidly darkening to purple at the tender skin of haunch and top fesse, where Trina had stroked hardest. Emily gasped for air, her breath a rasping gurgle, slamming her titties against the hardwood bench. Trina put her hands on her hips and bent forwards, facing the audience, with her naked teats dangling beneath her face. She too gasped, the sweat dripping from her brow and the points of her nipples, which stood swollen and erect to the stares and cameras of the rednecks; the gusset of her shorts was slimy with her own come, dripping into the cunt-juice oozed by Blush Coynte, so that Trina's vulva and perineum slithered as she stood up with the oil lubricating her anus.

Heidi and Alice stared, smiling, with their legs apart and fingertips just above their cunt-fleeces, already glistening with a dew of come; Harriet too had her hand between her legs and was openly masturbating, flicking her eyes from Trina's breasts to Emily's scarred bare nates. Long lenses waved from the panting rednecks to the cunts of the masturbating girls. She raised her cane for the next set of Emily's hundred, then gasped. Zealla squatted with her skirt folded up, then placed herself beside Harriet and put her hand between the maid's legs, touching her quim. She began frotting her, while Harriet took Zealla's nipples between her two thumbs and fingers, rubbing and pinching them until the big plum nipples stood fully erect. Zealla's free hand crept beneath her thighs and clamped the lips of her own vulva, peeking beneath her skirt; she began to masturbate vigorously and openly. Trina's clitoris throbbed; panting, she slashed the air.

Vip! Emily's bare buttocks reddened and heaved.

'Ah! No, please! Oh . . .'

Vip!

'Ah . . .'

Vip! Vip!

'Ahh!'

Trina settled into the rhythm of her caning, spacing the sets with a minute's gap, and delivering sets of ten stingers in quick succession, so that Emily's nates writhed and squirmed as harshly when free of cane as under stroke. The reddened flesh was everywhere deepening to jagged dark welts and ridges, highlighting the puffy, mottled skin on either side of the weals. Emily's shrieks mellowed to a low, continuous sobbing, heightened by snuffles and wails. Her cunt streamed with a copious flow of come, and between her wails at cane's impact were soft little yelps and moans. Her writhing loins rubbed her vulva on the teak, and at the fifty-sixth stroke Trina demanded if she was masturbating.

'Aren't you, mamselle?' Emily sobbed. 'Doesn't everyone get off, seeing a girl's butt caned?'

Trina looked round; redneck couples were openly embracing and caressing each other genitally, with some of the women engaged in solo masturbation of their exposed cunts. Blush, Julie, Alana, Heidi and Alice and the custodians – all were frotting themselves, or each other; Zealla and Harriet practised heavy tribadism, with Harriet squatting and her face between Zealla's thighs, exposed under the billows of her dress, and panties at her knees, while Zealla caressed Harriet's cunt with her booted foot. Zealla looked up at Trina, licked her teeth and nodded towards Trina's own quim; her shorts were soaking wet with her come. Sweat poured from Trina's breasts and brow; she closed her eyes as her fingers crept down the front of her shorts, dallied in the rich curls of her cunt-fleece and impacted the erect, throbbing clitoris.

I can't stop myself. What have I become? A flogger, a masturbatrix, a diddler . . .

Trina poked three fingers into her come-slopped cunt and, with jerking motions of her hips, began to thrust her clitty against the heel of her hand. She touched her swollen nipples with the cane, rubbing the whole length of the wood across them, with the wood still hot from Emily's flogged bottom. She drew the cane back and flicked her nipples with its tip; then slapped her breasts with the shaft of the cane, harder and harder, until the thwacks of her tit-flogging echoed through the courtroom. Thin stripes appeared on her teats, crossing the areolae and streaking the nipple-buds. Emily twisted her neck to gaze at the teat-jellies and lustfully rubbed her cunt on the flogging bench in a sweeping motion. Trina gasped, tore her cane away from her glowing bare titties and lifted it over Emily's bare ass. Vip! Vip! Vip!

'You fucking bitch!' she hissed. 'How dare you masturbate!'

'But, mamselle! We're *sub specie modestiae*! Please –'

Vip! Vip! Vip! Three stingers, all on top fesse, striping unwealed skin. Emily howled, and her whole body jerked rigid as her naked buttocks quivered like automata.

'Oh! Oh!' she screamed.

As she stroked, Trina masturbated with firm, vigorous rubs of her clitty. Her fingers slopped with her own gushing come and she paused in her frottage to rub her come into her bare ass-melons, tight under Blush's shorts, and with Trina's knuckles crawling mole-like under the fabric as she kneaded the hard ridges scarred by her own bare-bottom floggings. She moaned, panting harshly.

'Ohh!' Emily squealed as three cuts lashed the very same weal, deepening it to a jagged trench across her pumping top buttocks, just below her rubber restraint strap.

Vip! Vip!

'Ooh! Ahh!'

Hsss . . .! A second jet of piss spurted from Emily's cunt, this time oily with rainbow globules of her copiously oozing come. Her thighs, vulva and ass-cleft were bathed in the fluid, and her wriggles made slopping sounds. Vip! Vip!

'Ahh!'

'Dirty little fuckpig!'

Vip! Vip!

'Uh! Cane harder, mamselle,' Emily whimpered. 'Please, mamselle, fast, all together, all together . . .'

'Sassy bitch!'

Trina drew up her cane and gave Emily ten in quickfire succession, using alternate backhand and forehand strokes, and squeezing her clitty while three fingernails clawed the wet walls of her cunt-pouch. Her titties flapped together as she flogged, the skin cracking with a wet, slapping noise; her belly heaved as she watched Emily's bare croup, a sullen kaleidoscope of weals, squirm and shudder at each wealing canestroke.

'Ah . . . ah . . . ah . . .' Emily cried; a gush of come flooded her thighs, and her cunt and belly slapped up and down on the wood as Trina delivered the last two strokes.

Vip! Vip!

'Ahh . . .!' Emily shrieked as she writhed in orgasm.

Dazzled by camera flashes, Trina raced her fingers on her clitoris as the girl's flogged bare continued to jerk and quiver. She bit her lip and sobbed as her belly exploded in the flood of her own climax. She reached out with her flogging hand and touched Emily's scalded bare bottom as the ripples of her orgasm caressed her cunt. She let her fingers draw through Emily's cane wounds, brushing the crusted dark skin of the ridges and welts and tracing the painting her cane had made on the soft bare flesh.

Emily was left strapped to her flogging bench while the cases of the other malfeasants were heard. Sweating, Trina draped herself in her robe, and heard a litany of plaints and defences. None of the offences was as grave as panty despoliation, nor even of treason: they concerned insolence, bedwetting, failure to leave the latrines clean, nail-biting, smiling on parade. Zealla assured her that she could defer the sentences until the morrow, with the prisoners given to the custody of the watch, thus saving her flogging arm. She indicated the relevant pages of Mamselle Flageolet's reglements. Her quim still dripping come, and an electric flicker shooting in her cunt as she passed sentence, Trina read out the fates of the sullen maids, one after the other:

Clara Latasse, to receive twenty lashes of the whip, bareback, and twenty canestrokes on bare fesses, the strokes to be taken freestanding and strapped by wrists only, with toes touching the floor; Prudence Vile, fifty canestrokes on bare fesses, *chevauchée*, meaning riding a rail with her naked quim on the crossbar, wrists raised above her and ankles strapped to the base of the rail; Beulah Beaucoup, sixty lashes on the buttocks from a nine-thonged leather quirt, taken in horizontal suspension, wrists and ankles roped from a gibbet, her mouth filled with gravel, and her teats weighted with two three-pound rocks; Jewel Persimmon, forty lashes of the rattan cane on bare fesses, in upside down suspension from the gallows, legs apart, the quim filled with sea anemones and the anus with clams, both orifices sealed with duct tape; Florence Glow and Virginia Marble, their shaven pubic hillocks glued with sweet gum, and jointly suspended by the right wrists, with the left wrists in half-nelson, bound to spiked collars; Devora Dykes – Trina paused, looking at the insolently smiling face of the malfeasant, and closed the rule book, breathing deeply before pronouncing – Devora Dykes was to be publicly hanged, racked, flogged in suspension from the gallows, to one hundred with the cattle whip on bare back, and one hundred with hickory switch on fesses, the floggings to be dealt simultaneously, with a mouthful of rocks, and spider crabs in both cunt and anus, the orifices taped shut for three hours after cessation of chastisement, and her naked body to be displayed on the gibbet in Republic Place during that time. Devora bowed low and whispered, 'Thank you, mamselle.' Trina trembled as she looked up, crossing her legs repeatedly and with new come seeping in her cunt still hot from orgasm.

'We need some volunteers, mamselle,' Zealla said, 'for Emily's crushing, under *peine forte et dure*. Those trulls should do. Shall they doff their underwear, mamselle? Naked crushing is more shameful for the prisoner.'

Trina watched Devora twitch at her bra and slither her panties down until large tufts of her pubic forest peeped beneath her navel; she agreed to their nudity and the malfeasants stripped naked. Blush and Julie removed the flogged prisoner from her bench but left her wrists and ankles strapped behind her, so that her body was arched, with the titties, belly and cunt thrust in a crescent. They pushed her to the floor and Blush planted her heel in Emily's vulva, then poured a vessel of sweet gum all over her body. The malfeasants lined up in order of sentencing, and Clara flung herself on Emily's belly with a sticky thud, followed by Prudence and Beulah, the three bare bodies covering Emily completely and muffling her shrieks. The cameras of the spectators continued to flash. Jewel, Florence and Virginia threw themselves on the naked pile, and the squeals of the first crushers, slapped by new naked bodies, rose above Emily's wails. Devora was last, taking a run and hurling herself on the heap of writhing bare bodies, spreading her arms to embrace them. The pile writhed, slippery with sweat and sticky with sweet gum, as Devora stroked the bare fesses inches from her nose and her fingers brutally penetrated two open, squirming cunts. Looking back and smiling, she proceeded to masturbate the two maids, whose heads were hidden in the throng.

'Mamselle Pure,' Trina cried to Zealla, 'I must protest – this is just a spectacle for rednecks?'

Zealla shrugged.

'It's what they pay for, mamselle,' she replied, 'and, begging your pardon, the execution of sentence is my responsibility, as directress of discipline. Custodians Felt, Acajou, add your bodies to the crush pile.'

The two maids stripped and threw themselves on to the mass of bare bodies, wriggling and vibrating as fingers probed open helpless cunts and rammed squirming butt-holes, while mouths chewed bare skin. The bodies glistened with oily come, sliding amongst the rivulets of sweat and sweet gum. Beneath the throng, Emily's frantic shrieks yelped higher and higher. Devora's arm dived into the tussle and jabbed, until Emily's squeals turned to long wailing sighs; Devora continued to jab with her fist as she masturbated Emily's exposed cunt amid the thighs of Jewel and the teats of Prudence.

Heidi Absorb threw aside her robe and straddled Devora's buttocks, ramming her forefinger into the wrinkled plum of Devora's asshole and making her squeal; she penetrated the anus to the knuckle and began to ream Devora's anus, while her teeth fastened on her left nipple and bit savagely. Alice climbed on and straddled Heidi in her turn, getting her fist into the maid's writhing cunt and pumping until her wrists flowed with Heidi's glistening come, and at the same time she masturbated her own swollen, exposed clitty.

Trina crossed and uncrossed her stockinged legs, with the seep of come now a flow slithering into the stocking fabric and drenching her thighs and pubic fleece. Her long pubic tendrils were oily and damp amid the folds of her perineum and tickled her anus bud. She clenched her sphincter muscle hard, several times, but only succeeded in drawing the hairs up into her anus, which became unbearably ticklish. She gaped as Prefect Alana Funger threw off her own uniform and plunged nude into the morass of limbs, her eyes and lips glistening and her pussy oozing come. Zealla looked pointedly at Trina's dripping cunt and stretched her arm towards the naked pyramid of girls in invitation.

'Yee-haw!' cried the rednecks as two females shed their skirts and halter tops, ripped off their bras and soiled panties, squashing the garments on to their menfolk's faces, as they vaulted the rail and slapped their naked bodies on to the buttocks atop the throng.

'Wait . . .' Trina groaned.

'*Sub specie modestiae*,' murmured Zealla, pulling Trina's arm forwards. 'You know you want to, mamselle.'

'No . . .'

'I do.'

'Oh, yeah, do me . . . do me . . . diddle my cunt . . .' sobbed Emily Cawdor, way beneath the throbbing mass of bare bodies, as rivulets of come streamed from her cunt at the bottom of the crush pile.

'Uh!' Trina gasped as she fell heavily on to the fleshy mountain of squirming bare nates.

She squashed her face against the churning buttocks and bit hard, rewarded with a shrill cry of agony. It was Devora; she bit again and again, with come from the bitten girl's cunt flowing into Trina's nostrils. Zealla's bare breasts slapped her back and she felt the girl's full weight astride her, riding her and with fingers groping for her quim.

'No!' cried Trina, trying in vain to close her spread thighs as Zealla succeeded in prising open her gash-flaps, getting three fingers inside the already slopped quim, and began to frot her vigorously, with vicious slaps to the rock-hard, extruded clitty.

'Uh . . .' Trina gasped, 'Oh, you bitch, that's so good, oh, fuck me, don't stop.'

Her thighs clamped Zealla's penetrating fingers as the blonde maid fist-fucked her and juice squirted from Trina's gushing cunt until the invading flesh was slippery with her come. She continued to bite Devora's buttocks, getting closer to the cleft until she got a sliver of perineum skin between her teeth and chewed hard. Devora groaned and swivelled her cunt-basin to present Trina with her gushing slash, the lips swollen and red and the come bubbling in a shiny ooze, soaking her rampantly stiff clitty. Trina clamped her teeth on the clitoris and bit; Devora howled and wriggled, slamming her wet cunt against Trina's face. Trina would not let go but opened her jaws to take the entire vulva between her teeth and bit, locking the cunt in her mouth while she began to suck the gash-flaps and tongue the hard clitty.

Devora began to moan, swivelling her hips to push her cunt further into Trina's face, while Zealla, riding Trina like a horse, punched her fist again and again into her wet slit, getting in right to her wrist and slamming the neck of Trina's womb with each thrust. Trina's cunt sucked and squeezed Zealla's arm, while her leg jack-knifed, pressing her foot inside Zealla's open cunt, and her stockinged toes began to mash Zealla's stiff wet clitty. The discipline directress writhed on top of Trina, and cascading come washed Trina's wriggling bare ass as Zealla moaned. There were thuds as further bodies impacted the huddle and redneck girls began their fevered probing of cunts and buttholes. Trina groaned as the weight twisted her neck and squashed her titties flat, yet still she bit, caressed and writhed in response to Zealla's fistfuck; her belly heaved in the onset of spasm.

'Yee-haw!'

'What the –?'

The huddle of girls tumbled as limbs were wrenched from the throng. Trina blinked through come-drenched eyes and saw a redneck male, naked and with a giant stiff cock fully erect. The male grabbed her and heaved her forwards, swinging her like a club. Trina shrieked as she was slapped on to the guardrail, with her feet on the spectators' side, her buttocks high and her cunt and anus spread, as if for punishment.

'Now wait –'

A hairy hand clasped her mouth shut, while a second plunged into her streaming cunt, and palmed a handful of her come.

'Mmm!'

Trina writhed in a frenzy of pain as fingers prised open her anus bud and the helmet of the huge cock, oiled with her own come, penetrated her anal shaft. Two hard thrusts and the monstrous flesh was slamming the root of her anus. The male enculed her with vigorous, rapid thrusts, withdrawing his slimed cock all the way from her hole and nuzzling the anus bud before driving into her again; her anus began to slime with ass-grease and contract around the invading tool, the soft greasy elastic of her anal chamber caressing and squeezing the swollen glans as it penetrated her. Hands gripped her at shoulders, hips and ankles and, despite her shuddering, her slippery body was trapped, the guardrail poking painfully at her pubic bone as her cunt-basin slammed up and down. The man's belly slapped her jerking bare ass-globes, as his ass-greased cock pierced her anal elastic.

'Stop . . . you'll split me in two,' Trina groaned.

'Rufus, this bitch is hot for cornholing!' cried the male hoarsely. 'She could get jism outta *your* dick!'

'Then you spurt your tiny fuckin' peckerwad, Billy, and let a real man go,' said his companion. 'I gonna fill her up till she fucking floats away.'

'No!' Trina yelped. 'Don't hurt me. Please, sir.'

Billy bucked harder, not leaving the anus but withdrawing only an inch or so before ramming again against Trina's bruised anal root. Trina groaned, feeling the first hot droplets of sperm drip from his peehole, and then he grunted and a hot flood of sperm spurted from his cock into her rectum.

'Mmm,' Trina grunted into the palm covering her lips, 'Mmm, mmm . . .'

Her legs buckled as come flooded her cunt and she writhed in orgasm with the hot jet of sperm bubbling at the lips of her writhing anus pucker.

'Oh! Yeah!' she gasped, as the hand left her mouth, and steadied herself against the rail – 'Ooh!'

A second cock, that of Rufus, stabbed her sperm-slimed anus and succeeded in penetrating her with a single thrust, of which he proudly advised Billy.

'She's hot, this pig,' he said. 'See them whupmarks? She's hotter than hot, she's begging for it . . .'

Vap! Vap! Vap! Vap!

A rain of spanks showered on Trina's naked, quivering buttocks and she howled as Rufus began a ruthless buttfucking. His cock was bigger than Billy's and left little play for Trina's squeezing sphincter. He fucked her ass vigorously for over a minute as she screamed, wailing, and finally stammered;

'You're so big! You'll burst my asshole!'

'Now you know, lady,' growled Billy. 'This is real Mississippi cornhole, I ain't no Yankee candy-ass like that fuckin Duane Carvalho. Guess you've had his snake up that turd highway, bitch – slut like you, can't get enough, always falls for that sombitch.'

'I swear, I've never met Duane Carvalho,' Trina gasped.

'Fuckin liar! That butt stud made you grease up pretty good in the pomade factory, what I hear.' He pronounced it 'po-made'. 'You sluts are all the same. It's treason, fuckin' the enemy, and I am gonna punish you, bitch.'

'Oh! You're hurting me!'

'Yeah! Hurt her good, Rufus,' shrieked a female voice.

'Fuck her till she faints,' added another.

'No, wait, please,' Trina gasped, but already Rufus had his sperm risen and the first cream of his jet was spurting over the remains of Billy's.

Trickles of sperm overflowed from her anus on to her thighs, and women howled in glee as a third stud mounted her, buttfucked her, spurted and gave way to another. There was a fifth cornholer and a sixth before Trina lost count. Trina's anus was raw, bubbling with sperm and her own gushing ass-grease. Her bare buttocks danced under heavy spanking, the slaps falling mostly on her tender haunches until the skin was ribbed and crusty and the flesh blackened. Her body shuddered in orgasm three times more under her spanking and enculement, until she was left to slump, sobbing, to the floor. The girls surrounded her, masturbating, with a bruised and sullen Emily Cawdor in their midst, kneeling before Devora Dykes and tonguing her clitty; Heidi Absorb and Alice Frequemme frotted each other's cunts, while Zealla sat on Harriet's face, big toe inside Harriet's juicing bare cunt, which she foot-frotted as Harriet sucked her slit.

'I swear, I've never fucked Duane Carvalho,' Trina sobbed.

'Are you sure?' Zealla asked. 'A filthy trull like you is certain to, unless we consign you to a carcer which will sicken you of lustful perversions forever. I've plenty to hang you on, poor foolish spy. I was looking forward to chastising you to the max, as your abeyant penalty, for conspiring to corrupt public servants Acajou and Felt and for masturbating a prisoner of the republic.'

'She had her fingers in my pussy and tongued my nubbin, and everything!' blurted Blush Coynte. 'She said that's what they did every day on New Albion – so she must be a spy.'

'You'd have had short rack plus vigorous caning, say eighty strokes, maybe suspension, Trina,' Zealla continued. 'Now I have you on gross indecency, masturbation and anal sex, caught *in flagrante delicto*, before witnesses! I can have you racked, whipped, hanged and gagged, till you scream.'

'We are in court!' Trina blurted. 'What about *sub specie modestiae*?'

'You're not in court,' Zealla snapped. 'Your feet are over the guardrail, on the public side.'

She turned to Rufus and Billy.

'Any of you men fancy a second shot? Where she's headed, this bitch needs all the practice she can get. And you can use this, in case your hands get sore.'

She tossed a rubber scourge of nine thongs, which Billy caught, slapping it twice across Trina's naked croup, which made her cry a sharp, piercing cry, then bringing it down across her naked breasts, not once but over two dozen times. Trina screwed her eyes tight and wailed as each lash of the thongs laid red weals on her bare titties, the tips of the thongs catching her nipples. Zealla bent closer to Tina's face, contorted in pain as the quirt lashed her shuddering, bare teat-jellies.

'Hurt much? Keep quiet about what Emily said, or I'll tell Mamselle Wand to hurt you much more at the Stella Maris. I know another thing . . . on the boat bringing you here, Elvis fucked your cunt, you filthy, depraved bitch.'

Thwap! Thwap! The scourge continued its flogging of Trina's naked titties until they were purple with weals.

'Oh!' she cried, as a hot spurt of piss flooded her cunt and squirted her thighs, puddling the floor as her eyes streamed tears. 'Oh, no . . .!'

The piss was followed by a plop-plop of dung pellets shooting from her anus. The cleft of her buttocks widened as the dungs hissed from her grease-slimed pucker, and her ass-globes rose, jerking.

'Look at those flapjacks,' cried Blush. 'A New Albion spy, for sure.'

'Yee-haw!' chorussed the rednecks, and cameras clicked as Trina's bare cheeks were spread again.

From the Journal of Mlle Augustine Flageolet, anno 1760 12

I am increasingly convinced that New Arras shall be the perfect society, based on reason and female submission to the male principle, yet self-sufficient in all things, including our deepest female desire to submit. Caning and whipping of our tender parts is not so much pain, though painful it is, as the symbol of our submission, whose marks our skins bear long after the ceremony of chastisement. The baring of the nates for the shameful penetration of the nether hole by the erect male member is a ceremony, I believe, almost equal in importance to that of bare-bottom caning. Yet, so often, unreasonable female lusts overwhelm our modesty, and the desire to submit becomes a desire for sensual gratification.

I learn that here aboard ship, swivings take place outside the rules of the virgins of Ishtar, and that some girls actually open their juicing pudenda to the poking of the brute male organ. That is only acceptable when properly sanctioned, according to my reglements. Reason, I have decided, must be accompanied by order. There is no shame in despotism, if the despotism is enlightened. On our island of New Arras I shall be intendant, ruling for the common weal, through committees which shall convey the wishes of my people to me, who shall transmute their base metal into gold. As for gold, I possess a fortune beyond fantasy. After a youth spent conniving with bankers over the disposition of my estate and learning their tricks, I shall found my own bank of New Arras! Having skirted the Antilles, we are nearly at the Orleans territory of America. We must be perfect on arrival, and that applies to me. The guardian of the treasure may not be above reason. I must offer myself as a virgin of Ishtar.

13

Strap-on

'There's no need to tremble, maid,' said Hazel Wand, crossing her nyloned legs and sharpening the dagger point of her purple-polished index with a silver nail file. 'It makes me squirm to think what a reputation we have from idle tongues and vicious rumours.'

The directress of the Stella Maris was a tall blonde of twenty-one, with an untamed mane of yellow tresses, her prominent breasts and derriere encased in a filmy uniform of shiny grey cotton, with a pearl necklace nestling in her deep cleavage where three undone shirt buttons bared her breasts almost to the big strawberry nipples in stark relief under the thin, damp cotton. Beneath the cotton, a purple waspie corset was visible, squeezing her waist to nineteen inches. Her skirt was pulled up her thighs to show a tuft of pubic hair, for the directress was pantiless and braless, the waspie thrusting her teats up to firm jellies and accentuating the swelling of her buttocks. Sprawled in a cane chair, she was fanned by two sweating girl slaves, both barefoot, wearing only a bra and panties of coarse hempen hair and with their manes tied back in ponytails. Each slave had her bare feet locked in a wooden hobble bar, three feet long. Their hairy panties were scarcely more than a thong pulled tightly between their gash-flaps, whose folds swelled on either side and left their melons almost totally bare; vivid pink stripes the width of the cane on Hazel Wand's lap streaked their buttocks.

Hazel sighed and tossed aside a sheaf of papers, Trina's dossier; then stood and bent over Trina, looking into her eyes. Nude, Trina squatted before her, buttocks on calves, with her ankles in a hobble bar. Her arms jutted rigid before her, with her waist fastened in a wooden hobble, a bar of solid teak fastened to a steel coil around her waist and locked at the small of her back. Beside the waist hobble, two taut chains stretched down her belly, joining clamps around her nipples to those on her cunt-flaps. A third, smaller chain, linked the two to hold a clamp gripping the clitoris and pressing it to extrusion. The various clamps cupped the skin so that the nipples ballooned from pincers at the areolae and the cunt-flaps swelled bulbously below the extruded clitoris; any motion on Trina's part would savagely wrench her nipples and gash-lips. Trina shook her head to brush her mane across her eyes and wipe the beads of sweat. Behind her stood a guardian of virtue in black uniform of a tabard top and frilly skirtlet, her legs and feet bare. From her fist dangled a loose chain fastened to Trina's spiked neck ring.

'You are a puzzle, mamselle,' Hazel said. 'However, I may not enquire into your provenance any more than your dossier advises. Directress Pure is displeased with you. Gross indecency, behaviour unbecoming a scholar, conduct to the detriment of the morals of the republic ... I shudder. Your titties and ass seem bruised, so I surmise you are one of those submissive perverts who crave the lash on her intimate body. Wise of you to waive right of appeal; malfeasants caught in the act enjoy little leniency from the supreme court. You'll emerge from your stay with us purified and thoroughly reasonable, won't you?'

Panting in the heat, Trina did not respond.

Stripped of the intendance, that bitch Zealla again in control, and I'll bet she's the supreme court, too. I'm not even a scholar, but a slave ...

Vip! Hazel's cane slapped her full across the clamped, swollen nipples and Trina cried out.

'I said, "won't you"?'

'Yes, mamselle,' Trina sobbed.

'That's better. Now, I'd invite you to join me in a cup of herbal tea, only I see it might be awkward for you – if we get business over soon, you'll be in time for our *table d'hôte* in the slaves' refectory. Slaves at the Stella Maris are known only by their number, not by name, so our first task is to assign you a number.'

'Slaves, mamselle?' Trina blurted, her eyes filling with tears. 'In the republic of reason?'

'Technically, a thrall of this institution. "Slave" is a conceit of Mamselle Flageolet's – charming folklore. I shall assign your slave number after a test, determining your suitability for the corrective regimes we offer: hard labour, hospitality and rigorous corporal punishment. Hard labour is the most sought after, as it involves diving and other healthy aquatic pursuits. Hospitality is next; prescribed chastisement is mainly for maids with bottoms bare of stripes, easily caned to repentance. We had one the other day, a timid, tearful trull who blurted slanders about our new intendant, that she was a flapjack spy, a lesbian – worse, a submissive who would do anything for a bare-ass flogging. I haven't the honour of knowing our intendant, but I caned the trull a hundred on the bare for her vile slander.'

She stroked Trina's bruised nipples, gently rubbing the points until the plums stood to erection.

'Mmm . . . did I hurt your breasts?' she murmured.

'Yes, mamselle. Nothing I haven't taken before, in this . . . this place. What sort of test, if you please?'

Hazel bent down and stroked Trina's buttocks, then passed her fingers, dancing, along the outer and inner thighs, brushing the lips of the clamped cunt.

'Good girl meat,' she murmured, 'strong, firm, muscled, skin satin-smooth, and ripe for thrashing.'

She stood and flexed her cane.

'That is a Georgia yew sapling, one of the strongest yet most supple woods, and most painful in a cane,' she said, stroking its gleaming yellow surface. 'It's a little longer than a whipple and thicker, too. The whipple is more for close-up work, but I prefer a good reach. I'll be interested in your reaction. Your dossier says you are accustomed to bare-bottom caning with numerous rods and that your vulva juices under punishment. Correct?'

'What kind of a question –?'

Vip!

'Ah!'

Trina jerked as the cane lashed her upturned soles.

'I don't know . . .'

Vip!

'Uh! I guess so,' she wailed.

Hazel placed the canetip at Trina's cunt, prising the lips apart to reveal glistening pink meat.

'Mmm,' she said. 'The test is simple, mamselle, and is actually a trick of mine for your benefit. I must report all chastisements you receive, with copies to the committee, a privately annotated copy to the directress of discipline and to the public watch. A test, however, is *in privilegio proctoris*. I shall cane you on bare, a caning you may halt at any time, and the number of strokes you take shall be your slave number. The higher your number, the more privileges you shall receive under my domain. Guardian of virtue Beth Dudge shall observe your expressions of distress to ensure that you can take my strokes. No girly wriggling or yelling, mind, or the stroke isn't counted. High numbers serve as my thralls, while the low numbers like Wendy and Marietta here . . .'

She gestured at the hair-pantied maids who continued fanning her, and lashed her cane between Marietta's legs. The girl shuddered and she took the stroke in full vulva, without a sound. Wendy winced and closed her eyes, before a similar stroke slashed her across the teats, ripping her bra. Hazel laughed.

'They have no privileges,' she said. 'So afraid of cane, they'll endure any shame to spare their bottoms. They are the lowest hospitality girls, taking cock in anus, or sucking cock – or both – ten times a shift, when they have only to accept a clean beating to escape. Let's do it.'

Beth Dudge pulled Trina to her feet and made her shuffle across the room to an iron flogging rail, three feet high in its wooden frame. Beth thrust Trina across it so that her face was on the floor, with the flogging rail biting between waist hobble and pubic mound. Her hips took her weight, with the iron rail grinding her and stretching her belly chain so that her cunt-flaps and nipples were pulled to whiteness. The waist hobble touched the floor at such an awkward angle that she had to strain her back to keep her head up. Her legs were splayed behind her, feet on tiptoe, and her bare bottom thrust into the air. Trina moaned as Hazel flexed her cane, letting it spring back with a whistle.

'Please, mamselle? About the test – have I any choice?'

Hazel stooped and put her face an inch from Trina's. She placed the purple talon of her index at Trina's cleft and rammed, piercing the anal pucker to the full depth of the fingernail. Trina's buttocks clenched, trapping the fingernail inside her anus, and Hazel slowly reamed the elastic as she whispered.

'Get a clue, bitch,' she hissed. 'I own you. I own your cunt and your ass and what's inside. Anything I say is official and anything you say is trull's slander.'

Beth raised her leg high, her skirt falling away to reveal the thin thong of her rubber string panties biting deeply into her thick, oozing cunt-lips; she put her foot at the base of Trina's spine, grinding hard on her spinal nubbin while Hazel penetrated Trina's butthole with the whole of her index finger, right to the knuckle, and began a series of swift jabs. Trina's ass-cheeks clenched and she groaned, her cunt- and teat-clamps wrenching her swollen flesh as she writhed. Hazel withdrew her finger from Trina's anus and clawed the full length of her cunt-lips, raking the quim from clitoris to the perineum. Trina howled.

'Sorry,' Hazel said, 'but you might have been one of those perverts. I can see you are a submissive belle gone astray, and really don't get off on pain. Shall we begin?'

'Yes, mamselle,' Trina answered, then groaned as Beth's heel ground her spinal nubbin.

'I didn't hear that,' Hazel said.

'Yes, please, mamselle.'

Hazel nodded, smiling, and raised her Georgia yew to the full reach of her arm over Trina's trembling bare. Beth removed her foot and squatted in front of Trina. Her face flushed, she stared at Trina's grimace of anguish; beneath her skirtlet, framing the tight rubber thong, her naked cunt-lips drooped, heavy, swollen and tangled in shiny, dripping hairs. The cane whistled and impacted Trina's quivering naked melons, the strokes slicing fully across both fesses. Vip! Vip! Vip! Trina's buttocks squirmed.

'Oh!' she moaned.

'That's three,' Hazel said. 'Is it OK to give you tracks of three? Most maids prefer to get it over fast. I sometimes prefer the delicate delivery, each stroke savoured as its caress eats into the flesh and the melons trembling so sweetly – the tight fruits of a girl's bottom, quivering helplessly, are the artist's perfect canvas. Your fesses are such a canvas, mamselle. Perhaps we may savour the slow pleasure in future.'

Trina's buttocks clenched as her back shivered, and three pink welts coloured her bare buttock meat.

'Yes, mamselle,' she sobbed, choking. 'Threes are fine.'

'Good.'

Vip! Vip! Vip!

'Ooh!'

'Remember what I said about girly wriggling, and screeching and stuff.'

'But, mamselle, you cane so tight . . .'

'Tighter than Zealla?'

'Oh, yeah.' Trina sobbed. 'My ass feels on fire, it smarts so. You're crueller than Zealla.'

'Why, thank you.'

Vip! Vip! Vip!

'Ahh!'

Trina's flogged buttocks jerked in spasm as the cane whipped her three cuts. By nine strokes, the bare fesses were fiery with the pink weals, darkening fast to crimson, and with trenches of puffy flesh already rising to flank the bruises made by the whippy little yew sapling. Trina's groans grew in counterpoint to the rhythmic vip-vip-vip of Hazel's cane. Pinioned, she could do no more than twitch her fesses as the bare flesh reddened under striping. Once in every dozen strokes, Hazel had to reprimand her for undue clenching and tell her the stroke would be disallowed in her tally.

'You poor baby,' she said, stroking Trina's bare and running her purple fingernail down the freshest and rawest of Trina's grooved welts. 'It must hurt so. Say it's over, and it shall be over – but you won't have a high number. You do want one?'

'Yes, mamselle,' Trina gasped. 'Please, how many have I taken?'

'Such a juicy, full bottom, and quivering so painfully. That's the beauty of no clenching – the caner can only guess at the pain her lash causes. How many? Not enough, mamselle.'

Vip! Vip! Vip!

'Ahh!'

The caning progressed, until Trina's naked fesses glowed red, mottled with purple streaks, mainly at the haunches and top buttock. She sobbed and wailed; her titties wobbled helplessly as her body jerked to the cane. Her trembling turned to clenching, with strokes disallowed. At last, she sobbed that she could take no more.

'Very well.'

Vip-vip-vip-vip-vip-vip!

'Oh! Ohh . . .'

Hazel released a flurry of cuts to the mottled mid-fesses and Trina clenched her nates frantically, her whole body squirming and jerking in her bonds. Hazel's fingers stroked her buttocks once more, rubbing gel into her bruises and into the crevice of her perineum. She massaged the anus bud and stretched cunt-flaps, while poking one, two and then three fingers into Trina's wet slit.

'You took two hundred and forty-one strokes,' she said, 'so that's your slave number. Wendy here is number 138, and Marietta 144.'

She put her come-slimed fingers into Trina's mouth.

'You juice well under cane, number 241. I can only remember one number coming close, and that was 239. She was a juicer, too, a disgusting pervert like you. Time for you to hobble to your luncheon in the refectory, and then to the hospitality suite – you'll stay nude until you earn a seduction dress, for basic hospitality doesn't permit time for dressing, flirtation and the like.'

'My privileges of high number, mamselle?' Trina groaned.

'Perhaps you misunderstood, slave,' Hazel sneered. 'Nudity is your only privilege. A high number indicates tolerance and craving for the cane – you are a degenerate, naked for shame, who has no privileges at all.'

'That's not fair!'

Vip! Vip! Vip! Hazel's cane lashed Trina's naked breasts.

'Ahh! Oh!' Trina cried, as her teats wobbled.

She was released and her arm hobble removed, but not her cunt-chains, nor her ankle hobble. Beth Dudge led her on all fours to the refectory and cast her inside.

'Say, it's mamselle the fucking intendant!' cried a voice, to raucous laughter, and Trina spluttered as a bowl of ordure was poured over her head.

'Please,' she groaned, wiping the rotten slop from her face, 'there's been a misunderstanding . . . ooh!'

A second bucket of slop cannoned into her teats, slopping garbage all over her breasts, belly and cunt. She looked up and saw a circle of maids standing over her, including Jennifer Tans, Dolores Henek and the former POW Odette van Kram. Odette's voice had greeted her.

'I'm a fucking citizen now, you fucking illegal alien bitch!' she cried.

All wore bra and panties sets of skimpy, clinging pink latex, hinged with silver, and with peekaboo openings at the nipples and quim. Each girl wore black fishnet nylon stockings, one foot unshod and the other encased in a high, platformed surgical boot of black rubber.

'241, huh?' said another girl. 'Sumpweed and goosefoot, that's your lunch, you fucking submissive bitch. Eat what we give you, suck the cocks you're told to suck, take it in the ass without a squeak, and your whippings too. You prove you're 100% slut, maybe you get to wear seduction dress, stockings and all, and you're allowed to masturbate and keep a quarter of your tips from the fucking rednecks.

You squeal, we'll ram your hobble up your asshole and tape you fucking shut. Catch you diddling after stripes, we'll buttfuck you with a hot brick. Mamselle Hazel hates fucking submissives. We hate fucking submissives. Get it?'

'I'm not a submissive,' Trina sobbed.

A surgical boot rose, looped itself behind her jouguette, and jerked, wrenching Trina's quim-lips and nipples.

'Oh! that hurts!'

Another boot dug into her stretched teat-flesh, while the heel of a third dug into her crotch and mashed her clitty and gash. Trina doubled up, choking.

'Get it, cunt?' demanded the girl.

The speaker was Corporal Cindi Kock. Sobbing, Trina nodded.

There were over twenty girls confined in the Stella Maris, of which only two were sub-sluts. The other official sub was Jolene Bracken, a tow-haired girl of nineteen from Pine Bluff, Arkansas. With Trina, Jolene ate, chained naked to the post in the refectory, formerly a stable. Like Trina, she wore a slave ring on her neck. Superior slaves, those who had earned seduction dress, threw scraps of sumpweed or chitterlings, with an occasional spoonful of mushy grits slopped on their faces or poured into their clamped-open cunts. Monitors guarded the proceedings but there was no rule against talking, save that every now and then a monitor would select one girl for a thrashing, bend her over the gnarled hickory table and whip her bare until she pissed all over the spread food. Jolene said it was better than living in a trailer park with her bad cousins. She was strung up on the gallows every morning beside Trina to receive a 'livener' of twenty-five lashes from a rubber quirt with four-foot thongs, before they got their crusts for breakfast. The floggings were alternately on back or buttocks, and Jolene said she didn't mind which as it gave her an appetite and made her frisky for her day's work. She had been a slave for thirteen months, refusing the offer of seduction dress and a place at table.

'Guess I am one of those submissives,' she said. 'I don't want to be uppity, like those whores in panties. Who do

214

they think they are? Just buttfuck sluts like the rest of us. Even back home, I didn't feel right unless one of the menfolk whaled me bare-ass every day. Never could enjoy diddling unless my ass was ribbed. Mamselle Hazel offered me one of them lewd bikinis, and a place at table, but I feel better naked and squealing like a hog. I like being whupped and buttfucked. A girl should be honest about herself. Don't you like being a slave, Trina?'

'No! I've never been so degraded! I've reached the pits,' Trina gasped. 'Jolene, what *are* you?'

'What's any of us? A female, fit for whupping and juicing and coming, that's all.'

One rule, almost the only rule, was never to ask a girl's offence. Rumours abounded – that Cindi had offered her bottom to unlimited caning in order to cause a run on the currency, that Jennifer and Dolores had planned to kidnap Sophie Petrarque and sell her as a slave to Lady Juliet Gorges of New Albion. Such fancies were immaterial, serving merely to enliven the sameness of every day. Activities were the lash, hard labour and duties in the cathouse, as the vast, airy service building was nicknamed.

Each girl was assigned her cubicle in the great hall, the spaces separated only by canvas sheeting, and there she awaited her guests. Walkways at each open end of the cubicle permitted customers to scrutinise the girlmeats on offer in the intervals between clients – or even in the act, if the client agreed. Cane-wielding monitors patrolled the floor of the hall and the balcony above. Slaves were forbidden all speech during their service. They had to obey every order their visitors gave, understanding that any humiliance, however vile, had Hazel's approval.

Each girl had to keep a selection of canes and dildos in her cubicle for use on her person. New slaves were kept nude and received the busiest traffic. After four days of intensive pleasure service, Trina was released from her hobble and cunt-chain. Hazel was pleased that she had serviced forty-three clients, of which eighteen were female, in those days: mostly, she took anal sex, often with a strap-on dildo, and gave oral sex, whether to male or female. That did not count the canings and hand spankings most visitors chose to apply to her naked bottom. Thereafter, her average of clients fell to a median eight per day, drawing praise from Hazel, who complimented Trina on her compliance under cane and fellatio and her prowess at feigning orgasm under buttfucking.

'I wish it was feigned, mamselle,' said Trina bitterly.

She divided her time between her cubicle and the ocean or the potato fields, where maids scrabbled for tubers with their bare hands. Diving duty meant scouring the sea-bed for crustaceans, and a diver had to spend at least two minutes under water, on pain of a pertinent caning on the wet buttocks. At first, Trina was caned after every dive, until her lungs got used to long airlessness. The divers were nude and clients watched, sometimes paying extra for fellatio administered under water: most days, Trina was obliged to suck cock with her head under water and her bare melons raised for a whipping with flails of knotted seaweed, studded with shells and driftwood fragments – forbidden to rise apart from necessary breaths until she had swallowed a full load of sperm, however long it took to bring the male to orgasm. When she surfaced, mouth dripping with molluscs and sperm, males plastered her titties with mushed-up hamburger so that gulls swooped to claw her teats, as they seized the raw meat. For this treatment she had to stand rigid, hands clasped on her head, and the males liked to pepper her bare ass and vulva with broken clamshells fired from slingshots. Far away on the horizon, through her tears, shimmered the golden slab of New Albion.

After a scanty lunch of slop, she went straight to duty in her cubicle where, mutely obedient, she bared and spread for cock after cock in her anus. There were no sleeping quarters: slaves had to bed down without blanket on any patch of privacy they could find or secure. There were furious catspats as nude slaves gouged and kicked each other in titties and cunt, arguing over a secluded spot, stinking of piss and spiders, beneath some staircase. Those discovered fighting were yoked on an outside gallows, flogged on the back and buttocks and left overnight, to be flogged again at dawn on the breasts. Trina took to bedding down with Jolene outside in the sultry air, with coverlets made of palm leaves, rushes and dried seaweed. Jolene made some secret Arkansas liniment that kept the bugs away. Naked, they watched the turtles lumber up from the sea to lay their eggs, and shivering at the wails of gibbeted escapers. Slaves dreamed of escape, but the 'SM' ring round their necks, requiring a hacksaw for removal, made recapture almost certain. Even in the maze of streets in the old quarter of New Arras, it was impossible to evade spies or the security corps, and a removed slave ring left an imprint on the flesh for several days.

Stella Maris was surrounded on land by walls forty feet high, with broken glass, and escape from the sea meant swimming a mile out to circumvent the breakwaters of sheer rocks. Spies inside Stella Maris were just as eager for reward. Gerdie Nichols had swum to freedom and, recaptured in a wine shop by the security corps, had been brought back in chains. Before the assembled slaves, all hobbled and yoked for Gerdie's crime, she had been whipped two hundred lashes, tarred and feathered, then had stinging sea anemones stuffed in her cunt and crabs in her anus, both orifices sealed with duct tape, before being hoisted on the gibbèt on the beach. Mouth gagged by two pairs of soiled panties, she was whipped thrice daily for a week until the lash had denuded her body of feathers, her only sustenance a pint of rainwater per day and a single mouldy crust. Twice a day her holes were untaped to permit her evacuations, then at once refastened. For days after Gerdie was released, her body covered in livid weals and bruises, her cubicle was the most popular.

Crouching below the dining table, Trina heard snippets of gossip. There was to be an assault on New Albion, and all the slaves were to be freed to form a shock battalion in the vanguard of the invasion; Zealla Pure was to be commander, having ousted Alice Frequemme from command of the armed forces. She had ousted Heidi Absorb from direction of Stella Maris, and Heidi was already a slave amongst them, disguised in a perruque and pubic wig. Hazel had her own cubicle in the cathouse, and could be seen giving head and taking it up the ass after midnight. Jolene told Trina to ignore such rumours, except the last.

'Only assault going to come is from New Albion,' she said one night in Trina's tenth week of enslavement, as they lay naked under the stars, with the sobbing of a gibbeted escaper and the swishing of the waves.

Idly, they discussed their duties of the day past: Trina had taken ten cocks in the ass, compared to Jolene's six, and sucked seven, to Jolene's five.

'I can still get the guys, even a lifer like me,' Jolene said.

'Some guys I can do without,' said Trina. 'Rufus and Billy – filthy fucking rednecks. Oh! No offence meant.'

'And none taken,' Jolene said.

'They come in and do me every other day, and they got me in here in the first place. Motherfuckers.'

'Trina, you got yourself in here, for being a wicked, forward girl, just like we all did,' Jolene said. 'Cindi Kock, she used to be a real vile sub and a lesbian, and now she's the worst snitch and worst whipper among the slaves – though that's all the slut will ever be. She's marked. Righteous bitches, think candy won't melt in their ass-holes, and they just disappear, you know? Not back into the population, just . . . somewhere. Sold back east, is what I think. Rich dudes in Boston pay a fortune for a Southern slavegirl, you know? Millions of people gotta go to food centres in this country – slavery ain't so bad, compared. Rufus and Billy – they the ones who shout "yee-haw"?'

'I know them.'

'Good cocksmen, you gotta agree. I always come when they cornhole me. Fuck my ass raw, like Southern gentlemen, you know? They're slavers.'

Her hand caressed Trina's bottom.

'Say, I'm no lesbian – but, you know, if I was, then you'd be my choice.'

'I was going to say the same thing,' said Trina, her hand creeping to enfold the lips of Jolene's gash.

'You want we should masturbate? I know it's unlawful, but who'd know?'

The only monitor was Beth Dudge, drowsing by her campfire. Gingerly, the two naked slaves began to caress each other on breasts, bottoms and cunts until their fingers were bathed in oily come.

'I've wanted to for a long time,' Jolene gasped, wriggling her cunt-basin against Trina's probing fingers as Trina slid three digits into Jolene's slimy pouch. 'Your ass-welts are so lovely and crisp and hard, and I just love your pussy. Don't you miss a good pussy-fucking? Cornholing is fine, and I'd hate to be without cock for my asshole, but it gets to hurt all the time.'

'Me too, to all of that,' Trina murmured, wriggling down to get her lips around Jolene's clitty.

'Oh, yeah,' gasped Jolene as Trina chewed the stiff nubbin and poked four fingers into the wet cunt. 'Yeah . . .'

Their nude, sweating bodies slithered as the two girls gamahuched until, by frottage of the clitoris, oral sex and knuckle masturbation of the cunt-pouch, they had each climaxed twice. Both girls' fists were slopped in come. Trina whispered that she had a plan for escape, if Jolene wanted to come along, and Jolene clapped her palm over Trina's mouth.

'No more!' she hissed. 'I don't wanna go and I don't wanna know.'

Suddenly, both girls were pinioned to the sand.

'Plotting escape?' hissed a female, next to Trina's ear.

'It was me! Jolene knows nothing,' Trina cried. 'I swear.'

'Whip the bitch anyway,' ordered Zealla. 'I like to hear redneck flesh sliced while I fuck.'

Her nude body towered over Trina, gleaming in the moonlight. The knots and striations of her giant phallus quivered, buckled to her waist.

'You like my strap-on?' she sneered, jerking Trina's cunt upwards with a booted foot in her gash. 'You won't even feel cock in your anus, once I've fucked you with this baby.'

Vip! Vip! Vip!

'Ohh!' cried Jolene.

A cane began to work on her naked melons as the pinioned girl writhed, her mouth full of sand. Zealla wrenched Trina up by the hair and forced her to crouch, doggy style.

Vip! Vip! Vip!

'Oh, mamselle,' she moaned, as canestrokes welted her upthrust bare, 'fuck me, but please not the cane.'

Vip! Vip! Canes sang on the two helpless bare croups. The canes striped the naked fesses of the two girls for minutes, and the air was rent with sobs and shrieks as their asses squirmed. Then only one cane whistled, lashing Jolene. Zealla crouched and pushed the tip of her dildo into Trina's anus bud. She straddled Trina, resting her full weight on her shoulders, and thrust hard. The dildo penetrated Trina's anus halfway.

'Oh! It hurts, mamselle . . . Oh!'

A second thrust, and Trina screamed as the dildo sank to the root of her anus. Grunting, Zealla began to buck vigorously.

'Ever had cock like that?' she snarled.

'Oh! No, mamselle!'

'Not even from Elvis?'

'That's not fair!'

'Say it! My wood's better than his! Bigger, more hurtful . . .'

Zealla's hips slapped against Trina's squirming bare nates as she corkscrewed the dildo into the anal elastic, withdrawing it fully, dripping with ass-grease, for each new penetration.

'Oh! Yes! It is . . .'

'Then you won't mind, mamselle . . .'

The naked male behind Zealla's croup grasped her hips, slid his organ into her cleft and found her twitching ass-pucker. He slammed his cock into her shaft to the root of her anus. Zealla grunted as the male enculed her in time with her penetration of Trina's butthole.

'Bitch is sassy, Elvis,' she grunted.

'Ram her ass good, then, mamselle,' Elvis replied.

The force of his thrusts pumped Zealla's strap-on harder into Trina's hole, matching the rhythm of Jolene's caner, who stroked the girl's bare with geometric precision. Jolene

220

writhed, gurgling and shrieking, her jerking cunt-basin pinioned to the sand, and her ass-cheeks crimson in the moonlight. A trickle of come seeped from her slit into the sand, leaving a dark damp patch. Zealla's come spurted from her bucking cunt to trickle down Trina's ass-cleft. She fucked Trina's anus for fourteen minutes, with Elvis buggering her, and Trina pissed herself twice during that time. The cane did not cease to lash Jolene's bare. After nine minutes, Zealla removed one supporting hand to masturbate, and the flow of come wetting Trina's skin became more copious as she accompanied her buttfucking by shrieks and gasps.

'Yeah,' she moaned. 'Yeah . . . I always wanted to fuck you, bitch.'

'You only had to ask, Zealla,' Trina groaned.

'Call me 239, slut! Asking's no good. Only fun in fucking is power. You hurting, bitch? You feeling my power?'

'Yes . . . Uh . . . Enough . . . Oh, stop, please.'

Abruptly, Jolene's caning stopped and the thrashed girl lay sobbing and writhing on the sand, her hands rubbing the red bare melons of her flogged croup. Her caner crouched low with her head between Trina's thighs, and Trina wailed as teeth fastened on her erect, piss-soaked clitoris. The girl swallowed Trina's flowing come, mashing her lips on Trina's clit and nose-fucking her cunt. She wiped her nose rapidly up and down Trina's slimy slit-lips, ramming its tip deep into her cunt-pouch. Her bare ass wriggled on the sand as she thumbed her own clitoris. Zealla, masturbating, buggered Trina's anus as she herself groaned under Elvis's buttfucking. Trina's belly heaved.

'Oh . . .' she gasped, 'I'm going to – Oh! Oh!'

Come spurted in a torrent from her cunt over her gamahucher's face as her loins shuddered in spasm, accompanied by grunts and hisses from Zealla, masturbating herself to simultaneous climax. Elvis panted and his bucking of Zealla's anus grew fierce until Zealla put her hand to her anus to smear his sperm-froth from her pucker and wipe it on Trina's face. The girl slopping Trina's cunt withdrew, licking her glistening lips.

221

'Harriet!' Trina moaned, as Harriet rose, piniowed her mistress, and roped her wrists behind her back.

'Colonel Harriet to you, citizen,' she said. 'Of the New Albion strategic intelligence bureau.'

From the Journal of Mlle Augustine Flageolet, anno 1760 13
My head concealed in a muslin bag, I offered my bare bottom, crouching beside four other bagged girls, trembling nervously, as was I. I felt the joy of pure, orderly nature, with five naked bottoms presented to be used, like a fivefold trough at which any horse might drink. Far from our quivering bare fesses the smirks and dissemblances of flirtation and intrigue! We were submissive animals, ready to be used, as all females crave.

The worship of Ishtar lasted from midday to five p.m., with two breaks for refreshment. I felt the first matelot grasp my hips and, without ceremony, thrust his naked organ against my compliant buttocks. He quickly found my nether hole, which I spread for him to the best of my ability, groaning at the speed of his penetration and the massive stiffness of his member. I saw myself again in that English stable, with my muddy ostler, stinking of male power. He began to buck – I thrust to meet his strokes, unable to stifle my gasps of pain as I felt his organ slam my root, nor my sweats and shivers of submissive pleasure. There was a delicious tingling in my belly, as intense as masturbated ecstasy. Too soon, he spurted his cream, bathing my hole in hot fluid, and withdrew, leaving my belly fluttering.

No sooner did his member plop from my squeezing hole than another took its place, swiving me for longer and its massive girth bringing me close to fainting. The third matelot tipped me over into spasming pleasure and my moans were genuine as, I knew, were the groans of the swived girls around me. Thereafter, I lost count of the organs I served, save that each brought me to new heights of pain and pleasure mingled. My anonymity as a naked female animal for the use of males was more potent as a lustful stimulant than any potion or perfume.

At last, a voice broke the silence, and I recognised Capt Stouplois. He said I was a trull, or trollop, and deserved whipping for my lewdness – this as his organ, more massive than any other, was stabbing my innards, and at his words I came to spasm once more. I made no protest as he dragged me to the deck and roped me naked to the mainmast. Still bagged, I did not see the crowd of jeering watchers, male and female, as I was whipped one hundred on the back, then caned one hundred with a stout willow rod, as I later learned, on the buttocks.

I had never known such a dreadful, sublime flogging. Every nerve of my tortured bare flesh screamed stop, while my heart swooned in joyous submission to the male's lash. I shrieked in pain and ecstasy. When the captain drew the bag from my head, I saw we were coming into the harbour of New Arras. He said we had passed the island of New Albion, settled by English barbarians from Maine, but that the sounds and spectacle of my flagellance had cowed their raiding party, and my stripes were the salvation of New Arras. A true priestess of Ishtar must sacrfice all dignity and comfort for the good of the public weal!

My maids looked at my bruised flesh, more scarred than any other's, and applauded with heartfelt vigour. Having decided that New Arras needed a male as custodian of public order and administrator of punishments too severe to besmirch female hands, I offered the post of public executioner to Capt Stouplois, who accepted. That post, it was agreed, remained in my personal domain, as did the person of its holder.

14

Whipped to the Bone

'What are you doing to me?' Trina wailed.

'Making you comfortable for the night,' said Zealla.
'String you up; then in the morning you'll be whipped,
tarred and feathered, and yoked on the gibbet.'

Jolene helped Zealla and Harriet plaster sweet gum on
Trina's pubic fleece.

'My, how your bush has grown,' Zealla said. 'So gross!
You left this behind.'

She held up Trina's pubic *vison*, rich with the shorn hairs
of Devora Dykes, and pressed it to her groin until it stuck
firmly to her natural growth; then slathered more sweet
gum to the artificial pubic hair. Jolene pulled a meathook
down from the gibbet, while Elvis dug holes in the sand.
Trina lay on her back while her bound wrists were buried
in one hole and her ankles quickly roped in the second.
Jolene winched up the meathook, drawing Trina's body
into an inverted U and suspending her, crablike, with her
weight taken by her glued groin, unless she chose the agony
of supporting herself on her arched back, legs and arms.

'Ah! Ah!' Trina shrieked, her breasts flopping over her
chin.

'Hurts, I guess,' Jolene said, piling rocks over Trina's
buried feet and hands.

'Jolene! How could you . . .?' Trina sobbed.

'How can anyone do anything?' Jolene replied.

'We'll leave you something to remember,' Zealla said,
taking a springy whipple cane and lashing Trina's breasts.

Vip! Vip! Vip!

'Ah!'

The cuts took Trina on the milky underside of her dangling teats; her body shuddered, jerking the rope and wrenching her pubic fastening.

'Jolene – the nipples – if you've no objection?'

Jolene grasped Trina's flailing breasts, cupped them and squeezed them, holding them erect so that the big plum nipples stood out, bulging.

Vip! Vip!

'Ah! No! Jolene, please . . . Zealla's a traitor.'

'What do I know?' said Jolene. 'I'm only a sub-slut.'

The cane sliced each squeezed nipple across the bud, and Zealla continued the titty-flogging to forty cuts, until Trina's breasts were striped with livid red weals. Her torturers left her, sobbing and swinging from her hook. Her only companions on the beach were the crabs that scuttled up and down her flesh and into her gaping cunt, and the turtles lumbering up and down from the waves. Trina gritted her teeth, raised her groin an inch, then sank violently downwards, wrenching her pubic wig. Her eyes streamed with tears as she repeated the manoeuvre, shuddering up and down, until the hair of her false pubis ripped noisily from her groin, taking tufts of her real fleece with it, and she collapsed between her imprisoning rock-piles. For two hours, she waggled her feet, inching them from the sand and pushing aside the rocks one by one, all the time wincing as clusters of tiny crabs crawled in and out of her cunt, biting and nipping her pouch walls. At last she sat upright, her limbs free.

It's all gone so wrong . . . why me?

She staggered into the sea and splashed, drenching her naked body until her eyes cleared. She rubbed her ass and smoothed her inflamed anus pucker with a fingertip, cursing and withdrawing sharply as her skin met the swollen anal elastic extruded by Zealla's buttfucking.

Why me . . .?

She clambered on to the back of a turtle and let herself float out to sea, watching the dwindling lights of New

Arras. When she tried to steer the turtle, it was no use – the beast was newly alert, preparing to dive. When it slid into the depths, Trina was left floating on her back in the warm Gulf waters. She lay looking up at the stars, inert and with her limbs stretched, the saline fluid washing her open holes and lapping over the welts on her whipped breasts. Her tears ceased and she drifted into numb, hopeless sleep. It was not yet dawn when hands plucked her from the ocean and hauled her aboard a boat.

'You are a sassy bitch,' Zealla said, 'and dumb. Why didn't you just wait?'

'You were going to tar and feather me, and flog me!' she sobbed. 'I wanted to escape . . . to New Albion.'

'Naw, mamselle,' Elvis said, turning round from the ship's wheel. 'Mamselle Zealla wanted to fuck you before you were shipped out, that's all. Jolene's one of her spies, see. So's Mamselle Harriet, only she's a counterspy, a double agent, got her pecker right in that Lady Gorges's asshole, in a manner of speaking.'

'Shipped out!' Trina cried. 'Where am I going?'

Harriet extracted two wriggling crabs from Trina's gash, licked them, and threw them into the sea.

'New Albion, mamselle,' she said. 'All this time, where did you think you were going?'

It was dawn when the craft entered the deserted rocky cove. On the hills high above, cannon faced out to the ocean in the direction of New Arras. They disembarked and Trina shivered in the brisk sea air. The trees here were slanted to the gale, and the dark grey rocks were barren of mosses. Zealla murmured her approval that the bay was undefended. Trina stumbled over the rocks with the others until they all shrieked as the rocks erupted in an earthquake. Flung to the ground, the intruders had no time to rise before a platoon of New Albion soldiers, nude but for waist flails, tit- and ass-spikes and spiked cunt-traps, apprehended them.

Trina squealed as a beefy New Albion commando coolly swivelled her hips and delivered a flurry of stinging spanks to Trina's bare with the swaying metal cords extruded from her ass-cleft. All around them, the rocks stirred and opened with a whisper of zip fasteners; hard shells crumpled to soft bags and, from their cocoons, more naked soldiers emerged. A tall, coltish blonde, wearing captain's insignia, sauntered to Trina and placed the tip of her spiked jackboot in her anus, giving it a twist. Trina writhed.

'Welcome to your future home, ladies,' she spat. 'We know what to do with saboteuses, here on New Albion. A diplomatic incident – a show trial – perfect excuse for our invasion. I'm Captain Musquonset, of the palace guard, and you'll be seeing a lot more of me – or my whip.'

Trina gaped at the bay, moments ago deserted but for rocks, and now swarming with soldiers. The bay was by now denuded of rocks, all of which had opened and shrunk, leaving serried ranks of heavily spiked girl soldiers busy tending the the fabric of the rocks as it reshaped itself into a flotilla of attack boats. They attached outboard motors revealed by the crumpled rock fabric to the back of the craft and pushed the boats into the sea, then boarded them in platoons.

'Wh-what . . .?' Trina stammered.

'Our secret weapon, no longer secret,' said the captain. 'Camouflage body bags, from El Segundo, California.'

She looked at her watch.

'Very good exercise, halberdiers,' she barked. 'Next time, the real thing. Form up! Quick march, at the double, hup! Let's get these saboteuses back to the palace, and then you can draw lots for the honour of torturing them before their trial. How I love to see candy-butts writhe. The stinking trulls . . .'

Halberdier Donnette Spinks interrupted her with a cry from the deck of Elvis's boat. She held up a bulky package wrapped in oilskins. From each end protruded tips of wooden twigs, gleaming grey in the sunshine.

'What?' cried Abby Musquonset. 'Secret weapons? Armed and dangerous, indeed!'

'For display purposes only,' Elvis said. 'They are just a few samples. Springy birches, superior to – oh!'

Zealla kicked his ankle, silencing him.

Donna Spinks approached, bearing her package; she said the hold was full of them. Abby looked inside, paled, then smiled nervously.

'Beautiful weaponry,' she said, rubbing her buttocks. 'That'll do to hang your ringleader. Or worse, if she's whipped to the bone with one of those. Such an arm could upset the whole social structure of New Albion, cause a revolution . . .'

'I'm no revolutionary, mamselle,' Elvis drawled. 'I just deliver things.'

Abby ordered her female captives roped together and paper bags placed over their heads. She lifted her cane and dealt a blow to the bare buttocks of each female. None squealed. Donnette shouldered the oilskin package and Abby took Elvis by the groin.

'Now, hup ho!' she cried.

'Yes, ma'am,' said Elvis.

Lady Juliet Gorges watched her soldiers frogmarching their captives across her front patio. She slipped a pig's trotter into her mouth and sucked at the gel, then gulped her Old Aroostook ale. Watching the nude bodies of the captives, pricked on by the whip of Abby Musquonset, she let her fingers brush aside her robe and touch the gaudy rich bush of her quim, then penetrate the pink folds to find the clitoris. She wore a velvet robe of rich purple, pinned only at the waist and its pleats open at the front; no shirt, but a boned corset of purple, laced to eighteen inches and leaving her massive teats bare and bunched. At her waist dangled a four-foot ashplant cane, and her feet rose proudly on black stilettos. She sipped, while playing with herself, fingers brushing both slimy quim and stiff nipples, with her eyes fixed on Trina's melons, bobbing and jerking as soldiers took turns to lash her with their butt-spikes.

'So that is our scapegoat, the cause of all our troubles,' she mused, to her sergeant. 'Zealla tells me she is resilient under torture. I'm so looking forward to seeing her squirm.'

She contemplated the lanky form of Elvis, contriving to stroll with nonchalant dignity, and rolling his hips under his blue jeans with an unashamed bulge at his crotch, caressed by Abby Musquonset's fingers; he grinned at the bare spiked bottoms of his captresses, beaded in sweat and bouncing as they trotted. Juliet rubbed her clitty.

'I do like Duane,' she said, 'but it seems they are bringing a replacement.'

Feet clattered up the staircase and Abby led in her captives. Lady Gorges ordered them unbagged, but still roped, with her sergeant, Donnette Spinks and Abby as guards. Halberdier Claudine Butreaux was despatched to organise refreshments. A feast arrived, with pots of ale and tea carried by a naked slave, her ankles in a three-foot hobble bar. Her bare buttocks and breasts bore livid welts, the same colour as Lady Juliet's corset and robe. There were tears in her eyes as she served the captives, but she did not look up, and neither Harriet nor Trina made a sign of recognition. The slave was Jewel Persimmon. Lady Gorges invited her captives to chow down.

'An army marches on its stomach,' she said, 'and that's why your French candy-butts are no match for us. I am so glad you have seen reason, Zealla dear. Cold showers, hot canes and a brisk diet makes us the soldiers we are. Have a mutton pie – mashed turnips, awfully good – some Maine chowder?'

The others ate, but Trina had just a cup of hot tea, with milk and sugar. Abby unfolded the oilskin package and Juliet gasped. She extracted a sheaf of gleaming silver birch rods and began to stroke them.

'I've never seen anything like this,' she whispered. 'We must keep utmost secrecy, Captain Musquonset. Any tattle-tales shall kiss the gunner's daughter . . .'

'So you are New Albion agents,' Trina said listlessly to Harriet and Zealla.

'*She* is!' each hissed.

'What to do with Trina?' Juliet said. 'A show trial, of course, during which Harriet and Zealla shall receive the Gorges Medal. After Trina's torture and exemplary chastisement, I suppose a punishment battalion, or the nylon factory.'

She touched Trina's bare ass-melons, now goose-bumped and shivery; her naked breasts trembled too, with her nipples erect and downy hairs in her areolae bristling. Juliet put her fingernails in Trina's tit weals and clawed gently as Trina winced. Then she stroked her ass, letting her fingers rest inside the ridged welts of flogging. She put a hand into the flaps of her own cunt, pinching the skin from the inside, and squirted a plume of come from her gash. She giggled and began to masturbate her clitoris with firm, slow strokes as she touched Trina's shivering flesh. Her hand went to Trina's cunt, parted the flaps and delved in the pouch; Juliet brought her fingers out wet, and put them in Trina's mouth.

'Such a lovely specimen,' she murmured, 'already wet at the thought of naked flogging. A true submissive slut . . . I shall enjoy watching your naked fesses wriggle, Trina, precious, and the tears in your eyes as my whips flail you – it shall be very painful – and your shame at your golden rain as you piss yourself on my cannon. Beauty unwhipped is not true beauty and whipping, unless of beauty, is not true whipping. As for Elvis –' she reached out and stroked the bulge at his groin, which swelled to her touch, at the same time parting her robe as she masturbated her naked clit '– males are always useful, in their way. Nevertheless, someone must kiss the gunner's daughter.'

Drip, drip, drip . . .

'Ahh . . .' Trina sobbed. 'Please, no . . .'

There cannot be so much pain in this world . . .

Drip, drip, drip . . .

'Ahh!'

The dungeon echoed to her scream. She could not see through the tears blurring her eyes as she hung, naked and upside down, beneath the cauldron of melted wax, continually replenished by the ring of candles.

'Save your voice for your birching, mamselle,' said Zealla.

Nude, but for a seventeen-inch purple corset and high jackboots, she poured the wax into Trina's exposed holes: anus and quim, pegged open by surgical speculums. Both orifices were half-full of the solidifying wax. Harriet held the cauldron on her shoulders. Lady Juliet Gorges and Abby Musquonset looked on, gashes bare and masturbating each other while their fingers played on the groin of Elvis's jeans.

'My ambassador is returning from New Arras via Biloxi,' said Lady Juliet. 'He shall join us at any moment.'

'That varmint!' hissed Elvis.

Zealla looked at him with an icy stare.

'I hear Duane is no different from you, sir. A pimp that fucks any woman's hole. Higher, Harriet. Yes . . .'

She sluiced wax into Trina's cunt, ignoring Lady Juliet's frown.

'Ah! Ah! For pity's sake . . .!' Trina screamed.

'Is hot wax awful inside your cunt? Just tell us where the treasure is,' said Juliet. 'The treasure of Mamselle Flageolet. That's what you were sent to Louisiana for, isn't it? Your birching will go easier, yet not without glory – it will be the first birching on the cannon.'

'I don't know what you're talking about.'

'Birch her,' snapped Lady Juliet.

Harriet tipped the cauldron so that hot wax dripped on to Trina's quivering bare nipples; the torture continued until Trina's cunt and anus overflowed with lava-like furls of solidified wax and her breasts quivered under a two-inch crust. The wax dribbled over her titties on to her belly and also down her back, until her whole torso was encased in a waxen sheath with its tendrils grasping her neck and chin. Moaning and crying, she was lowered to the floor, gyved in hobble bars at wrists and ankles and made to stumble, buttock-whipped by the canes of halberdiers Spinks and Butreaux, until she emerged on to the patio.

On the parade ground, the national guard of New Albion stood stiffly at attention, facing the cannon overlooking the sea – the gunner's daughter. Trina stumbled through the ranks of spiked buttocks, wincing as Donnette's cane flicked the nubbin of her spine or the edge of her top fesse. She cried out only once, when a soldier suddenly swivelled and slapped Trina right across the bare with her full buttockload of quivering spikes, then turned to leer. It was Devora Dykes. Beside her, also smiling, was the nude, spiked Cindi Kock. Pouring with sweat, Trina hobbled up the hillock and, wailing, allowed herself to be divested of her hobbles, then hogtied naked to the gun barrel, her thighs and arms spread so that her wrists and ankles met beneath it, knotted in a single rope. The high noon sun beat on her uncovered head and she wriggled as the heated gunmetal burned her naked titties, squashed against it, and melted her waxen crust. As she squirmed, driblets of wax sprayed from her filled cunt and butthole.

'Troops,' announced Lady Juliet, 'you will see how New Albion punishes malfeasants, and by a device of their own importation. The saboteuse of New Arras thought herself invincible with this new weapon – but it is now ours. Our Maine birches are still standard infantry weapon, of course, but our shock troops shall bear the new springy birch.'

She turned to Zealla, in the cluster of maids overlooking Trina's bare ass, as well as Elvis and Duane Carvalho, both stripped to the waist and chewing tobacco.

'You must return and ensure the export of your entire stock, Zealla. You, Harriet, must seize the supply lines, wherever these items come from. The malfeasant, her *nom de guerre* Trina Guelph, shall receive an unlimited flogging, whipped to the bone, until she reveals the state secret of the Arrasiennes – the location of their purloined treasure, rightfully the property of New Albion. My troops, we shall break the candy-butts.'

'Hail Gorges!' roared the soldier girls.

'I swear, I don't know what you mean,' Trina blurted.

'Let the whipping commence. Whip her hard, hangman.' Swish!

'Ahh . . .'

The birch rods descended full across Trina's naked buttocks. They clenched frantically, and her legs stiffened as she screamed. Duane Carvalho chewed laconically as he raised his arm for the second stroke.

Swish!

'Ahh! No . . .!'

Swish!

A tattoo of livid crimson weals adorned the whole expanse of Trina's bare buttocks, which writhed and wriggled, slamming her cunt against the gun barrel. The springy birch's length and its long handle allowed Duane to flog from four feet, thus maximising the impact of his strokes on the unprotected bare flesh.

Swish! Swish!

'Oh . . .! Oh!'

Trina gasped, her buttocks and spine flailing on the hot metal as her cunt slammed repeatedly on to the gun, and her cleft deepened in the frantic clenching of her wealed ass-cheeks. The birch crackled. Swish! Swish!

'Ahh!'

Juliet's eyes met Zealla's and turned away; both had their hands at bare quims, and frotted clitty, while Harriet, nose close to Trina's squirming ass-cleft, joyously masturbated with a full four fingers stroking inside her wet cunt-pouch.

'All you have to do is tell us where the treasure is,' Juliet hissed. 'Then, you may have an endstroke at a hundred. A mere hundred with birch on bare! Mild chastisement, for a vile, submissive slut.'

Swish! Swish! Swish!

'Ahh!'

Trina's buttocks squirmed bright red; her cunt hissed and she expelled a powerful jet of golden piss, streaking the shiny gunmetal and splattering Lady Juliet's toes.

She made a moue of distaste. 'So that is your answer,' she spat.

Swish!

'Uh . . . uh . . .'

'The treasure?'

Swish!

'Ohh! Lady Juliet, I'd tell you if I knew. Please stop my beating. It smarts worse than anything I've known.'

233

Swish!

'Ahh!'

Trina's squirming bare mottled to purple, the birch rods imprinting the bare satin flesh with a lattice of deep weals. Duane continued the beating until Trina's whole buttock-flesh, and the tops of her thighs, halfway to her knees, were covered in vicious dark welts. Trina gazed at the monstrous bulge in Elvis Lesieur's jeans and, as the birch strokes rained on her helpless bare ass, a stream of come began to slime the gunmetal beneath her twitching cunt-basin. Zealla, Harriet and Juliet continued to masturbate while the troops stood stock still at attention, their nude, sweating bodies gleaming in the sun and juice seeping from their shaven cunts. At the eightieth stroke Juliet, still fingering her throbbing, extruded clitty, bent to Trina's ear and asked her real purpose in coming to New Arras, if not to find treasure. Trina did not answer.

Swish!

'Oh . . .'

Swish!

'Ohh . . .'

'Tell me, Trina. Fess up, and you could rise above the nylon factory. You could be on my personal staff and wear nylons . . . many pairs! Why did you come to Arras? We could continue birching your bare back – another first . . .'

Swish! Swish!'

Trina's buttocks flamed dark crimson, streaked with rapidly crusting purple ridges; a steady stream of come flowed from beneath her soaked pubic forest. Her hips writhed, in the bath of her cunt-slime.

Swish!

'Ahh! It hurts . . . so . . . much . . .'

'Why, Trina?'

Juliet's fingers twitched her red, throbbing clitty as come poured from her gash; Zealla had her fingers inside Harriet's cunt as Harriet thumbed Zealla's extruded clit. Both girls gushed with come.

Swish!

'Oh!'

'Why?'

Swish! Swish! Swish!

'Ohh . . .!'

A naked birching . . . If only I could see myself . . .

Trina's back arched and her buttocks rose to slam her clitoris against the metal; her throat bubbled in squeals as her belly heaved, fluttered and mashed her dripping cunt and extruded stiff clitty against the gun in a pool of her own flowing come. Drool slimed her lips and she sobbed more and more shrilly; then her sobs rose to piercing cries of orgasm. Duane splattered her asshole and cunt-lips with a jet of tobacco juice that mingled with her come in a brown oily stream.

'Submissive fuckin' bitch, huh? Whup her ass, she wets her panties, and comes too! Let's birch that pretty little girl-ass. Right, Elvis?'

'Let's do it, Duane. I'm just the mailman, mind.' Elvis shrugged, grasping a second birch.

The two males birched Trina's shuddering bare body, Duane working on the buttocks and thighs, while Elvis took the shoulders and mid-back. Swish! Swish!

'Ahhh . . .!' screamed Trina; then sobbed, 'Is there no end?'

'No, bitch,' spat Juliet. 'Duane, birch her square on the asshole. She's had so many cocks in there – Elvis mustn't look, or he'll see his second home damaged.'

Swish! Swish! The birch crackled on Trina's cunt-lips and anal pucker. Trina's melons clenched violently and she wailed, her wail descending to a choked, whimpering sob as the birch lashed her pucker and gash again.

'*What* did you say?' Zealla hissed, her face pale.

Juliet turned to her with a sneer.

'Why everybody on the seven seas *knows*, missy. Your Elvis isn't exactly yours . . .'

'And your Portuguese man o' war? My asshole could tell his meat in the dark.'

'You fucking whore,' cried Juliet, leaping on Zealla and flooring her, with her knee slamming her groin and a flurry of slaps clawing her titties.

Both females were buttfucked for over twenty minutes, bringing both of them to orgasm, while their alternate tonguings of Trina's birched cunt brought her off twice more. Duane pulled Zealla's head away and withdrew his cock from her asshole, then thrust her lips around his engorged glans, pushing until she took his ass-greased cock to the back of her throat. Her head began to bob like a pigeon's as she sucked his cock; Elvis treated Lady Juliet the same, pushing his peehole into each of her nostrils before ramming his helmet and shaft into her mouth, and getting his glans deep in her throat. Lady Juliet gurgled as her lips, greased by her own slime, fellated the monstrous organ. Crack! Crack! Both asses writhed as the males spurred the fellatrixes with spanks. The males grunted, and copious creamy sperm frothed at the mouths of Juliet and Zealla, their bare buttocks red with livid spankmarks. Harriet leaped on to the crest of the hillock, brandishing a springy birch.

'Troops of New Albion,' she cried. 'See the disgrace of your leader. I proclaim the free state of New Albion, with peace between our islands forever.'

Also birch-wielding, Abby Musquonset pushed her aside.

'Don't listen to this renegade. I proclaim myself the new sovereign. War! We shall trounce the candy-butts!'

Still at attention, the troops began to murmur, until Devora Dykes and Cindi Kock broke ranks and cried out in support of Harriet, to be joined by the whole army. Harriet lashed Abby across the breasts with her birch; Abby stumbled and fell, and Harriet pounced. She clawed tits and cunt, kicked and punched, until she had ripped off Abby's purple corset and the ravaged nude blonde submitted, sobbing.

'Yee-haw!'

Warriors burst from the forest, waving birches, as they ripped green camouflage sheaths from their spiked bodies. Emily Cawdor and Blush Coynte were in the van. They mowed through the wheeling ranks of New Albion troops, lashing and slicing, the defensive spikes no protection, until the parade ground was a mass of writhing soldier girls, clutching wealed bare bottoms and teats. Leading Sergeant Merlene Makings, Beulah Beaucoup and Alana Funger, Blush Coynte bestrode the hillock and put her hand on Trina's flogged bare. Below them, Felt and Acajou supervised the collection of surrendered weapons and obliged the surrendering troops to crouch, faces to the ground and bottoms in the air for the removal of their spikes. When their croups were defenceless, the New Arras commandos began a systematic birching of every bare bottom; the parade ground glowed crimson.

'Good work, mamselle,' Blush said.

'Those are . . . Goody Baggs!' Trina gasped. 'How . . .?'

'We've had Goody Baggs at New Arras for ages, thanks to Zealla's twin sister, Kimmi. She visited with us, and she and I became . . . special friends.'

Blush turned, and showed her bare croup, fingering two especially deep welts. She licked her teeth.

'Dear Kimmi! We of the directorate planned the invasion months ago. It was Mr Lesieur who got us our ultimate secret weapon – Canadian birches, from Arlette Sobovica, in Biloxi. They were the dowry for her daughter Yveline to enrol at our academy, although Yveline –' she pointed to one soldier's ripe bare fesses '– would have passed her croup test easily. Harriet Stooplaugh purchased the birch forest in New Brunswick, so now we have assured supply. She's a Canadian.'

'What?' Trina sobbed, wriggling in her ropes. 'I thought you were from Savannah, Georgia.'

'Canadians are devious, mamselle,' said Harriet. 'My name is not Stooplaugh, but Stouplois. Henriette Stouplois, Comtesse de Saguenay et Marquise de Trois-Rivières.'

The New Arras committee of public safety arrived in scholar's uniforms, but wearing dress canes and with their rear skirts undone, showing bare. They curtsied to Blush Coynte, and she took each girl's cane to lay it softly on her bare, after which Alice, Heidi, Sirena and Dorita murmured, 'Thank you, directress.' They turned to Abby Musquonset.

'Quite a good show, this time round,' said Abby.

'What will you do with Juliet?' Heidi asked.

'A spell in the nylon factory will do the bitch good,' said Abby.

Juliet howled and burst into tears, rubbing her bruised bottom.

'Abby, is there somewhere we can go to sort out the peace treaty?' said Alice Frequemme. 'It'll be different from last time, as these new birches kind of give us the edge, armament-wise. Keeping the cycle, though – unified state, revolution, war, unified state. Until one of us finds the treasure . . .'

'Let us hope we never do,' said Abby. 'We can go to the throne room and I can sit on the throne awhile, if Lady Harriet will permit. And your mailman, Mr Lesieur . . . would you let him buttfuck me? Please? I can't help thinking of the night my ship was captured, and he whipped me, and . . . oh, it was a girl's dream come true.'

'Milady?' said Alice.

'Oh, sure,' Harriet said, turning to Trina's scarred bare fesses. 'But our intendant never answered Juliet's question. What did you come here for?'

'To run New Arras and produce Goody Baggs,' said Trina bitterly. 'Seems I'm the victim of deception.'

Harret put a fingernail inside her anus and clawed her anal elastic.

'What did you really come for?'

'Oh! I told you, Harriet!'

Harriet picked up the birch.

'I don't think so.'

Swish! Swish! Trina's flogged bare buttocks squirmed, blackening with new welts.

'Ah! I told you!'

Swish! Swish! Trina's melons jerked, trembling at the caress of the springy birch rods to her naked flesh.

'Ooh! It hurts so!'

'Yes,' said Harriet.

Come oozed from Trina's wriggling cunt-lips. Harriet birched her to twenty swishes, then thrust her fingers inside Trina's soaking cunt, squeezed the clitty and began to masturbate her.

'Mmm . . . oh . . . mmm . . .' Trina moaned, her cunt squashing Harriet's fingers.

Crack! Crack!

'Uh . . .'

Harriet raised her hand over Trina's birched bare, and began to handspank her, laying her strokes on the new, open weals of her birching. Her fingers pummelled Trina's cunt and clitty, with Harriet's wrist now slopped in Trina's gushing come.

'Mmm . . . yes . . . don't stop. Spank me, fuck me . . . Oh, Harriet! Oh!'

Her bare-bottom spanking of eighty slaps brought Trina to orgasm and she gurgled, her cunt writhing on the spear of Harriet's fist.

'Answer the question,' said Harriet. 'Here's a clue. You haven't once asked to be released from your bonds, bitch. Or from your Stella Maris slave's neck ring. Why did you come here?'

Crack! Crack!

'Why?'

'Oh! Oh!' Trina sobbed. 'I wanted to become a submissive belle, milady.'

'Beg pardon, milady,' said Emily Cawdor, curtseying to Harriet. 'The troops wish to know, is mamselle still our intendant?'

'Of course,' said Harriet.

Emily picked up the birch and held it in front of Trina's face. She curtsied again.

'Please, mamselle intendant,' she said, 'if it wouldn't be too much trouble . . . my bottom hasn't been flogged for ages. Could you give me fifty strokes on account?'

'Mr Lesieur,' gasped Trina. 'If you've no objection?'

Elvis made a moue and took the birch. He bent Emily over the gun barrel and parted her thighs, lifting her pubic mound to raise her bare melons. He lifted the birch to his arm's full extent and Emily's fesses began to tremble. Her cunt, between the spread ass-globes, was swollen, fleshy pink and oozing juice.

'I hope this won't inflate the currency,' Trina said,

240

'What do I know, mamselle?' Elvis drawled. 'I'm only the mailman.'

From the Journal of Mlle Augustine Flageolet, anno 1776 14
So many factions, so many departures from the doctrine of pure reason! Yet, my present uncertainty can only be temporary. Only I hold the key to the treasure of New Arras, upon which our credit rests. My spies are everywhere; my secret alliance with milady Gorges, and her barbarians on New Albion, is my trump card. As insurance, I have contracted an altogether subtler alliance with Cordwainer Carvalho, a strapping native of New Bedford, Mass., who is milady's public executioner and who attends to the submissive propensities of my anal chamber with refreshing northern vigour. I understand the barbarians well – after all, they too are refugees from oppression, having fled the New England puritans for the bracing disciplinary climate of a new Maine. Every day, we recruit new loyal maids from Mississippi, Alabama, the Carolinas and the Orleans territory, even as far away as Kentucky, longing to be trained as 'submissive belles', in their piquant American idiom. I know I have allies on the committee of public safety, and can count on the loyalty of Caleb Lesieur, my new executioner, as virile and dedicated as Capt Stouplois, who, after valiant service in the cause of reason, sailed to seek his fortune to the north. Lesieur's virility only seems to grow, no matter how much he swives me in the nether hole and chastises naked girls. The public watch I am not sure about, but I know I can count on the security corps and, most important, the Bank of New Arras, where the bankers of Biloxi and their rivals in the Orleans Territory think my treasure is lodged. If only they knew the truth of my treasure! That treasure secures most credit, whose glory is unseen, as Louis XIV used to say . . . I take care to spread rumours that it is the treasure of the Knights Templar, filched from its Pyrennean cache, or else the treasure of Eldorado. But, like all treasure, its value is in the mind. As I look at the perfect ranks of my naked maids' bottoms, arrayed for mass ceremonial caning, I

look at my inexhaustible treasure. It is the naked buttocks of young maids, eternally fresh, eternally juicy under cane, and eternally submissive. New Arras, the republic of feminine reason, shall last forever!

15

Submissive Belle

'Trina,' cried GG Baggs, 'You're always so well dressed . . . so together!'

'Oh, I just throw on any old thing,' Trina said, pouring her boss's coffee. 'This is one of Allan's shirts, you know? And barefoot is more comfortable.'

Trina wore only the man's shirt, open to her navel, and with her naked breasts swinging free above her waspie corset. The shirt's hem just covered the bare bottom and vulva, and tufts of cunt-hair dangled moist at the front.

'It's the corset I was looking at. What a pink! I mean, kind of pinker than pink! And how do you get it so tight? Doesn't it hurt?'

'That's the point, GG.'

'How is Allan?'

'I see him for lunch, sometimes. He's very gentle these days. I think he's met some bully broad. Poor Allan.'

'You should have introduced him to Kimmi,' GG said.

'Well, he flies to Paris. He can go see her at GG-Box.'

'Trina, could I ask your advice?' said GG. 'It's about Gwendoline.'

'Have I failed to satisfy her?'

'Trina . . .' GG wagged a finger. 'You know I never pry.'

'I mean, in the office.'

'On the contrary, she thinks you're great.'

'Yeah, we get on pretty good. She's a great masseuse and therapist. We see each other, evenings.'

'I'm just wondering if Gwendoline is a tad too aggressive ... Too unpolished, like a diamond in the rough.'

Triina smiled, blushing.

'Oh, she can be pretty rough.'

'I mean, businesswise, with the salesmen.'

'I surely wouldn't know.'

'Thing is, they're macho guys, and they appreciate a tough babe.'

'She's that, all right.'

'A babe tough enough to be a submissive belle, Trina. Like you.'

'I should help her find her deeper nature?'

'Yeah. Then, a little field work might be right for her. She's twenty already, high time to learn. When I bought Jive Sacks of El Segundo, last year, I found they owned an island in Hawaii. Just right for a Goody Baggs factory.'

'Like New Arras?'

She stretched herself and yawned, letting the shirt fabric fall from her torso and expose her naked breasts, wobbling over the flatness of her corsed belly.

'Oh!' she said, 'how rude of me, boss.'

'It was, a little,' GG said. 'You're demanding, ever since you came back from Louisiana. I guess you want ...?'

'Not want, boss,' Trina said. 'Deserve.'

She placed her hips at the corner of his desk and flicked up her shirt tail, exposing her bare bottom. She parted her thighs fully and showed her hairy perineum and cunt-lips, glistening in the morning sun, then stood with buttocks thrust upwards and her hands on the desk.

'Paddle? Hairbush? Cane?'

'Hairbrush, please. It's maximum pain, for your least effort.'

GG took a silver-backed hairbrush from his desk drawer.

'Just a hundred, boss, I have work to do. Those floors won't polish themselves. And I've all your shirts to launder.'

Whap! Whap! Whap!

The hairbrush smacked the quivering globes of Trina's bare bottom, which reddened rapidly with big red welts. Whap! Whap! Whap!

'Ooh! That's good!'

'It's supposed to hurt, Trina.'

'It does. Can't you see my . . . you know?'

The beating lasted four minutes, and by its end Trina's face was as flushed as her scarlet bare. Her quim glistened with oozed come.

'Thanks, boss,' she said. 'Truth told, I don't feel right unless I get a morning spanking.'

'You won't forget about Gwendoline?' said GG, and Trina smiled, a dreamy, secret smile.

That evening, she was on her balcony, nude, with the twenty-year-old, and overlooking a perfect sunset. Gwendoline was blonde, coltish, with firm, conic breasts and a pear-shaped croup. Trina sat in her lap, her hands between Gwendoline's thighs, wiping the seeping come from her cunt. Gwendoline's fingers squeezed Trina's erect nipples. Her hand played over Trina's bare bottom, lightly pinked by recent spank marks.

'We're not lesbians or anything,' Gwendoline said. 'I mean, it's so natural and empowering for women to pleasure each other, isn't it? Men! Nothing but cocks and sperm bags. I can't think why you let GG walk all over you, Trina. And wearing that corset, like a token of bondage. You are so submissive.'

Trina grabbed Gwendoline by the hair and wrenched it hard.

'Ow!' Gwendoline squealed. 'What –?'

'Some of us like to be proper ladies,' Trina snarled, 'and not forward girls, like fucking lesbians. Like you, bitch.'

She pinioned Gwendoline's neck between her thighs and stuck her wriggling buttocks up in the air. Reaching behind her, she grabbed her studded leather belt from her jeans, and folded it double.

'Let me go!'

Thwap!

'Oh! That hurt!'

'Yeah, bitch, not just some cissy spanking.'

Whap! Whap!

'Ah! Stop!'

Gwendoline's buttocks squirmed frantically as the naked skin reddened with livid welts from the belt studs.

Whap! Whap! Whap!

'Ooh!'

Come began to ooze from the wriggling girl's cunt. As Trina continued the thrashing past fifty, Gwendoline's yelps softened to gurgles, then moans, and her gash writhed on the cane chair, rubbing her clitoris. Whap! Whap! Whap! Trina reached under Gwendoline's buttocks, found her juicing cunt and mashed the clitty.

'Oh . . . what are you doing?'

'Diddling you, whore. You're a fucking lesbo trull. You need real cock, a good eleven-incher, stuck up your sassy lesbo cunt. Better still, your asshole.'

Whap! Whap! Whap!

'Ahh! No! Oh! Don't stop! Oh, yes!'

Gwendoline's belly began to heave.

Whap! Whap! Whap!

'Ohh . . . yes . . .'

Trina abandoned the belt and drew Gwendoline's thighs towards her, pushing her head below the chair and squashing her face to the floor with her bare foot on Gwendoline's neck. Trina's face dived between the red wet gash-flaps, took the cunt between her teeth and bit, then began to chew. Gwendoline moaned, mewling, as her cunt squirted copious come. Trina got her tongue on the extruded clitty and began to suck it; in moments, Gwendoline gasped, then shrieked as her belly shuddered and her cunt trembled in orgasm.

'Oh,' sobbed Gwendoline, 'you lovely, lovely bitch. My ass is on fire. How many did I take with that dreadful thing?'

'A hundred and three,' said Trina. 'Feel better?'

'How did you know . . .? I've never come like that before! The pain – it's a whole new dimension. And you insulted me, so . . . *powerfully*. My pussy's so wet.'

Trina shifted on the deck to scratch Gwendoline's weals with her fingernails.

'Oh! Don't! I mean, yes, do.'

She grabbed Gwendoline's bare teat, pinched the erect nipple and bit savagely. She put a finger inside Gwendoline's anus, plunged it to the root and began to ream.

'Oh! yes . . . More. Harder. I want to come again . . .'

'Gwendoline,' said Trina, chewing hard on the naked titties.

'Oh, that's so good. Whip me again, Trina? Please?'

'Sure. If you'll try on my pink corset.'

'OK, Trina. Just whip me?'

Gwendoline slipped into the corset, gasping, as Trina fastened it to the tightest aperture. She bent over and touched her toes with her legs spread, showing gash. Trina lifted her whipple cane over Gwendoline's upraised bare buttocks. She lashed the quivering melons.

Vip!

'Ooh!'

'Good?'

'You know it is. Oh! It hurts.'

Vip!

'Yes . . . harder!'

Trina lifted the cane again.

'You're going to love Hawaii,' she said.

NEXUS BACKLIST

This information is correct at time of printing. For up-to-date information, please visit our website at www.nexus-books.co.uk

All books are priced at £5.99 unless another price is given.

Nexus books with a contemporary setting

ACCIDENTS WILL HAPPEN	Lucy Golden ISBN 0 352 33596 3	☐
ANGEL	Lindsay Gordon ISBN 0 352 33590 4	☐
BARE BEHIND £6.99	Penny Birch ISBN 0 352 33721 4	☐
BEAST	Wendy Swanscombe ISBN 0 352 33649 8	☐
THE BLACK FLAME	Lisette Ashton ISBN 0 352 33668 4	☐
BROUGHT TO HEEL	Arabella Knight ISBN 0 352 33508 4	☐
CAGED!	Yolanda Celbridge ISBN 0 352 33650 1	☐
CANDY IN CAPTIVITY	Arabella Knight ISBN 0 352 33495 9	☐
CAPTIVES OF THE PRIVATE HOUSE	Esme Ombreux ISBN 0 352 33619 6	☐
CHERI CHASTISED £6.99	Yolanda Celbridge ISBN 0 352 33707 9	☐
DANCE OF SUBMISSION	Lisette Ashton ISBN 0 352 33450 9	☐
DIRTY LAUNDRY £6.99	Penny Birch ISBN 0 352 33680 3	☐
DISCIPLINED SKIN	Wendy Swanscombe ISBN 0 352 33541 6	☐

- - - - - - ✂ -

Please send me the books I have ticked above.

Name ....

Address ....

....

....

.... Post code..................

Send to: **Cash Sales, Nexus Books, Thames Wharf Studios, Rainville Road, London W6 9HA**

US customers: for prices and details of how to order books for delivery by mail, call 1-800-343-4499.

Please enclose a cheque or postal order, made payable to **Nexus Books Ltd**, to the value of the books you have ordered plus postage and packing costs as follows:
UK and BFPO – £1.00 for the first book, 50p for each subsequent book.
Overseas (including Republic of Ireland) – £2.00 for the first book, £1.00 for each subsequent book.

If you would prefer to pay by VISA, ACCESS/MASTERCARD, AMEX, DINERS CLUB or SWITCH, please write your card number and expiry date here:

....

Please allow up to 28 days for delivery.

Signature ....

Our privacy policy.

We will not disclose information you supply us to any other parties. We will not disclose any information which identifies you personally to any person without your express consent.

From time to time we may send out information about Nexus books and special offers. Please tick here if you do *not* wish to receive Nexus information. ☐

- - - - - - ✂ -